BOOK ONE

BOOK ONE

RUINED

RUINED SERIES

BY T.O. SMITH

1

Three sexy, tattooed, alpha presidents . . . and she's at the center of them all.

The one man who always promised to love me - to take care of me - ruined me.

Joey? He's my hero.
Joey saw me - broken, barely surviving - barely breathing - and he taught me how to breathe again.
He gave me a purpose.

But we were oil and water. And Joey? He was the oil - trapping me, smothering me.
But I love him - I love this man with every fiber of my being.

He's made me promise to keep him with me because without him, I'm not living. I'm dying.

And when River steps into my life?
He teaches me how to live all while Joey reminds me how to breathe.

But throw in Tristan - my first love - and it's all one big, screwed up mess.

For Riley, my reason for everything that I do.

And for every woman who has ever felt completely misunderstood and unloved – may you find hope again in this book.

Cover Design: Noxity de Lucora (Special Edition Hardcover ; available at Barnes & Noble) & Tiff Writes Romance

Editing: Tiff Writes Romance

Proofreading: Taylor Jade

E-book ASIN: B08R6NVLBW

Paperback ISBN: 979-8722003300

Hardcover ISBN: 979-8489367202

ONE

ADELAIDE

"Come on, Adelaide, it's time to go," Joey told me, a scowl settling over his features as I continued dancing on top of the table, not paying him a bit of mind – purposely ignoring him.

I was in a right fucking mood, and I *really* just wanted to forget what this day was – what it meant to me. And Joey was doing his best to shit all over that.

Joey was a control freak, and though I loved the man with every fiber of my being, he was overbearing – too much for a woman like me that *needed* freedom and independence – needed to be able to make her own decisions without the Sons of Hell's President breathing fire down my neck all of the time.

Joey and I didn't mix – never had – no matter how much we wanted to. We were oil and water. And Joey was the oil – always smothering me.

"You're fucking wasted, pretty girl." *Oh, that sweet name.* That name would forever melt my insides. "Get your ass down here *now*." He snapped up at me. I only continued to ignore him, and though I knew it was pissing him off, I couldn't bring myself to care. I just wanted to be left alone, to forget the pain and heartache in my chest.

"Loosen up, Joey. Let the girl have fun." I heard his twin, Jessie, snap at him. "You're always up her ass. She's not your girl – not right now. You two ended that." She reminded him.

Her words felt like a slap across my face – a sore reminder that Joey and I just couldn't ever get it right together.

"She needs a goddamn man to put her in line." Joey snapped back at her. "This shit has gone on long enough."

I clenched my jaw, my body momentarily stopping before I forced myself to start again, forcing myself to block out the familiar pain of losing my best friend – exactly one, torturous year ago – on my fucking birthday.

My birthday had become a series of tragedies, and it was now a day I longed to just forget about.

"Am I interrupting something?" I heard a voice that I hadn't heard in *years* ask us.

I abruptly stopped dancing so quickly that I instantly lost my footing since I was so wasted. A shriek left my lips as I fell forward, my arms flailing for something to grasp onto. Everyone turned to stare at me, and I screamed as the floor came closer to my face. With a muttered curse, Joey quickly caught me in his muscular arms before I could face plant on the floor – always there to save me from my own shit – shit that I tended to always get myself into.

Always my savior – my hero – the reason that I'm still breathing today.

Despite the rage that I could see in his eyes, he gently set me on my feet on the floor before he released me, the muscle in his jaw ticking furiously. "I told you to get off of that table, Adelaide." He snapped down at me, his frame easily towering over my shorter one.

Momentarily forgetting about our visitor, I grinned up at my for-the-moment-ex as I sloppily pressed my finger to Joey's lips. He released a soft sigh, his eyes softening for the tiniest moment before they hardened again. "*Shh*," I told him, drawing out the sound. He narrowed his eyes at me. "You're such a party pooper." I slurred.

Joey rolled his eyes at me, but I saw a smirk twitch at his lips for a moment. He'd never been one for joking and messing around, but somehow, I seemed to kind of bring out the brighter side of his personality. But that was probably due to the sort of strange dynamic we had together.

Oil and water – always smothering me, trapping me, holding me down.

But fuck if we didn't deeply care about each other. I have never loved another man as much as I love Joey Dirks – the president of Sons of Hell.

Joey was always so damn serious, but I was the woman who smoothed out his rough edges, who made him feel human again because, in our world, too many feelings could kill you.

I was eighteen when Joey had taken me under his wing, giving me a reason to live, to fight. And it was my twentieth birthday when my best friend lost her fight to cancer, and I started my downwards spiral – getting deeper into the life of an outlaw.

But Joey had never left my side – never left me to fight on my own. It didn't matter if we were on the outs, not getting along. This man in front of me *never* let me down.

"It's been a fucking year, Adelaide." Joey snapped down at me.

I narrowed my eyes at him, fire lighting up my dark eyes. Joey clenched his jaw, a look of regret passing through his eyes before he smothered it, evenly meeting my burning gaze, not intimidated by me in the slightest – not like his other men would have been. "You really want to do this?" I snapped at him, my words still slurred, but that one sentence sobered me up a tiny bit.

It was my birthday today – my twenty-first birthday at that – which meant it was exactly a year since I'd lost my rock to cancer. It had been an entire year since I'd walked into her apartment and found her dead - lifeless - on her couch.

Joey clenched his jaw. "We've all been waiting for you to come around, Adelaide, but enough is fucking enough." I could have breathed fire at that moment as I glared up at him, my hands tightening into fists at my sides. "You're twenty-one fucking years old today. It's time to get your shit together."

I sent a right hook against his face, not giving a fuck about the consequences. Joey could be violent if he wanted to. He'd never hit me, but he was an MC president, and shit like I'd just pulled couldn't go unpunished.

His face swung to the left, and I instantly saw blood well up on his lip and trickle down his jaw. He turned his blazing, dark eyes to me, danger glittering in their depths. I swallowed thickly, knowing how volatile Joey could be. Jessie quickly grabbed him, pulling him back from me before he could retaliate like I knew he wanted.

I felt large, calloused hands settle over my bare shoulders, sending a shiver racing down my spine as his cologne wrapped around me. I would know those hands anywhere - could pick up the smell of that cologne in any setting. He hadn't changed.

Tristan Groves.

My best friend's brother that I had once been madly in love with.

But that was before he shattered my heart on my eighteenth birthday.

After last year, I was beginning to think my birthdays were cursed.

"Why don't you go cool off, Joey?" Tristan suggested, his voice filled with so much coldness that some of the people around us stopped dancing and turned to see what was going on. They never paid Joey and I much mind - knew we fought all of the time. But someone daring to stand up against Joey – another MC president at that?

It was very possible that blood was about to be spilled.

I flung Tristan's hands off my shoulders, stepping closer to Joey. He reached out and pulled me against him, his left arm wrapping around my shoulders, holding me protectively to his body. We may be oil and water, but he didn't rip my goddamn heart out of my chest. I could *always* count on Joey when it came down to it.

Tristan? He took one of the worst times of my life to fuck me up.

"How about you get the fuck out of my clubhouse, Grim?" Joey snarled at him, using Tristan's street name. "And keep your fucking hands off of my woman," Joey growled, his arm flexing around me. I slid my hands under his cut, keeping him calm, holding me with him.

That was the one promise he made to me – that I would *always* be able to keep him with me, no matter what happened between us.

I squeaked in shock when Tristan quickly grabbed me and pushed me behind him before he stepped toe to toe with Joey, both of their heights evenly matched, though Joey was just a bit more muscular – and a little older. "I was here to make a deal, Joey." Tristan snarled at Joey. "But I can always change my fucking mind and instead spill blood all over your fucking carpets."

What the hell was Tristan talking about? A deal?

Joey had cut ties to the Sons of Death as soon as he found out what Tristan did to me. I hadn't even been under Joey's care for a week, but Joey quickly cut all connections, and they'd been enemies since.

Before I could begin to voice my questions – to try to figure out what the hell Tristan was on about – I leaned over and vomited all over the floor.

"Fucking hell, Adelaide!" Joey snapped as Jessie quickly gripped my shoulder and held my hair back out of my face. "You're cleaning this shit up!" He barked at me.

"Ignore him, sweetheart," Jessie told me softly, rubbing my back soothingly as I retched again. "You alright?"

I nodded at her, not admitting weakness. I never would – especially not in front of Tristan. Standing back up to my full height, I glared up at Tristan. "Why are you here, Tristan?" I demanded. "This club doesn't make deals with the Sons of Death. They're actually *loyal* to the people they care about."

Pain momentarily flashed in Tristan's eyes, but honestly, I didn't care. "I'm here to make a deal with Joey." He turned his gaze to Joey, ignoring me. "In exchange for us leaving your crew and your territory alone, I want Adelaide. You deny me this, and I'll fucking wipe your goddamn club off the face of the earth."

Joey's face lit up with an almost uncontrollable fury, as did my own. This was my home – my family – my fucking crew just as much as it was Joey's. "Over my fucking dead body, Grim." Joey snarled. "Adelaide is *mine*."

I swallowed thickly. Why the fuck did Tristan want me? He'd tossed me aside three years ago as if I had never meant shit to him.

Tristan's eyes darkened with rage. "Let me make this clear, Joey," Tristan said with chilling softness. My heart pounded hard in my chest, my eyes nervously flickering to Joey. This wasn't the Tristan I remembered. This was a monster. "I will be leaving with Adelaide tonight with or without your consent." I narrowed my eyes at Joey in a silent warning. He better fucking protect me. I would *not* be fucking leaving with Tristan.

An understanding passed between us as Joey flickered his eyes to me; Joey would do what he could to keep me with him.

That was all that I could ask for. "We can do this civilly, or I can start dropping bodies until you give in." Tristan snapped at Joey, not missing our silent exchange. "Which is it?"

"Hold on!" I shouted, holding up a hand. "Don't I get a fucking say in this?" I snarled up at Tristan, my eyes blazing with rage.

Tristan shook his head at me. I sneered at him, and his lips twitched up into a smirk at my rage. I couldn't fucking believe his audacity. I didn't want him – didn't want to be with him.

He had fucking ruined me. Because of him, I was a mess of a fucking woman.

He turned his attention back to Joey. "Well, which is it?"

Suddenly, something hit me hard in my temple, and I let out a cry of pain, my vision quickly darkening as I began to crumple to the floor.

"Adelaide!" Joey roared.

The last thing I remembered was gun shots and Tristan's muscular arms wrapping around my body before I could completely drop to the ground.

■ ■ ■

My head was throbbing, and I could taste stale vomit in my mouth, not to mention it felt like I'd chewed on fucking cotton balls all night.

Fuck, I had partied way too hard last night.

I slowly ripped my eyes open and cursed softly as I quickly took in my surroundings. This certainly wasn't the fucking clubhouse.

And normally, I woke up with Joey's arm thrown over my waist as he snored next to me. But Joey wasn't anywhere to be found. He never left me alone after a night of partying.

So, where the fuck was I?

The bedroom door opened as I began to push myself up into a sitting position, my head spinning at the movement, nausea rising fast in my throat. I swallowed it back down – a master at keeping myself from getting sick after so many nights of losing myself at the bottom of a liquor bottle.

Tristan strode into the room, a disgruntled scowl settled on his features. Rage rose hot and fast in veins. Why the fuck was I *here* – with him?

Fucking hell, I hadn't seen him in three years – not since he had ripped my heart out and stomped all over it in his steel-toed, black boots on my eighteenth birthday *at my birthday party* that *he* had organized for me.

I hadn't even seen him at my best friend's funeral – his twin's funeral.

"Morning, Addy." He said, shooting a devilish smirk my way that still had my stomach twisting into knots. Fury laced through my veins at myself.

Christ, he couldn't really still be able to affect me like this, could he? It was unfair – life was fucking unfair – and half the time, I felt like it was laughing at me in my face.

I didn't want to feel anything for Tristan but anger and hatred.

"Why am I here?" I demanded to know, wincing when the sound of my voice just made my head hurt so much worse than it already did.

Tristan silently strode over to me and grabbed a bottle of medicine off of the nightstand and a bottle of water. Different emotions swirled in my gut. He had thought about how I would feel when I woke up – enough to set medicine and water near me so I would have quick access to it when I was finally awake.

I hated that it made me long for more of that care. Tristan had never been this attentive when we were together. He just took care of me, but I had been hopelessly in love with him back then – so in love that I overlooked how bad of a boyfriend he was.

"Here." Tristan gruffly spoke up, holding out two pills and the now opened bottle of water.

Silently, I took the medicine, keeping my eyes steady with his. I didn't care how he made me feel. I was here because of him. I wanted to know why the fuck I wasn't with the Sons of Hell – with Joey. "Well?" I demanded.

He shrugged. "I found out that for the last three years, you've been with Joey's crew." He informed me, his anger twisting his features into a snarl, but he didn't intimidate me. Instead, I only got angrier at the fact that *he* thought he had *any* right to be pissed about what I've been doing with my life when *he* was the one that brutally ripped my heart and soul apart.

"I brought you back here where you belong." I opened my mouth to snap at him, but he kept going. "Why the fuck were you with Joey's club?" He snarled down at me.

"Because three years ago on my fucking birthday, Tristan, you fucking ripped my goddamn heart out." I snarled at him. His face paled slightly at my words as he swallowed thickly. "I wanted you to hurt as much as you'd hurt me," I admitted angrily. "So, I fucking betrayed you by joining the one fucking crew you can't *stand*." I lied. In all reality, Joey had offered me a night of fun, and I'd taken it with both hands, just wanting to forget about my heartbreak.

But later that night, when he had gotten ready to drop me off at home and saw where I lived, he just shook his head and drove back off.

"I'm not letting you stay in a fucking trap house – not when you're of legal age now." Joey had told me. "You're coming home with me."

"What the hell?!" I shouted at him. "Joey, turn back around! I'm not going home with you!"

He turned those dark eyes at me, settling the unease in my gut. I didn't know how he did it, but those dark eyes had been soothing me all night. "Pretty girl, you're eighteen now. Any man in that house could now take you, and you'd probably lose the rape case because men get away with that shit all of the time. I won't let you be a victim."

I helplessly tossed my hands up in the air before letting them drop down to my lap. "Well, I don't have anywhere else to go, Joey."

He smirked at me, melting my insides. "You do now, pretty girl." He stopped at the stop sign at the end of the street and reached over, cupping my cheek in his hand. "You have me, pretty girl." My bottom lip trembled, tears burning in my eyes. His words were so sweet, and I was doing my best not to cling onto them, but it was so hard. "You'll always have me."

He glanced behind us at the house we had left behind. "Besides, with how tormented your eyes have looked all night, I have no doubt in my mind that you'd lose yourself inside of every drug you can find in that house, and I won't let you do that to yourself." A tear slid down my face. I had actually planned on doing just that. How had he known?

He leaned forward and brushed his lips to my cheek, catching the tear. "I'm going to teach you how to breathe again, Adelaide."

"Did Helene know?" Tristan demanded, the muscle in his jaw ticking with his outrage as he dragged me out of my head, out of that sweet memory with Joey.

A smirk twisted my lips, my heart squeezing painfully in my chest. "She told me it was a fucking great idea." I retorted, lying straight through my teeth, but he didn't need to know that. Helene had thought Joey would be a good rebound guy for me - nothing more. She hadn't expected nor wanted me to get in so deep with him and his club. "She hated you for doing that to me." I reminded him. He had always loved his sister; I knew that much. They used to be two little peas in a pod.

And I planned to use that to hurt him as much as I could. I was a sadistic bitch, but he had destroyed me.

His face fell the tiniest bit. "I know." He said quietly. "I fucking remember." He admitted.

I shook my head and slid off of the bed. "I need to get back," I told him, not wanting to continue with our conversation. What happened between us was done – it was over – and I had no urge to rehash old feelings, to reopen those wounds deep inside of me. It would do nothing but make me destructive – self-destructive at that.

"You're not going anywhere, Adelaide," Tristan informed me, using my full name.

I narrowed my eyes at him. "Who the fuck are you to dictate my goddamn moves, Tristan?" I sneered. His features darkened, but I wasn't afraid of him. I had faced worse – much worse. Chills slid down my spine at the mere thought of the hell I had recently endured. "I'm fucking grown. I'm no longer that naive little eighteen-year-old girl that begged you to stay and love her." He flinched. "I have shit I need to do, and I can't fucking do that if I'm here." I snapped.

Tristan glared at me as he shook his head. "You're here now, Adelaide. You're done in Joey's crew, got that?"

I picked up the closest thing to me – which happened to be a lamp – and threw it at him. He ducked, letting it crash against the wall and shatter into pieces as it fell to the floor. "I'm not fucking done any goddamn where, Tristan Groves!" I shouted at him, my chest heaving up and down with rage. Who the fuck did he think he was?

He was *not* keeping me from Joey. I would lose myself if I lost Joey.

Tristan made it clear three years ago how he felt about me. I turned to someone else, and that someone else actually cared about me and loved me in his own fucked up way.

Joey and I may clash heads, but he had *never* fucking abandoned me – not like Tristan had done.

Tristan stormed over to me, his eyes almost black as they swirled with rage. I swallowed hard, remembering the kind of rage Tristan kept under the tight composure that he always wore. I tilted my chin up defiantly despite my heart pounding hard in my chest. Tristan had never put his hands on me before, but I'd seen what he was capable of doing to other people – had seen the aftermath – and it had never been a pretty sight.

If he put his hands on me, he would quickly realize why I was Joey's woman.

I was fucking dangerous – lethal. Joey had created a monster to make sure I continued breathing. He had given me a purpose.

He gripped my chin in his grip, his face a mask of absolute rage. "Don't you *dare* do something like that again, understand?" He softly snarled down at me.

I let a smirk twist my lips. "Or what?" I taunted.

I squeaked in shock when he gripped a fistful of my hair and yanked my head back, covering my lips with his. In one quick step, he had me pushed against the wall, his hand sliding around to hold the back of my neck as his other hand tightly gripped my hip. I gasped, opening my lips under his demanding ones as my body surrendered to his. My nerve endings curled tightly, and desire swept through my core, leaving me throbbing and wet as his tongue slid along mine.

Fucking hell, I had forgotten what it was like being with Tristan – being claimed and taken by him.

And I couldn't resist kissing him back. All of those old, buried feelings rose inside of me, and I gripped his cut in my fists, kissing him back just as hungrily.

The shrill ringing of my phone jerked me out of the moment, and with a gasp, I shoved him back from me, my eyes widening in horror.

What in the *hell* had I been thinking – doing?

Tristan cursed, his chest heaving up and down as he tried to catch his breath. "What the fuck is that noise?" He heatedly demanded.

"My phone," I grumbled, moving towards the sound only to find it on the floor beside the bed.

Jessie.

I answered the phone with a drawn-out sigh. "Yes?" I asked.

"Adelaide, you know I've tried protecting you from Joey for the last year since you went off the rails, but I can't do anything this time." She told me right off the bat, her voice sounding slightly panicked.

"What now?" I demanded to know.

"You're with Tristan." She told me. I grunted. It sure as fuck wasn't by choice. "Joey is *pissed*, Adelaide. You can't come back, Adelaide. Promise me that you'll protect yourself." She begged.

I snorted. "Jessie, Joey and I have fallouts all of the time –" I tried reassuring her, but she quickly interrupted me.

"No, Adelaide, this time it's different." She told me. I clenched my jaw, glaring at the sheets of the bed as I sat down, my heart thumping crazily in my chest. My throat burned with tears. He couldn't be doing this. He promised me that I could always keep him with me.

"He's destroyed your entire fucking room, and he's got a meeting this afternoon with a hired hitman." She informed me. I swallowed hard. My life just took a major downward spiral; Joey had officially turned his back on me. "You need to stay hidden."

"Thanks, Jessie, but I can take care of myself." I reminded her quietly.

I hung up, clenching my jaw to hold in my emotions. I quickly pulled up my texts and went to Joey's number, a smirk twisting my lips as I prepared to piss him off even further. I couldn't help it. I was hurting.

I was self-destructing.

Can't wait to see what you've got planned, Joe- Joe. Love you! - Adelaide.

My phone pinged with a text message a moment later, and I felt Tristan hovering over my shoulder as I opened it and read it.

What the fuck are you talking about? -Joey

"What the fuck is going on?" Tristan demanded to know. When I didn't answer him, he gripped my arm and swung me around to face him, his face a mask of rage. My heart was splitting in my chest, the pain billowing out through the rest of my body. "Fucking answer me, dammit." He snarled down into my face, his eyes narrowed down at me.

I shrugged, moving back from him. My heart and mind started going nuts when he touched me. I hated it. I couldn't let him affect me like he used to. I wasn't that same young, foolish, naive girl anymore.

I wanted Joey, but he was giving up on me.

My phone pinged again, this time with a text message from an unknown number.

Wherefore art thou, Adelaide? Tick. Tick. Boom.

"Fuck!" I shouted, gripping Tristan's wrist in my hand as I pulled him towards the bedroom door.

"Addy, what the fuck?!" Tristan shouted, trying to pull me to a stop.

"We've got to get out, Tristan. This place is about to fucking explode!" I barked at him over my shoulder, my heart pounding hard and fast in my chest as adrenaline rushed through my veins.

Something in my gut told me this wasn't Joey's doing. He wouldn't have had time to have a talk with a hitman yet, nor to set up any kind of plan.

Someone was after Tristan.

Or me – there was no real way of knowing. I'd pissed off a lot of people in the past three years.

We rushed out of the old, rundown house right before the ground shook with an explosion. The last thing I remembered was Tristan throwing me to the ground and covering his body with mine before everything went dark.

TWO

I released a soft groan when I turned my head to look over at Tristan, a wince flashing across my face as pain stabbed through my neck from where I'd slept wrong. It was dark outside, and the only sound was the soft purr of the car engine and the tires rolling over the asphalt of the highway. Tristan was driving the car, one hand on the steering wheel, the other on the stick shift between us.

A pang pierced my heart for a moment as I remembered him always giving my knee a gentle squeeze before he used to switch gears.

He had always preferred manual cars over automatics.

"Good to see you awake." He spoke up, glancing over at me before he focused his eyes back on the road.

I rolled my eyes and rolled my neck around, groaning as my neck popped, but that ache finally eased off. "Where are you taking me?" I asked him.

Tristan tapped the steering wheel with two of his fingers, looking in his rear-view mirror before he switched lanes to go around a slower car. "To my cousin's since my house got blown up." He informed me.

I rolled my eyes at him. "Should have kept your nose in your own business." I retorted.

Tristan clenched his jaw. "You don't belong with the Sons of Hell, Addy." Tristan snapped at me. "You belong *here* - with me."

I snorted. "One, stop fucking calling me Addy. You lost that privilege three years ago." Tristan's hand tightened on the steering wheel, his jaw clenching so tightly that the muscle in his jaw began to tick. "Two, I belonged with them a hell of a lot more than I belong with you." I snarled.

Tristan shot a dark look in my direction. I only narrowed my eyes at him in return. He didn't intimidate me anymore, nor did he scare me. "You never used to be like this, Adelaide." Tristan snapped back at me. I snorted. He didn't know who the fuck I was today. He'd been gone for three goddamn years. I wasn't sweet anymore. I was a fucking monster. "What the fuck is going on with you?"

I rolled my eyes. "Did you seriously expect me to still be the same sweet, innocent girl you were with three years ago?" I asked incredulously.

Tristan shrugged, almost as if he actually had been. I rolled my eyes. "The Sons of Hell aren't known for allowing their women to get caught in the dirty shit."

I barked out a laugh. Tristan had no idea how shit operated with the Sons of Hell. I was not only Joey's off-again-on-again girlfriend, but I was also his right-hand woman. "I was in the *middle* of all of the dirty shit, Tristan," I informed him. He clenched his jaw at that information, his eyes flashing with anger. "I smuggled their drugs back and forth across the Mexico border, and I fought when I needed extra cash. I blew shit up, and I delivered hired hits. You don't know a fucking thing about me."

Tristan shook his head, fury lighting up his eyes as he changed lanes again. "I don't know which to be more pissed about." He growled. "You smuggling drugs, or you fighting. Helene refused to tell me about the shit that you were caught up in."

22

"It wasn't any of your fucking business." I retorted. And it wasn't. When it came down to it, Helene protected my secrets, even if she didn't agree with them. And I knew she never spoke to her brother about what I was doing nor what was going on with me. She had at least agreed with me that Tristan didn't deserve to know a damn thing about me after what he had done to me.

"It *was* my fucking business!" Tristan finally roared, slamming his hand on the steering wheel. I clenched my jaw, getting ready for a fight. "Goddammit, Adelaide, I broke your heart all those years ago for your own fucking good, but two weeks ago, I saw you attached to Joey's hip, and he was introducing you as his fucking girl to Vin."

I flinched at Vin's name.

If I thought Tristan had ruined me, then Vin had fucking destroyed me - killed my soul.

Joey was trying to set up an alliance with Vin, and he knew Vin had a soft spot for me. I grimaced as I remembered that night, how I had barely escaped with my life.

Yeah, Vin had a soft spot for me alright.

"What's that look for?" Tristan demanded as I grimaced.

Fuck, he was way too perceptive for his own good.

"Nothing." I snarled, looking out the window. I was done talking to him. "Are we almost there?" I asked as Tristan took an exit.

"Almost." He snapped, still aggravated and pissed off at me for being so secretive. He had no damn right to be pissed, though. Had he seriously expected that he would pop back up into my life and I would fall into his arms again as if he had never hurt me, as if he had never ripped my fucking heart apart and tossed the pieces at my feet? "We'll be at Noah's in about ten minutes," Tristan informed me.

I sighed and leaned my head against the window, looking out at the darkness surrounding us. There were no lights off of this exit, leaving everything encased in a pitch-black color.

"Why couldn't anyone from your crew take us in?" I asked him.

Tristan shot me a deadpan look. "My crew is the first place that whoever is after us is going to look. I need to keep you safe until I can deal with this problem, Addy."

Every time he called me by my nickname, my heart skipped a beat in my chest, and I fucking hated it. I didn't want to react to him at all. I wasn't that weak girl anymore. I was stronger now.

"I can take care of myself, Tristan. I've been doing it for three years now." I reminded him. He clenched his jaw angrily and tightened his grip on the steering wheel, his knuckles turning white. "And stop calling me Addy." I snapped at him. "My fucking name is Adelaide. Start fucking using it."

Suddenly, Tristan yanked the car over to the shoulder of the road, threw it into neutral, and pulled the emergency brake up. He firmly gripped my chin in his hand and brought his face close to mine. My breath hitched in my throat, nervousness filling my gaze.

"Three years ago, I let go of the most important person in the entire world to me to keep her safe from my enemies." My breath hitched in my throat as my heart began to rapidly beat at his words. "Two weeks ago, I found that same woman in the middle of a deal with one of the most feared men of Mexico." I swallowed hard, knowing he was talking about me.

"It took everything in me to not to put a bullet through Vin's head that night, Addy. But that night, I vowed to have you back with me, in my arms, by my side, where you fucking belong and where I know that I can keep you safe. You can fight me on this all you want, Addy, but my mind is set, and I *will* get what the fuck I want."

He ran his thumb over my bottom lip, and I couldn't help the little sigh that escaped my lips at his touch as I closed my eyes, hating that he still affected me so strongly, yet not being able to help leaning

24

into him, wanting more of that strength and security that he was offering me. "And I will not stop calling you Addy, because you are mine, baby girl, whether you like it or not."

With that, he threw his car back into first, put down the emergency brake, and pulled back into traffic. I drew in a shaky breath.

That, ladies and gents, is the possessive, controlling Tristan at his finest.

■ ■ ■

I released a tired sigh and stretched my body out as I stepped out of Tristan's old '67 Mustang. Noah, Tristan's cousin who I remembered as being more like a brother than a cousin to Tristan, stepped out of his small, brick house. I had always thought that Noah was extremely attractive even though Tristan had always held my heart, as much as I hated it at this moment. Noah was also a lot more laid back, and he enjoyed getting on every single one of my nerves.

Noah was wearing only a pair of faded, worn, blue jeans that were hanging low on his hips. He didn't have a shirt on, leaving all of his muscles and abs on display. I flashed him a wicked smirk, and he grinned back at me, his eyes lighting up.

"Adelaide, it's been a while," Noah commented as he strode down his porch steps towards me as Tristan came around the hood of his car to stand next to me, a disgruntled look on his face.

I rolled my eyes. "It hasn't been long enough." I snarkily retorted.

"Ignore her," Tristan told his cousin. Noah turned his amused eyes to his best friend. "Adelaide has been in a very pissy mood since she woke up a little while ago."

I glared at Tristan. "Bite me." I snarled, making Noah bark out a laugh.

Tristan's lips tilted up into that devilish smirk that always made my belly twist with need as he leaned in close to me. My breath hitched in my throat at his proximity. "Don't tempt me." He breathed. I swallowed thickly, my heart pumping blood so fast through my veins that I could feel the rapid beats in my throat. "Because I know the perfect place to bite you in." He huskily reminded me as he reached up and ran his calloused index finger along the curve of my neck where it met my shoulder.

I shuddered at his touch as my eyes locked on his. His eyes darkened at the need shining in my own that I couldn't hide from him no matter how hard I tried to.

But I would fight that need with every fiber of my being.

"Anyway, if you two are done eye-fucking each other, I've got something to tell you two that I don't think Adelaide is going to like too much," Noah commented as he rocked back and forth on his heels, an amused grin on his features as he shoved his hands into the pockets of his jeans.

"What?" I snapped at him, dragging my heated gaze from the man I still somehow wanted more than anything.

And wanting Tristan was dangerous.

"I only have one extra bedroom, and my brother, Josh, is crashing on my couch, so you guys are going to have to share a room," Noah informed us, his grin widening at the rage that flashed in my eyes.

My gaze narrowed on him, my hands twitching at my sides to fucking hit something. Noah held his hands up in a surrendering gesture as he took a step back from me. I looked up at Tristan, but his smirk only widened as he winked at me.

I fucking hated them both.

"Don't look at me like that, Addy, because you know I'm going to take advantage of this arrangement as much as I can." Tristan reminded me.

I stepped up to him and jabbed my finger against his chest, making sure my nail hit him hard. He flinched and reached up to rub his chest. I was seething. "I'd rather fuck Vin again than let you touch me." I snarled up at him, lying through my teeth. I'd never fucked Vin willingly, but Tristan didn't know that.

But I wanted to hit this son of a bitch where it fucking hurt.

Tristan wrapped his larger hand around mine that was still against his chest and tugged me closer to him. Leaning in close to me, he finally spoke, his voice a deadly whisper that chilled the blood in my veins. "The only man touching you in any fucking way will be me, do I make myself clear?"

Not being able to come up with a snarky remark when he was looking down at me so intensely, I just wordlessly nodded my head.

Oh, boy, what have I just been dragged into?

■ ■ ■

I sighed in irritation as I looked at the single, full-size bed in the center of the bedroom.

Why couldn't Noah at least have had a queen size bed?

With Tristan's bulky frame, there was no way we were going to sleep on this bed tonight without touching each other. I knew that Tristan wasn't going to mind in the slightest, considering for some reason he was trying to stay as close as possible to me – wanted me back as his – but I couldn't have that. I had to protect myself and my heart from him at all costs, no matter how hard it was going to be.

At this moment, I missed Joey more than I ever had before. I knew what to expect with Joey. We fought, we fucked, and we were good for a few days. It was like a routine.

I fucking craved that.

"Well, this is nice," Tristan stated as he came into the bedroom, a devilish smirk tilting his lips. I scowled at him. "Ready to cuddle, Addy? It'll be just like old times." He stated, wiggling his eyebrows at me.

My scowl deepened, only causing his smirk to widen.

This was about to be a long night.

"I'm not sleeping on that bed with you." I snapped, pointing down at it.

He clenched his jaw, his amusement quickly disappearing. "Oh, yes, you are." He told me, his voice firm.

I clenched my jaw. I was just about seething, and he didn't want to see how lethal I was when I finally lost my shit. "No, I'm not." I snarled.

His eyes lit up with fury as he stormed over to me in all of his dominating, masculine glory. "Oh, yes, you are." He snarled back down at me again as he gripped my upper arms and yanked me against him. My heart began to rapidly beat in my chest at his proximity. I swallowed nervously. I hated not knowing what to expect with Tristan. "Your life is in danger, and I am *not* letting you out of my arms while we sleep and are at our most vulnerable." I opened my mouth to protest, but he put his finger over my lips, silencing me as his eyes bored into mine.

"You are the most important person to me, Addy, and I will *not* risk anything."

As much as I hated it, my heart melted, my destroyed soul crying out for him to heal us and to put us back together again.

THREE

It was my eighteenth birthday when I first met Joey – the same night that Tristan decided to destroy my heart – decided to leave me in pieces. I was at my birthday party that Helene was throwing me at their place, and I was a fucking mess. I was drinking away my sorrows in a corner, crying into my hands when Joey had knelt in front of me.

He'd seen a broken girl filled with pain, and he'd wanted to help her.

"Hey, gorgeous, aren't you the birthday girl?" He asked me.

I looked up at him through my tears, sniffling unladylike. Nodding slowly, I answered him. "Yeah," I whispered, taking another swig from the bottle of whiskey that I had snatched from the kitchen. His lips twitched, his eyes lighting up in surprise as the liquid burned down my throat, but I never flinched.

"Why are you crying on one of the biggest days of your life?" He asked me, taking a seat beside me on the floor. I flinched, casting my eyes to the floor as I remembered my heart being ripped apart not even an hour ago. "You're too beautiful to be sitting here crying on your birthday, pretty girl."

I blushed at his words even though my heart was filled with so much pain, I wasn't sure if I was capable of feeling anything else. "My boyfriend of three years just broke up with me." I admitted, more tears sliding down my cheeks. He frowned. "I don't know what I did wrong." I pathetically sobbed, everything suddenly spilling from my lips. "We were so happy earlier, and then all of a sudden, he's telling me he doesn't want to be with me anymore, and that he's been miserable for the last year."

"Well, he's a fucking asshole." The guy next to me admitted. I snorted. "Is he still here?" At my nod, he sighed. "Is that why you're hiding in this corner when you should be enjoying your birthday party?"

I nodded again. He pursed his lips, and then stood up, a smirk twisting his lips. My breath hitched in my throat. God, he was hot as fuck.

And I was clearly a little drunk.

"How about this, pretty girl?" He asked me. I arched an eyebrow at him, my tears drying up. "My name is Joey, and I think it's time to let loose and forget about this asshole of an ex for a little while. What do you say? Want to get out of here?"

I nodded at him, desperate for some kind of relief from the pain in my chest. He held his hand out to me, and I placed my hand in his, letting him pull me up to my feet. He wrapped an arm around my waist, a mischievous twinkle lighting up his eyes that almost had me swooning. "It's time to have some fun on the wild side, pretty girl. What's your name?" He asked me.

"Adelaide," I informed him.

"Gorgeous name for a gorgeous girl." He commented.

That night led to many more nights filled with "fun" on the wild side.

But honestly, Joey might have saved my life because back then, I wasn't sure if I could survive without Tristan to lean on.

■ ■ ■

I sat on the bathroom counter, trying to put off dealing with Tristan for as long as I could. I knew he was waiting on me to come out and come to bed before he went to sleep.

But he was going to be waiting a hell of a long time. I'd sleep in this damn bathroom before I slept in the same bed with him again.

I stared down at Jessie's name on my phone. She was calling me again, and I was sorely tempted to answer it. She and I had always been close, especially after Joey and I had started clashing heads a lot a few months after the first few months we were together. She'd always had my back after one of our huge fights, and I knew at the end of the day, she was one of the people that I knew I could always rely on.

Then again, I'd thought that about Joey, too, and that quickly, he'd turned his back on me just because I was with Tristan.

Sighing, I pressed the answer button on my phone, putting it up to my ear. "Hello, gorgeous," I commented, a smirk twisting my lips, actually kind of happy that I would be hearing her familiar voice.

"I figured you'd answer her call and not mine." Joey drawled on the other end of the line. I cursed softly, the smirk dropping from my lips. He sighed softly, sounding extremely tired and worn out. A frown tugged at my lips as worry wound around my heart for the man.

"You actually think you can run from me, pretty girl?" He asked, using his old nickname for me.

"Not really running, Joey," I grumbled, being honest. I mean, I was in a way, but I was running from whoever was after Tristan – or me – still trying to figure that one out.

He snorted. "Right." He sarcastically retorted. I swallowed thickly. "I'll pretend that you didn't just try to fucking lie to me." He snapped. I grimaced. If Joey hated anything, he fucking hated a liar. "Tell you what, pretty girl," he said, calling me by that old, familiar nickname again. I swallowed thickly. God, I missed him. "You come back to me by tomorrow night, and I'll fix all of this bad shit between us. We're good as hell together, pretty girl, and you're in too deep in this shit to try to run away now." He reminded me.

I swallowed hard, all of those old feelings rising in me. Joey had drawn me out of the funk that I had fallen into after Tristan and I had broken up. He was my rebound in a way, and after a few months, he became a lot more than that to me. Although we were toxic as fuck together, I couldn't deny that I still deeply cared about Joey – always would. He was my rock.

"Joey, you know that I would never rat on you." I reminded him. "I went through hell and back to protect you and your secrets." And he knew what kind of hell I'd gone through. How many times had I finally come back home to him, beaten to within an inch of my life to protect him? It was certainly more times than I could count on one hand,

He sighed. "You leaving right now was a really bad choice, Adelaide. You need to come back home, pretty girl."

"Why, Joey?" I angrily demanded. He knew how much I hated being given the run-around.

"Pretty girl, I've got a lot of explaining to do, alright? Just . . . fuck, I always seem to fuck up with you." He admitted. "Pretty girl, I know what Jessie said to you. *I* never put a hitman on you. I tried to set up a meeting to get one off of your back, but it didn't fucking work." I swallowed thickly. "There's a man that's supposed to be bringing you back to me, but he's not going to hurt you. He's supposed to protect you until he can get you back here to me."

"But Tristan's house -" I started.

"Vin is after you." Joey interrupted me.

My hand tightened around the phone, and I swallowed down vomit. Now wasn't the time to be throwing up. "V-Vin?" I stuttered, my face paling. Even his name left a nasty, bitter taste in my mouth.

I could picture Joey running his hand down his face in my mind. "Yes, pretty girl. I had no idea what the fuck Vin was doing to you. I had no idea he fucking raped you." I flinched and squeezed my eyes shut, resisting the urge to whimper as his malicious face popped into my mind. "I know it doesn't make up for shit, Adelaide, but I'm *so* fucking sorry that I didn't protect you better." He apologized. I resisted the urge to cry. God, I hated it when Joey felt guilty about shit that happened to me – especially shit that wasn't his fault. "He told me he was using you for some fights – that's it."

I swallowed hard. "I was the only one to escape him, Joey," I whispered.

"I know, pretty girl. I need you to come back home, alright? Fucking hell, at this point, I wouldn't give a fucking shit if you brought Tristan with you. You need protection until this Vin situation can be dealt with. The more protection you have, the fucking better. I won't lose you, Adelaide – especially not to fucking death."

The bathroom door opened, and Tristan stood there, his expression murderous. I glared back at him, defiance gleaming in my gaze. "Why the *fuck* are you talking to Joey, Addy?" Tristan snarled at me.

"Let me talk to him, pretty girl," Joey told me gently. "Don't fight him, Adelaide. Just let me talk to him."

With a sigh, I slowly held my hand out to Tristan, offering him the phone. He glared down at it, not reaching forward to take it. He instead looked back up at me. "Tristan, please," I whispered.

I just wanted to go back home where I knew I was okay, back to the man that I knew what to expect with – the man that I knew would never, truly let me down – not where it truly counted.

Tristan's expression softened when he actually paid attention to how terrible I looked at the moment. Wordlessly, he took the phone from my hand. Stepping between my legs, he wrapped his free arm around my waist, tugging me up close to his hard, muscular frame as he put my phone to his ear.

I hated myself for it – knew I shouldn't want it – but I leaned into him, allowing Tristan to silently comfort me. I closed my eyes, allowing myself this one, small moment of peace between us.

"What?" Tristan grumbled into the phone.

I could hear Joey explaining everything to Tristan as best as he could. Tristan's body tensed against mine, and his eyes flickered down to me more than once, fury lacing their depths as he held me tighter against him when Joey told him about Vin.

"We'll be on our way back in the morning," Tristan informed him. "I'll have my crew meet us at your place. The more protection on her, the better."

"I agree," Joey told him.

"Just let me ask this." Tristan started, his fingers absentmindedly running up and down my spine. I sighed softly, my eyes beginning to slide closed. He remembered one of the ways to calm me down. Tristan used to do this all the time when we were younger, and honestly, I missed his soft, soothing touch. "Why are you all of a sudden being protective over Addy?" He demanded to know.

"I've always been protective of her in my own way, Tristan," Joey told him. And he had. "Adelaide and I have a silent agreement of sorts. She hates being doted over, and she wants to be free to make her own decisions. I protect her from the background, and I only step forward when something drastic is happening – like now." Joey told him. "She's not the same girl whose heart you broke three years ago, Tristan. She's changed, and she's grown into a hell of a woman."

I couldn't stop the smile that crossed my lips at Joey's words.

"Whatever," Tristan grumbled, obviously not pleased by that bit of information. "I'll text you and let you know when we're on the road," Tristan informed him, hanging up the phone right after.

After a few silent moments, Tristan finally looked down at me. "What kind of history do you and Joey have?" Tristan asked me, his voice gruff.

I tilted my chin up defiantly as I leaned back from him, every one of my guards going back up against Tristan – hard. He was digging too deep into something that wasn't his fucking business. "I don't think that fucking concerns you." I snapped at him.

Tristan placed a hand on either side of me on the counter and leaned down so his face was only a couple of inches from mine. My breath hitched in my throat at his proximity. His eyes almost undid me as he let them meet mine. "It *does* concern me when I'm back to claim what's mine," Tristan informed me softly. I swallowed thickly, my heart racing in my chest at his words, but whether from hope or fear, I wasn't sure. "And believe me when I say this, Addy; I will have you back no matter who or what I have to hurt or destroy to get my way."

With that, he stood back up to his full height and walked out of the bathroom.

I dropped my face into my hands, my heart racing in my chest at his words.

When did my love life become so fucking complicated?

■ ■ ■

I stepped into the Sons of Hell's clubhouse, the familiar smell of cigarettes and liquor instantly infiltrating my nostrils. Tristan was walking close behind me, his Vice President, Sergeant at Arms, and

Treasurer following close behind him while his other men stayed outside.

I found Jessie working the bar, so I walked over to her, leaning over the bar to grab my own bottle of Vodka. "Hey, gorgeous." I greeted. "Where's Joey?"

She jerked her head in the direction of the back where the combat ring was set up. "There's a fight going on out there right now. Joey's out there handling bids." She informed me.

I shot her a smile, and she snatched the bottle of Vodka back out of my hands, her eyes playfully narrowing at me. "You've got to stop drinking all of the Vodka, gorgeous." She lightly teased.

I rolled my eyes at her. She only laughed as I walked off towards the back of the clubhouse, feeling Tristan following close on my heels. I pushed open the back door, and sure enough, two men were beating each other bloody in the ring, and Joey was handling the money as he held a conversation with his Vice President, Charles.

Joey looked up when I stepped out of the clubhouse onto the gravel, a smile tilting his lips the slightest bit, warming that spot in my heart that would always solely belong to him.

I quickly walked over to him, and he instantly wrapped me up in his arms, pressing a kiss to my temple. I sighed softly, my body relaxing as I sank into his familiar, safe embrace. "Good to have you back home where you belong, pretty girl." He murmured. He brushed his finger over a bruise on my cheek from the house explosion. "You alright?" He asked me, a wave of slight anger flashing in his eyes before he smothered it.

I nodded at him. "I'm fine," I assured him.

Tristan gripped my arm and pulled me back from Joey, holding his hands over my shoulders. I scowled as I reached up to brush his hands off my shoulders. "Let me just make this clear," Tristan said, his voice coming off calm, but extremely cold. It sent chills down my spine just at the sound of it. "Adelaide is mine." He snapped at Joey. "Keep your goddamn hands off of her."

"I'm no one's." I snarled, ripping myself away from Tristan, throwing him a harsh glare as I did so.

He narrowed his eyes at me. "Remember what I told you?" He asked me, making me swallow hard.

No matter who or what I have to destroy to get my way.

"You're a fucking sadistic asshole." I snarled up at him.

He smirked, but it lacked any humor, instead coming off cold. It made my stomach turn as I stepped back slightly into Joey. Joey silently settled his hands over my hips. "Always have been, Addy." Tristan retorted. He narrowed his eyes where Joey was lightly gripping my hips, but he kept his mouth shut.

The urge to punch him was still strong, though.

I turned to Joey. "I want to fight," I told him.

He inclined his head to me. "You sure?" He asked me. I nodded. "You've been through a lot of shit lately, pretty girl." He gently reminded me, knowing how I could get in the ring when I was overwhelmed.

I clenched my jaw, glaring at him. "Joey . . ." I warned softly.

He nodded with a shrug of his shoulders. "Alright then, pretty girl. Go change. I'm giving you five minutes to get in that clubhouse, change, and come back out. Rachel just came back, and she's itching to fight you."

I nodded once in understanding. Tristan gripped my arm as I went to move past him, and his eyes narrowed on mine when I looked up at him. "You're not fucking fighting." He snarled down at me.

I ripped my arm from his grip, glaring up at him as I did so. "You don't fucking own me, Tristan." I snarled at him. "You want me, you take all of me just the fucking way I am, got that?"

I stormed into the clubhouse before he could get another word in. I was so sick of him trying to control every little damn thing I did. I'd found myself, found my fucking independence. I didn't need a damn man dictating every single thing for me anymore.

And Tristan better figure that shit out quick.

After changing into a black sports bra and a pair of sweatpants, I slid on my black high tops and threw my hair up into a messy bun, not caring if it was perfect or not. I planned to have blood coating my hands by the time this match was over. How I looked as I did it was the least of my fucking concerns.

I was a fucking monster, and Tristan was going to see that very quickly.

I walked back out of the clubhouse to see Tristan sitting on one of the tables beside Joey, his VP Jesup flanking his side.

Joey looked up at me as I walked over to him. "Ready?" He asked me. I nodded. He ran his eyes over my face for a moment before he nodded. "Alright, remember to keep your face and your stomach covered. Rachel's not going to go easy on you."

I nodded in understanding. "Got it," I told him.

Tristan gripped my wrist before I could spin away to go to the ring, his eyes intent on mine. I could see worry for my well-being shining in their depths, and I swallowed hard, my heart skipping a beat at the unfamiliar, tender look. "Be careful up there, alright?" He murmured.

I nodded, shooting him a small smile. I could take care of myself. Tristan didn't know who I was today, but if he stuck around long enough, he would quickly find out.

And though Tristan got on my fucking nerves, I could deal with him being an asshole. It was familiar territory for me because it was easy as fuck for me to be bitchy back.

But when he got all caring? I didn't know how to deal with him. It made my heart skip beats as my stomach fluttered.

Reluctantly, Tristan let me go. I walked up to the makeshift ring, waiting for Joey to announce me and Rachel into the ring.

■ ■ ■

TRISTAN

Fucking hell, she was so much sexier than she'd been at eighteen.

In the three years that I had been gone, she had filled out into a beautiful, young woman, and she'd eventually shaped into a fucking goddess. The woman standing at the edge of that ring was fucking magnificent. No one could ever compare to her.

I could tell she worked out a lot by the defined muscles of her abdomen, and I could see the hint of muscle in her arms. She was light as a feather; I knew that from carrying her, but I had no damn idea that she was this fucking fit.

"She'll do alright," Joey assured me.

I just pretended to not hear him. I hated that he knew her better than I did – hated that when she was near him, she leaned into him without realizing it. She instantly sought him out in a room.

She looked at him like she *used* to look at me.

And yeah, I had ruined that shit between us, but I was back now. I was back to fix this shit with her.

I just needed her to stop fighting me every step of the damn way.

With a grunt, Joey got up and walked up into the ring. "Alright, first up we have Rachel Keen. She's a guest here from one of our other charters." Joey announced, looking at the far corner of the ring.

A few cheers went up, and I watched as a girl with blonde hair stepped into the ring. She was wearing a bright pink sports bra with a pair of tight pink workout shorts that showed her ass cheeks. I heard some whistles come up around the crowd, and I scowled.

She had absolutely nothing on Addy.

"And next, we all have your favorite – Adelaide!" Joey roared, reaching down to help her up into the ring.

Adelaide came up in the ring, and a roar went up in the crowd surrounding the ring, the noise almost deafening.

"She's not the same girl, Grim," Jesup said, calling me by my street name.

I nodded in agreement. "Trust me, I know," I grumbled. "The old Adelaide would have never even *thought* about violence like this," I admitted.

And that thought made me sick to my stomach. Just who was Adelaide today?

"You ladies know the rules," Joey told them. "No hair pulling, no biting. Fight fair. The winner leaves here with a grand in their pocket."

They both nodded in understanding. Joey stepped out of the ring. "Fight!" He roared.

Adelaide quirked an eyebrow at Rachel, a smirk twisting her lips. I felt my blood chill at the sight of that smirk. This version of Addy was cold – she was a true fighter.

"Are you sure you don't want to back out while you've got a chance?" Addy taunted her. Rachel scowled. "I see you wrapped your pretty little knuckles up." She laughed.

I looked at Rachel's hand, and sure enough, her knuckles were wrapped in bandages to keep them from getting scarred.

Adelaide's hands were bare, and I suddenly realized why she had so many scars covering her knuckles and her hands.

She fought bare-handed.

Rachel curled her lip up at Adelaide. "Watch me beat your ass like Vin did." She snarled.

Adelaide snapped.

Before Rachel had time to react, Adelaide slammed her shoulder into Rachel's abdomen, sending them crashing to the matted floor. Rearing her fists back, Adelaide sent repeated blows against Rachel's face. Rachel was so blinded by panic that she couldn't figure out how to fight back.

Adelaide was a fucking monster in that ring.

Blood was splattering the white mat around them, and Adelaide wasn't showing any signs of stopping. Even after Rachel had knocked out unconscious beneath her, Adelaide kept swinging.

Joey and I made it into the ring at the same time, and he stayed back while I gripped Adelaide's shoulders, pulling her off of Rachel. She jammed her elbow into my ribs, and I coughed out a breath, locking her arms against her sides as I held her to me, her back pressed to my front.

"Adelaide, chill." I snapped into her ear. Her chest was heaving up and down, her expression a mask of pure rage. It was almost as if she wasn't even in the ring with us anymore. "Addy, you need to close your eyes and take a few deep breaths." I coaxed.

She shook her head. "Get the fuck off of me." She snarled as she tried kicking backward, though I thankfully dodged her foot just in time.

Gripping her chin, I turned her head, pressing my lips to hers. I instantly felt the tension leave her body as her lips worked with mine, a soft moan falling from her lips. My cock hardened in my jeans at the sound, and though I desperately wanted to deepen that kiss, I slowly pulled back after a moment, opening my eyes to look down at her beautiful face.

She was calm again – or at least back here at the clubhouse with us – her cheeks flushed and her lips a bit swollen from me kissing her so hard.

"You good?" I asked her gently, brushing a stray hair out of her face that had fallen from her bun.

She swallowed hard and nodded before she looked down at Rachel. Her face paled slightly. "Get me out of here, Tristan." She whispered. She swallowed hard. "Please." She added on at the end, her voice pleading with me.

I nodded and led her to the side of the ring. Joey looked at me before he ran his eyes over Adelaide, concern in his eyes. "Take her to her room in the clubhouse. She'll want a good shower." He told me.

I nodded in understanding. I hated that he seemed to know so much about her, but at the same time, I was a bit grateful for it because I was honestly a bit terrified that I wouldn't be able to handle Addy in this state.

The Addy I remembered was sweet and innocent. She blushed when I so much as looked her way, and she *hated* violence with a passion after growing up in a trap house.

This Addy had just beaten a girl into a bloody pulp in pure rage.

No matter who she was today, I knew she was still my Addy. I just had to learn to be patient and wait for her to come around to me.

FOUR

ADELAIDE

I nodded my head to the beat of the song coming through my radio, lightly tapping my fingers to the beat on the steering wheel of my car as I drove aimlessly down a random back road.

After my fight earlier, I had scrubbed myself down in the shower and escaped through the window in my room to go for a drive.

I had to get the fuck away from there.

I knew how destructive I was – how much of a monster I could be. But I had almost killed Rachel in that ring.

And that? That wasn't me – not if I wasn't trying to survive. But I had heard Vin's name, and I snapped – I lost control of myself.

I glanced up into my rearview mirror but did a double-take when I saw someone was coming up fast on my ass. I cursed at the black Charger. Its windows were illegally tinted, and there was a slight mark on the front end that alerted me that the person following me was the one from my fucking nightmares.

The only person I knew that drove a black Charger with illegally tinted windows and that mark on the front end was Vin.

He'd fucking found me.

I instantly tightened my hand around the steering wheel and floored my black Camaro, looking for the next side road. I knew my way around this area, and I knew that I could easily find my way back to the clubhouse.

It would bring shit on the Sons of Hell, but I had no other choice. Vin would fucking slit my throat if he got his hands on me, and I knew Joey would protect me if I could get to him.

I refused to let that asshole get his grimy fucking hands on me again.

I would fucking kill myself before I allowed that shit to happen again.

I almost missed the next road since it was kind of hidden in a curve, and I cursed, hitting the brake as I whipped my wheel, my back end sliding as I made the sharp turn onto the road at the very last second. I saw Vin fly past me, but as he was passing me, I saw him hitting his brakes.

I floored it again, looking for the next side road that would lead me to the clubhouse. I knew this road. Joey liked to use it when he was bringing in guns and drugs. The next road that led to the clubhouse was hidden well, only used by the club since it ended at the back of the Sons of Hell's property.

A couple of minutes later, I swung my car onto the next road that led to the back gate of Joey's crew. My heart was pounding as I saw the gates up ahead. They were locked tight, and there wasn't anyone standing guard.

"Here goes nothing," I whispered.

My phone switched to a song with more base as I laid on my horn, warning whoever was on the other side of the gate that I was about to crash through the fucking thing and to get the fuck out of my way.

I jutted forward in my seat as I slammed through the gate, the seatbelt locking around me, stealing the air from my lungs as I slammed my forehead onto the steering wheel. My airbags burst out, filling the air around me with white powder. I coughed as I pushed it out of my face. I had so much adrenaline running through my body that I didn't even feel the pain.

My door was ripped open, and I blinked up at Tristan, slightly dazed as the white powder floated out of the car. "Are you out of your damn mind?" He barked at me as he reached over me to unsnap my seatbelt.

I slowly turned to get out of the car, and Tristan gripped my upper arms to help me out. I stumbled slightly, my vision blurring as I stood on my feet.

"You're bleeding." He muttered, reaching up to wipe a little bit of blood from my forehead.

"Vin," I muttered. "He – Vin was following me." I managed to get out.

"Here, sit down, Addy." Tristan gently said, easing me onto the ground so that I could lean back against my car. "You're in shock."

"Guard that fucking gate!" I heard Joey bark at someone as he came over towards us. He leaned into my car and turned it off, shutting off my music. He knelt in front of me, his dark eyes running over my face, taking in the blood trickling from my forehead and down my cheek. "What happened, pretty girl?" He gently asked me.

"Vin was following her," Tristan informed him as I leaned my head back against my car, finally registering the pain in my head from where I had hit my steering wheel.

"What in the fuck were you doing off of the clubhouse grounds to begin with, Adelaide?" Joey demanded. I slowly rolled my head around to look at him. "You were supposed to be resting after that fight."

"I had to get away," I told him quietly, knowing he would understand. Joey sighed, a frown tugging at his lips.

"Getting away almost got you killed, Addy," Tristan spoke up. I looked up at him. His arms were crossed over his broad chest, making the muscles in them bulge a bit. Joey rested a hand on my knee and gave it a gentle squeeze - a silent reminder that Tristan wouldn't understand.

He didn't know the woman I was now.

"You told me you were going to sleep after you got a shower." Tristan reminded me, an accusation in his tone.

I shrugged. "You should learn that what comes out of my mouth usually can't be trusted." I snarkily retorted, not being able to help but piss him off further.

"I should have fucking known you wouldn't have rested after blacking out like that," Joey grumbled. I slowly looked over at him. His eyes were tender and understanding as he met my eyes, but there was slight anger in their depths as well. "But Adelaide, you can't just run off like that without *at least* letting someone know. What if Vin had been able to catch you? We might not have been able to save you in time."

I sighed. "I got it," I grumbled. "I fucking got it."

Before Joey could respond, I heard gun shots ring out around us. Tristan cursed as he dropped down to the ground beside me, him and Joey pulling guns out of their cuts at the same time. Tristan wrapped an arm around my waist, tugging me close to him. "Can you use a gun?" He asked me.

I nodded in answer to him. He thrust a pistol into my hand and pressed his lips to my forehead - the part that wasn't bleeding. Despite the dangerous situation we were in, my heart fluttered in my chest. "If someone that's not one of my men or Joey's men comes near you, fucking shoot them." He harshly ordered.

I watched as Tristan inched around the car, crouching at the hood. He started firing back, Joey right beside him. I kept my eyes trained on the area surrounding me. Soon, the gun shots died down, and I heard cars tear off of the lot, giving up for now. Tristan stood up and came over to me. "You alright?" He asked me.

I nodded, pushing myself up off of the ground. "Vin?" I guessed.

Tristan nodded in answer to my question. Joey came over to me. "You need to get in that clubhouse." He instructed me, his eyes hard, still in his President mode. I clenched my jaw. "I'll get one of the men to get your car over to the garage to get fixed."

I narrowed my eyes at him. "You know no one works on my car besides me, Joey." I snarled at him.

He stepped towards me, our toes touching as he towered over me, his eyes narrowing down at me. I tilted my chin up at him defiantly. "Get the fuck over it." He snarled at me. I bristled. Joey was worried about me, and he was itching for a fight. "Twice in the past ten fucking minutes, your life has been jeopardized. Get your fucking ass in that goddamn clubhouse!" He barked down at me, pointing his finger in the direction of the clubhouse.

I spit in his face. He slowly closed his eyes and stepped back from me, using his shirt to wipe my spit off of his face. "You better watch who the fuck you're talking to." I snarled at him. "In case you've fucking forgotten, I still hold a goddamn gun in my hand."

He opened his eyes and arched an eyebrow at me, anger flaring in his eyes. "You threatening me, pretty girl?" He asked me, his tone low and dangerous – the true, terrifying criminal within him coming to the surface.

I stepped up to him, glaring up into his handsome face. I wasn't afraid of Joey. He knew that. "I'm making a promise." I seethed. "If you ever talk to me again like you just did, I will fucking shoot you, understand? I'm not one of your goddamn men."

"Get the fuck out of my sight." He snarled.

Tristan gripped my arm and pulled me back from Joey when I reached up to jab my finger into his chest, ready to spew some more shit at him. "Come on," Tristan told me, trying to deescalate the situation. "You both need to calm down."

"Don't tell me what the fuck I need to do." I snarled up at him, ripping my arm from his grip.

He gripped my upper arms and snatched me against his hard, muscular frame, glaring down at me. I swallowed hard. I still wasn't used to this side of Tristan. "I'm not Joey, Addy. Watch yourself." He snapped at me.

I let a careless smirk twist my lips. "You going to hit me, Tristan?" I asked him – almost taunting him.

He leaned his head down so his lips brushed against my ear. I shivered, my breath hitching in my throat as my eyes closed. *Oh, God, what the fuck was he doing to me?* "I'm not that kind of man, Addy, but I will throw you over my shoulder, drag you into your room, and fuck you senseless." He breathed into my ear.

My eyes snapped open as white-hot desire rippled straight down to my core. He leaned back up and reached up with one of his hands to brush the pad of his thumb over my bottom lip. My breath hitched in my throat. "Got it?" He asked.

I wordlessly nodded my head, currently lost for words.

■ ■ ■

I silently watched as Tristan leaned his muscular body over the pool table with his cue stick in his hand, getting ready to break the triangle of balls on the table. I couldn't help but let my eyes linger on his ass for a moment.

For a man, he really was gifted with a great, toned ass. It was the kind you wanted to sink your nails into – or hell, even your teeth.

"You stare at that man any harder, gorgeous, and you'll burn holes into his ass," Jessie commented as she leaned over the bar to hand me another beer.

Dragging my eyes away from Tristan, I turned my head to smirk at her. "At least this way I can check him out without him trying to fuck me every time I turn around." I retorted. She released a loud laugh. "It's been three years since I've seen him, much less been with him like that." I reminded her. "I don't exactly know how to deal with him." A soft frown pulled at her lips as her eyes filled with concern for me. "He's ten times cockier than he was when we were eighteen."

Jessie sighed. "Maybe that's a good thing, gorgeous. You need some sexiness like him in your life again." She told me, trying her best to lighten the mood again.

I pursed my lips. "I don't know. I think I've got enough of that in my life with your brother."

Jessie snorted. "Look, I know Joey is my brother and all, but you don't react to him the way you react to Tristan. That man comes within five feet of you, and everyone around you can see just how much he affects you."

I rolled my eyes. "He does not -" I started, but I cut myself off, my anger roaring through my veins when I saw Lacie – one of the club women – saunter up to Tristan and press herself against him, a flirty smile on her lips.

"Oh, he doesn't affect you, hm?" Jessie asked me, a knowing smirk on her lips.

I ignored her as I guzzled half of my beer down as I watched him smirk down at her and whisper something into her ear that had her blushing and giggling. I clenched my jaw. "Two can play at this fucking game." I snarled, getting up from my stool.

Worry for me flashed in Jessie's eyes. "Don't do anything stupid, Adelaide."

I only shot her a smirk before I turned around to go to the pool table, sliding up to Joey's side. I could feel Tristan's eyes on me, but I completely ignored him as I smiled up at Joey. "I'm sorry about earlier," I murmured. I knew I was trying to make Tristan feel what I was feeling, but I did mean those words to Joey. I truly was sorry.

Joey gave me a soft smile as he wrapped an arm around my waist and kissed my jaw. "I know, pretty girl. We were both pissed at each other. I'm sorry, too." He apologized.

This was one of the things I loved about Joey. He knew he had his faults, and he wasn't afraid to admit that he had fucked up with me, just as I wasn't afraid to apologize to him when I acted like a class-A bitch.

I splayed my hands over his muscular chest, looking up at him from under my lashes. "Makeup sex?" I asked him softly.

He smirked, his eyes flaring with his need for me. "I'll never turn that down, pretty girl." He thrust his pool stick at Charles. "Charles is taking my place." He announced to Tristan. "I've got something to tend to."

I could feel Tristan's glare on my back as I laced my fingers through Joey's and tugged him towards his room, but I didn't give a fuck. I might have originally started out wanting to piss Tristan off, but now, I wanted Joey.

I wanted that normalcy I'd always had with him, and I knew Joey would give that to me – would take care of me like I needed.

Joey would always be the one man that I knew I could rely on in my time of need.

■ ■ ■

TRISTAN

I gently pushed the blonde woman away from me, clenching my jaw as I watched Adelaide disappear down the hall into one of the rooms with Joey. I wanted to rush after them and fucking rip him away from her – bash his fucking face into my knee.

The blonde pouted up at me. "Tristan." She whined.

I was so sick of club women. The only fucking woman I wanted was Adelaide, and she didn't fucking want me.

Every rejection from her cut me deep.

"No." I snapped at the blonde, not able to control my temper. She flinched back from me, her eyes widening with fear. "I'm not fucking interested. Go fuck someone else." I snarled.

She glared up at me as she recovered from her shock. "Getting tangled up with Adelaide will only get you killed." She spit up at me.

This girl was treading on dangerous fucking waters. She had no fucking clue what kind of woman Adelaide was.

Do you even know who she is? My mind snapped back at me.

I stepped towards the blonde, my eyes narrowing dangerously at her. Her face paled, and she quickly stepped back from me. I could see her pulse jumping erratically at the base of her neck in fear. "Unless you've got something nice to say about Adelaide, I'd advise you to keep your fucking mouth shut." I quietly warned her, my voice deadly and frightening – a clear warning that talking shit about Adelaide was off fucking limits.

I turned on my heel and stormed over to the bar, not interested in playing pool anymore. Jessie arched an eyebrow at me as I plopped onto one of the bar stools, a scowl settled over my features. "Something strong?" She guessed.

Wordlessly, I nodded. She grabbed a glass and filled it with ice, pouring hundred proof vodka into the glass afterward. I caught the glass as she slid it towards me, the ice making a clanking sound in the glass. "If it makes you feel any better, she only went to fuck my brother to make you jealous," Jessie informed me as she raised her dark eyes to meet mine.

I arched an eyebrow at her. "Who said I give a shit about Adelaide?" I retorted.

Jessie smirked and leaned forward on the bar, propping her chin up on her hand. "It's written all over your face, sweetie." She told me. She leaned back up and shrugged. "Adelaide saw you with Lacie, and she got pissed."

I pinched the bridge of my nose with a rough sigh. Most of the time, I didn't know how to even begin to deal with Addy. She was so different from the girl I fell in love with so many years ago. I missed the old her so fucking much – missed the girl who was sweet and kept me grounded.

Adelaide now? She was wild – untamed – and completely fucking dangerous.

"I love that woman more than I should." I grumpily admitted, swallowing some of the Vodka in the glass, not even making a face as the alcohol burned down my throat.

Jessie shrugged. "I could see the love you have for her when you laid your eyes on her the night of her birthday party," Jessie told me. I grunted. "But I'm going to warn you now that Adelaide has been through some shit, and she doesn't love easily anymore. Not after what you did to her, and especially not after your sister died."

She informed me. I couldn't hold in my flinch. The loss of my twin sister was still fresh.

"When Helene lost her fight to cancer, it seemed like Adelaide lost the last part of her that made her human. Sometimes, I swear she doesn't feel anything." Jessie's eyes lifted from the bar and met mine. "Well, until you came along, that is."

"Helene was always her rock," I remembered, that familiar sadness ringing through me as I thought of my younger twin sister. She'd been the light of everyone's life, and she had been Adelaide's only friend. Growing up in a trap house like Adelaide had, friends were few and far between, and having someone that she could trust was even rarer.

"Look, I love my brother to death," Jessie informed me, "but I'm going to be honest with you here. I love Adelaide - she's like the sister I've never had, and I want what's best for her. She and my brother are toxic as fuck together, but he also knows how to keep her grounded - keep her alive. If it weren't for Joey always bringing out that fire in Adelaide, I'm not even sure she would be alive today." I swallowed thickly. "But Adelaide also needs someone to bring her out of that fucking hole she's in, and I know that you can do that if you can just manage to get past that wall that she's built up against you."

"How did she even get like this?" I demanded to know. "She used to be so sweet and innocent."

Jessie sighed, and judging by her face, I knew I wasn't going to like the sound of whatever she said next. "Not going to lie to you, Tristan, it all started with you." I flinched. "When you broke up with Adelaide on her birthday, Joey met her, and he gave her the freedom that she needed, but he also got her caught up in some fucked up shit to bring her out of her funk. Adelaide was dead inside - you killed a part of her." Pain lanced through my chest. "The first time I met

Adelaide, she and Joey had been together for three months, and she was snorting a line of coke up her nose."

I roughly ran a hand down my face, hating myself now more than I ever had before. I had left Adelaide so that I could protect her – had destroyed her heart to keep her safe.

But I only drove her into the arms of just another form of the devil that I was already trying to protect her from to begin with.

Fucking hell.

"Apparently, Adelaide had been doing runs for Joey for a while." I shook my head in disgust. Women weren't meant to be a part of this shit. "I met Helene that same day. Your sister had come into the clubhouse to find Adelaide, and she instantly started yelling at Adelaide for snorting that line of coke up her nose. Helene helped her get clean, but your sister wasn't enough to help your sister heal."

"Adelaide told me that Helene got her caught up with Joey – said she even encouraged Adelaide."

Jessie shook her head with a bitter laugh. "She thought Joey would be a great rebound guy for Adelaide, but nothing more. She was pissed as hell when she found out that Adelaide was caught up in this life, but by the time Helene found out, Adelaide was already in too deep to get out even if she wanted to. But she didn't; Adelaide *needs* this."

"Fuck." I whispered. What the fuck had I done to the sweet, innocent girl that used to be Adelaide?

"The two years between her eighteenth birthday and Helene's death, Adelaide seemed normal for the most part after she got clean. She did the runs for Joey, and she fought when she needed extra money." Jessie released a sad sigh. "But Adelaide lost the last part of herself that kept her sane when Helene lost her fight to cancer on the morning of Adelaide's birthday."

I fucking remembered that day like it was yesterday.

I had been sitting in my clubhouse, staring at Addy's picture on the background of my phone, wishing I had everything figured out so that I could go back and claim her as mine again. I had been daydreaming about the day that Adelaide would be mine again.

Then, I had received a call from the hospital.

Helene was pronounced dead when paramedics got to her apartment.

"She won't celebrate her birthday anymore, Tristan," Jessie informed me.

I swallowed hard. "I can guess why," I muttered. Not only had Helene passed away on her birthday, but I had destroyed her.

I wouldn't want to celebrate my birthday either after that kind of luck.

"She was so happy when she got up that morning and drove over to Helene's apartment. I was with her." Jessie told me. I swallowed thickly as I stared down at the bar. I knew this was shit I needed to hear – needed to know if I wanted any chance of understanding Adelaide any better – but it sure as fuck didn't make it any easier to know. "We were all going to go shopping, eat out, and party our hearts out at a club that night, but when we got there, Helene wasn't responding to the knocks on her door."

I swallowed hard. "Don't tell me," I whispered.

"Adelaide unlocked the door and found her on the couch, but Helene was already gone." Jessie continued. "I called 9-1-1, and Joey had to come to get Adelaide because she was losing her fucking mind. She was screaming and crying, not making any sense. I didn't know how to help her." Jessie drew in a deep breath. "Joey saved her that day. She was ready to end her life to be with Helene."

She'd found my sister, and in one day without ever knowing it, I'd almost lost Adelaide, too.

I dropped my face into my hands, blowing out a harsh breath.

"Are you okay?" Jessie asked me, as if I deserved any kind of kindness after the hell I had put Adelaide through.

I nodded. "I hadn't realized it was her that found Helene," I admitted. I should have known, though. "The doctor only told me that a friend of hers found her and called 9-1-1. I can't even begin to imagine what the fuck that did to her."

"The girl you saw beat the fuck out of Rachel earlier," Jessie commented, "that's the Adelaide we all know now. She's a fighter, and she's vicious as fuck – deadly. Even Joey treads carefully around her sometimes, but Tristan – be careful around him. Joey will destroy the fucking world over her. They may scream and yell at each other, and sometimes, Adelaide might even throw shit at him, but Joey loves her in his own twisted, fucked-up way. He made her into a monster to help her – and she *is* a monster, Tristan. She's destructive."

"That scary?" I asked her.

Jessie shook her head, looking over towards the hallway as Addy emerged, her face twisted into a scowl as she hollered something over her shoulder.

"Nope. Just that unpredictable." Jessie muttered.

"Don't fucking be a bitch when you were the one fucking using *me* to get to him!" Joey roared after her as he came out of the hallway as well, his eyes narrowed on her back.

"Go fuck yourself!" Adelaide yelled back at him.

"I don't need to fuck myself, sweetheart, when there's plenty of other women in this clubhouse willing to fuck me in your goddamn place!" He roared down at her as he gripped her arm and spun her around to face him. She glared up at him, jealous rage shining in her eyes at his words. My heart sunk to my feet. Even fighting, she still wanted him. "I am second best to *no one*, Adelaide. You best fucking remember that." He growled.

"Well, fuck." Jessie grumbled, watching the scene unfold in front of us. I clenched my fists, wanting to bash Joey's face in for the way he was treating Adelaide.

Adelaide's hand came up and flew across Joey's face with a resounding slap that sent his face swinging to the side. "Fuck!" I heard Jessie yell.

I jumped up at the same time that Jessie jumped over the bar, rushing towards the two of them. Joey roughly shoved Addy away from him, sending her crashing into a table and down to the floor.

I saw fucking red.

I stormed over to Joey and slammed my fist into his face, sending him crashing back into one of the pool tables. Joey spit out blood, glaring up at me. "What the fuck?" He snarled up at me.

"Keep your fucking hands off of her." I snapped down at him.

He chuckled, spitting out more blood as he pushed himself up off of the floor and rose back up onto his feet. He looked deadly – like the monster everyone described him to be. "You go ahead and deal with that fucking whore." He snarled. "I'm done with her."

This time when I punched him, he slumped to the floor, knocked out cold, though I was pretty sure it had more to do with the liquor in his bloodstream rather than my fist hitting his face.

I turned to Addy, only to see Jessie already helping her up from the floor. "You sure he didn't hurt you too badly?" Jessie gently asked Addy.

Adelaide nodded. "Yeah. I'm good." She grumbled, her eyes flickering to Joey for a moment before she shut her eyes, drawing in a deep breath.

I walked over to her and let my eyes run over her, checking to make sure that she was truly okay. "If he ever touches you again, I'll fucking put a bullet through his skull." I snarled, drawing her into my arms as she stood up to her feet.

She sighed, relaxing into me. I tightened my arms around her, not one to let a moment like this pass me by. I knew there would be very few of them. "I hit him first." She defended him.

I sighed. She fucking loved him, and that shit gutted me. "Addy, baby, if you hit me, the most I would do is put you over my knee and spank you into submission." I heard a low moan release from the back of her throat, and I smirked. I could still affect her just as I had when we were younger. "You don't deserve to be treated like that, Addy."

She shrugged. "You get used to it."

I clenched my jaw, wanting to break Joey's neck at that moment, but I restrained myself, knowing that if anything would drive Adelaide away from me, that would be it. "You should have never had to get used to it, Addy."

She stayed silent, and I tightened my arms around her again, pressing my lips to the top of her head. We stayed like that for a moment, letting her draw strength from me.

After a moment, I leaned down so my mouth was at her ear. A shiver ran down her spine as my hot breath blew over her ear. I smirked. "I bet I could have you scream my name a hell of a lot louder than he did, Addy."

Her fingers twisted into my shirt as her breath hitched in her throat. I silently pressed a kiss to her rapidly beating pulse.

Patience. I had to have patience.

I knew I would have her where she belonged soon enough.

FIVE

I bounced on the balls of my feet as I swung my fist forward, connecting it with the punching bag in front of me. I quickly swung my other fist forward, bringing my leg up right after.

I was aggravated beyond belief.

After everything that happened yesterday with Vin, I was on lockdown. To say that I was already going stir crazy in less than twenty-four hours was a bit of an understatement.

Joey had even left me behind this morning when he went on his run. We woke up everyone in the clubhouse during our shouting match. Now, he was going to be gone for three days, and the last words I'd said to him were that I fucking hated him.

I was sorely regretting my words now. I knew he wasn't ever guaranteed to come back from a run, and if something were to happen to him, I would hate myself.

Because no matter how much we fought, Joey was one of my rocks. He kept me grounded – fuck, he kept me *alive*.

After I'd shouted at him that I hated him, he had simply left me with strict instructions that I wasn't supposed to leave the clubhouse. And to ensure that I followed the rules that Joey set, Tristan had set up one of his men at each entrance and exit of the clubhouse – which included the fucking windows so that I couldn't escape like last time.

I'd sent Joey a text to apologize since I knew he wouldn't answer his phone while he was on a run, but he hadn't responded to me yet.

"Beating the hell of that punching bag isn't going to make you feel any better, love," Jesup stated as he stepped into the workout room, a beer held loosely in his grip as he watched me take out my aggression on the swinging bag in front of me.

I clenched my jaw, hating that he was disturbing me when all I wanted was to just be alone. "It's better than punching some people in the fucking face." I retorted, swinging at the bag again.

"You tried talking to anyone instead of just letting all of that aggression just simmer inside of you?" Jesup asked me as he took a seat on the bench across from me as I continued hitting the bag.

I shook my head. "All I want to do is beat Joey's face in until he's not so fucking handsome anymore for locking me in here, but I want him to fucking talk to me as well. We left shit on a bad note." I swung again as Jesup grunted. "And I also want to beat the hell out of your perfect fucking president and boot him and the rest of you mother fuckers back to where you came from."

Jesup took a swig from his beer, not seeming bothered by my words. "You mean that?" He asked.

I clenched my jaw, grabbing the punching back as it swung back towards me. I turned my head to glare at him. "I was handling myself just fine before Tristan dropped back into my life and snatched me up," I told him. "Tristan did all of his damage three years ago – let me know how he fucking felt the night of my eighteenth birthday. He should have fucking stayed gone."

"Tristan has always loved you, Adelaide," Jesup told me. I snorted. "He never stopped."

I narrowed my eyes at the VP, clenching my jaw so hard that my teeth ground together. Three years later, and that wound was still raw as hell. Tristan had sent me on a downwards spiral. The only fucking reason that I was still standing here today was because of Joey.

"Could have fucking fooled me when he told me that he was tired of the relationship - that he couldn't fucking deal with my neediness anymore." I snarled at him. Jesup sighed as he shook his head. I threw my hands up into the air in exasperation, glaring at Jesup. "Jesup, he fucking kissed some random whore right afterward. I fucking *begged* him not to do that shit to me, and he fucking did it anyway."

"He did what he needed to do to keep you safe, Adelaide."

I released a humorless laugh, throwing my arms out to the sides. "Obviously, I could fucking do that myself if he had just stopped fucking babying me." I snarled at him. Jesup rolled his eyes. "I've been taking care of myself since the moment he dumped me and I met Joey. So, don't you *dare* try that fucking shit on me."

"When he broke up with you, Adelaide, you were still young and naïve," Jesup told me bluntly. I narrowed my eyes at him in a warning. Jesup knew the kind of shit that I grew up in. I wasn't fucking naïve. I grew up in a goddamn trap house. "You still needed emotional support. You have to admit that. Tristan needed to protect you, and he did what he needed to do for that to happen." Jesup tried to reason with me.

"From what?!" I finally yelled at him, losing my cool. "What the *fuck* did he need to protect me from so badly that he had to fucking break me like that?!" I screamed.

"Vin." Tristan's voice rang through the workout room. I swung my angry gaze to his. "I was trying to protect you from Vin."

My eyes widened in shock as I looked up at him, but then I glared at him, clenching and unclenching my fists at my sides.

"Obviously, you didn't do a good enough fucking job." I snarled at him. "Because guess who the fuck is *still* after me? Fucking *Vin*."

Anger flashed in Tristan's eyes as he narrowed his dark, gleaming eyes at me. "Oh, I did." He corrected me. "Your precious *Joey* got you in this fucking situation all by himself. I owed Vin a shit ton of money, and he was threatening those close to me to get what was owed to him." Tristan stepped further into the room, and Jesup slipped out, leaving me alone with Tristan. "Remember that day that I didn't show up to school?" He asked. I swallowed thickly. I remembered it well. I had been panicking all day because Tristan *always* showed up to school – even if he was so sick that he could barely stand – to make sure that he was there to protect me from assholes. "When you finally saw me that night when I came home, my face was bruised and bloody." He reminded me.

I nodded my head, my heart clenching in my chest as I remembered him collapsing in the foyer of his house as soon as he shut the door behind him – collapsing and giving in to the pain where he was finally safe. "Vin had finally gotten his hands on me that day, and he threatened to hurt you."

That had happened a week before my eighteenth birthday.

"I did what I had to do to protect you from him, Addy," Tristan told me quietly, his dark eyes swirling with protectiveness. He stepped closer to me. "I never stopped loving you, Addy baby. Everything I said to you was to protect you from my shit."

I shook my head at him, my heart beating so fast in my chest that it physically hurt. Everything he was telling me – fuck, it was so overwhelming. "How – what?" I started, not being able to actually complete a sentence. I was shocked as hell.

He really had done all of that to protect me.

And I had been such a fucking bitch to him when he finally came back.

But dammit, I'd been hurt. I had buried all of that pain that he had caused me for *years*.

I felt tears fill my eyes, and I squeezed my eyes shut, turning away from him as I drew in a deep, shaky breath, desperately trying to calm myself. I didn't want him to see me cry – to see me break down like this.

"Why didn't you just tell me that to begin with?" I asked him, hating that my voice came out weak and shaky.

Tristan's large, calloused hands settled over my shoulders. Warmth slid through my veins, unthawing the ice around that part of my heart that had always been his. He slowly turned me around to face him. A tear trickled down my cheek as I looked up at him, unable to keep it from sliding down my cheek.

He had never stopped loving me.

His face fell as he watched the tear slide down my cheek. With gentle hands, he quickly reached up and wiped it away, but kept his hand on my cheek afterward. "Because if I had told you what was going on, Addy, you would have never let me let you go." He told me honestly, and I knew he was right – hated it, in fact. "I had to break your heart in the worst way possible to keep you safe."

Another tear slid down my cheek, and my bottom lip trembled as I stared up at the man that had once held my entire heart. With a soft sigh, Tristan pulled me into his arms and pressed his lips to my hair. I quickly wound my own arms around him, pressing my body close to his, the steady thud of his heart keeping me calm – grounded.

"Did Helene know?" I asked him quietly.

Tristan shook his head. "No one but Jesup knew." He told me. I breathed a little easier now that I knew that my best friend hadn't kept such a huge secret from me. "I couldn't risk you finding out and trying to play the hero. I needed you to hate me." He told me. "It fucking hurt like hell to let you go – to let you down – but it had to happen."

I pulled myself tighter against him, taking in all of the warmth, strength, and comfort he was giving me, soaking it up. He slid his hand down my back, his other arm flexing around me in response.

I looked up at him, and his dark eyes met mine. "So, what are you going to do now?" I asked him. "Are you going to break my heart all over again – destroy me for good this time?" Since Vin was still around, I assumed that was Tristan's plan again. Sure, I had fought him every step of the way on this shit, but if he walked away again, I wouldn't recover.

Tristan shook his head. "I'm older, and I'm stronger." Tristan reminded me. "I've got the right men to back me, and my club is strong." His warm hand cupped my cheek, his eyes tender as he kept them locked with mine. "And we all protect our club women, especially our queen, Addy." I felt my cheeks heat up slightly at his words. "Vin won't get close to you ever again – not if I have anything to do with it. He's crossed me wrong for the last fucking time. I'm a hell of a lot meaner than I was when we were kids and fucking with you has deadly consequences."

My heart warmed at his words, my soul lighting up the slightest bit with hope – hope that he really wanted this with me, that he wouldn't fucking destroy me again.

And this time, when Tristan bent his head and pressed his lips to mine, I didn't want to pull away. I didn't want to fight him on it.

I succumbed to him.

With one hand on my lower back, Tristan pressed me closer to him as his other hand slid up into my hair, holding my lips to his. I gripped his shirt in my fists, obediently opening my lips beneath his.

A shiver ran down my spine as his tongue slid against mine, making me moan softly. I slid my hands under his cut, feeling the rippling power of his muscular frame.

The door crashing open ripped us apart, both of us breathing a bit heavy as we looked to see who had intruded on our moment.

"Sorry, Grim." Jesup apologized. "I know you guys were having a real heart to heart in here, but we've got a fucking problem." I pulled back from Tristan, my attention now fully on Jesup. My stomach twisted, a gut feeling that something was wrong spreading through my body like ice. "Joey has been shot, and he's being rushed to the emergency room," Jesup informed us.

My heart dropped to my feet, pure panic rushing through my veins.

I couldn't fucking lose him - not Joey.

I moved past Tristan and ran out of the room, heading for the clubhouse exit. Jessie met up with me at the door, tears rushing down her face. I was still panicking, too shocked and terrified of losing Joey to cry yet.

"I've got my car keys." She informed me as she desperately tried to hold herself together, but I knew she was freaking out as much as I was. "Ink and York are riding with us for protection."

I was shaking. All I could do was rush after her to her car, praying that I wasn't losing Joey.

I heard Tristan barking orders behind us at all of his men, but I was already rushing out of the door towards Jessie's car, not paying him any mind. Once my ass hit the passenger seat, she took off towards the hospital, barely giving me time to close the door.

My heart was painfully pounding in my chest, stealing my breath, making it extremely hard to breathe.

God, I know I'm a shitty person, but please don't make me lose him. I won't survive it.

■ ■ ■

When we got to the hospital, I rushed inside, instantly demanding the receptionist on duty to let me know which room Joey was in.

"I'm sorry, Miss, but he's currently in surgery." I swallowed down vomit. Surgery. That was bad. That was really fucking bad. "You can have a seat in our waiting room and wait for the doctor to let me know that he's out of surgery and into a recovery room."

Numbly, I nodded, moving to the waiting room. Jessie took a seat in one of the hard, plastic chairs, but I couldn't sit. I paced back and forth across the floor. If I sat still, I would lose my fucking mind.

Ink took a seat beside Jessie and wrapped his arm around her, pulling her into him as he tried to console her. She cried into his shoulder.

I wished I could cry. Right now, I was numb – teetering on the edge between sanity and losing my damn mind. I didn't know what to do without Joey.

I hate you.

Those had been my last words to him, and right then, I fucking hated myself for letting him get hurt with those being my last fucking words to ring in his head.

I looked up when the double doors opened, and Tristan stepped in with Jesup hot on his heels, their familiar President and Vice President patches adorning their cuts, letting everyone around know who they were.

Tristan frowned when our eyes connected. Without a word, he opened his arms to me, giving me the option to take his comfort. With a choked sob, I rushed into his arms and collapsed against his chest as his strong arms wrapped around my slender frame, holding me together as best as he could.

"I can't lose him, too, Tristan." I sobbed.

"Joey is strong, Addy baby." Tristan soothed as he brushed his calloused hand over my hair. "It's going to take a lot more than this to take him out," Tristan assured me softly, pressing his lips to my temple.

But for some reason, I couldn't believe him. Any other time, I would agree, but something in my gut was telling me that this time wouldn't be like the others.

I cried into Tristan's chest as he stood with his back facing the wall, his arms tight around me as he let me cry it out. Jesup stood next to us, his eyes staying focused on his surroundings. "Joey Dirks?" A male voice asked as he entered the waiting room.

Jessie jumped to her feet and rushed over towards the doctor who was still in his surgery scrubs. "I'm his sister." She informed him. "Is he okay?"

The doctor gave her a sad look, and I instantly knew.

I'd lost Joey, too.

"I'm sorry, Miss, but we did everything we could." He softly told her.

I wailed as I collapsed to the floor, my arms wrapping tightly around myself. Sobs wracked my body, my screams bouncing off of the walls. "No!" I screamed, my fists pounding the floor. "*Joey!*" I screeched.

Tristan dropped to the ground next to me, dragging me into his arms, holding me tight to him as he rocked me, doing his best to calm me back down. I tightly wrapped my arms around his torso, loud cries ripping from my lips as I begged Joey to come back to me.

Tristan gripped my face in his hands, shaking me gently as he forced me to look up at him. His expression shattered as he ran his eyes over my face. "No, baby, not now. I need you to breathe, Addy." He told me firmly. "Focus on me." He commanded. "Come back to me, baby. Joey wouldn't want you to be like this."

I whimpered, my chest aching.

Tristan gave me a gentle smile. "Come on, baby girl. In. Out. Breathe." I followed his instructions as he ran his thumbs over my cheekbones. "That's it. Slowly, Addy. Breathe."

"I-Is he really gone?" I asked, my voice coming out weak and strangled.

Tristan slowly nodded and drew me into his arms as silent tears trickled down my cheeks.

Who else was I going to lose before all of this shit was over?

■ ■ ■

The clubhouse was silent as I walked in with Tristan right behind me. Some people were silently crying while others were staring blankly into space.

This club had just lost one of their greatest presidents.

I had just lost one of the greatest men I'd ever known.

"You know this is your fault, right?" Charles asked from his position at the bar. I looked over at him silently, a blank expression on my face and in my eyes. "Joey would still be alive if Vin hadn't fucking gone after him for protecting you."

Tears welled up in my eyes at his words, shattering that numbness that I so desperately needed now. "I'm sorry." I choked out to both the club and Joey.

It was all my fucking fault.

Tristan's hands settled over my shoulders as I felt him press himself against my back, guarding me and protecting me the best that he could. "Watch your fucking tone with her." Tristan snarled at Joey's VP – now the president of Sons of Hell.

"He's right." Jessie snapped at Charles. "This isn't her fucking fault."

"How the fuck is it not?" Charles snarled at her. I flinched at his words. "She's been nothing but fucking trouble since Joey took her from her birthday party when she was eighteen." Charles looked at me, rage covering his features. I swallowed thickly. "As the new president, I'm ordering you to leave." He snapped, pointing his finger at me. I sucked in a sharp breath at his words. "Get your shit and get the fuck out of my clubhouse. You're no longer a part of this fucking club."

"Now hold the fuck up!" Ink roared from his position beside Jessie. "You know Joey never wanted her to leave this fucking club, Charles! She's one of us! She was *his*, for fuck's sake."

"Not anymore she's not!" Charles roared at him. I rolled my lips into my mouth, resisting the urge to whimper. "Now shut your fucking mouth when speaking to me!" He looked back at me. "Get out, Adelaide."

I tilted my chin up defiantly, refusing to show weakness to the asshole in front of me. Wiping my expression clean off my face, I nodded at him. "Alright, Charles, I'm leaving, but note this." I snarled, shrugging Tristan's hands off of my shoulders as I strode forward until I could feel Charles's hot breath on my skin. "This club will turn against you, Charles. No fucking new president ever goes against what the old president wanted. It's called respect for the fucking dead."

Charles tightly gripped my arm, yanking me closer to him as a disgusted snarl twisted his features. I brought my knee up, kneeing him in his dick. He quickly released me and dropped to the floor, holding his balls in his hands, his expression white with pain. I spit on him, clenching my fists at my sides. "Mark my fucking words, Charles. You ever fucking come near me again, and it won't be my knee on your balls. I'll shoot your fucking dick off, you got me?"

I stepped over him and stormed to my room, not waiting for his bullshit reply. After yanking a duffel bag out of the top of my closet, I tossed it onto the bed and began throwing my necessary clothes into it along with any important documentation that I had. I could practically feel Tristan's eyes on me as I moved around the room, but he was silent, giving me a moment to gather myself.

"What makes you so sure that the club will turn on him?" Tristan finally asked me.

"No one here really likes Charles," I informed him. Tristan stayed silent, allowing me to continue. "He always wanted to go against Joey. Everyone here respected Joey as a President, and they respected his decisions. Him running me off, the one fucking person Joey ever gave two damn shits about, the one person this club ever respected like a sister, is going to cause problems – the club is going to turn on Charles."

"And what happens when the club turns on him?" Tristan asked me.

"It gets bloody," I told him. "And the club is very possibly over."

Tristan stayed silent after that. I zipped my bag up, and he grabbed it off of the bed. "Guess you're finally coming home where you belong." He stated softly.

I swallowed thickly but nodded, knowing Sons of Death was the only place I could go to now. I didn't have anyone else.

I looked across the hall to Joey's room as we stepped out of mine. Putting my finger up to signal Tristan to hold on a minute, I pushed open Joey's door, swallowing hard as I looked at the picture of us on his nightstand. I was about turn nineteen in a couple of weeks in that picture, and Joey had surprised me by making me an official member of his club and giving me my own room in the clubhouse.

We were standing right outside of the clubhouse, and he had his arms wrapped around me from behind. I was wearing his cut to show everyone that I was his woman, even though it basically swallowed me. Joey had on a blue and black flannel shirt with a pair of dark jeans, and he was grinning down at me as I laughed at something he had said.

If I wasn't mistaken, Jessie had taken the picture of us.

Even then, we had always clashed heads, but we loved each other in our own sick, twisted ways.

Silent tears trickled down my cheeks as I picked up the picture, a small, sad smile playing on my lips.

Fuck, I already missed him so damn much.

"I will always love you, Joey," I whispered, my words almost inaudible to my own ears.

I grabbed his cut one of the members had laid out on his bed, and I grabbed his knife that he always kept under his pillow. His father had given it to him, and he had always said if he ever had a kid, he would always give the knife to his child.

He wasn't ever given the option. Joey would never have a family, never have children.

I walked back out of the room, and Tristan looked down at the items in my hand. Deciding to stay silent, he just followed me out of the clubhouse without a word. He was strapping my duffel bag to his bike when Jessie rushed outside and threw her arms around me. I hugged her back instantly.

"I'll miss you, gorgeous." She whispered into my shoulder.

I squeezed her gently, tears stinging my eyes, but I wouldn't let them fall – not here. "I'll miss you, too, gorgeous," I whispered in return.

She pulled back from me, her dark eyes glimmering with unshed tears. "Promise me that you'll stay safe?" She asked softly.

I nodded. "You better do the same," I told her. She gave me a wobbly smile. "If things ever get to be too rough around here, call me. I promise I will come to get you – whether Tristan agrees or not." I assured her.

She nodded and kissed my cheek. "Please keep in touch." She quietly begged me.

I kissed her cheek as well. "Always, gorgeous."

With one last, sad smile, she went back into the clubhouse where Ink was waiting on her. I sighed and slid onto the bike behind Tristan as he turned the engine over, the bike rumbling to life beneath me as I sat down. He gripped one of my hands and brought it up to his lips, pressing a light kiss to my knuckles. I drew in a slow, deep breath before I tightly wound my arms around his midsection and pressed the front of my body to his back.

And we were off to the Sons of Death's territory.

SIX

I gagged when I woke up, vomit rising in my throat. I quickly jumped out of bed and rushed into the bathroom connected to Tristan's room in the clubhouse, barely making it in front of the toilet before I began to throw up.

I vaguely heard Tristan call after me, concern tinting his voice. I couldn't respond. I quickly dropped to my knees in front of the toilet, throwing up stomach acid since I didn't eat anything yesterday. Tristan was kneeling next to me instantly, his hand holding my hair back out of my face as his other hand caressed my back, whispering soothing words to me as I continued emptying my stomach.

Afterward, I sagged back against the wall in exhaustion and closed my eyes, ignoring Tristan's worried gaze as he studied my face. I didn't want the worry. I probably just had some kind of stomach bug. It wasn't even something to be worried about.

"When was your last period, Addy?" Tristan gently asked me.

I opened my eyes to look at the handsome man in front of me, arching my eyebrow at him as I did so. "What kind of question is that?" I asked in confusion.

"Just answer it." He told me, frustration tinting his voice.

I sighed as I thought about his question. I took a moment to do the math in my head, and my eyes flashed back open as tears welled up in my eyes when I realized I was actually late.

I was very possibly pregnant.

With Joey's baby.

Tristan sighed, sadness ringing in his eyes. "I thought so." He whispered.

Tears silently slid down my cheeks in quick succession as I looked down at my flat belly – my flat belly that was probably growing Joey's little kid.

I sobbed.

Tristan sat beside me against the wall and pulled me onto his lap, wrapping his arms around me. I burrowed against his chest, resisting the urge to wail. How cruel could God be?

"How can you not hate me right now?" I asked Tristan, my voice muffled against his muscular, bare chest.

Tristan sighed, tightening his arms around me. "I could never hate you, Addy." He admitted. I sniffled. Could he still love me so much that he was okay with me carrying another man's baby – another *president's* baby? "Does it make me upset that you're carrying another man's baby? Yes, of course, it does, but I can't be angry at *you*. You and Joey were having sex *way* before I stepped back into the picture." He told me, but there was a bit of bitterness in his tone. I knew he hated the fact that I felt so much for Joey, that I loved him so fucking much.

At the mention of Joey, my tears came harder. "I'm pregnant with his kid, and he'll never know." I sobbed. "I'll never get the opportunity to see him hold his baby. He would have been a fucking fantastic dad." I cried.

Tristan tightened his arms around me. "He would have been ecstatic about it, Addy." Tristan tried assuring me. "Joey would have gone above and beyond to make sure you and your baby were well and taken care of."

I wrapped my arms tightly around Tristan's torso as I cried harder. "What am I going to do?" I asked.

"I think you mean *we*." Tristan gently corrected me. I looked up at him in confusion, my tears clouding my vision. He reached up and gently wiped some of my tears off of my cheeks before he wrapped his arm back around me. "We're in this together, Addy baby."

I sniffled. "You're too damn kind for your own good," I grumbled as I buried my face back against his chest.

Tristan let out a husky, sexy laugh that had my belly twisting with desire for him, but I tampered it back down. "I just love you, Addy." I swallowed thickly as my heart skipped a beat. "That has never changed. If loving you means that I have to father a kid that's not mine, then that's what I'm going to do. I'll love this baby as if it were my own." He assured me.

What in the hell did I ever do to deserve a man like Tristan?

■ ■ ■

TRISTAN

I slowly slid out of bed the next morning, being extremely careful to not wake Addy up. Now that I knew that she was pregnant, I was going to make sure she got all of the rest that she needed and that she took extremely good care of herself. All of this toxic shit that she had been doing had to come to an end. She wasn't just thinking of herself anymore.

But I knew that was going to be a fucking fight.

BOOK ONE   RUINED

I walked into my in-suite bathroom and got a quick shower so I could go deal with club shit. I knew I needed to get a run organized and get ready to distribute funds at church today.

After getting dressed in a pair of black cargo pants, my black steel-toed boots, a black t-shirt, and my cut, I walked out into the bar room where Jesup was already behind the bar, talking to a couple of club women about cleaning up the mess from the welcoming back party last night.

Jesup arched an eyebrow at me when he noticed me. "You're up early." He commented.

I shrugged. "So are you." I retorted.

Normally after a welcome home party, all of the club members, including myself, slept extremely late – well into the afternoon.

There was too much shit on my mind today to sleep.

Jesup grinned at me. "I was expecting you to be balls deep inside of Adelaide for a while." He lightly teased. I scowled at him. "It's been years since you've been with her."

I shook my head, thinking about Joey's death, and then the fact that she had just found out that she was pregnant with his kid on top of it all.

No fucking way was I about to sleep with her, much less try anything like that. I was a bastard, but I wasn't that damn cruel.

I nodded in my head in the direction of the chapel, signaling for Jesup to follow me into the room. Once we were in the chapel, I shut the doors and locked them. Walking over to one of the windows, I crossed my arms over my broad chest and looking out at two of the prospects working on a car in the garage. "I think she's pregnant." I bluntly informed him, cutting straight to the chase.

"Woah, *what?*" Jesup demanded. I turned to face him. His face was a mask of absolute shock and disbelief. "You're fucking serious?" He asked after a moment. "She's fucking *pregnant?*"

I shrugged with a deep sigh. "She woke up in the middle of the night last night to throw up. Probably a bit TMI for you, but I asked her when her last period was since she didn't seem sick to me – no high temperature, not throwing up actual food since she didn't eat anything yesterday. Her period is late." Jesup's eyes widened. "I'm going to take her to Dr. Howard when she wakes up so he can run a pregnancy test. She needs to know for sure."

"Holy fuck, man." Jesup breathed as he ran his hand through his hair. "How do you feel about that?" He asked me. That was the question I was dreading. He shook his head. "On second thought, how the fuck does *she* feel about this?" He asked me.

I was dreading that question even more.

I sighed and stuffed my hands into the pockets of my cargo pants. "I'll step up and do what I need to do for her," I told him, though I knew Jesup already figured that much. "I love Addy. I always have. If she's pregnant with Joey's kid, it's not going to change how I feel about her." I swallowed hard, blowing out a harsh breath as I glared at the table in the center of the room that had the club emblem engraved into it. "As for her – well, she fucking cried herself to sleep last night on the bathroom floor," I told him quietly, pain lancing through my chest as I thought about how fucking heartbroken she had looked last night. "So, I don't know how the fuck she's feeling about this shit. She just lost Joey, only to find out she's probably carrying his kid."

Jesup leaned against the wall, crossing his ankles and his arms as he steadily regarded me with that unnerving gaze of his. "What's the plan if she is?" Jesup asked me.

I let my eyes meet his. "We protect her and that baby at all costs," I told him. He nodded. "And we keep the Sons of Hell intact as much as we can because in about nineteen years, that club is going to fall into that child's hands."

Jesup nodded in understanding. "Charles looks like he might become a problem," Jesup commented.

I nodded. "Addy has already warned me," I told him. He raised an eyebrow at me. Adelaide had been in a lot deeper than he or I had originally thought, and she knew how that club worked. "When that club does fall apart, we'll do what we have to do to make sure that the Sons of Hell stays a club."

Jesup pursed his lips. "You think they'll make Addy a president since she's carrying Joey's kid?" He asked me, knowing that was a possibility since she had been an actual club member.

I clenched my jaw. "Over my fucking dead body." I snarled. Jesup smirked. "The life of a president is too fucking dangerous, and she's a mother before anything else if she's pregnant. Her only worry and concern will be to make sure that child is safe, protected, loved, and taken care of. Nothing else. If the Sons of Hell eventually need a fucking leader, we'll patch them over, but I will not have Addy as the president."

Jesup nodded. "Understood."

"I don't know who the fuck you think you're talking to," I heard Addy snap at someone through the closed chapel doors, "but you better back the fuck down before I give you a goddamn reason to need plastic surgery."

"And she's awake," Jesup said with a chuckle as he opened the door and we rushed out of the meeting room to stop Adelaide from getting into a fight.

Addy was glaring at Emma, one of the newer women, and Emma was glaring right back at her. I let my eyes run over Addy, taking in her curvy figure. She was wearing a pair of jeans that clung to her round ass and thick thighs, and a black t-shirt with her black combat-style boots. I swallowed hard.

Fuck, I was never going to get over how fucking sexy she was.

"I don't think you understand how things work around here." Emma snarled at her. Adelaide sighed in aggravation. I noticed River gently push Adelaide back, giving her a stern look to stay back. My blood pounded in my veins, but I tampered it down. It wasn't like he was hitting on her. He was merely keeping her ass out of trouble. "The president doesn't allow women to fucking call on him. He gets us when he's ready to have one of us. So, no, you don't need to know where the fucking president is." Emma snarled at Adelaide.

Emma wasn't wrong, but Adelaide was different.

Before I could stop Addy, she grabbed River's half-empty beer and threw it at Emma. Emma shrieked and ducked down right before the bottle could hit her in the face, letting it crash against the wall instead.

"Woah; everyone chill the fuck out!" I roared, coming up behind a seething Addy. River stepped back, letting me take control of the situation. Jesup's sorry ass was too busy laughing at the entire situation to be of much help.

I laid my hands over Addy's shoulders, feeling some of the tension drain out of her shoulders as she subconsciously stepped back against me. "Grim, she's fucking crazy!" Emma shouted, calling me by my street name.

"Watch your tone with me." I snarled at her, making her flinch back and cast her eyes away from me. Adelaide snorted. I gently squeezed her shoulders, warning her to tamper her attitude down. "Now, what's going on?" I demanded to know.

"I'm about to break her fucking fake nose." Addy snarled, the tension entering her shoulders again. "That's what's fucking going on."

I massaged her shoulders gently. "That's not what I asked," I stated calmly, knowing that arguing with Addy wouldn't get me anywhere. The woman was hotheaded as fuck. "I asked what was going on."

"She demanded to know where you were, Grim," Emma stated. "I told her what you tell all of us – not to ask for you."

"You really don't have any fucking idea who I am, do you?" Addy asked Emma as she tilted her head to the side the tiniest bit.

"Obviously not." Emma snarled at her. "But judging by the way Grim is with you, you mean something to him."

"Smart girl," Jesup commented. I sighed. He really didn't help situations much. "I knew Grim kept you around for a reason." He lightly teased Emma.

I rolled my eyes at Jesup. "Adelaide, meet Emma." I introduced. "She's one of the newer additions to the club. Emma, meet Adelaide, my old lady."

"Your old *nothing*." Adelaide snarled, snatching herself out of my grip as she turned her angry eyes on me. I vaguely heard River snort in amusement, but I turned my gaze to his. He only raised his fresh beer to me before rolling his lips into his mouth, staying silent.

I looked back down at Adelaide. Fuck, she looked so gorgeous when she turned that fiery gaze on me. "I'm no one's goddamn old lady, Tristan, and you better get that through your thick fucking head."

I narrowed my gaze at her. I hated when she fought this shit between us. We could be great together if she would just stop fighting me every damn step of the way. "You are *mine*, Adelaide," I said, my tone coming off cold, but there was a hint of a warning there for her to stop while she was ahead.

She stepped up to me, jabbing her finger against my chest as she glared up at me. Fuck, she really wasn't scared of anything. "I am *no one's*, Tristan. I can be a girlfriend, but I am not *yours*, and I am certainly *not* your old lady."

I gripped her finger in my hand and yanked her against me, wrapping an arm around her waist as I dipped my head down, covering her lips with mine. She instantly kissed me back, her hands gripping my cut tightly in her fists as she tugged me closer to her, a low moan sliding from between those perfect fucking lips.

God, she was fucking addicting.

I pulled back enough to stop kissing her, but my lips still brushed against hers as I spoke. "You are *mine*, Adelaide, and to claim anything different will only get you fucked into submission, understand me?"

Her breath hitched in her throat at my words as she nodded her head. I released her, stepping back as she drew in a deep, shaky breath. Jesup barked out a laugh. I glared at him, but Jesup had known me for so long that he didn't even heed my silent warning to shut the fuck up. "I swear, even though she's obviously not the same girl that she was when she was eighteen, the effect you have on her is still the same."

Addy scowled at him. "Watch yourself." She snarled at him, not amused by him in the slightest.

He held his hands up in a defensive gesture, but the smirk didn't drop from his lips. She sneered at him before she turned her beautiful eyes back to me. "Want to go to the doctor?" I asked Addy.

She swallowed hard, and I saw fear flash through her eyes as the fight inside of her quickly disappeared, leaving behind a frightened, vulnerable woman. I stepped closer to her, resting my hands over her upper arms as I ran my hands up and down them, trying to soothe her. "You need to," I told her quietly. She drew in a deep, shuddering breath. "I'll be by your side the entire time; I swear," I promised her.

She swallowed hard again but nodded her head. I grabbed her hand in my own and laced my fingers through hers as I pulled my bike keys from my pocket. "Jesup, can you hold everything down here?" I asked him, though I knew he could without me having to ask.

He nodded, his eyes flickering to Addy for a split second before he returned them to me. "Got it, Grim."

■ ■ ■

Addy nervously bounced her leg up and down as we waited for Dr. Howard to come into the little room that we had been placed in. I knew that nothing that I could say would calm down her nerves right then, so I just sat behind her on the little cot with her between my legs as I held my arms around her, pressing light kisses to her neck and shoulder in a silent reminder that I was still with her – that she wasn't alone.

A light knock came on the door, and Dr. Howard stepped in with a warm smile on his face. Judging by the way Adelaide tensed in my arms, though, it did nothing to soothe her. "Good to see you again, Tristan. How's your collarbone?" He asked me.

About a year ago, I'd had a motorcycle accident that had broken my collarbone. But after months of physical therapy, I was perfectly fine. I didn't even have a scar from the accident.

I shrugged. "Never been better," I told him. "Able to function perfectly again."

Addy shot me a questioning look, but I just shook my head at her. She sighed and turned her attention back to Dr. Howard. He smiled at her and held out his hand for her to shake. She slowly took his hand in hers. I pressed a light kiss to her shoulder, wishing I could help calm her in some kind of way, but I knew nothing was going to work right then.

"I'm Dr. Howard – Tristan's only trusted doctor within a two-hundred-mile radius." I rolled my eyes, though it was true. I didn't trust anyone else. "You're Adelaide Berkeley, correct?"

She nodded in answer, only bouncing her leg faster as she did so. I pressed a gentle kiss to her neck as I momentarily tightened my arms around her. Dr. Howard sat on his stool and looked up at her. "You are pregnant, Adelaide." He confirmed, not beating around the bush.

Her body went rigid in my arms. I pressed another kiss to the side of her neck as I tightened my arms around her. "Breathe, Addy," I told her gently. "I'm right here," I assured her. "It's okay, baby."

She drew in a shaky breath, her hands coming up to grip my forearms in a death grip, her nails digging into my skin. "Is Tristan the father?" Dr. Howard asked her.

Adelaide shook her head in answer. I could practically feel her body struggling to hold in her tears as her nails dug further into my arm, almost drawing blood. I ignored the pain. "Do you know the family history of the father?" Dr. Howard asked her.

Adelaide nodded silently. I drew in a deep breath. She was on the verge of breaking; I could feel it.

"We need to write down any history of diseases on the father's side. Can you do that for me?" He asked her, sensing her sadness.

"If you're not ready, just say so," I told her gently before she could answer him. "You need time to heal." I softly reminded her.

"I can do this." She whispered.

I pressed another kiss to her shoulder as Dr. Howard began asking her questions about Joey's family history. Fuck, she was so goddamn brave. I didn't know anyone who could do this so soon after losing someone so close to them. "Is he going to be in the picture?" Dr. Howard asked her after a few minutes of asking her questions about Joey's family history.

That was all it took. She fell apart. Dr. Howard swung his alarmed gaze to me. I just shook my head at him wordlessly, and he nodded, stepping out of the room to give us some privacy. I wrapped my arms around Addy tightly, dragging her tight against me. "Hey, calm down," I told her gently. "Stressing yourself out isn't good for the baby." I quietly reminded her, hating her being so upset.

"S-sorry." She hiccupped. "It's - it's just . . ."

I pressed my lips to her forehead. "I know, baby girl," I assured her gently. She whimpered, her fingers clenching my cut in her fists. "It's okay to cry, but I don't want you to work yourself up too much. You have a little one to take care of." I reminded her, grabbing her hand and placing it over her still flat belly, pressing my hand on top of hers as she looked up at me.

She sobbed, and the sound was so fucking broken that it tore at my soul.

She leaned up and kissed me softly. I knew she was using it as a distraction, but I took full advantage of the kiss. I groaned, instantly moving to deepen it. It was the first time she'd kissed me on her own, and it fucking drove me insane for her that she was finally moving forward me with that tiny bit, even if every part of me was telling me that she was just looking for something in that moment to make her feel better.

"Promise me that you're going to help me get through this?" She asked me softly.

"I promise, Adelaide," I swore, letting my eyes meet hers. "I'm not leaving your side."

A few moments later, Dr. Howard came back into the room, acting as if nothing had ever happened, and for that, I was grateful. "Alright, Adelaide, we're going to do an ultrasound to check on your little one, okay? Based on the date of your last period, you're almost six weeks along, so you should be able to hear your little one's heartbeat if you'd like."

She nodded at him. "Alright. You two - follow me." He instructed.

Addy stood up, and I did as well, instantly lacing my fingers through hers as we followed Dr. Howard down a couple of halls to a dark room. A huge TV screen was on the wall, and beside the little cot in the room was a machine with a couple of wands attached to it with a small screen and a tiny printer. He told us that he would see us back in the room we had just come out of once we were finished here before he dipped from the room.

A lady came out from behind a curtain, a smile lighting up her face. "Hi!" She exclaimed, overly chipper. "My name is Alyssa, and I'll be doing your ultrasound today." She explained to Addy. "I just need you to lay back on the cot and pull your shirt up and unbutton your jeans. Just slide them down for me a tiny bit, okay?"

Addy nodded and did as she was instructed. I stood beside the cot, holding one of her hands in mine as I slowly ran my fingers through her hair. Alyssa squeezed some gel on Addy's belly and then pressed one of the wands against her skin. Instantly, a gritty image popped up on the screen. Everything around it was gray, and there a black looking hole.

Addy squeezed my hand tightly, and I could feel her rapidly beating pulse through her hand. I gave her hand a gentle squeeze in return - a silent reminder that I was still here with her.

Suddenly, two tiny balls popped up on the screen. Alyssa stopped the screen, taking what seemed to be measurements. "This is your baby," She said, pointing an arrow to it on the screen and typing the word 'baby' "and this is the yolk sac." She said doing the same thing.

Alyssa smiled over at Addy who was rendered speechless. "Would you like to hear the heartbeat?" She asked.

Addy nodded. There was a couple of taps on the keyboard, and then suddenly, I heard it.

Whoosh-whoosh. Whoosh-whoosh. Whoosh-whoosh.

It wasn't even my kid, but at that moment, I fell in love with Addy's baby, and I was jealous as fuck of Joey, even if he was no longer with us.

Tears streamed down Addy's cheeks. She looked up at me, a small, breathy laugh falling past her lips. The beautiful sound warmed the darkest, coldest parts of my soul. "She's real." Addy breathed.

"She?" I asked, not able to stop the smile that spread across my lips.

Addy nodded. "I have a damn good feeling that I'm going to have a girl, and she's going to have Joey's eyes and attitude."

My mood soured at the thought of Joey, but I knew Adelaide needed this. And if it made her happy, then so be it. I would suck it up.

Alyssa smiled and handed Addy three pictures. "You can go through that curtain there," she said, pointing to a small curtain, "and clean the gel off of your belly."

Addy handed me the pictures as she got off of the bed, disappearing behind the curtain. "You two are very lucky parents. The baby seems very strong and seems to be developing extremely well. Congratulations on being parents." She said as Addy came out from behind the curtain.

I looked to Addy, smiling at her warmly, so happy to see a small smile on her face after looking so sad ever since Joey passed. "Thank you. I'm just happy to be having a baby with a woman as incredible as her." I told Alyssa, though my words were solely for the beautiful woman in front of me. Addy's smile widened at me as she allowed me to grab her hand and link our fingers together. "Should we just head back to Dr. Howard's room?" I asked the ultrasound technician.

Alyssa nodded. Once we were back in Dr. Howard's room, Addy leaned up to kiss me again. Fuck, she was finally loosening up with me, and I was loving every second of it. I needed my Addy baby back. "Did you mean what you said in there?" Addy asked me softly.

I looked down at her and nodded. "Of course, I did. Addy, this baby may not be mine, but the moment I heard that heartbeat, I fell in love with it." I told her. Her beautiful eyes welled with tears. "I want to be here for you every step of the way - through the mood swings, through the morning sickness, even the labor and delivery. I want to help you raise this baby, Addy."

Tears slipped down her cheeks at my words. "You're too damn amazing, Tristan." She whispered, her voice hoarse.

I reached up and wiped the tears from her cheeks, giving her a warm, soft smile. "Only for you, Addy baby," I told her, and it was true. For anyone else, I would have booted them to the curb.

For Addy? I would fucking do anything to keep her by my side.

Dr. Howard stepped into the room., breaking our heartfelt moment. "Alright. Well, your baby looks extremely healthy, and it's developing well, Adelaide." He handed Addy a thick folder. "This is everything you can expect every week while you're pregnant - with your body as well as how the baby is developing. I've also added in a list of over the counter medications that are safe to take while you're pregnant, and there's some information on some prenatal yoga classes, some parenting classes, etc. if you're interested."

He looked at me. "If something is happening, and it's worrying you, you know how to reach me after hours." He reminded me.

I nodded. I had Dr. Howard's private number, and if something were happening with Adelaide, he could bet on a phone call. I wouldn't take any chances – not with her or her baby.

He looked back at Adelaide. "Here's a prescription for some prenatal vitamins that you need to begin taking tomorrow morning." He told her as he handed her a prescription paper. She put it in the folder. "You look as if you already exercise – what do you do?" Dr. Howard asked her.

"I normally fight," Addy told him. I sighed. That was going to have to stop.

He shook his head at her. "I wouldn't do that anymore if I were you." Adelaide pursed her lips in distaste. "Some boxing with a punching bag probably won't hurt, but no more actual fights." He informed her. "Light walking and jogging are good, but the moment you begin to feel tired, call it quits. You're pregnant, and you don't need to overdo yourself."

She nodded in understanding, though she looked as if the idea of no longer fighting left a sour taste in her mouth. "Three meals a day is extremely important with some light snacks in-between. No more caffeine, and drink plenty of water. I want you to come back in a month for a follow-up appointment."

"Anything else?" She asked him, looking a bit overwhelmed with all of the information he had just crammed into her brain.

He shook his head and gave her a warm smile. "I'm pretty sure Tristan will make sure you take care of yourself. I look forward to seeing you in a month, Adelaide." He told her before he left the room.

It was real. My Addy was becoming a mother.

SEVEN

ADELAIDE

I was sprawled out on the couch in the clubhouse bar room with my headphones plugged into my ears, my music turned all the way up as I listened to an old hip-hop song. Tristan was sitting at the bar with Jesup, and the entire club was waiting on Tristan's North Carolina charter to ride in for a run later in the evening.

The lyrics hit a sad note about someone passing away at a young age. I swallowed hard, realizing how hard the rapper's words hit home for me. For three years, I'd watched numerous people close to me die.

Numerous people had even died at my *own* hands.

Joey was only twenty-four.

And I had already lost him – lost one of the closest people to me.

How many more people would I lose before all of this shit was over?

The clubhouse doors opening caught my attention, and I watched as Troy Hilton – the president of North Carolina Sons of Death's charter – stepped in, his Vice President Kyle following closely on his heels. A few of their other members followed in behind them.

Tristan stood up from his seat at the bar to greet his cousin, Jesup standing up as well. I pulled my headphones out of my ears, watching as Tristan walked up to Troy, both of them shaking hands and pulling each other into a one-armed, manly hug.

"Good to see you, bro," Tristan said as he stepped back from Troy. "I appreciate you riding out here on such short notice."

"Not a problem," Troy assured him as his eyes moved over the room, not taking notice of me yet.

But when he would finally notice me, I would be ready. Troy and I had always butted heads, especially since he was already in the life of an outlaw with Tristan, and I was just the girl that grew up in a trap house, not part of anything in particular.

I had always been considered dangerous – unreliable.

Emma strode over to me. With a sigh, I turned my attention to her. She had been wearing on my damn nerves ever since I had gotten here. "Are you going to help us serve drinks or just sit here like you're better than the rest of us?" She smarted off, crossing her arms over her chest.

I arched an eyebrow at her. "Emma, why don't you go fuck off?" I snapped up at her. She knew who the fuck I was to Tristan, and yet, every time that she thought he wasn't paying attention, she had some snide remark to say, or she sent me a nasty look.

I was getting damn sick of it.

She sneered down her nose at me. "All of us women have been trying to get Tristan's attention for as long as we've been here, so fucking forgive me if we don't appreciate the special fucking treatment you get from him." She snarled. I snorted. "You don't belong here, Adelaide. You're nothing more than Joey's whore."

Wrong timing, bitch.

I stood up, clenching my fists at my sides. The doctor may have told me no more fighting, but I didn't give a fuck. I was about to knock this bitch right off of her fucking feet and onto her knees in front of me. "You want to fucking repeat that?" I demanded, my voice coming out cold, my warning clear: she had better shut her mouth before I shut it for her.

She laughed. "Oh, you think no one knew?" She asked. "Why don't you fucking run back to your fucking *master*, Adelaide? I'm sure Joey fucking misses you. After all, he's got to be the only man who will ever really want you. He did make you into his fucking dog, after all."

That was all it took.

My fist swung out, and I punched her in her nose, sending her crashing back against one of the tables. She shrieked in pain as she hit the floor with a thump. I yanked her up by her throat, my eyes glaring down into hers, ignoring Tristan as he shouted at me to let her go. Her eyes were filled with fear. I smirked down at her, watching as all of the blood drained from her face.

Tristan couldn't protect her ass every fucking time, and unlike the rest of these bitches around here, I wasn't afraid of Tristan.

Because she had one thing right. Joey had trained me, and he had trained me well.

"I *can't* go back, bitch!" I barked down at her. She flinched. "You want to fucking know why? Because he's fucking dead!" I screamed down at her. I shook her, not giving a shit that her face was turning blue as she clawed at my hands around her neck. "You inconsiderate fucking *bitch*!" I snarled.

I managed to land another punch to her face before Tristan grabbed my arms and yanked me up from her, forcing me to release her. I was seething, my chest heaving up and down with my rage as Emma sobbed on the floor, blood trailing from her nose and down her chin.

Just for spite, I spit on her face.

Jesup began to help her up from the floor as Tristan roughly swung me around to face him. I glared up at him, my eyes gleaming with rage. "What the fuck happened?" He demanded to know.

"Why don't you ask the fucking whore who told me to go back to my fucking master?" I snarled up at him, still absolutely furious. She had no fucking idea what Joey and I had together, and it pissed me the fuck off that she thought she had the fucking right to assume shit about me and the man who had honestly saved my goddamn life.

"What goddamn master?" He asked me, clenching his jaw as anger sparked in his dark eyes – anger on my behalf.

"She doesn't belong here!" Emma screeched. Tristan tightened his hands on me, keeping me rooted in my place as I made a move to face her again. I was seething. "She's Joey's bitch -"

"Shut your fucking mouth!" Tristan roared at her, making her flinch and cower back against Jesup who shot her a dark look for talking shit about me. "I didn't ask you a goddamn question! Speak only when you're spoken to!" He looked at Jesup. "Get her the fuck out of my sight. I'll fucking deal with her later."

"Tristan -." Emma began again, but he growled, his eyes flashing dangerously as he turned his gaze on her again, effectively shutting her up.

Jesup steered her down the back hall. Tristan brushed my hair out of my face. "Are you alright?" He asked me gently, his mood doing a complete one-eighty on me.

I nodded, blowing out a soft breath as I flexed my fisted hands, forcing them to relax. "I'm fine," I grumbled. "She just caught me by surprise."

Tristan pressed his lips to my forehead, and I closed my eyes, drawing in the comfort that he was offering me. "Have you eaten anything for dinner yet?" He asked me. When I shook my head no, he shot me a disapproving look. I scowled. "You're not just looking after yourself anymore, Adelaide." He gently scolded.

I rolled my eyes with a sigh. "I'll eat when I'm ready to, Tristan," I told him, placing my hands on my hips.

"She's a hell of a lot feistier than I remember," Troy commented as he strode over. "Not the same, sweet Adelaide we all remember, huh?" He asked, looking down at me.

I bristled, putting my guard up against Troy. "You should know the answer to that considering it was *your* VP that I shot in the shoulder." I snapped at him.

Kyle scowled down at me, but I only smirked in return. Tristan sighed as he ran a hand down his face. "Thanks for that, by the way." Kyle snapped at me. My smirk only widened. "It took me three months of physical therapy to be able to properly use my shoulder again."

"Why did you shoot Kyle in the shoulder in the first place?" Tristan asked me, his eyebrows pulled together, a disturbed look passing over his face before it became practically impassive again.

I shrugged before I crossed my arms over my chest. "I was at a drop, and Troy was there with Kyle and a couple of their men waiting to sabotage the entire exchange and lose the Sons of Hell one of our best clients," I informed him. "It was a million-dollar deal. I wasn't letting anyone fucking sabotage it."

Tristan clenched his jaw and shook his head. "I keep forgetting that Joey had you in the middle of all of that shit." He snapped. I glared up at him, a silent warning for him to tread carefully. He clenched his jaw, dropping the subject before he turned to Troy. "She's no longer with the Sons of Hell," Tristan informed them. Pain sliced at my chest.

Troy shrugged. "Guessed as much by the fact that she's here with you," Troy commented. "I heard Joey is currently MIA."

I swallowed past the sudden lump in my throat, hating the swarm of emotions that warred inside of me at the thought of Joey being dead.

God, I fucking missed him. Hell, I fucking *needed* him.

Without a word, I turned on my heel and stormed off towards the bar. I could feel Tristan's gaze on my back, but I ignored him, not even bothering to turn to face him. "Fucking hell; I wish I could have a drink right now," I muttered as I walked up towards the bar. I looked up at Jhenna as I reached up to rub my temples where they were beginning to throb. "Hey, Darlin', get me a cold water," I told her.

She arched an eyebrow at me. "Just a water?" She asked, almost as if she couldn't believe that I would want water on the night we were having a club party.

I narrowed my eyes at her. She instantly cowered back from me a little. "Did I fucking stutter?" I snapped at her. Her face paled the tiniest bit. "Get me a fucking water," I ordered.

With a nod, she spun around to the fridge and pulled out a bottle of water, handing it to me. I strode away from the bar and towards my room. However, before I could reach my room, my phone began to vibrate in my back pocket. With a disgruntled sigh, I pulled it out.

Time is ticking, gorgeous.

"Fuck!" I yelled, dropping to the floor as the ground beneath my feet shook, and the glass from the windows exploded, raining all around me.

Whoever had exploded this place did it with perfect timing – where I would be separated from *everyone*.

"Addy!" Tristan roared, his voice filled with panic.

I coughed, the air filling with smoke. It didn't take long for me to realize that the building was on fire from whatever had exploded outside. I quickly pulled my shirt up to cover my nose and mouth, desperately trying to see through the smoke.

I could feel the heat wrapping around me, and I cursed. I couldn't see past any of the flames and the smoke. I coughed again, my eyes burning from the smoke and the heat.

Was this really how I was going to go out?

"Adelaide!" Tristan roared. "Baby, if you're alive, please fucking answer me!"

"Tristan?!" I called out, coughing again.

"Fuck, Addy, where are you?" I heard him yell.

I screamed as a board fell from the roof, and I jumped out of the way just in time before it collapsed on top of me. "I'm trapped!" I told him as I realized it myself, fear gripping my chest.

I placed my hand over my belly as I began coughing so hard that I was gagging, my shirt not doing much to help with the smoke in the air. "Tristan, it's hard to breathe!" I managed to choke out.

"I'm coming, Addy. Just hang in there, baby." Tristan told me, panic clear in his voice.

I couldn't fucking breathe.

I dropped to my hands and knees, clawing at my chest.

Joey, babe, I'm so fucking sorry that I couldn't protect your kid.

Everything went dark.

■ ■ ■

TRISTAN

She was no longer responding to me. My heart was racing so fast that I was sure I was either going to have a heart attack or a stroke.

I had to fucking get to her before it was too late. The part of the building that she was trapped in was already burning high and hot.

"I'll go through the back," I informed Jesup. "The fire shouldn't be too bad in there."

He nodded, still speaking to the 9-1-1 operator on the phone. I rushed around the back of the building, Troy hot on my heels. I was terrified that something had happened to Adelaide. I could barely fucking think straight past the panic in my head.

I looked at Troy as we got to the back of the building. "If I'm not out in two minutes, something happened," I told him.

Troy nodded. "Be careful, bro."

I nodded, rushing in. The heat and the smoke were almost unbearable, but I pushed through, desperate to get to Addy. She was the only one who hadn't been able to get out.

And then I saw why.

There were burning boards all around her, blocking any escape route she could have taken. She was passed out on the floor, but I knew she wasn't going to last much longer if I didn't figure out how to get her the fuck out of there.

Whoever had set up that explosion had done it perfectly. It kept Adelaide from being saved.

And something in my gut told me that was the plan all along. Someone wanted to shut Addy up.

"Troy, I need help!" I roared.

I heard him behind me a moment later, and he cursed. "What's the plan?" He asked me as he looked around the burning building, trying to find a way to her.

"We've got to get one of these boards out of the way," I told him, the panic in my mind making it extremely hard to think straight. All I knew was that I fucking needed to get to her before it was too late.

He nodded in understanding.

Fucking hell, please let her be okay.

I couldn't lose her.

"Help is here!" Jesup roared into the burning building.

I was conflicted. I knew the firefighters could get her out, but I couldn't bring myself to move – to leave her here by herself.

Troy grabbed my arm when he realized that I wasn't making any plans to move. "I know you want to get her out, but you've got to let the firemen do what they can." He told me. "We're only going to be in their way. She'll be alright, man." He tried assuring me.

But I wouldn't feel better until she was back in my arms and out of danger.

Troy managed to get me out of the building, and a couple of minutes later, one of the firemen strode out, carrying Addy in his arms. I instantly rushed forward. "Give her here," I commanded.

"Sir, she needs help—"

"And she'll get fucking help!" I roared at him, finally losing my fucking cool. "Give my fucking woman here so I can take her over to the fucking paramedic!"

Without another word, he handed her over to me, and I strode over to the ambulance, pressing kisses to her sooty forehead as I did so. Her breaths were shallow, and I knew if she'd been in there any longer, she'd have died.

I almost lost her.

"Sir, we have to take her to the hospital to get her proper help." The paramedic informed me as he listened to her breathing. "Her lungs are filled with too much smoke. Do you want to ride with her?" He asked me.

I nodded, jumping into the back of the ambulance, sitting beside her head as they hooked her to an oxygen mask. I knew Jesup could take care of everything. It was one of the reasons he was my VP.

There was no way in fuck I was leaving her side unless a doctor ordered me to.

"Is there anything we should inform the hospital of?" The paramedic asked me as he began to check her vitals.

"She's pregnant," I informed him as I brushed my fingertips over her cheek.

Please, just let her be okay.

I couldn't lose her, too.

■ ■ ■

ADELAIDE

I coughed, pain gripping my chest as I came awake. I ripped my eyes open, squinting them at the bright light in the hospital room. Tristan was passed out in the chair next to me, his hand wrapped loosely around my own with his head resting on the bed. Jesup was passed out on another chair on the other side of my room, the hood of his black jacket thrown up over his head, soft snores sounding from his lips.

Both of the men were covered in soot, and they looked exhausted as hell. I pulled the oxygen tubes from my nose and winced at the beeping sound that instantly filled the room, jerking both men from their sleep.

Tristan snapped his head over to look at me, a relieved smile stretching his lips as his eyes landed on my open, tired eyes. God, he looked like he'd been through hell and back.

"You're awake." He breathed.

A nurse burst into my room before I could nod my head at him, and she blew out a relieved breath when she realized that I was awake. "Good to see you're awake, Miss Berkeley. I'll let your doctor know." She informed me as she turned off the machine that was beeping before she strode back out of the room in search of my doctor.

"How are you feeling?" Tristan softly asked me as he gently ran his thumb over my cheek.

"Tired," I admitted a bit hoarsely, leaning my face into his hand as I closed my eyes again. "What happened?"

"You passed out after inhaling too much smoke," Tristan informed me. I grunted. That would explain why my chest and throat hurt so damn bad. "I tried to get to you, but I couldn't." He sounded guilty as fuck. I looked up at him. He swallowed thickly. "The firefighter got to you just in time."

I sighed softly. "It was Vin," I told him quietly. "It had to be. No one else makes sense."

I felt his hand tense on my cheek, and I slowly opened my eyes to look up at him. His eyes were blazing with fury, and his jaw was clenched tightly. "How do you know?" He asked me, his tone quiet but terse.

"I got a text right before the place exploded. It said 'time's ticking, gorgeous'. Besides Jessie, Vin is the only one to call me gorgeous, and he only does it in threatening messages."

"Fucking hell." Tristan cursed right before someone knocked on the door – most likely my doctor. "Come in!" Tristan called, stepping back from me as a doctor stepped into the room.

The doctor gave me a warm smile as he moved over to my bed. "How are you feeling, Adelaide?" He asked me.

I shrugged. "Kind of burns when I breathe, and I'm still really tired," I informed him.

He nodded. "That's to be expected. I want to keep you here tonight to observe you since you are pregnant, and we'll see how everything looks tomorrow." I sighed. I hated hospitals. "I did an ultrasound while you were passed out." He informed me. I looked up at him expectantly. "The baby seems fine as of right now, but if you begin to notice anything that seems the tiniest bit abnormal, hit the button for the nurse." He told me sternly.

I nodded in understanding. He smiled. "Let us know if you need anything." He instructed before he left the room.

Tristan turned to Jesup. "Call River and Tank. I want them outside of this hospital room door. No one gets in this room besides you and me, the doctor, and her nurse on duty." Jesup nodded, pulling his phone out of his pocket. "Tell Dray and Wren that I want them on surveillance around this hospital, and one of them is to keep an eye on this hospital room window at all times. I'm not taking any more fucking chances. Not a goddamn soul comes near her without first being approved by one of the club men."

"Got it," Jesup told him, pulling his phone to his ear.

I looked up at Tristan. He looked exhausted and stressed, but under all of that, I saw how worried he was that he wouldn't be able to properly protect me from Vin. I grabbed his hand in mine and tugged him closer to the bed. "Lay with me," I told him softly, giving him a small smile.

It was dangerous as fuck to want to be close with him like this, but I needed his comfort. Too much shit was happening back to back lately, and my rock was gone.

With a soft sigh, he kicked his boots off and laid on the bed beside me, pulling me into his arms without a single complaint. I sighed softly in contentment, nuzzling closer to him as I began to drift off to peaceful oblivion again.

My mind slid to Joey, and I frowned for a moment.

Somehow, Joey, I know you're looking over me.

He always had - somehow, someway - Joey always found some way to protect me.

I just wish he were physically with me.

I wanted *him* – just him. I covered my belly with my hand, tears threatening to fall from my eyes.

Joey, baby, why?

EIGHT

I absentmindedly tapped my fingers on the bar, listening to the sounds of the construction crew finishing up the rebuilding of the part of the clubhouse that had burnt. Tristan was holding church, and the club girls were most likely still passed out in their rooms after the party that was held last night in celebration of my coming home from the hospital.

Zyla came out of the back, fully dressed and showered, her hair done perfectly, her make-up on point – just like she always used to be. She was Jesup's ex, and she had taken off with another man who had more money a few years ago. I honestly wasn't shocked to see her back here. Besides, we all went through our own shit. I wasn't one to judge.

"Good morning." She chirped.

I tiredly ran a hand down my face. "I wish it was," I grumbled. "I'm exhausted. I've been up since two this morning with morning sickness." I admitted to her.

She gave me a sad smile, pain flashing in her eyes for a moment before she smothered it. "Shit sucks, doesn't it?" She asked me.

I cocked my head to the side, my curiosity piqued. "You ever been pregnant before?" I bluntly asked her.

She swallowed hard, looking down at the bar as she picked up a random glass and began to wipe it down, removing fingerprints and watermarks. "Once upon a time." She informed me, leaving it at that.

Before I could respond, a loud bang on the clubhouse doors drew my attention, and Zyla and I both looked at each other before I grabbed my gun from the small of my back. I slid off my barstool and moved towards the door. River motioned me to stand down, his blue eyes warning me to heed his order. With gritted teeth, I stood back, watching as he shoved the door open, his gun drawn in front of him.

I gasped when I looked down at the body lying in front of the door. Joey was laying on the concrete, his face bloody and beaten.

"Joey!" I screamed, not bothering to question how the fuck someone who was supposed to be dead was currently laying on the ground in front of me.

Joey was here.

I set my gun down on a random table and looked over to Zyla who was staring with wide, shocked eyes at the man lying at my feet. River crouched down next to Joey, pressing his fingers to his neck for a pulse. "Get Tristan!" I barked at Zyla as I grabbed Joey under his arms and dragged him into the clubhouse, not waiting on River to help me.

Joey was alive.

He was fucking alive and here – with me.

The doors to the chapel flew open, and Tristan rushed out with Jesup hot on his heels. "Zyla, get me a first aid kit," I ordered as I sat on the floor, placing Joey's head in my lap, unable to pull his heavy body any further. I noticed River slip out the clubhouse doors, most likely to go check the grounds and the surrounding area for anyone else.

"Joey, can you hear me?" I asked him, my hands shaking as I ran them over his body, tears clogging my throat and burning at the backs of my eyes.

Nothing. Not a sound.

My heart constricted in my chest.

"Tank, Dirk – go with River to check the grounds," Tristan instructed the two men. Tristan placed a hand on my shoulder, dragging my tearful eyes up to his. "Let me and Jesup get him on the couch, Addy. It'll be more comfortable for both of you."

I nodded. Tristan and Jesup lifted him from the floor, and I watched as they carried him across the room to the couch. I quickly sat down on the worn furniture, placing Joey's head back in my lap as Zyla brought me a first aid kit. I began cleaning up his face, grimacing at the deep cuts.

Someone wanted to hurt him – not kill him. They wanted to send a clear message.

"Jessie . . ." Joey grumbled a moment later.

"Joey, what's wrong?" I gently asked as I ran my fingers through his soft, dark-blond hair.

"Adelaide, get Jessie." He grumbled, his eyes slitting open to look up at me. I knew he was telling me because he trusted me to save her – trusted me more than he trusted his own men.

I looked up at Tristan, hoping he heard Joey's command. I couldn't bring myself to leave Joey's side – not after getting him back so soon. It was selfish of me, but I didn't care.

I wasn't leaving him.

Tristan nodded once at me. Pain flashed in his eyes for a moment before he smothered it. I swallowed thickly. I knew he hated seeing me with Joey like this, but I couldn't – would never – turn my back on Joey.

"Hey, man, we're on it. Do you know where she's at?" Tristan asked him.

"With Charles," Joey mumbled, beginning to pass back out.

I looked back up at Tristan. "Go," I told him. "Tank and River will hold everything down here," I assured him.

Tristan leaned down and pressed his lips to mine. Pain lanced through my chest as I kissed him all while my fingers momentarily tightened on Joey. Now that Joey was back with me, it felt wrong – like I was betraying the man who had saved my life three years ago. "Call me if anything happens," Tristan instructed.

With that, he and Jesup strode out of the door before I could respond.

I looked down at Joey. Cupping his face in my hands, I leaned down and brushed my lips with his, not giving a fuck who was in the room and witnessing it.

"Thank you for coming back to me," I whispered.

Joey slowly brought his hand up and laced his fingers in my hair, deepening the kiss for a moment. My heart swelled in my chest, and tears spilled down my cheeks as I eagerly kissed him back, so fucking happy that he was back with me where he belonged.

"I'll always come home to you, pretty girl." He rasped.

His eyes shut again, darkness pulling him back under.

■ ■ ■

TRISTAN

Jessie slid off the back of my bike, wincing in pain as she did so. She was beaten pretty badly. Charles had fucked her up badly. When we got to the Sons of Hell clubhouse, it had been vacant, but I'd found Jessie tied up in the basement, bloody, beaten, and naked.

Honestly, had Joey not come to Adelaide for help, Jessie might have died there.

And the woman had no idea that her brother was still very much alive. Hell, I wasn't even sure if she was aware that *she* was still alive. Jessie was basically a shell of herself.

But hell, none of us had known Joey was alive. If any of us had known, it would have saved Adelaide all of the pain she had gone through.

It had killed a part of her to think that Joey was dead.

When she had dragged him into the clubhouse, her beautiful, dark eyes had lit up with a true fire – a fighting fire – something I was beginning to realize only Joey could bring out in her.

I was beginning to wonder if he had become the other half of her soul.

And that shit cut me deep.

"How did you know where I was?" Jessie asked me as we strode towards my clubhouse.

"Your brother," I informed her. She swung her wide, shocked eyes to mine. I released a quiet sigh. "He's alive, Jessie. He came to Adelaide for help."

"How is he alive?" She choked out, disbelief coating her voice.

I shrugged at her. "I don't know," I told her honestly. "He only woke up long enough to inform me and Adelaide of where you were."

I strode into the clubhouse, my eyes instantly landing on Adelaide, who was still sitting on the couch. She was talking to Joey. He looked to be mostly awake, but he looked exhausted and in a shit ton of pain. He had taken a hell of a beating, that was for sure.

"Joey!" Jessie exclaimed.

Joey jerked his head up to look at his twin. "Fucking shit, he fucked you up good." He breathed as he pushed himself up off the couch with a pain-filled grimace, opening his arms up to his sister.

"I'll be fine." She choked out as she wrapped her arms around him.

I walked over to Adelaide. "How are you feeling, Addy?" I gently asked her, knowing her morning sickness was beginning to seriously kick her ass. Instead of it being only in the morning, it was becoming a fucking all-day thing.

She leaned her head back against the back of the couch, a tired, weary look in her dark eyes. "Exhausted." She admitted, her tiredness seeping into her voice.

I knelt in front of her, running my hands over her jean-clad thighs. Her eyes flickered towards Joey for a moment, but she didn't push me away, for which I was relieved. "Have you eaten anything yet?" I asked her.

She nodded. "I just threw it up right back up, though." She admitted to me. I frowned at her. "My stomach has been upset since two this morning." She reminded me, as if I could forget spending half the night sitting in the bathroom with her.

"You need to rest," Joey said to her. "You always had a problem with resting to get better."

Adelaide snorted. "Going to take me about another eight months to get over this." She informed him, her dark eyes clashing with his, dropping the bomb of her pregnancy like it was nothing.

Joey sucked in a harsh breath at her words, and then he narrowed his eyes at me, anger flashing in his dark depths. "That goddamn fast you got her knocked up?!" He roared at me.

I clenched my jaw, reining in my temper. I wouldn't fight with him – not over this, and not with Adelaide sitting here to witness it. She had just gotten him back. I wouldn't put her through this stress.

But it didn't mean that I wouldn't put him in his goddamn place – give him a reality check. "Not me." I snarled at him as I stood up to my full height. "You fucking did."

Joey looked like I had punched him in the gut. His wide, shocked eyes snapped to Addy. Adelaide clenched her jaw and stood up from the couch, running her hands down her face in exhaustion.

"How far along are you, Adelaide?" He asked her quietly.

"Six weeks." She informed him.

He swallowed hard as he stared at her. "Fuck." He finally whispered.

Addy suddenly gagged, her hand flying up to her mouth as she rushed past me and down the hall to the bathroom. I rushed after her, getting there right as she dropped to her knees in front of the toilet, throwing up stomach acid since she hadn't been able to keep anything down all day.

Once she was finished, I reached forward and flushed the toilet, lifting her into my arms. "I think it's time for you to get some rest." I gently told her.

She nodded in agreement, resting her head against my shoulder. "Don't let him leave." She mumbled, already beginning to drift off. "I don't want to lose him again."

I swallowed hard at her words, but I quickly reminded myself that I was the one she was currently with – not him. But I couldn't deny that she loved him – that she would always love him.

And it was going to take me some time to come to terms with that.

"I won't, Addy baby." I gently assured her as I laid her on my bed.

But she was already passed out, not hearing my words.

When I walked back into the bar, Joey was swallowing a mouth full of beer, and Jessie was helping Zyla clean up, though they seemed to be holding a pretty good conversation. I understood Jessie's need to do something although she looked like death rolled over. She was trying to have normalcy. It was a normal reaction to a traumatic situation.

"Bit early to be drinking, isn't it?" I asked Joey as I took a seat next to him.

He just shot me a dark look. "I just found out I'm going to be a dad, not to mention the fact that the woman I'm madly in love with is carrying that kid and that she's in love with another man." He chuckled, shaking his head as he took another swallow of the beer in his hand. "I always knew I would lose her to you someday." He admitted, sounding like he had just lost one of the greatest fucking things in his life.

Fuck, I was going to need a beer for this conversation as well.

I got up and walked around the bar to the fridge, grabbing two beers – one for me and another one for Joey since he had just finished his off, and it looked like he was definitely going to be needing a second.

"What's your plan for her?" I asked him.

Joey popped the top off of his fresh beer with the bottom of a lighter. "I'm doing what's right by Adelaide and that baby." He informed me. "She may be with you, Grim, but I will be there for her as well." He let his dark eyes meet mine. "You're going to have a miserable relationship with her if you make her give me up." He warned.

I clenched my jaw, jealousy sparking in my veins. I tampered it down, though. There a baby in the picture now. I *had* to learn to get along with Joey for the baby's sake – and Adelaide's.

Because Joey was right. I couldn't ever force her to give him up. She would choose him over me.

"I'd be pissed if you weren't," I told him. "Takes two to tango and all that shit. This baby is your responsibility, too."

"Which means you and I are working together from now on, Grim." He informed me. I grunted in agreement, though I didn't like it. "The past? Out the fucking window. Clean slate."

He was fucking serious about this shit because Joey didn't let go of grudges for anything, not unless he gave a fuck about something.

And he gave a fuck about Adelaide.

"And your club?" I asked him.

Joey smirked – a cold- calculating smirk that chilled my bones. Sometimes, it was hard to forget just how ruthless and destructive Joey could be. "I'll put a bullet in the head of every mother fucker that dared to follow Charles – that dared to fucking cross me wrong," Joey informed me. "And I'm taking my fucking club back." He swallowed another mouth full of beer. "No one watches over Adelaide unless it's me, you, or Jesup." He informed me. "I won't take any chances with her safety. She's our priority. Not a goddamn thing comes before her."

I nodded in agreement, glad that we could at least agree on something. Jesup came out of the back, but he halted in his steps when his eyes landed on Zyla. He swallowed hard, and I cursed, setting my beer down.

He had no idea that his ex-wife was back, nor that she was here seeking refuge from her crazy ass husband. Right when both he and Zyla turned eighteen, they went to the courthouse and got married. We hadn't even graduated high school yet.

And only a few months after their marriage, she left him.

"What in the hell are you doing here?" Jesup snarled at her.

"Ooh, drama," Joey said as he grinned at the scene in front of him. I glowered at him. He only shrugged. "What? I've been getting the shit beat out of me for the past few days – cut me some slack." He grunted.

"J -" Zyla started, but I cut her off.

"Jesup, let's go talk," I told him as I slid off of the barstool.

Joey got off his stool. "I'm going to go check on Adelaide. Where is she?" He asked me.

"My room," I told him. "Can't miss it. It has President on the door." I pointed a finger at him. "Don't disturb her," I ordered.

He rolled his eyes. "I'm not a fucking idiot." He smarted off. I glowered at his back. Joey always ran by his own book, and he never gave a fuck whose toes he stepped on in the process.

These next few years were going to be fucking exhausting and a real damn test of my patience.

"How the fuck are you even alive right now?" Jesup demanded as Joey walked past him.

Joey shook his head at Jesup. "I did die, but they were able to revive me. I told them not to tell anyone I was alive because I've known for a while that Charles has been plotting against me." He clenched his jaw, looking over at his sister. "And he's been working with Vin this whole fucking time." He quietly snarled, letting his voice trail beyond us three.

"Fucking hell," I swore. If Vin had been working with Charles, then that only meant that the entire time Joey had been trying to protect her, Vin had been one step ahead, and he might still be depending on where Charles was.

Joey nodded. "It's why my sister looks like she does." He informed us. "Charles and Vin have been selling her out."

With that, he walked down the hallway to go check on Adelaide.

I stared after Joey for a moment, trying to make sense of what might be going through his head, but I knew it was useless. Joey was unpredictable and dangerous.

I looked over at Jesup. "Come on," I told him, pushing open the chapel doors. I knew this was going to be a tense conversation. Jesup had loved – hell, still did – Zyla with every fiber of his being. She had cut him deep when she took off with Rodney.

"Why is she back here?" Jesup demanded to know as soon as the doors were closed back behind us.

"She came to me last night – showed up during the party. She's lost everything, Jesup. She just needs a place to stay until she can get back on her feet." I told him.

Jesup shook his head. "Not here, Grim." Jesup snarled. "She fucking left. She demanded the divorce. She can figure her shit out on her own."

I crossed my arms over my chest. "Jesup, it's just for a little while, alright?" I told him. Zyla hadn't told me what happened, but the look in her eyes as she begged me for help? She was looking for safety, too. Something had happened, and I wouldn't turn her away if she needed help. "You don't even have to converse with her."

Jesup clenched his jaw. "I don't even want to see her fucking face, Grim. She's got a month. That's it. If she isn't on her feet in a month, I want her gone." He snapped.

With that, he strode out of the room, not giving me a chance to respond.

■ ■ ■

ADELAIDE

I slowly opened my eyes, locking them on Joey's darker ones. He was knelt beside the bed in front of me, his eyes running over my face. "Hey, pretty girl." He quietly greeted me as he reached up to run the tips of his fingers over my face.

"Hi," I whispered. I swallowed thickly, tears burning in my eyes. "I missed you." I croaked. "It hurt so fucking much to think that you were gone -."

"Easy." He soothed as he cupped my cheek, brushing his thumb over my cheekbone. "You know I'll never leave you." He reminded me. "That has always been my one promise to you. Always remember that promise, pretty girl."

I sniffled as a tear ran down my cheek. "You're my rock, Joey. I can't ever lose you."

He gave me a tender smile, one that warmed my heart and melted my soul. "I'll be your rock for as long as you need me to be." He told me. I smiled at him - a broken smile. "Always so fucking pretty." He breathed. He leaned forward and soothed his lips over mine. I softly sighed into the kiss, reaching up to clutch his shirt in my fist, holding him with me.

"We may fight; we may clash heads, but you fucking hold me with you for as long as you need me, pretty girl." He told me. Another tear ran down my cheek. "Tristan tries, baby, but he doesn't see *you*. So, you hold me with you for as long as you need."

"Lay with me?" I quietly asked him.

I slid over, allowing him to slide into bed with me. He instantly wrapped his arms around me, holding me close to him. I snuggled further against him, desperately needing every part of him wrapped around me at that moment. "I know things are different, Adelaide." My throat closed up with tears. I wasn't ready to hear this. "It's not just me anymore. I know that. But something in my gut tells me that it's not going to be just Tristan, either. It doesn't end with him, pretty girl."

"It may," I whispered, my voice breaking. All I knew at that moment was that I wanted Joey, though. To hell with everyone else.

Joey shook his head. "The vibe between you two – it doesn't sit right with me. You've changed – changed too much for you two to ever fit together again." He drew in a deep breath. "Adelaide, when that man comes along that warms your soul – that sets you on fucking fire – you *need* to let this go between us."

I clutched his shirt in my fist, shaking my head. "Never." I croaked.

Joey sighed as he brushed his lips to the top of my head. "You will; I know you will." He said quietly. "Just go to sleep, pretty girl."

I shut my eyes, not wanting Joey to know how much he was ripping my heart apart. I knew things were coming to an end between us.

But I would hold him with me for as long as I could.

NINE

ADELAIDE

Zyla blew out a harsh breath as she stepped up behind the bar where I was currently mixing a drink for one of the new girls. "I knew he was going to be upset about me being back, but I didn't know it was going to be like this." She told me as she grabbed a glass and filled it with Jack before she tossed it back, her face screwing up at the burn.

Zyla had never been much of a drinker, and it looked like that had never changed.

"You were the love of his life." I reminded her. She sighed, closing her eyes at the reminder, pain momentarily flashing across her face. "And you ripped his heart out when you divorced him for Rodney."

She swallowed hard. "I did it for a good reason, Adelaide." She told me quietly as she stared down at the counter. I glanced over at her, intrigued. "I'm still madly in love with him, but I wouldn't change my decision to destroy him. I did what I had to do."

I handed the new girl her drink and watched as she sauntered off towards one of the club men. I turned back to Zyla, turning my body in her direction. "Then why did you leave him, Zyla?"

She grabbed a beer out of the fridge for one of the men. "Promise you won't say anything – not even to Tristan?" She asked me.

I nodded. "You've got my word, Zyla."

She blew out a soft breath as she handed the beer to the guy who had asked for it. "Rodney got out of jail." She told me. I nodded, at least knowing that much. Rodney had been her ex when she and Jesup got together. They broke up when she was sixteen when he went to jail for a felony drug charge, and she met Jesup a few months after that. "And he wanted me back. He threatened to kill Jesup if I didn't go back to him, Adelaide." She drew in a shaky breath. "I couldn't take it if something happened to Jesup because of me."

I handed another guy a beer. "Then, why are you back now?" I demanded to know. If she did all of that to protect Jesup, why would she come running back here? Wouldn't that just put him in the same danger she had originally tried to protect him from?

She shook her head, a humorless laugh spilling from her lips, sounding almost hysteric. "Our place got searched by the FBI – Rodney got locked back up. I know he's going to get out on bond, and he'll probably get off with a slap on the wrist since he has so many damn connections these days, but I'm running before he has the chance to get out." She swallowed hard. "So, I came back here for a few days, just until I can figure out where to go." She informed me. "I can't let him trap me again."

"You got money?" I asked her.

She nodded. "I took all of Rodney's cash. He kept a few million in his safe. The FBI didn't find it."

I studied her for a moment. "Where do you plan on going, Zyla?"

She shrugged, pouring a drink for one of the girls. "I don't know right now. I'm still working that out." She blew out a breath.

"Somewhere far, though. I don't want him to ever find me again."
She shrugged. "Might have to learn to live off the grid, to be honest."
I frowned. I hated this for her.

"Zyla, why don't you just explain everything to Jesup?" I asked
her. I knew he would protect her if he knew what had happened -
knew why she did what she did.

She instantly shook her head. "No." She snapped. "It's out of
the fucking question."

I clenched my jaw at her stupidity. "Jesup is still in love with
you, Zyla. I can tell you right now that man has never stopped loving
you. He can take care of himself, Zyla. And he can take care of you,
too, if you would just give him the chance. This could be your chance
to not have to spend the rest of your life running from Rodney."

She shook her head. "I killed his kid." She told me quietly.
My eyes widened in shock. "I couldn't let Rodney know I was
pregnant, and I'd never gotten the chance to tell Jesup. So, I had an
abortion." She shook her head. "I can't ever go back to him, Adelaide
- not with that weighing down on my shoulders." She blinked back
tears. "How could Jesup ever forgive me for something like that?"

"Give me something that's going to fuck me up." Jesup
snapped as he stepped up to the bar. "And I want Adelaide to make
it." He snarled when Zyla got ready to pour him a drink. She flinched.
I scowled. "I don't fucking trust you to make me a damn drink, you
traitorous fucking bitch."

Zyla swallowed hard and stepped back from the bar, pushing
through the door that led to the kitchen. I glared at Jesup. "I think
you owe her a fucking apology." I snarled at him.

Jesup barked out a laugh. "Me, owe *her* a fucking apology?" He
demanded. "Girly, you're out of your fucking mind. I don't owe her
a goddamn thing. *She* left. *She* betrayed our marriage. I didn't do *shit*.

She doesn't deserve a goddamn apology. She deserves every bit of shit that I'm throwing her way."

I wanted to snap his neck at that moment. I could take one look at Zyla and know that she was running from something. Tristan could, too, otherwise he wouldn't have allowed her to stay here.

Jesup was either blind as fuck, or he was choosing to ignore her silent pleas for help and protection.

"Then, you're out of your goddamn mind if you think I'm making you a fucking drink." I snapped, grabbing Zyla's drink and throwing it in his face.

"What the fuck?!" He roared, jumping up from the barstool, sending it clattering loudly to the floor.

"There's your fucking drink." I snapped at him.

"What the fuck is going on here?!" Tristan roared as he walked up.

I glared at Jesup. "Get your fuckard of a VP out of my goddamn face." I snapped at him before I turned and pushed through the kitchen door where Zyla had disappeared to.

I found her sitting in the corner near the fridge, her knees pulled up to her chest, sobbing into her hands.

"He hates me." She cried when she looked up at me.

"Come on," I told her gently, helping her up off the floor. "I think you need a good, stiff drink and to forget about what a cunt Jesup is."

I led her back out behind the bar, and I poured her a glass of Jack and Coke. "Liquor doesn't fix anything, but it sure as hell makes you feel better for a little while," I told her as I handed her the glass. How many times had I lost myself in a bottle to forget about all of the bad shit in my life for a while?

Her phone went off in her pocket, and she pulled it out, her face paling to a sickly white color. She jerked her eyes up to mine, fear like no other covering her features. "He's out." She whispered in horror.

I snatched her phone from her, answering it for her, a twisted, cruel smile playing on my lips. "Where are you, Zy?" Rodney asked as soon as I put the phone up to my ear.

"Zy." I hummed. "I've never been called that. I think it fits me." I said, my smirk widening when Rodney made an annoyed sound in the back of his throat.

"Adelaide Berkeley." Rodney snarled.

My smirk widened. "The one and only." I sang. "How can I help you, Rodney boy?"

He growled. He had always hated that damn name, and I lived to piss off my enemies. "Where the fuck is Zyla?" He snarled.

"She's currently naked in my bed," I told him. Zyla's eyes widened at me, fear flashing in their depths. I knew Rodney was practically steaming, and I was enjoying every second of playing with him. "I always did have a thing for her," I told him.

"You fucking bitch!" He roared.

Pointers for me for knowing that Rodney was possessive as fuck when it came to Zyla.

I tsked. "That's not very nice, Rodney boy." I teased as I leaned against the counter.

"You tell that traitorous bitch that she has two hours to get back to my house with all six million of my cash, or I will destroy everyone she holds dear."

I let out a low whistle as I arched my eyebrows at Zyla, a proud smile playing on my lips afterward. The girl had robbed Rodney. Six million in fucking cash was a goddamn lot of money.

I snorted. "Sorry, Rodney boy. I can't relay that message since she's actually already on her way somewhere overseas, very far away from you. She left me her phone so that you couldn't track her. Good luck getting all of that money back." I taunted. "She's long fucking gone."

He released a snarl. "I always fucking hated you, Adelaide." He sneered. I laughed. "You better hope dear old Joey knows how to keep a leash on you because the moment I get my fucking hands on you, you are *dead*." He snarled. "I'm going to fuck you in every position, and I'm going to enjoy listening to you as you beg me to stop before I slit your throat."

My blood chilled in my veins as the line went dead. I set Zyla's phone on the counter. "That went well," I commented dryly.

Zyla's eyes flickered over my shoulder, and she paled even further. I turned around to see what she was looking at and cursed. Tristan's eyes were blazing with fury. He pointed at both of us. "Chapel - now." He snarled.

I blew out a harsh breath and followed him inside the chapel. Jesup and Joey were already in the room, both of them sitting at the table. Joey's eyes were cold and flat. I clenched my jaw, knowing this was about to be a fucking fight. "Sit the hell down." Joey snarled at me.

I placed my hands on my hips, tilting my chin up at him defiantly. "Who the fuck do you think you are?" I snapped at him.

Despite his injuries, he jumped up from his chair, slamming his hands down onto the table as if he weren't hurt. I saw Zyla jump in her seat, but I just arched an eyebrow at him, staying on my feet. None of the men in this room scared me. "The father of the fucking kid you just put in danger." He snarled at me. I narrowed my eyes at him in my deadliest glare. "So, sit the fuck down."

"*Now*." Tristan breathed in my ear, his tone not allowing any room for argument.

With a harsh glare at both of the men, I sat down in a random chair, crossing my arms over my chest. Joey sat back down in his seat, his eyes steady on mine, knowing how I could get. "Want to fucking explain to us why you just had a conversation with Rodney Hill?" Joey snapped at me. "How many times do I have to fucking tell you that man isn't one to be fucked with, Adelaide?"

I sneered at him. "Numerous times, apparently." I snarled, wanting to piss him off further.

Tristan slammed his hand on the table. I swung my angry gaze to him. "Enough!" He roared, jabbing a finger in my direction. I sneered at him. "One of you better start fucking explaining yourselves." He ordered as he looked between me and Zyla.

"My question is," Jesup stated, his voice eerily calm – the calm before the storm, "is why the fuck he was calling *your* phone, Zyla."

"He didn't -" she started, but Jesup slammed her phone on the table so hard that it shattered the screen. Tristan must have grabbed it while we were walking towards the chapel.

Zyla flinched, swallowing hard.

"One more fucking lie, Zyla." He warned.

I looked over at her. "Zyla, if you don't want to tell them anything, you don't have to," I assured her. "You left the club. You don't owe anyone at this table an explanation."

Jesup jumped up from his chair, sending it flying against the wall behind him. Joey jumped as well, pressing a hand to Jesup's chest, a warning for him to stand the fuck down.

"For once, shut your fucking mouth, Adelaide!" Tristan roared at me.

I jumped up from my chair as well, glaring down at Tristan. "You want to fucking know why the fuck I was talking to Rodney?" I snarled at him. He stood up from his chair, glaring down at me, but I wasn't intimidated by him. "I'm doing what Jesup failed to fucking do. I'm protecting Zyla."

I stormed over to the door, but Tristan beat me to it, blocking my exit. I glared up at him. "You are not walking out of this fucking room until one of you explains every fucking thing that's been going on." He snarled down at me. "Fucking try me, Addy." He warned when I sneered up at him.

"Or what, Tristan?" I angrily demanded. "Are you going to fuck me into submission?" I taunted. "I doubt I'd even enjoy it."

His features twisted, revealing the monster Tristan had grown into. I bristled, but I didn't stand down. "Don't fucking test me, Adelaide." He quietly warned.

I roughly jabbed a finger into his chest. "No, *you* don't fucking test *me*." I sneered up at him. "I've had it with you, and I've especially had it with this overbearing *bullshit*."

"Adelaide, just sit the fuck down," Joey spoke up, his voice a bit calmer, knowing I was almost past the point of reasoning.

I glared at him, the words falling from my lips before I could stop them. I knew it was only my anger talking, but I was past the point of giving a fuck. Had it been just Zyla talking on the phone to Rodney, they wouldn't have given two shits. Joey had no reason to give a fuck, so I couldn't fault him for that. But Jesup? Tristan? They should have cared about why Rodney was contacting Zyla. The only reason they were concerned was because I had talked to him, and that shit pissed me clean the fuck off.

"I wish you had stayed dead." I snarled at Joey. He looked like I had slapped him. He clenched his jaw, anger flaring up in his eyes. I glared up at Tristan. "And you and me? We're fucking *done*, Tristan. Your priorities are fucked up, and I'm done with you and this entire fucking club. Now move the *fuck* out of my way."

He glared back down at me. "No." He snapped.

I snatched his gun from him when he wasn't expecting it, pointing it at him. His eyes flashed with shock for a split second before he smothered it. "Move the fuck out of my way, Tristan," I told him. "Now, or I swear, I will pull this fucking trigger and move you myself."

"Let her go," Joey spoke up. Tristan didn't remove his eyes from mine. "Trust me, man. She just needs to cool off. She's way past the point of reasoning right now. She just needs a little bit."

With a clenched jaw, Tristan moved out of my way, and I stormed out of the clubhouse. I slung his gun on the floor as I did so, making numerous girls scream in fear.

And honestly, I had every intention of coming back into the clubhouse in a little bit with a more level head, but fate – cruel, twisted fate – had other plans for me.

TEN

RIVER

I frowned at my phone screen when I saw Adelaide's name flash across the top. I only had her number and vice versa in cases of emergencies only.

A bad feeling settled in the pit of my stomach. I'd been doing my damnest to protect her without drawing too much attention to what I was doing without my president's orders, but the woman had a knack for getting into some shitty situations. It honestly had to be some kind of fucking talent she had.

I had been attracted to Adelaide ever since she popped back up at the clubhouse after all of these damn years. The woman was full of fire – full of life – and she didn't take any shit from anyone. She had an air around her that instantly drew your attention to her when she stepped into a room.

She would make a hell of a good old lady one day. I was just biding my time until I could make my move. No matter how long it took.

Because I could be a patient man for the right things.

And Adelaide? She was someone you were patient for – something Tristan didn't understand, though I could tell that Joey kind of understood her. He was trying, but he couldn't seem to get it right yet.

You learned a lot by standing on the outside looking in.

"Adelaide?" I asked. "Darlin', what's wrong?"

"Help." She whispered. "River," she whimpered, "everything hurts."

I stood up from my couch, moving towards my apartment door. I wasn't much of a partier – never had been. So, when the club started getting rowdy earlier, I came home to come to drink a beer in the silence of my apartment.

"Darlin', where are you?" I asked her. "Can you tell me where you are?"

Her breathing was shallow. Fear for her safety pulsed through my veins, but I locked it away, focusing on finding her. "I don't know." She whimpered. I heard something hitting her phone. "My location is on." She told me, her voice fading in and out. "River, find me." She begged.

The line went dead. Rage soared through my veins, and I vowed to get justice for her. I would slaughter whoever the fuck put their hands on her.

Darlin', I'm coming. Just hold on for me.

■ ■ ■

TRISTAN

I looked down at the bar as my phone vibrated beside my elbow, showing a call from the hospital. A bad feeling spread through my gut, and I answered the call quickly, praying it had nothing to do with Adelaide, though my gut was telling me otherwise.

"Tristan Groves."

"Um, Grim, Adelaide was just rushed into surgery." River informed me, his voice cold. River was a damn good club member, but sometimes, I worried where River's loyalties actually lied. But I knew if I needed him to do something, he would – no questions asked. He was a cold-blooded kind of man. I wasn't even sure if he really had human emotions.

And as stupid as it was of me, it didn't even occur to me to ask him why and how he knew Adelaide was being rushed into surgery.

"Fuck!" I roared, hanging up the phone, panic gripping my heart. I pointed my finger at Joey. "Had you just fucking let me handle her, she'd fucking be here safe and sound." I snarled, pulling my bike keys out of my pocket.

"What the fuck happened?" Joey demanded to know as he got up off of the couch with a pain-filled grunt.

"Adelaide is in the hospital." I snarled, running out of the door, not giving a fuck if he decided to follow me or not.

Addy, baby, I'm so sorry that I keep fucking up with you.

■ ■ ■

I stared at the doctor, barely hearing him through the blood pounding in my ears. River was gone by the time I got to the hospital, but he'd been proactive enough to inform the front desk that Joey and I would be coming to the hospital, and we were in charge of her care.

Adelaide had been beaten to within an inch of her life.

She had multiple stab wounds in her lower abdomen.

There were signs of being strangled.

She lost the baby.

She was raped – most likely numerous times.

The doctor's words: "she's extremely lucky to still be alive."

"Grim," Dink called, coming over to me with his laptop. "I found this."

He showed me a video. "Got this from one of the traffic cameras." He told me.

The video showed Adelaide being thrown out by a dumpster, her phone tossed out beside her. She hit the ground unconscious. There were no markings or plates on the van.

"Fuck." I snarled, running my hands through my hair. We had no way of knowing who the fuck did this to her, but something in my gut told me it might be Vin.

Joey came out of the back from visiting Adelaide. When she had been released from surgery, he was the first person back there to see her.

His jaw was clenched, and he looked murderous - like the cold-blooded killer people said Joey really was. "She's asking for you," Joey told me.

I shook my head at him. "I can't go see her right now," I told him, guilt swirling in my gut. "Not knowing that I fucking let her walk out like that - that I'm part of the reason she's in this goddamn situation."

Joey shook his head at me, anger flashing in his eyes. "Man, if you don't go see her, I think it's going to send her toppling over the edge. She doesn't even give a shit that she's lost a baby, Tristan. She's at the point of breaking completely, and I don't want to see her become that kind of monster. Don't be selfish. Fucking go see her."

"She won't," I told him, getting up from my chair, ignoring the last part of what he had said.

Joey glared at me. "Then you don't know that woman at all. She's destructive, Tristan, and right now, she's on the verge of shutting it all off." He shook his head.

I ignored him. Adelaide wasn't that kind of woman. I just needed a few hours to come to terms with what the fuck had happened – what I had failed to protect her from – then, I would go see her.

■ ■ ■

I'd never felt more like an idiot in my life.

I should have just fucking listened to Joey, swallowed my guilt, and went to go see her.

She fucking disappeared.

I stood with Jesup and Joey as we listened to the doctor. "She left sometime in the middle of the night." He informed us. "I don't know how the hell she managed to walk out, but she's gone. With her kind of injuries, she shouldn't have even been able to move off of the bed. I have no idea how she slipped past the nurses on duty, either. Security footage doesn't show anything. She was by herself."

I swallowed hard. Joey chuckled, but it was humorless. He shook his head. "I fucking told you, man." He laughed again. "I fucking told you!" He shouted.

Then, his fist connected with my jaw, knocking me off my feet. He was dragged into cuffs, but he only grinned at me, looking slightly like a maniac – like a man possessed.

"I created that monster to keep her from dying, Tristan." I spit out blood on the floor. "You should have fucking just listened to me, and she'd still be here." He snarled at me before he was dragged away by the officer.

I fucked up.

Adelaide was gone, and this time, *no one* knew where the fuck she'd gone.

Addy, baby, I'm so, so fucking sorry.

She had done exactly what Joey said she would do.
She had shut it all off, and she had left.

ELEVEN

I walked into the bar where Vin had set up our next exchange. A year had gone by since Adelaide had left, and it was like she'd disappeared off of the face of the Earth. There was no fucking trace of her anywhere. Honestly, if we couldn't still find proof of her driver's license and social security number, it would have been like she'd never existed.

Vin had mellowed out – shockingly, but I still had a feeling he knew where Adelaide was, and I also had a feeling he had hurt her. I'd tried to go after Rodney, too, but someone had beat me to it. When I confronted Joey, he'd been as shocked as I'd been. Someone had shut Rodney up before either one of us could, but we just put that down to the dumbass having too many enemies.

So, a couple of months after Adelaide had disappeared, I set aside my pride and formed a truce with Vin in the hopes that I would find Addy before it was too late to save her.

"Fuck, this place is a disgusting ass strip club," Jesup muttered, following me back to the small booth in the very far corner where it was the darkest – where Vin always decided for us to sit. He didn't like being able to be seen.

A roach crawled across my shoe. I flung it off, disgust crawling down my spine. I was glad this place didn't serve food, but I seriously

worried about the alcohol the patrons were consuming. Jesup wasn't
joking. The club was disgusting and dirty.

Vin came out of the back, his suit immaculate, a stark contrast
to his strip club. "Welcome, boys." He commented as he took a seat.
A waitress dressed in practically nothing sauntered up to our table,
and Vin ordered three rounds of Vodka shots, but I wouldn't be
drinking mine, that was for sure. I may be an outlaw, but I had
standards, and cleanliness was one of those standards.

It was silent around the table for a few moments. Vin liked to
do this - let the silence linger. It made him feel powerful - like the
big man in charge.

The song playing over the speakers switched, and the blonde
girl that had been up on the stage walked off as another dark-haired
girl came on the stage. She was wearing a red ensemble that barely
covered her. She looked starved - way too fucking skinny. Hell, I
could see her ribs from my table, and we were in the far back corner.

She turned her face our way, and I sucked in a harsh breath,
the need for blood to be spilled pulsing through my veins. "Grim, is
that -" Jesup started, but I snatched my gun out of my cut, pushing it
against Vin's temple. He hadn't had any warning, so all he could do
was sit still and just hope that I didn't blow his fucking brains across
this booth.

"Why the fuck is Addy on your stage?" I snarled at him.

Vin's lips tilted up into a smirk. "She's mine now, Grim." He
informed me, using my street name.

"Not anymore she's not. She's *mine*." I snarled. I pulled the
trigger, his blood splattering my clothes and my cut. I roughly booted
his dead, lifeless body out of the booth and stood up, glad that I had
my silencer on my gun. No one had noticed the commotion, but
everyone was soon going to see the blood splattering my clothes.

I couldn't even bring myself to give a fuck about that, though. I'd found Adelaide, and right then, that was all that mattered to me.

I stormed up to the stage. A man blocked my way, crossing his arms over his chest. "No one is allowed up on the stage with the girls." He told me gruffly.

I was past the point of giving a fuck about his goddamn rules.

I quickly put a bullet in his chest, and then I stepped over him, storming up onto the stage. Addy snapped her eyes over to me, stumbling in her heels as her dark eyes widened in shock. Her face paled at the blood covering me.

"It's time to come home, Adelaide," I told her.

"I - Tristan—" she stuttered, not able to form an entire sentence in her shock.

"Hey, you've got to wait for your fucking turn!" A disgusting man barked from the foot of the stage. I clenched my jaw and closed my eyes, my patience fucking gone. "I paid two fucking grand for her tonight."

Jesup snapped the man's neck, shaking his head. "I would hope she's worth more than two grand." My VP grumbled in distaste as he spit on the man's lifeless body.

Addy stumbled, her eyes rolling to the back of her head as she passed out. I caught her before she hit the stage and lifted her into my arms. Fuck, she was light - too light. She'd lost so much fucking weight that it was a miracle she was still alive.

"Good thing we brought the van," Jesup commented.

I silently agreed. We'd originally planned to leave here with guns, but I had cargo in my arms that was way more important. I would send a couple of other men to get my weapons. I had to get Addy back to the clubhouse where it was safe and where I could keep an eye on her.

I carried Adelaide out of the back entrance of the club to where the van was parked. Addy grunted quietly, her eyes slowly opening as she began shivering when the cold air slid over her exposed skin.

I got into the van with her still cradled in my arms, and Jesup jumped in the driver's seat. "It's c-cold." Adelaide stuttered.

Jesup silently tossed me my jacket from the front seat as he pulled onto the highway. I covered her up with it, cradling her closer to me, not able to bring myself to care about the fact that I was covering the side of her body in Vin's blood.

"You're covered in blood." She grumbled after a moment, almost as if she were just beginning to realize it herself.

I shrugged. "Shit happens," I said bluntly.

"You do that a lot now?" She asked, looking up at me with her gorgeous, dark eyes.

I just grunted.

I had turned into a ruthless bastard when she left.

I wasn't the same man she'd left behind.

But I wasn't the only one who changed.

Adelaide's soul had gotten ripped apart. I just didn't know it yet.

■ ■ ■

When we got to the clubhouse, I carried Adelaide straight to my room, not giving two shits about the numerous eyes that followed me as I did so. "Why are you bringing me back here?" Adelaide asked me.

"This is your home, Addy," I told her gruffly.

She stayed silent, which was unnerving. The normal Addy would have at least tried biting my head off.

134

Silent Adelaide? It made my gut twist with anxiety.

I set her on her feet, watching as she slipped off her heels, making her height drop almost six inches. "It's not my home anymore, Tristan." She finally spoke up, but there wasn't fire in her voice anymore. She sounded lost – broken. "I'm not the same woman that left." She informed me.

"Like hell that this isn't your home, Addy," I growled. "This will *always* be your home."

She looked up at me, slowly undoing the buckles and chains to her outfit. I swallowed hard as I let my eyes trail over her as she allowed her outfit to drop to the floor. God, even though she'd lost so much weight, she was still the most beautiful woman I'd ever seen in my life.

My cock strained against my jeans, begging to be buried deep inside of her.

"What do you want from me, Tristan?" She asked me softly, stepping towards me. She ran her hands under my cut, gently pushing it off my shoulders. I swallowed hard. She wasn't even giving a fuck about the blood.

"You want to fuck me, don't you? Want to sell me out?" She asked huskily. "I'm a fantastic way to earn the club some extra money."

There it was. I let my eyes meet hers, but hers were dead – lifeless. She was cold – detached.

My blood roared in my veins. Whereas I had just been ready to let her have her fucking way with me, now I was seeing fucking red.

I stepped back from her, watching as she just let her hands fall back to her sides, not even giving a fuck that she was naked as she stood in front of me. "What the fuck has gotten into you, Addy?" I demanded.

She shrugged. "I told you that I wasn't the same woman that I used to be." She informed me. "Vin made damn sure of that."

"I could shoot him a second fucking time." I snarled.

She shrugged carelessly. "It's not his fault that I'm like this." She told me. *Like hell it wasn't.* "I went to him willingly, Tristan. I asked him to make me forget who I was." She let those beautiful eyes meet mine. "I was tired of hurting."

I didn't believe that shit for a second.

I shook my head and walked over to my dresser, rage like no other roaring through my veins. I yanked open my drawers, grabbing her one of my t-shirts and a pair of my sweatpants. "Get a fucking shower." I snarled at her, shoving the clothes at her.

She crossed her arms over her chest, that old spark lighting up in her. There she was – there was my woman. "Make me." She seethed, getting angry.

Without a word, I moved to the bathroom, knowing my door was locked, and Jesup had put two men outside of my door and my window. She wouldn't be going anywhere anytime soon. She wasn't escaping again.

After turning the shower on, I stripped out of my clothes and walked back into the bedroom. I didn't miss the way her breath caught in her throat as she ran her eyes over me, but I was beyond giving a shit anymore.

She wanted me to make her get a fucking shower?

Fine.

I wasn't being the fucking nice guy anymore.

I gripped her wrists and shoved them behind her, thrusting her chest out so her nipples brushed against my chest. My dick instantly went hard, but I pushed down my desire for her, instead grabbing a pair of cuffs from my dresser.

"Tristan, what are you doing?" She demanded, panic seeping onto her face and into her voice, but I couldn't bring myself to care. She was always pushing buttons - that had at least not changed with her.

I leaned down so that my face was level with hers, my eyes boring into her own. She swallowed thickly as she slightly leaned back from me. "You're not the only one who's changed, Addy baby, and I promise you that I will bring the old you back." I quietly swore.

"I'd like to see you try." She snapped at me, trying to hide her panic, but I needed her to break down, needed her to come back to me.

I smirked down at her, making her swallow nervously. "Oh, you will, Addy, and I'm going to break you down as I do," I promised her.

I cuffed her wrists behind her and dragged her to the bathroom. "Get in the shower," I ordered.

"Go fuck yourself, Tristan." She snarled at me, her breathing picking up speed.

Without a word, I swept her off her feet and stepped into the shower with her. "I fucking hate you." She snarled up at me, those beautiful, brown eyes sparking fire at me.

A humorless smirk twisted my lips as I set her on her feet. "If that's the case, baby girl, your hatred is only going to grow," I informed her.

She glared at me with nothing but cold hate and disgust shining in the depths of her eyes, but I swallowed down my guilt.

If I wanted Adelaide back - my Adelaide - I had to break her down, no matter how much it pained me to do so.

She would understand it in the future, and she might even thank me for it.

■ ■ ■

"You're a mother fucking asshole!" Adelaide shouted from my room after I shut the door to my apartment in the clubhouse behind me. I hated leaving her like that, but I didn't trust her to not run away again. I needed her to stay – needed her to stay with me so that I could fucking help her.

Jesup arched an eyebrow at me. "Sounds like everything is going swell." He sarcastically stated.

I ran my hands down my face, exhaustion and guilt weighing down on my shoulders. "I have to do it to her," I said quietly. "I hate it, but I don't know how else to bring the real her back."

"Tristan, get your ass back in here and uncuff me!" Adelaide screamed.

Jesup barked out a laugh. "You cuffed her?" He asked, his eyes shining with humor.

"To the bed," I informed him.

Jesup only laughed harder.

You'll forgive me for this later, Adelaide.

■ ■ ■

ADELAIDE

I squeezed my eyes shut, desperately trying to fight the panic attack that threatened to overwhelm me. I *needed* to be uncuffed. God, I would do whatever Tristan wanted me to do if it meant I got uncuffed. I couldn't stand being restrained anymore – not after everything that I had gone through.

He had to come back to uncuff me.

"Tristan!" I shouted, squeezing my eyes shut again.

I watched as Vin stepped into the room, his heavy boots making soft thudding noises as he continued walking closer to me.

I pulled at the shackles that held my wrists to the wall, my breathing picking up as panic began to settle in. Vin officially had his hands on me, just like he'd always wanted.

He was going to ruin me – destroy me.

Vin was going to break me in the worst way possible.

"You know you're mine now, right?" Vin asked me as he pulled his shirt off, revealing his heavily muscled form.

"What is your obsession with me?" I choked out, fear thudding hard in my chest. My heart was beating so fast that I was surprised I didn't fucking die from it.

"You're the only one to escape me, love." He reminded me. Tears slid down my cheeks. "And I can't have that."

"Vin, please." I choked out, tears streaming down my face.

He undid his belt. "Oh, I'm going to love listening to you beg me to stop." He huskily spoke.

I yanked at my cuffs, tears streaming down my face. I looked down at my clothes, tears of relief streaming down my face.

I was still dressed.

I wasn't naked.

I was on Tristan's bed. I was okay. Vin couldn't hurt me here.

I squeezed my eyes shut, turning my face to the side as silent tears streamed down my face.

Unable to fight it, another fucking flashback dragged me under.

■ ■ ■

A scream tore from my lips as I woke up, my heart pounding hard in my chest. The door flew open, and Zyla rushed in with Tank and River. "Please get me out of these." I sobbed, my eyes searching out River's. I'd paid enough attention to River a year ago to know he would go against his president – wouldn't give two fucks about the consequences as he did it, either.

River ran by his own book.

"Let me help her." River said softly as he gently moved Zyla aside so that he could reach me. Zyla nodded.

Tank put a hand on River's shoulder. "You know Tristan will be pissed." He warned his friend.

"You think I give a fuck?" River growled. "This is fucking inhumane, Tank. She doesn't deserve this shit. What Adelaide needs is fucking love and support, and Tristan is being a goddamn dick."

I squeezed my eyes shut, desperately fighting against the images wanting to rise to the surface. A sob ripped from my throat, and I pulled at my cuffs again, losing the battle.

I fell into my tortured memories again. But before I completely succumbed, I felt River's lips brush my forehead. "Just come back to me, Darlin'." He whispered before I disappeared inside of my head completely.

■ ■ ■

TRISTAN

When I walked into my room, I did *not* expect to see Adelaide no longer cuffed to my bed.

And I was even more shocked to see Tank leaning against the wall beside my door while River sat on the floor with Adelaide in his lap, gently rocking her as she sobbed, her entire body shaking. Zyla was whispering soothing words to her.

I didn't know whether to be pissed or jealous. She was clinging to River as if he were her lifeline – clinging to him in a way that she had never done with me. His forehead was resting against hers as he whispered soothing words to her, being her rock – taking my place and doing what I should have been doing.

But once again, I was fucking failing her.

"What the hell happened?" I snarled as I stepped further into the room, glaring down at River.

"She flipped the fuck out, Grim." River grumbled. He swallowed hard, shaking his head. His arms flexed protectively around Adelaide. "Someone fucked her up bad, Grim." He glared up at me. "Cuffing her to the bed triggered *numerous* flashbacks, so real good fucking job there, Prez." He sarcastically snapped at me.

Adelaide jumped up from Zyla's lap and rushed over to me before I could lose my shit on River for putting his hands on my woman, shocking the fuck out of me. I caught her before she knocked us both to the ground, instantly wrapping my arms around her, my body relaxing as I held her tight to me.

"Please don't cuff me to the bed and leave me like that again." Addy sobbed into my chest. Guilt swirled in my stomach. "Please don't." She begged me, drawing my attention away from River.

I soothed my hand over her hair. "I won't." I softly promised, feeling like such a jackass now.

What the fuck had I done?

Zyla, Tank, and River left the room, closing my bedroom door behind them quietly. I sat on the bed with Adelaide in my arms, leaning against my headboard with her cradled on my lap.

"Don't let him hurt me," Adelaide whispered as she clutched my cut in her hands, her head falling onto my shoulder.

Before I could ask who, she passed out in my arms, her soft snores letting me know that she was out cold.

As I looked down at her, I realized then that everything she had said to me when she had gotten there had been a lie.

Someone ruined her – that someone being Vin.

TWELVE

ADELAIDE

I looked up at Tristan as he stepped back into the clubhouse. He'd been out most of the day working in the garage, but he hadn't cuffed me to the bed again, for which I was thankful.

I needed a way out. This shit with me and Tristan was toxic as fuck. I couldn't do this – not again.

Where the fuck was Joey? Why wasn't he here? Why hadn't Tristan told Joey that I was here – that I was back home?

My eyes caught River's from across the room. His lips tilted up the slightest bit in my direction, warming my heart, giving me strength that I hadn't even known I'd been seeking.

I'd always thought that River was attractive, but the way he'd held me yesterday when I had completely fallen apart? My heart skipped a beat in my chest. He was warm and strong – safe – something I hadn't been in a year.

Zyla handed one of the guys a beer, her lips tilting up a little as Jesup walked in behind Tristan. "Things changed a lot, didn't they?" I asked her, noting the way Jesup shot her a wink that had her cheeks burning red.

She shrugged as she turned her attention to me. "You were gone for a while, Adelaide." She reminded me.

I was only supposed to be gone for a couple of hours at most, but Rodney had found me.

I glanced at River again. His eyes were on me, and when they caught mine, they softened slightly, understanding and strength for me in their depths. My chest swelled. I hadn't been looked at like that – well, *ever*.

River had come to my rescue that night. I didn't want to call Tristan - didn't want to call Joey.

I wanted someone who never looked at me with judgement – someone who looked at me without pity.

River jumped out of his truck, his boots making a soft thud on the dirty ground. He had made it to me in record time, just as I knew he would. When he'd given me his number in case of an emergency, he'd told me anytime day or night, call him.

I was so glad that offer still stood.

"Fuck, Darlin'." He breathed as he knelt next to me, but there was no pity in his eyes. Instead, there was a burning rage in them. "It's going to hurt like fuck for me to move you, but I need to get you to the hospital." He told me.

"Okay," I whispered.

He eased his arms under me and easily lifted me against his chest, his arms flexing around me. He wasn't wearing his cut, and he had a beanie on his head, mostly concealing his identity from anyone that might see him.

I whined in pain, my breaths shallowing out. He brushed his lips to my bloody forehead. "Easy, Darlin'." He soothed. "I've got you. You're not alone; I'm here."

Tears slid down my cheeks. "I feel like I'm dying." I choked out as he set me in the passenger seat of his truck.

He gripped my face in his rough, calloused hands, locking those beautiful, blue eyes on mine. "Live for me, Adelaide." He told me. I swallowed thickly at the raw emotion in his eyes. "Can you do that? Can you live for me?"

I nodded. He brushed his thumbs over my cheekbones. "No matter what hell you endure, Darlin', live for me, yeah?" He brushed his lips over mine. I sobbed, everything hurting so much, but he was doing his best to soothe me. "Just live."

Troy and Kyle stepped up to the bar, drawing me out of my memories – that sweet, bittersweet memory where River gave me a taste of what it was like to truly be cared about.

Live for me.

I'd fucking lived – not a goddamn thing else, but I fucking lived. I kept my promise to him.

"You here to stick around this time, Adelaide, or are you just going to leave and fuck everyone up again?" Troy demanded to know as Zyla slid him a beer.

I clenched my jaw. He didn't know *shit*. "Watch yourself." I snarled at him.

"She's not going any fucking where." Tristan snapped. I fisted my hands but forced them to relax. I just needed a plan to make Tristan fucking get rid of me for good. I needed to destroy him. I couldn't keep going in this endless cycle. Vin was dead. The threat hanging over my head was gone.

I just wanted out – away – from this endless, heartbreaking cycle.

I got up from the stool and sighed. "I need my own clothes," I informed Tristan.

He smirked. "I like you in mine." He informed me.

I huffed in aggravation, not enjoying his playfulness. "I still need my own." I retorted, not playing his game.

He blew out a breath. "Give me fifteen minutes to grab a shower, and then, we can go shopping."

"Shopping?" I asked incredulously. "I just need you to take me to my place to get my things," I told him. I didn't want him spending a dime on anything. I had clothes at the apartment Vin had housed me in. Since I was now gone and Vin was dead, I doubted anyone was guarding it, waiting on me to come home.

Tristan shook his head at me. "I'm not taking you anywhere near Vin's territory, Addy. It's too fucking dangerous considering I just potentially started a war by shooting him yesterday. So, we're going shopping." He told me.

"Whatever," I grumbled, not in the mood to argue with him further. I was still tired, my body still begging for rest.

"In the meantime, ask Zyla if she's got something you can wear." He told me. "You two should be about the same size."

I only closed my eyes as I turned away from him.

I needed out - needed freedom.

I felt eyes burning into the side of my head, and when I turned, my eyes locked with River's again.

■ ■ ■

As it turned out, Zyla and I were the exact same size since I had lost so much weight in the year that I had been gone. I hadn't been properly fed - only allowed to eat when Vin allowed me to. He'd done everything in his power to tear me down, to make me weak.

And he had accomplished it. Vin had ruined me.

I opened the door to Tristan's room to find him buckling his belt, his shirt tossed on the bed. I swallowed hard, my grip tightening on the door handle as my eyes trailed over him. I may not want to be in a relationship with Tristan, but I couldn't deny that he still turned me on. He was well built, his muscles rippling with every move he made.

"You continue to fuck me with those pretty eyes, Addy baby, and we won't be going shopping for a few more hours." Tristan huskily warned me.

My eyes snapped up to his, and I subconsciously licked my lips. I wanted this, at least. I wanted a distraction – something familiar.

And I was familiar with having sex.

With a muttered curse, Tristan walked over to me, his hand sliding into my hair as he tilted my head back, his lips sliding against my own.

I moaned softly, my body curving into his as he closed the bedroom door, pushing me against it as he easily lifted me against it, his lips attacking mine. I wrapped my legs around his hips, my hands clutching at his shoulders as his tongue slid against mine, making my body shudder against his.

This – this was what I needed for at least a little while. There was nothing to sex. It didn't require much thought.

He grabbed the bottom of the shirt I was wearing and tugged it over my head, tossing it to the floor. I whimpered as he ran his rough, calloused hands over my smooth skin.

He was distracting, but not distracting enough. My mind kept flickering to other shit, burying me further in my internal torment.

In no time, my clothes were on the floor, and Tristan had me on my back on his bed. His hands ran over my body, and he kept teasing me by going so close to where I wanted his fingers the most and then retreating.

I released a frustrated sigh, and finally, he moved over me, his eyes meeting mine. He slowly slid into me, and I cried out his name, arching my back off of the bed as my walls clutched at him, my body desperate for a release – a release that was all my own – of all my own control.

With a gentleness that Tristan had never really possessed when we were younger, he made love to me, bringing me over the edge over and over again, until exhaustion was weighing me down like a brick.

And I cried.

■ ■ ■

Tristan was sitting at his desk when I woke up, a pair of sweatpants riding low on his hips, his muscular upper body bare. He had the club books spread out in front of him, obviously working on budgeting and paying bills that needed to be paid.

I stretched out my body, feeling that familiar soreness of being used, but at least this time, I had wanted it. My movement drew Tristan's eyes over to me. He smiled softly. I felt my throat close up with tears. Tristan's smile no longer comforted me or made my heart swell like it used to. Now, it just made me feel trapped. "Sleep well?" He asked gently.

I nodded. "Extremely well," I told him, meaning it. I hadn't had any kind of decent sleep for a little over a year.

Tristan stood up and moved over to me, sitting beside me where I was lying. He brushed his fingertips over my cheek. My eyes slid closed as I reveled in his touch, wishing it still comforted me like it used to. Tears burned at the backs of my eyes, but I forced them not to fall.

I would not cry for something lost.

"I have to leave for a couple of days." He informed me. I opened my eyes to look at him again. "I'm leaving River here with you." He informed me.

My heart picked up pace in my chest. River – the man that I was pretty sure I was gaining feelings for. The man who hadn't judged me when he'd saved me.

His words rang in my head. *Live for me.*

"Where are you going?" I asked Tristan.

"Joey needs me at his club for a few days to deal with an inside problem." *Joey.* Oh, God, I fucking missed him. "He knows you're back, but he asked me not to bring you – not until he dealt with this problem." I frowned, my mood dimming again. "He'll come to see you when shit is taken care of on his end."

I sat up, shaking my head as I held the sheet around my chest, hiding my body from Tristan, suddenly feeling vulnerable. "I'm capable of taking care of myself, Tristan. I want to come with you." I told him.

Tristan shook his head. "Out of the question, Addy." He told me, his voice stern.

I glared at him as I slid out of bed, beginning to slide my clothes back on. I didn't even give a fuck that he was staring at me. I was angry – furious.

Hold me with you.

Well, Joey, I really fucking need you right now, and you're not letting me hold you here with me.

"Try and stop me." I snapped at Tristan as I tugged my jeans up my legs.

"That a challenge, Addy?" Tristan asked quietly, quiet anger in his voice.

I tilted my chin up at him, a defiant gesture that I knew Tristan both loved and hated. "I'm coming with you, Tristan," I told him.

He snatched my shirt from my hand, tossing it onto the bed. I swallowed hard as he took a step closer to me. Fear spiked in my veins, but I hid it from him. "I'll be damned, Addy." He snarled softly.

"And I'll be damned if I'm going to be kept a fucking prisoner in this mother fucking clubhouse." I snapped back at him. I'd been a prisoner long enough. I would *not* be one now.

"For the love of all that is holy, Addy, why the fuck is it always so fucking hard for you to just *listen* to me?!" He shouted.

I clenched my jaw and shook my head, backing down. "Fine." I snarled, giving in. That's what he wanted, right? For me to be a good old lady and shut my fucking mouth?

He sighed. "Addy -" He started, but I shook my head, hating him at that moment.

Trapped. I was always fucking *trapped*.

"I said *fine*, Tristan!" I shouted at him, snatching the shirt off of the bed and pulling it over my head.

I stormed out of his room, slamming his room door shut behind me with a resounding slam that shook the walls and silenced all of the voices in the clubhouse.

■ ■ ■

"Adelaide, it's getting dark." River stated as he stepped out of the garage office from where he'd been sorting through some of the books. His long legs carried him over to where I was currently working on a junk bike, trying to keep my mind off of the shit that I was always buried in. "I think it's time to call this quits until tomorrow, Darlin'."

My heart rate picked up speed in my chest at the sound of that familiar term falling from his lips. I had noticed he never called any of the other women that name - almost as if he reserved it solely for me.

Stupidly, it made me feel special - special to him.

"Don't want to be out here, River, then go on inside." I snapped at him. I needed to work on this bike - to keep myself busy.

Or I was going to self-destruct.

He sighed, opening the fridge in the garage and grabbing a beer out. "I can't leave you out here, Darlin'. You know that. Strict instructions from the president himself." He said, though he sounded sour about following orders. River had always struck me as the kind of man that ran by his own book. It always shocked me that he was a member of a club and not its president.

I looked up at him. "You ever thought about telling your president to shove his fucking commands up his ass?" I questioned seriously.

River barked out a laugh, his blue eyes glinting with humor. "Numerous times, Darlin', but that's not something you do if you don't want a damn good ass beating to remind you of your place." He reminded me.

"You ever get sick of playing babysitter?" I asked him.

He shrugged. "Zyla got on my nerves a lot," he admitted, "but you're a breath of fresh air, Darlin'."

My breath hitched in my throat at his words. I sat back on my heels and let my eyes run over the man in front of me. River wasn't really a looker. He was rugged - not as handsome as Joey or Tristan, but there was something about him that drew me in - made me crave him.

I couldn't deny that I was attracted to River – that I wanted to be his in some kind of way. It was fucked up. I loved Joey; I loved Tristan. Yet, here I was, falling for yet another man.

I was a fucking mess.

I knew River had to be from somewhere in the south because of his southern accent, and he wore flannels better than any other man here, Tristan included. Tattoos swirled over his skin, disappearing under the sleeves of his flannel, appearing back on his neck. He was broad-shouldered, and his arms flexed with each movement he made.

Why the fuck hadn't I made a move on him before?

Because right now, I wanted him – badly. I wanted him to claim me as his, but I knew that would be asking too much from him. I'd never seen River show any real interest in a woman.

But I would have him in any way that I could.

"River, you got an old lady?" I asked him as I grabbed a wrench from the floor, yanking my eyes from him.

"Nah. Tried that once. She divorced me six months after we got married." He informed me, but he didn't seem too bothered by that fact.

"That's got to suck," I commented as I began to continue taking the bike apart.

I saw him shrug from the corner of my eye. "It was five years ago, Darlin'. I'm over it."

I stood up, deciding to take a chance. Fuck it. The worst that River could do was deny me. But I wanted someone to distract me from the shit my life had become – someone that wasn't Tristan.

That someone being River. If I could have this with him, I would take it. He'd shown me kindness – shown me what it was liked to truly be cared about.

Not in fucked up way Joey did.

Not in the tainted way that Tristan did.

I walked over to River, swallowing nervously as I did so. He only watched me, and his blue eyes didn't give anything away. "Want to do me a favor?" I asked him, stopping when I was a couple of feet in front of him.

He tilted his head to the side the tiniest bit as he studied me with an unreadable expression on his face. "Depends on the favor, Darlin'."

"Make me forget?" I quietly asked him.

His eyes softened all while they blazed with a lustful heat that made my nerve endings curl. Understanding passed over his features, and I knew right then that he wouldn't turn me away.

He wanted this, too.

"You trying to get me in trouble, girly?" He huskily asked me, as he set his beer on the toolbox next to him.

"No one has to know," I told him. "It can be a secret."

His eyes darkened at my words. "We'll keep it a secret if that's what you want, Darlin', but I fucking want you, and I frankly don't give a fuck who knows about us."

With that, he gripped the back of my neck and crashed his lips to mine before I could respond. His other hand gripped my hip tightly, yanking me against him. I gasped as I felt his hard, powerful frame press against me, a soft moan falling from my lips as I completely lost myself in him and the sensations already running through me.

Gripping my hair in his fist, he tilted my head to the side, pressing hot, open-mouthed kisses to my jaw and neck, nipping lightly at my soft spot.

"River." I gasped out, my hands gripping his cut in my fists.

"You sure you want this, Darlin'? I'm not going to be gentle."
He warned me, his voice husky. He drew back some to look down at
my face, those gorgeous, mesmerizing, blue eyes locking on my own.

"Yes." I breathed, feeling like I may lose my fucking mind if
he didn't finish what he had started.

"Fuck." He cursed, his lips molding with my own again as he
knocked everything off of the work bench behind me.

Tools clattered loudly to the floor, but he gave no fucks as he
lifted me and set me on the cold metal, his lips moving back down
my neck. His hands gripped the bottom of my shirt, and I lifted my
arms, allowing him to pull it over my head. With quick, sure fingers,
he unsnapped my bra, tossing it down on the concrete floor with my
shirt.

I moaned his name as his rough, calloused hands slid over my
body. I curved into him, a whimper escaping my lips as he trailed his
rough fingertips around the swell of my breast. "River, please – oh,
fuck!" I gasped out as his lips closed over one of my nipples, his hand
molding my other breast.

"You're fucking perfect." He muttered huskily as his lips met
mine again. My heart swelled in my chest at his words.

He quickly unsnapped my jeans and tugged them and my
panties down my legs. I quickly pushed his cut off his shoulders, and
I began fumbling with the buttons on his flannel as he peppered hot
kisses all over my skin. I gasped. I needed to feel his skin on mine.

"Oh, fuck it," I grumbled right before I ripped it open, the
buttons popping everywhere, scattering across the floor.

River released a husky laugh before he gripped my chin,
bringing his lips to mine as I ran my hands over his hard chest and
his rippling abs.

Fuck, he was carved beautifully.

He let me push his flannel shirt off of his shoulders, and I pushed his jeans down his legs a moment later, licking my lips in anticipation as his cock sprung free.

Oh, God made him absolutely perfect when he created him.

"Last chance to back out." River warned me.

I shook my head at him, letting my eyes meet his. There was no fucking way that I could walk away now.

He pushed me back on the worktable so that I was on my back. He spread my legs, and in one swift thrust, he was buried deep inside of me. My back arched off of the table, his name falling from my lips as I clutched at his forearms. He felt like Heaven inside of me.

"Fuck, Darlin'." He choked out. "You feel a fuck ton better than I thought you would." He growled.

He set my feet on the table so my legs were bent and spread wide, and then, he gripped my shoulder, proceeding to ruin me for every other man.

And I fell hard for him because even though he was fucking me hard, he was still treasuring every bit of my body and this moment between us.

I was ninety-nine percent sure that River was the one Joey had told me about.

THIRTEEN

My eyes were instantly drawn to River as he stepped into the bar room, freshly showered and ready to start another day. He was dressed in a red and black checkered flannel shirt with the sleeves rolled up to his elbows, revealing his tattooed arms. He adjusted his cut as he fully exited the hallway.

God, why was he so damn perfect?

His eyes met mine from across the room, and a slow, sexy smile tilted his lips the slightest bit, making my cheeks flush and a throbbing start in my core.

He had taken me over and over yesterday in the garage, and I had enjoyed every single moment of it. And then, he'd sat on the floor of the garage after tugging our clothes back on, and he'd held me in the dark silence. Not a word was spoken between us, and yet, he comforted me more than any other person in my life ever had.

"Adelaide, Tristan is trying to get in touch with you," Zyla stated as she came out of the kitchen, her phone held in her hand, Tristan's name on the screen.

"Tell him I said to go fuck himself." I snapped, knowing very well he would hear me himself.

"Watch yourself, Addy, or I swear when I get back—" Tristan snarled, Zyla obviously having him on speaker.

"You'll what?" I demanded angrily, snatching a bottle of Vodka from under the counter. River's eyes darkened momentarily at the unfinished threat, but he held himself in check. "Fuck me into submission?" I demanded heatedly. "Handcuff me to your fucking bed again?"

"This will hold until I get back." Tristan sneered.

I twisted the top off the Vodka bottle, glaring at the phone in Zyla's hand, wishing he were in front of me so that I could slap him. "Touch me when you get back," I dared him, "and I will personally chop off every single one of your fingers," I promised before I moved away from the bar, storming to the clubhouse doors, the bottle of Vodka still in my hand.

But I didn't miss the proud smile on River's face as I walked out, and it made my chest swell with pride.

"Morning, Adelaide." Jacob greeted from under the hood of one of the cars in the garage.

"Not now." I snarled, storming into the office.

"Little early to be drinking, Darlin'." River drawled as he stepped into the office with me, shutting the door behind him.

I snorted before I took a long drink from the bottle. "This is the longest I've been fucking sober in a year, River," I informed him. River stayed silent, that unnerving, blue gaze locked on my face. I frowned down at the bottle in my hand. "He pissed me the fuck off." I quietly admitted.

"He used to be your entire world, Darlin' – him and Joey, that is." River reminded me. I swallowed thickly, my heart throbbing as I thought of Joey, and a distant ache starting in my chest at the thought of everything that *used* to be between me and Tristan. "You used to never even look in another man's direction with them around. What changed?"

"I changed, River," I told him as I turned to look at him. There was no judgement in his eyes, just a tenderness that I was clinging to. I never wanted to lose that tenderness. "I'm not the same young girl that he was in love with four years ago, and I'm certainly not the same woman he loved a year ago. I changed. It was the only way to survive."

River quietly locked the office door, striding over to me after checking to make sure the blinds were closed. I watched with nervous, uncertain eyes. Anyone could see us, and I didn't want him to face the end of Tristan's gun if word got back to Tristan about us.

River gently took the bottle of Vodka from my hand, setting it on the desk behind me while I stared at him, my breathing picking up pace slightly.

"What . . ." I swallowed hard as he cupped the side of my neck and wrapped an arm around my waist, drawing me against him, "what are you doing?" I breathlessly asked him, my heart pounding hard in my chest all while anticipation curled in my belly.

"One night with you wasn't enough – it'll never be enough." He huskily admitted right before his lips molded against mine.

My mind shut down as I wrapped my arms around his neck, my fingers plunging into his soft, damp hair, tugging gently on the dark strands. I pressed my body closer to his, needing to feel him against me.

He groaned softly, his arms flexing around me. A knock sounded on the door, bursting our little bubble. I sucked in a sharp breath, abruptly yanking myself from River's arms as he cursed softly, clenching his jaw, anger flaring up in the beautiful, blue depths of his eyes. He drew in a deep breath before he cupped my face in his hands, soothing his lips over mine. My body instantly relaxed, my anxiety calming.

Oh, God, he was so fucking perfect.

He released my face and walked over to the door, quickly unlocking it and swinging it open as I grabbed the bottle of Vodka from the table and tipped it back.

We had almost gotten caught, and I wouldn't be able to live with myself if River got a bullet between his eyes because of me.

"River, we've got a problem," Dirk said. "We're a bar of coke short for the shipment tomorrow."

"Fucking hell." River grumbled, running a hand down his face. "I'll ride out there. I need you to tail me."

Dirk nodded, walking away. River pointed at me. "You – with me."

I rolled my eyes at him. He didn't have to drag me with him on this ride just because of Tristan's orders. Someone else could easily keep an eye on me. "I'm not going to run the fuck away, River."

He smirked at me, and every nerve ending in my body curled, making me want him just as badly as I had last night. "Oh, I know, Darlin'. I just want you on the back of my bike." He told me. "Now, bring your cute ass on so we can hit the road."

■ ■ ■

I was shocked to see Tristan, Joey, Jesup, and Tank at the warehouse when we got there, but I was excited to see Joey. He moved away from the desk as River parked his bike. River gave my hand a subtle squeeze as he looked at me over his shoulder, understanding in the depths of his mesmerizing eyes.

I slid off the back, taking my helmet off and handing it to River. Then, I dashed forward, jumping on Joey. He caught me easily, his arms wrapping around me as I locked my arms around his neck and my legs around his waist. "Hey, pretty girl." He whispered as he pressed a tender kiss to my temple.

BOOK ONE   RUINED

My bottom lip trembled, and I sniffled as tears burned in my eyes. "Easy." Joey soothed as he ran his hand over my hair, his other arm holding me just a little bit tighter.

"I'll close the doors - give you guys some privacy. Tristan will understand." River quietly spoke as he passed us.

I looked at him over Joey's shoulder. His lips tilted up the slightest bit, and I gave him a watery one in return. He nodded once at me, and somehow, I knew he understood.

My heart squeezed in my chest.

"Fuck, pretty girl, I've had people searching for you *everywhere*," Joey whispered. I closed my eyes and buried my face in the crook of his neck. "I was so fucking terrified that you were dead somewhere."

"River took me to the hospital that night," I told him quietly as Joey took a seat on his bike, keeping me wrapped around him.

He gently pulled my head off of his shoulder so he could properly look at me. His eyebrows pulled together in confusion as he brushed a tear off of my cheek that I hadn't realized had fallen. "What do you mean?"

"I called him," I told him quietly. Pain flashed in Joey's eyes for a moment before he smothered it. I swallowed thickly. "He asked me to live for him." Joey's eyes widened in shock. "So, I did. Vin found me pretty quickly, and he threatened to hurt all of you if I didn't find a way out of that hospital." I sniffled. "I wanted to die, Joey, but I lived because River asked me to."

Joey smiled at me. "Remember that one I told you about?" He softly asked me. I frowned, my heart squeezing painfully in my chest. He reached up and cupped my cheek in his hand, his smile now sad. "It's time to let me go, pretty girl."

I shook my head at him. "I'm not ready." I choked out.

160

He brushed the pad of his thumb over my bottom lip. "You can still hold me with you." He promised. A tear slipped down my cheek. "But this between us? You need to let it go, pretty girl. You've got a good man in there. I saw the way he looked at you – the way he's looked at you since Tristan took you back to his clubhouse a year ago. He's the one for you, Adelaide."

"I can't lose you," I whispered, my voice breaking.

He shook his head at me. "I'm forever with you as long as you'll keep me." He promised. "But you need to move forward with him."

"Promise?" I asked him quietly.

He nodded. Then, he cupped my face in his hands and took my lips in a savage kiss. I burst into tears as I kissed him back, my tears tasting salty on my lips. I sobbed as I gripped his cut in my fists, so much pain spearing through my chest.

"Keep me with you." He whispered. "But be with him, pretty girl."

■ ■ ■

"The fuck is she doing here, River?" Tristan angrily demanded as I strode into the clubhouse with Joey.

"Couldn't leave her at the clubhouse when I'm instructed to be by her side every damn second." River retorted. "You want me here? She comes, too."

Joey snorted. "So much for telling Tristan that she was outside with me." Joey retorted.

River only smirked at him. Joey rolled his eyes, but River's carefree attitude brought a small smile to my face. River's eyes caught mine, and his smile widened the slightest bit.

Tristan strode over to me, and I glared up at him, my hand tightening in Joey's. Joey drew me a bit closer to him. "Drop the fucking attitude, Addy." Tristan snapped.

"Go fuck yourself." I snarled up at him.

His eyes flashed with anger. My heart knocked hard in my chest, fear pulsing through my body for a moment. I instinctively stepped closer to Joey. "You're pushing your fucking luck, Addy baby." He swore quietly.

He reached out to grab me, but I flinched back, fear spiking in my blood. Joey stepped in front of me at the same time River stepped forward, Jesup grabbing River's shoulder to keep him in place. I stepped back a pace, swallowing hard. "Don't fucking touch me." I snarled at Tristan as I fought down the flashback that threatened to bring me to my knees.

"Fuck off, Joey. This is between me and Adelaide." Tristan warned him.

"Back the fuck up, Tristan," Joey growled, his voice cold and threatening. "Pretty girl, go on outside," Joey said, his voice more soothing, but he didn't turn to face me, instead keeping his eyes on Tristan as the two men stared each other down.

My eyes caught River's where he was standing beside the table that the bars of coke were sitting on, rage flashing in his eyes on my behalf. "Leave her be, Grim." River spoke up.

My eyes snapped back to Tristan's as he stared at me with hurt eyes before he quickly smothered it and shook his head, turning away from me and striding towards the table.

Did he know?

Joey turned to me and met my eyes. A sad smile flickered on his lips. He knew I'd been ruined - destroyed. "You alright, pretty girl?" He asked softly.

"I'm just going to get some air," I muttered, turning on my heel to stride out of the warehouse. I could feel someone's gaze on my back, and when I looked over my shoulder, River's comforting eyes met mine. Those blue eyes warmed me, giving me strength. I tilted my chin up slightly, and a small smile played on his lips before he turned his eyes away from me.

■ ■ ■

RIVER

I kept my eyes on Adelaide until she strode out of the warehouse and out of my sight. "Someone fucked her up – bad," Joey stated, shaking his head as he ripped his eyes from her as well.

I didn't know what had happened between them outside, but her eyes had been red and puffy when she'd come in with him, but judging by the way they'd been holding hands, it wasn't horrible – but it was probably heartbreaking.

"She won't fucking talk to me," Tristan grumbled. "I can't do anything if I don't know what happened."

I arched an eyebrow at my president. "Have you tried being nice to her instead of threatening her all of the time?" I asked him, most definitely overstepping my boundaries, but not really giving much of a fuck.

I never really gave much of a fuck about anything until Adelaide popped back up a little over a year ago. And the way he'd been treating her since he'd found her again? I'd lost count of the number of times I'd almost stepped over my boundaries and punched him in the fucking face, especially recently.

"I don't fucking threaten her, River," Tristan growled as he turned his dark eyes to me. "Learn your fucking place." He snarled.

I shook my head at him, keeping my mouth shut, not wanting Adelaide to catch heat if Tristan decided to think that I had feelings for her.

I mean, I did, but he didn't need to know that. Everything between me and Adelaide was only mine and Adelaide's business. She didn't want anyone knowing right now, and as long as she wanted it that way, I would keep it that way, no matter how much I wanted to openly claim her as my woman.

Jesup met my gaze from across the table, a knowing look in his eyes. I clenched my jaw, worried he may say something, but Jesup surprisingly kept his mouth shut, watching as Adelaide strode back into the warehouse.

"You've got company, boys." She stated, sounding careless, but I could see the fear in her eyes. I moved away from the table, my hand going for the gun in my cut.

Tristan moved from the table. "Who?" He demanded.

"Oh, brother, remember me?" Red asked, stepping in behind Adelaide, his gun pointed at the back of her head. I clenched my jaw in fury, stepping forward before Jesup clamped a hand on my shoulder. He gave a slight shake of his head at me to warn me to keep my cool. Reacting like this would set Tristan off.

And Adelaide didn't fucking want that.

But right then, she was in danger. I could give less of a fuck about how Adelaide felt about Tristan knowing about us. I would *not* let her get hurt just to save Tristan's feelings.

"Let Addy the fuck go." Tristan snarled. He knew Red was my brother - knew about the bad blood between us.

Red's eyes met mine, the same blue color as mine. "Grim doesn't know, does he, River?"

Fuck. *How the fuck did he know?* "Shut the fuck up, Red, and let Adelaide go." I snapped.

He shoved Adelaide onto her knees, the gun held at the back of her head. Her knees hit the concrete floor with a sickening thud. Her pulse was jumping wildly at the base of her neck, her eyes begging me to save her. I clenched my jaw, forcing myself to keep a clear head. Thinking with my rage would only get Adelaide hurt. "You going to suck my dick as good as you sucked River's, baby girl?" Red asked her, a taunt in his voice.

"How the fuck do you know?" I glared, ignoring the rage on my president's face. I would deal with him later. Adelaide was my main priority. I just needed to give one of these dimwits enough time to incapacitate my brother.

I watched Joey move out of the corner of my eye, but I didn't turn to look at him, not wanting to alert Red.

"Fucking with the garage doors open probably wasn't your brightest move, brother," Red smirked. "Especially with how loud she was screaming your name, begging for your cock."

I quickly raised my gun, pointing it at him. "Two seconds to let her the fuck go," I warned. And he knew I would pull the trigger.

Red smirked and kicked her to the ground with his boot to her back. I rushed forward, shoving my gun back in my cut, ignoring Grim's angry gaze on my back. Joey punched Red in the side of the head, knocking him out cold as I moved towards Adelaide and grabbed her off of the ground, drawing her shaking form into my arms.

"What the fuck, River?!" Tristan finally roared.

I pressed my lips to Adelaide temple. She shook her head, her hands grasping my face, tears building in her eyes. There was so much fear in her eyes - fear for me. "Go to Joey," I told her softly.

She swallowed hard. "I'm sorry, River." She whispered, hot tears sliding down her beautiful face.

I smirked down at her, trying to soothe her. I wasn't afraid of death, and honestly, if I was going out all because I loved her, then it wasn't a bad way to go. "I'm not," I admitted. "Now, go." I gently coaxed.

She moved over to Joey where he slung an arm around her shoulders and pulled her against his side, supporting her. "You fucked my woman?!" Tristan roared at me.

"She's not your fucking woman, Grim. You've been treating her like shit ever since she got back." I snapped at him. "How you could expect her to even *want* to be yours with the fucking way you've been treating her is fucking beyond me."

"I'm a hairsbreadth away from putting a bullet in your skull." Tristan threatened.

I continued. If I was getting a bullet in my skull, he was going to get a fucking wake-up call, and I hoped that Adelaide would choose to go back to Joey. The man had changed, and I knew he would finally love her how she deserved to be loved if he got the chance.

"If you would treat her right, Grim, you wouldn't ever have to worry about another man like me," I told him honestly.

He reached for his gun, and I clenched my jaw, my eyes flickering to Adelaide's panicked ones. "No!" She screamed, shoving Joey off of her before he could get a better hold on her. She roughly crashed against me. I stumbled with the force she knocked into me with, wrapping my arms around her as I steadied us to keep us both from falling to the concrete floor.

"You'll kill me first." Adelaide seethed at Tristan as she clung to me, using every bit of her strength to stay with me.

He clenched his jaw, hurt flickering in his eyes. "Why him, Addy?" He asked her, sounding broken. I almost rolled my eyes. How in the fuck could he be hurt about this shit when he had been doing nothing but treating her like shit? "The first second that I'm gone, and you hook up with the one man that I trusted with you mere hours after I just fucking had you in my damn bed."

"I'm not the same woman I was a year ago, Tristan." She told him. She sounded apologetic. I knew she still loved him – still cared about him. She didn't want to hurt him – didn't want him finding out this way.

I smoothed my hands over her back, holding her with me, giving her the strength that she needed.

"I don't give a fuck, Addy!" He roared, thrusting his hands through his hair. Adelaide flinched. I tightened my hold on her. "Fucking hell, woman, you know that I fucking love you! Why would you do this?!"

She swallowed hard, pain flashing across her face. I gritted my teeth. "You never saw *me*, Tristan." She told him quietly. "You saw the girl you wanted me to be – who I was before you ruined me on my eighteenth birthday." His face shattered, revealing the broken man beneath his mask – the man all of us knew he would be without her. Her bottom lip trembled. "Please, Tristan, if you love me, you won't kill him." She whispered.

With that, she reached up and trailed the tips of her fingers over my jaw before she strode out of the warehouse.

Tristan's eyes met mine. I was blown away by how shattered he looked. But this shit? It was his own fault. I didn't feel bad for him at all.

"You're banished from my fucking club, River." He informed me. I had figured as much. "You've got twelve hours to pack your shit, turn in your cut, and get the fuck out of my town. The only reason I'm not putting a bullet through your traitorous heart is because Addy cares about you, and I won't hurt her more than she already is." He looked towards the doors she had disappeared out of. "I've fucked her up enough as it is."

With that, he turned on his heel, disappearing into the office inside of the warehouse.

Joey looked at me. "I fucked up with her numerous times, River. That woman – she has a fucking heart of gold. Love her like she's always deserved." He drew in a deep breath. "She's going to fight you at first. The woman loves me more than she probably should, and she's going to do her damnest to try not to completely betray the love she feels for me, but I talked to her - tried to talk her into letting me go."

"She'll always hold you with her, Joey," I told him. He sighed as if he knew that, too. "That, I can bear." I shrugged my cut off my shoulders, holding it out to Jesup. He nodded once at me, and there was a proud glint in his eyes as he took my cut, almost as if he were proud of me for finally standing up for what I believed in. I looked back at Joey. "But as long as you make her happy, I don't give a fuck how long she holds you with her, even if that's the rest of her life."

With that, I strode out of the warehouse so I could go pack my shit and get the fuck out of Sons of Death's territory.

■ ■ ■

I threw my duffel bag onto the back of my bike and strapped it down, ignoring the sound of the pounding music from the clubhouse behind me. Tristan hadn't come back to the clubhouse yet, probably staying away until he got the word that I was gone.

Adelaide had disappeared from the warehouse before I had left, and I had only received a single text from her telling me she was safe and that she would see me before I left.

I straddled my bike, getting ready to strap my helmet to my head when I noticed a slim figure walking through the gates to the clubhouse, her arms wrapped around herself.

Those beautiful, brown eyes that I loved so much locked on me. "Leaving?" She softly asked me as she drew closer.

"Got to," I informed her as she continued walking towards me. "Grim's orders."

"I'm sorry." She told me quietly.

I grabbed her hips, pulling her towards me. Her hands settled over my shoulders. I slid my arms around her waist, drawing her between my knees. "Don't be," I told her. "I've been dying to have a taste of you since you came back from Joey's club," I admitted. "I'll never regret anything that happens between us, Darlin'."

"Where are you going to go?" She asked me, reaching up to run her thumb over the stubble on my jaw.

I shrugged. "Wherever the road takes me, I guess," I told her. But I had a feeling I would be going back home – home to Texas – home to the club I was born and raised in before family shit drove me away.

"You'll take care, right?" She asked me.

I reached up to cup her cheek. "Always, Darlin'."

She leaned down and pressed her lips to mine. I deepened the kiss for a moment, wanting this with her one last time. I knew she and I were destined to be together, but I had to be patient. She would come to me when it was time. And I knew when that time came, she would find me without even meaning to.

After a moment, I released her, strapping my helmet to my head as she stepped back from me, wrapping her arms back around herself.

"Live for me," I told her as I started up my bike.

She swallowed thickly, tears sparkling in her beautiful, brown eyes. "Always." She promised.

I peeled out of the lot, leaving the last bit of my happiness behind with her.

But I knew she would find her way to me.

FOURTEEN

ADELAIDE

I tapped my foot lightly on the floorboard of the taxicab in time with the beat of the song playing through my headphones as I stared out the window, watching the rain slide across the glass. It had been raining for a few days, but it was finally predicted to stop for which I was thankful. I normally walked to work but walking in the rain wasn't ideal. And this taxi fare was beginning to get expensive.

But I was honestly also kind of sad to see it go. It always made me feel a little bit better to see the world as gloomy as I was.

It had been three months since I had watched River ride off the lot, and two months and three weeks since I had left Sons of Death's charter with a small book bag on my back, ignoring Tristan as he begged me to stay, promised me to be better.

But I couldn't do it. I couldn't stay. I desperately needed to get away.

Joey had gotten me the money I needed to go somewhere – anywhere I wanted – to start off fresh.

I looked over my shoulder as the sound of a bike slowly reached my ears. I scowled, thinking it was Tristan, but my scowl lifted when my eyes locked on Joey and the familiar President patch on his cut.

"Walking somewhere, pretty girl?"

"Leaving," I told him. "I was going to call you once I got to wherever I end up."

He offered me a hand as he slowed to a stop. "Hop on, pretty girl. I'll take you wherever you need to get to." He told me. "No strings attached."

I breathed a sigh of relief. He was letting me walk away. He wasn't going to try to make me stay.

And I needed to go. I had to get away from here – away from all of this shit and all of the bad, painful memories.

I slid on the bike behind him and wrapped my arms tight around his waist, resting my head on his back. He took off, being careful with me on the back of his bike, though I remembered how to ride. I knew he was being careful because I didn't have a helmet, and his never fit me. Joey may have always been an asshole, but he was always serious when it came to my safety.

Once we got to the Greyhound station, he parked his bike and let me slide off before he stood off the bike as well, setting his helmet on the seat. I watched as he reached into his cut and pulled out a thick envelope, handing it over to me. "You're in luck, pretty girl. I just came back from an exchange. Take this."

I stared at him, my mouth hanging partly open in surprise. "Joey, I can't -."

He pulled me to him and slid the envelope into my back pocket. I swallowed thickly, tears burning at the back of my throat. Even after all of this time, he was still trying to take care of me.

"Trust me, my club will understand. They still worship the ground you walk on." He reached up and brushed the pad of this thumb over my bottom lip. I trembled as I tried to keep my tears at bay. "Do whatever you *need to for yourself, pretty girl."* My tears threatened to spill over. *"But don't ever forget that you have a home with the Sons of Hell."*

"I'm going to miss you," I whispered, my voice breaking.

He pressed a tender kiss to my forehead. I bit back a sob. "Hold me with you, pretty girl. I know you'll find River, but until you do, hold me with you. I am always just a phone call away if you need me." He promised. He squatted down some so that his eyes were level with mine. "Let him love you, pretty girl." A tear slid down my cheek. *"When you're with him, you look so fucking happy, and that's all I want for you, Adelaide."*

I reached up to trail my fingers over his jaw. "It's really over between us, isn't it?" I whispered brokenly.

He nodded, his dark eyes full of sadness. "The relationship part of us – yes. But I am always yours to command, Adelaide. Whenever you call, I'll be with you. Just hold me while you need me."

I nodded, more tears sliding down my cheeks. "I love you, pretty girl. I'll find you again when the time is right." He promised.

The taxi driver pulled up to the bar where I worked, pulling me from my last memory with Joey. It had been bittersweet, but it had been the good-bye that I needed to officially move on with my life.

I strode over to Lucky's, the bar that I was currently working at. It wasn't the best job in the world. My boss was a dick. The men were handsy and disgusting, but it paid my rent and other bills, so I couldn't complain too much. I was fairly compensated for the shit that I went through here, and I was close to purchasing a car due to being able to save a good bit every paycheck.

When I stepped into the bar, I walked straight behind the counter, going through to the kitchen where Brett was flipping burgers. "Evening, girly." He greeted with a warm smile on his face. I waved as I moved over to my locker. "Might want to be on your best behavior tonight." He told me, knowing I could get mouthy with some of the patrons. "The owners are here tonight." He warned me.

I had been informed when I had gotten hired that a biker club nearby owned the bar, and they occasionally came in to make sure things were being run properly.

What they didn't know was that I'd grown up in a trap house, seen so many drug deals go wrong growing up that not much shit fazed me anymore.

And then, when I turned eighteen, I got eyeballs deep in it with Joey – sometimes over my head.

I snorted. "Bikers don't scare me, Brett." I reminded him.

He shrugged. "Suit yourself, girly."

I put my bag and my hoodie in the locker, leaving me in my extremely short, jean shorts and my tank top that clung to my curves like a second skin and was cut low to reveal a lot of cleavage. I'd gained quite a bit of weight over the past few months, but it was my doctor's orders.

I was a little over three months pregnant, and my doctor had me on a strict diet to help me gain weight so I would be healthy enough to nurture my baby because when I'd gotten pregnant, I sure as fuck had not been. I was malnourished and extremely underweight.

I walked out of the back and began mixing drinks, putting them on a tray, and walking over to the table that had ordered them. "Jack and Coke?" I asked, without looking up from my tray to see who my patrons were.

"Right here." That man that I dreamed about every night said, his voice low and gruff.

My eyes snapped up in shock as I dropped the tray of drinks in surprise, my eyes locking on River's blue ones – the same ones that haunted my dreams every single night. He tilted his head to the side the slightest bit, his eyes running over me sensually. A shiver danced down my spine, my skin flushing beneath his gaze. His eyes darkened to a stormy blue color, his lips tilting up the tiniest bit.

But he was wearing a cut that clearly said President with Fathers of Mayhem under it.

He was the owner of the bar.

Fuck.

Fuck. Fuck. Fuck.

"I'm - I'm so sorry." I choked out, my heart pounding wildly in my chest.

I couldn't believe River was right here in front of me - had been right under my nose for *months*.

"Adelaide!" My boss roared, striding over to me. I snapped my wide eyes from River's to look at him, swallowing hard. Henry was a fucking asshole, and I tried to steer clear of him as much as possible. He was always making passes at me, and since I always shot him down, he'd been getting more aggressive.

"I'm sorry, River. She's normally not this dumb and clumsy." Henry apologized to River.

"It's fine." River grumbled, drawing my eyes back to him. "Take a seat, Darlin'." He told me, nodding towards the open seat next to him. "Henry, get someone to clean up that mess and bring me another drink, as well as a Watermelon Vodka for Adelaide," River ordered without removing his eyes from my face.

Henry nodded, sending me a hateful glare that River either didn't notice or didn't bother to pay attention to before he rushed off to go get one of the other girls to remake the drink orders.

"I didn't know you were in town, Darlin'." River drawled, bringing my attention back over to him as I cautiously took a seat beside him.

"I didn't know you were the president of another club." I shot back, feeling a tad bit defensive because trust me, if I'd known he was here, I would have sought him out.

Now, I was in my shit too deep.

"Watch your tone, girly." A guy a couple of years older than me spoke from the other side of the table, drawing my eyes to him.

He had blonde hair that hung to his shoulders and striking green eyes, his cut reading Vice President. He wasn't that bad looking, but danger rolled off of him in waves, and it made me edgy and wary of him.

But if I did anything, I loved playing with danger.

"Was anyone talking to you?" I snarled at him.

"Leave her be, Sam." River commanded. His VP swung his angry eyes to his president. "Adelaide is an old . . . friend of mine." He stated.

Friend, my ass. You went balls deep in my pussy over and over and cuddled with me afterward on the garage floor.

River ran his eyes over me as he reached forward and played with a lock of my brown hair. My pulse jumped. "You gained some weight, Darlin'." He noted. He let those mesmerizing, blue eyes lock on mine, sucking me into their beautiful depths. "Looks good on you." He informed me.

You don't want to know why, I admitted silently.

Fucking Hell, how do you tell someone they're going to be a fucking dad?

And I knew it was his. I had called Tristan when I had found out, and we'd had a DNA test done.

It wasn't Tristan's, though he offered to support me and the baby anyway. Needless to say, I turned him down flat and sent him back on his way to the Sons of Death.

"You couldn't find a better job than serving drunk, sleazy assholes?" River asked me as Natalia began cleaning up my mess on the floor.

I shrugged at him, my nerves feeling frayed as he continued to play with my hair. "It pays well, and I'm good at making drinks." I reminded him as Amber came with our drinks.

Amber set my drink in front of me, and I swallowed hard, knowing I couldn't have alcohol anymore. Not for another six months, at least – longer if I decided to breastfeed.

"Not going to drink your drink, Darlin'?" River asked me, his blue eyes intent on the side of my face as I stared at the Vodka in front of me.

I couldn't look at him. He would see right through me. I shook my head at him. "Not much of a drinker anymore." I lied, pushing the glass away from me.

He gripped my chin and turned me to face him. My bottom lip trembled under his scrutinizing gaze. "You're nervous." He stated, running his rough thumb over my cheek, soothing me whether he realized it or not. "Why?"

"I – I need to get back to work." I stammered. I jumped up from the table, needing away from him before he uncovered my secret. I wasn't ready to tell him.

I wasn't ready to tell River that he was going to be a father.

I felt his eyes on me as I rushed back behind the bar, but I did my damnest to avoid his table for the rest of the night.

■ ■ ■

I released a tired, exhausted sigh as I pushed my key into the lock on my apartment door, letting myself in. I dropped my keys on the kitchen counter and strode into my living room, jumping in fright when I saw River sitting on my plain, brown, leather couch, the lamp on beside it, casting his rugged features in a deadly shadow.

"You nearly gave me a heart attack." I snapped at him, putting my hand over my heart where it was beating rapidly. I swallowed down nausea. "What are you doing here?" I demanded. Anger. I needed to be angry. "Wait, on second thought, how did you know where I live and how the *fuck* did you get in my apartment?" I heatedly asked.

River shrugged and stood up from my couch. "I have access to all of my employee records." I swallowed nervously. This man was always one step ahead. "And since you were avoiding me all night, I decided this would be the best way to talk to you. You've never done well with the element of surprise, Darlin'." Damn him for knowing me so well. "And your lock is extremely easy to pick, which needs to be changed." I frowned. I never had to worry about someone breaking in until him. "As for why I'm here, well Darlin', I wasn't finished talking to you." He pulled my ultrasound pictures out of his pocket and tossed them onto the coffee table. I pressed my hand to my belly, tears burning at the backs of my eyes, a lump building in my throat. "Especially not now. We need to talk about this."

"River . . ." I started, my voice trembling as tears welled up in my eyes and spilled over onto my cheeks. I stared up at the man in front of me, terrified of his reaction. I hadn't wanted him to find out this way.

"Hey, hey." He soothed. He walked around the coffee table and wrapped his muscular arms around me, his hand on the back of my head, soothing over my hair as he held me to him. "There's no reason to get upset." He gently told me. "I'm not going to yell at you." He promised.

"How are you not pissed at me right now?" I asked him as I tilted my head back to look up at him.

He shook his head at me, a frown on his handsome features. "Have you ever really known me to lose my cool with you, Darlin', even when you do dumb shit?" He asked me. I shook my head. "I'm not Tristan, and I'm not Joey. You need to remember that."

"I know," I whispered as I finally wrapped my arms around him and leaned my forehead on his chest, soaking in everything that was River - his warmth, his strength - fuck, his safety.

"I missed you, Darlin'." He admitted softly. I slid my hands under his cut, and his body shuddered against mine. "Shocked the fuck out of me to see you serving drinks in my bar."

I laughed softly. "Imagine my shock when I realized you were the owner." I retorted, feeling much calmer now.

He shrugged. "When I came back home, my dad gave me the president cut. He was ready to step down - said he always knew I'd come back home."

"You were a biker baby?" I asked, looking up at him.

He nodded. "Through and through, Darlin' - born and raised to be one."

I yawned as I rested my head back on his chest. Suddenly, he hooked his arm under my knees, making me shriek in shock and tightly wrap my arms around his neck when he began striding down the hall to my bedroom. "River, what are you doing?!" I exclaimed.

He laughed softly at my reaction, his chest vibrating against me as he did so. "Taking you to bed so you can get some sleep, Darlin'."

I sighed softly, resting my head on his shoulder. "Will you stay?" I asked him quietly.

"For as long as you'll let me." He promised. He laid me on the bed, and then he pushed my shirt up, pressing a tender kiss to my belly. I sobbed at the tender moment, unable to help myself. My pregnancy was making me so fucking emotional.

River moved over me, his lips molding to mine. I moaned softly, my hands coming up to cup his face. "I never wanted kids, Adelaide, but as long as you'll let me be here, I'll be one of the best fucking dads to ever live on this Earth." He promised.

I cupped his cheek and pressed my hand over the steady beat of his heart as a small smile pulled at my lips. Joey's words rang in the back of my head. *Let him love you, pretty girl.*

"Stay with me," I begged River.

He turned his head and pressed a tender kiss to my palm. "As long as you'll have me." He promised.

FIFTEEN

My shower was running when I woke up, and the smell of freshly brewed coffee was wafting into my room. My bladder quickly reminded me of why I woke up, and I sat up, rubbing the sleep from my eyes. When I looked around, I noticed River's cut was laying on the foot of the bed, and his phone was still on the charger on my nightstand.

He'd stayed.

I got out of bed, striding to my bathroom. I could see River's muscular frame through the glass, and he turned at the sound of me entering the bathroom. "I have to pee." I sheepishly admitted when his eyes met mine.

He stepped out of the shower, leaving the water running. My breath hitched in my throat as I ran my eyes over him, locking on his hard cock. God, how did I already want him so early in the morning?

A knowing smirk tilted his lips, but he didn't comment. "Go ahead." He told me, pressing a kiss to my temple before he stepped out of the bathroom. Once I was finished, I called him back in as I stepped into the shower, sighing as the hot water ran over my tense muscles. God, the water was the perfect temperature.

This man was perfect for me.

"Fuck, woman, you're breathtaking." River stated gruffly as he drew me against him, leaning down to slant his lips across mine.

I moaned into the kiss and I ran my hands over his wet body until I grasped his cock in my hand. River growled softly as he shoved my knees apart with his thigh. Then, he slid his fingers along my pussy, dipping inside. I ripped my lips from his, crying out his name.

He pressed me against the shower wall, lifting me easily as he removed his fingers from me. I instantly wrapped my legs around his waist, moaning as he peppered kisses down my neck. "Fuck, I really want to draw this out—" he started, but I cut him off, grabbing his face in my hands and kissing him hungrily.

I needed him inside of me.

Muttering an expletive against my lips, he thrust up into me. "*River!*" I choked out, throwing my head back against the tiled wall.

He gripped my wrists and pushed them above my head. Holding my wrists in his large hand, and his other hand gripping my ass, he thrust in and out of me hard, his lips trailing kisses over every part of my body that he could reach.

I swear, when I came, I saw fucking stars.

■ ■ ■

I snatched my phone off the counter next to where I was sitting at my bar eating a bowl of sugary cereal. Henry's name popped up on the screen. I sighed, knowing he was calling me in to cover someone's shift. It was the *only* reason he ever called me. "Yes?" I asked when I answered, putting it on speaker as River set a cup of decaf coffee in front of me.

I shot him a thankful smile. He leaned down and softly kissed me in response.

"I know tonight is your night off, but one of the dancers called out. I need you to fill in." Henry informed me as River leaned back against the kitchen counter near my sink.

"Out of the fucking question." River snarled, alerting Henry to his presence. I swung my alarmed eyes to River's. I did *not* leave Tristan's club just to have my moves dictated by another man. "The only thing Adelaide will do at that bar is serve drinks. Find another dancer." He ordered.

"River, I don't have any other dancers -" Henry started, but River cut him off, his voice cold and full of authority.

"Are you fucking arguing with me right now?" River barked, making me swallow at the rage that spilled into his voice. He reached over and trailed his fingers over my cheek, soothing me, his eyes soft as they locked with mine.

"No, Prez." Henry quickly answered. "I'll find another dancer."

Henry hung up, and I looked up at River. "Was that necessary?" I asked him. "I could have used the extra money."

River leaned back against the kitchen counter again, taking a sip from his coffee. "You won't be dancing, Adelaide." He simply stated, as if that solved everything. I gritted my teeth. I was my own woman, and I was *so sick* of men dictating my fucking moves. "You're lucky that I'm letting you continue to serve drinks at that bar, but I understand your need for independence, so I'm not stopping you." Some of the fight left me at his words. "Dancing for a bunch of sleazy assholes is where I draw the line, though. And if you need extra money, that's what I'm here for. You're not alone anymore, Darlin'." He reminded me.

My heart warmed at his words.

He understood me. I hadn't been understood in a long fucking time.

A knock sounded on my front door, and River set his coffee down, moving to answer it. He came into the kitchen a moment later with his VP, Sam - the asshole from last night. "Sons of Death has finally gotten back with me," Sam informed River, making me jerk my eyes up from my bowl of cereal. My heart pounded hard in my chest at the thought of having to face Tristan again. I couldn't take the broken, betrayed expression in his eyes. It cut me deep. I knew I'd hurt him, but dammit, he'd hurt me numerous times, too.

"Tristan refuses to work with us, but Troy doesn't mind," Sam informed River. I grunted. River chuckled, knowing Troy and I always tended to butt heads. "He wants to set up an exchange three days from now."

River nodded. "Set up a time and location and get back with me on it." River told him.

"Already did," Sam informed him. "At the bar in a few days."

River looked over at me for a second before he nodded. "That works. I'll have Adelaide serve our table that night." River smirked at me. "Try not to drop the tray this time." He teased.

I scowled, making him chuckle. He leaned over and brushed his lips with mine. "Finish your breakfast, Darlin'."

■ ■ ■

"Hey, baby doll, bring your pretty little ass over here and get me a beer!" A man shouted through the loud noise of the bar, making me scowl at him as I snatched a beer from the cooler behind me and popped the top off for him.

I slammed the beer in front of him with a disgusted look his way. I fucking hated it when men gave me little pet names. The shit pissed me off.

Henry grabbed my arm and yanked me around to face him. "Kill the attitude with the customers." He snapped down at me.

"Get your fucking hands off of me." I seethed, glaring up at him, my hands clenched at my sides.

"Adelaide, table twenty-two is asking for you," Amber told me, her eyes nervously flickering between me and Henry.

Henry roughly shoved me away from him, and I caught myself before I collided with the counter, glaring at his back as he disappeared through the door that led to the back of the restaurant.

God, I fucking hated him.

Clenching my jaw, I walked over to table twenty-two, my eyes meeting River's as I approached. He ran his eyes over me, his eyes darkening at the red, hand-shaped mark on my arm from where Henry had grabbed me. He gently pulled me towards him. "Who the fuck put their hands on you?" He demanded to know.

"It was no one," I told him softly, not wanting to cause shit within his club. Henry and I had never seen eye to eye. The only reason he hired me in the first place was because I knew the drinks, so I didn't need training, and I was a good dancer.

River's eyes darkened in a warning, but I ran my hand over his hair, pleading with him not to do this right now. With a grunt, he leaned back in the booth again, but there was a promise in his eyes that we would continue the conversation later.

My gaze flickered around the table, my eyes locking on Troy and Kyle. "Well, well, well, been wondering where the fuck you disappeared to, Adelaide," Troy commented, letting his eyes run over me.

I bristled. "Put your eyes on my fucking face." I snapped at him, making Kyle snicker next to him.

He shrugged. "Figured since you seem to spread those sexy ass legs for just about anyone, I might get a taste of my own," Troy smirked.

"Watch your fucking mouth before Tristan has to find a new president for his North Carolina charter." River snarled at Troy, leaning forward threateningly.

Troy looked between us for a moment before he barked out a laugh. "Fucking hell, *you two?*" Troy demanded. "This is fucking priceless. Does Tristan know?" He asked, looking up at me.

"Don't know, nor do I give a fuck." I snapped at him. "Now, what do you want to drink?"

After taking their drink orders, I walked back over to the bar, making the drinks, knowing River wanted me to make them - not anyone else. He had club business to take care of, and he wouldn't want potential eavesdroppers. "Henry wants a word with you," Natalie informed me as she walked up. "I'll finish the drinks for you."

I shook my head at her. "That table will be fine, I promise," I assured her. "River is picky - doesn't want anyone else serving his table." She nodded in understanding as her eyes flickered nervously to the owner of the bar. "I'll be back in a minute."

I strode down the back hallway to Henry's office, which was next to the restrooms and the rooms that the dancers got ready in. "You called?" I asked as I stepped into his office. I hated being in the same room alone with him. It made my skin crawl with disgust.

I jumped in fright when he slammed the door closed behind me, shoving me back against it. My heart thundered in my ears as my mouth ran dry. "So, you can fuck my boss within *hours* of meeting him, but you ignore my advances for *months?*" He seethed. "I treated you decently, woman - took pity on you when you begged me for this job, and this is the fucking thanks I get?"

"River and I have known each other for a while. And I'll never fuck you, Henry, so fuck off." I sneered, thankful that my voice came out steady. I refused to show him how afraid I actually was.

Fear was a weakness in these situations. Men like him fed off of it.

I cried out in pain as his fist cracked against the side of my face, sending me sprawling to the floor. I felt blood well up in my mouth, and I gagged slightly at the metallic taste in my mouth, my stomach churning. My head was spinning from the punch, pain pulsing through my face.

Henry shoved me onto my back, straddling my hips as I fought against him. "Get off of me!" I screamed.

His fist slammed against my temple, and this time, it was lights out.

■ ■ ■

RIVER

"Get off of me!" I heard Adelaide scream from the back of the restaurant. People in the bar went silent, everyone trying to figure out who had screamed.

Troy stopped talking, but I was already on my feet, jumping out of the booth. I rushed down the hall as Sam, Troy, and Kyle got out of the booth. Slinging open Henry's office door, I found him straddling my fucking woman, his hand around her neck. She was bleeding, and her face was swelling.

Rage pulsed through me as I gripped him by the back of his shirt, slinging him off of her. He crashed against his desk, and Sam gripped my shoulder before I could go over and pummel my fists into his face. I clenched my fists, my breaths coming in short, quick spurts as I tried to control my rage.

No one put their fucking hands on my woman and got the fuck away with it. In fact, the last person that did that ended up in fucking *pieces*.

"I've got him," Sam told me gruffly. "I'll take him to the clubhouse. Deal with Adelaide. She needs you, brother." He said, breaking through my rage.

I rushed over to Adelaide, clenching my jaw at the bruising and swelling already popping up on her porcelain-like skin. "She's out cold," Troy informed me. "But she's got a strong pulse."

I just grunted in acknowledgment as I lifted her limp form into my arms, striding out of the office with her cradled against my chest. "Rick is right down the road with the truck," Sam called out from behind me as I was striding out of the office.

"She going to be alright?" Troy asked me as he walked down the hallway with me. I knew he gave Adelaide a lot of shit, but I knew he still cared about what happened to her. At one point, she'd been like a sister to all of them.

But times changed, and she changed with them.

I nodded at Troy. "She'll wake up with a massive headache, but she'll be fine," I assured him. "I'll have Sam set up another day and time for us to meet."

He nodded, taking his cue to leave as Rick rolled up with the truck. "Damn, Prez, what the fuck happened?" He asked as I gently set Adelaide in the passenger seat, leaning her seat back and strapping her in her seatbelt. Her face rolled to the side, still out cold.

"Fucking Henry." I snarled in answer. I ran my fingers over her cheek, using her to keep me grounded. I needed to be with her right now – not out murdering Henry. "I need you to manage the bar until I find a replacement," I told him as I strode around to the driver's side of the truck.

"Got it, Prez," Rick told me.

I threw the truck in gear and took off for Adelaide's apartment, silently thinking of the pain that I planned to inflict on Henry when I finally got my hands on him.

SIXTEEN

ADELAIDE

My head was pounding when I woke up.

With a groan, I slowly sat up, reaching up to rub the sleep from my eyes, sucking in a harsh breath as pain quickly flared up on my face, making me jerk my hand away. River's cut was laying on the foot of my bed, alerting me that he was somewhere in my apartment.

Judging by the pain in my face and my head, I had taken a fucking beating last night.

I walked into my bathroom, gasping at my face as soon as I looked in the mirror. The entire left side of my face was discolored and slightly swollen. "Holy fuck." I muttered, staring in horror at the battered woman staring back at me.

"Holy fuck is right." River agreed as he leaned against my bathroom door. I looked over at him as he moved off the wall, moving forward so he could gently cradle my face in his hands. "By the time my crew is done with Henry later, the mother fucker will be begging for me to put him out of his fucking misery." He quietly promised as he ran his eyes over my face.

I turned to look back at the mirror, sighing softly. "Make-up is definitely not going to cover this," I grumbled in disappointment. Henry had made sure he fucked me up good.

River walked over to the shower and turned the water on, pulling his shirt over his head. I swallowed hard as I ran my eyes over his beautiful, tattooed body, subconsciously licking my lips. Would there ever be a moment that I wouldn't want him?

River groaned softly. "Keep looking at me with those pretty, little fuck-me eyes, and I swear I will drag you to that bed and fuck you hard, Darlin'." River warned me, his blue eyes darkening.

I walked towards him, trailing my fingertips up his abs, over his hard, defined chest, and finally around his neck. I loved that he still found me attractive despite the ruined condition that my face was in. "Promise?" I asked him huskily.

With a slow, sexy smirk, he threw me over his shoulder, smacking my ass in the process. I squeaked in alarm. "That's always a promise, Darlin'."

■ ■ ■

I slowly untangled my arms from around River after he parked his bike outside of his clubhouse. I unstrapped the helmet he had for me and slid off, handing the helmet over to River.

"Go on inside." He instructed me. I sighed, looking over at the clubhouse. I wasn't sure about spending my day inside of one of these buildings again, especially around men I didn't know. "The club has already been informed you're going to be here today." He stood from the bike and gripped my ass in his hands, drawing me against him. My breath hitched in my throat. "Make sure you get you something to eat." He instructed.

"I'm not hungry," I told him.

He shrugged. "Tough." He told me, making me scowl. He rubbed my belly with one of his hands, softening my mood. How was he so fucking good to me – for me – without even having to try? "Got a little one to feed now, remember?"

I sighed, knowing that I wasn't about to win this argument. He kissed my forehead before giving my ass a light tap and releasing me.

"Darlin'," River called from behind me as I turned towards the clubhouse. I looked at him over my shoulder, "show 'em who the fuck you are." He told me with a smirk as he shoved his hands into the pockets of his jeans.

I tilted my lips up into a slight smile since smiling fully hurt too fucking much. He was telling me to stand my ground and that he would fully back me up in whatever – within reason, of course.

I strode into the clubhouse, walking into a round of arm wrestling. "A fighting ring would be much more fun to watch," I commented nonchalantly as I walked past.

"Women keep their mouths shut around here." One of the men stated.

I eyed him with distaste, taking in his brown hair and his beard that was the same color as his hair. He was muscular, and I rolled my eyes when he intentionally flexed his arm muscles as if that would intimidate me.

"Not this one," I informed him.

"Probably why your face looks like it does." A woman probably around the age of nineteen or twenty sneered.

River stepped into the clubhouse with Sam, and instantly everyone shut the fuck up and focused their attention on him. I snorted as I moved behind the bar to the kitchen. *What pussies.* I looked over my shoulder at River, and his gaze met mine, amusement shining in their blue depths.

I blew a kiss at him before I disappeared into the kitchen, rummaging for something sweet.

Cereal that had a ton of sugar in it, preferably.

I blew out a breath in frustration when I didn't find any. All they had were salty snacks, a bunch of fucking beer, and food that had to be cooked. All I wanted was unhealthy cereal and milk.

I pushed back through the kitchen door, finding River sitting at the bar, talking to the man with the beard from earlier. "River, there's no cereal," I grumbled, drawing his attention to me.

"So, find something else to eat, girly," the man snapped, annoyed at being interrupted. I glared at the man, a silent dare for him to continue. He was on a power trip, and I fucking *hated* men like that.

"Watch your fucking tone with her." River snapped. I smirked when the man scowled, but kept his mouth shut. "Mel!" River called, grabbing the young woman's attention from earlier. "Take this," he said, pulling a twenty from his wallet, "and go get a box of cereal – the sugariest you can find – and a gallon of whole milk." He instructed.

She nodded, taking the twenty from him and rushing out of the clubhouse doors. Henry stumbled out of the back hallway with a groan, drawing River's attention to him. River quickly got off his stool. "Oh, great, your finally fucking awake." He snarled.

And then, he slammed his fist against Henry's face, a sickening crunch sounding through the room. I gasped, watching as River slammed his fists against Henry's face over and over, well after the man was unconscious on the floor. I'd heard numerous bones break as River beat the fuck out of him.

He pointed a bloody finger at one of the men that had been arm wrestling. "Val, when he wakes up, I want his fucking cut. He's out of the fucking club. And I want him escorted off of my fucking territory."

"Understood, Prez." Val, a man with black hair and eyes just as dark, nodded his head at River.

River disappeared down the back hallway, and I quickly followed after him, finding him in the bedroom at the very end. His room was mostly plain. He had a black fitted sheet and a plain black comforter on the bed with a few pillows. The club emblem hung above his bed, and a single nightstand sat on the left side of his bed with a plain, black lamp on it. There was a dresser against the wall near the door, and the open door to the side of the room revealed the bathroom where River was currently washing the blood off of his hands.

"Never took the time to make this place feel like home, did you?" I asked him.

He shrugged. "Don't really have time to, Darlin'." He informed me as I leaned against the bathroom door jamb to watch him. "Being a president consumes most of my time, and when I'm not doing that, I'm normally out in the garage."

He turned the water off and dried his hands, turning to face me. "Feels a lot like home with you standing in the room, though." He admitted, a small smile tilting his lips the slightest bit, making my nerve endings curl.

Fuck, he couldn't just unleash his smile on me like that.

"Prez, you expecting company?" Someone shouted from up the hall.

"Fuck - no!" River called back. "Who the fuck is it?"

"Sons of Death!" The guy hollered back. "And ooh, boy, Tristan looks *pissed*."

My breath lodged in my throat as my heart rate picked up speed. I hadn't seen Tristan said I'd met him in another state to do a DNA test, not wanting him to know where I was staying at. The betrayal in his eyes that day had gutted me, and yet, he still asked me to come back home to him.

River clenched his jaw, looking down at my face as it drained of color. "You going to be alright?" He quietly asked me, reaching up to caress the good side of my face, his eyes running over me as he did so.

I shrugged, not knowing how to respond. River drew me into him, pressing his lips to the top of my head. I closed all the distance between our bodies, leaning on him for that one precious moment before my world got flipped upside down – my sanctuary broken into. We both jerked our heads up when we heard shouting. "Grim, you can't fucking go back there!" Sam barked.

"Fuck." River cursed, releasing me as he quickly stepped out into the hallway. "Tristan, you can get the fuck out of my clubhouse right now if you're only going to cause fucking trouble." River growled in a warning.

"Where the fuck is she, River?" Tristan demanded to know.

I slowly stepped out into the hallway, nervously looking up at Tristan. There was so much pain in his eyes as he ran them between me and River. Instantly, River possessively wrapped an arm around my waist, tugging me against his side.

"You left my club just to jump to his?" Tristan angrily demanded.

"He's the dad, Tristan," I informed him, swallowing hard at the hurt in his eyes. "And for your information, I've been supporting myself for the past three months. River just found me when he happened to come into the bar during one of my shifts." I explained, though I knew I didn't owe him any kind of explanation. But that hurt in his eyes was killing me.

"Yet, that quickly, you're in his bed and in his clubhouse." Tristan snarled at me. I flinched.

"Fucking lay off of her." River snarled, taking a threatening step forward as he pushed me slightly behind him.

I gripped River's arm, his bicep flexing under my grip. He swung his gaze to me, his eyes softening immediately. "Please," I whispered. "Not him."

River clenched his jaw but nodded at me, taking a step back from Tristan. I breathed a sigh of relief. River silently reached up and brushed his thumb over my bottom lip, understanding in his gaze.

We were the reason Tristan was hurting so much.

"What the fuck happened to your face, Addy?" Tristan asked, moving to step forward but deciding against it.

I pointed to where Henry was struggling off of the floor, his face covered in blood. "Hand over your fucking cut!" River barked, moving to where Henry was trying to struggle into a standing position, shouting in agony at the broken bones in his body. My stomach twisted.

"All of this over a random piece of pussy?" Henry bravely snapped at River from his position on the floor.

River wrapped his large hand around Henry's throat, lifting him off the floor as he slammed him against the wall. Henry screamed in pain. "Want to fucking repeat that?" River snarled at him, his voice deadly.

Henry choked, shaking his head no. River dropped him to the floor, and Henry sprawled at his feet, another scream of pain leaving his lips. My blood chilled in my veins. "Your fucking cut." River snarled, holding his hand out.

Henry managed to shrug it off, handing it over to River. "Val, get him the fuck off of my territory." River snapped.

"I would have put a bullet through his thick skull," Tristan commented as I strode past him and out into the bar room where River was handing the guy with the beard Henry's cut.

"Burn it." River ordered. The guy nodded before he strode outside, casting me a dirty look before he did. I glared back at him.

He was going to be fucking trouble.

I looked to the clubhouse doors as Mel strode back through holding two grocery bags. I grinned when she set them on the counter. "Oh, yes, finally," I murmured, rushing into the kitchen to find a bowl.

Tristan and River both sat at the bar as I made my bowl of cereal, both men silent as they watched me. I closed my eyes and moaned as I took my first delicious bite. River's eyes met mine, a smirk lighting up his face as my cheeks flushed under his burning gaze.

Tristan ran his hands down his face, and a bad feeling settled in the pit of my stomach, souring my mood again. "What did I do wrong, Addy?" He asked me quietly as he looked up at me with those sad eyes that always tore my heart apart.

I fucking hated myself for the pain that I caused him. I'd cheated on him and had gotten pregnant with another man's baby. I'd really fucking hurt him.

"I can probably answer that." River stated. I snapped my eyes up to River's face. "You confined her, Grim. You wanted to control her so much. I get it; you thought you were protecting her, but you slowly broke her, Grim. And she ran from you the first opportunity she got." River shrugged. "And you did the worst fucking thing possible by cuffing her to your bed when you got her back to try to keep her there."

Tristan's eyes met mine. "What happened, though, Addy? Fuck, I literally had you in my bed two hours before I fucking left that day." He reminded me.

I swallowed thickly, my heart throbbing for what used to be between us but could never - would never - be again. "I needed to

197

forget," I whispered, suddenly not hungry anymore. "And River was there to help me forget." I swallowed hard. "It was supposed to be a one-time thing," I admitted.

Tristan barked out a laugh. "One time, my ass." He muttered.

"Tristan -" I started, but River cut me off.

"You don't owe him a fucking explanation, Darlin'." He told me. I turned my eyes to him. He reached across the bar and gently gripped my chin. I blinked back tears. River's eyes softened with understanding. "He should have treated you better so that you wouldn't have to find comfort in the arms of another man. That's all it comes down to." He told me.

River stood up and came around the bar to where I was standing. He pressed his lips to the top of my head. I closed my eyes as I fisted his cut in my hands, holding him with me for a moment, just long enough to bring myself back together. He kept his lips pressed to my hair until I slowly released him.

"Finish your cereal, Darlin'." He instructed softly. He pointed a finger at Tristan. "You – with me. I want to discuss something since you've taken it upon yourself to barge onto my territory and into my clubhouse."

Tristan scowled but got up anyway, following River to a room off to the side of the bar room. I sighed, running my hands over my face tiredly.

Fuck, I just wanted to distract myself from this fucked up love triangle.

I loved Tristan – I did. But I hadn't been in love with him for a long fucking time. I fell out of love not long after I got tangled up with Joey.

I hated that I had cut him so deeply, but nothing short of something completely drastic would force Tristan to let me go.

So, I betrayed him in one of the worst ways possible. I slept with one of his most trusted men. But my plan had *not* been to fall in love with the man I slept with. But River? He looked at me differently – fucking treated me decent. And I fell hard – and fast.

I tossed my bowl into the sink after I forced myself to finish eating, striding out of the clubhouse and to the garage, determined to get elbows deep in some grease.

I needed a fucking distraction because all I could picture was Tristan's haunted eyes in my mind.

SEVENTEEN

RIVER

I smiled at the sight of Adelaide leaning under the hood of a white Nissan as I stepped into the garage with Tristan at my side. "Now, I bet if you fucking start the car, it'll run fine." Adelaide snapped at my prospect, Joseph.

Sure enough, when he started the car, it ran fine.

My woman was one of many talents.

"The starter was fine," Adelaide told him as she wiped her hands on a grease rag. "The spark plugs were shit, and the throttle body needed cleaning. I just saved the poor lady a couple of hundred dollars."

God, she was so fucking feisty, and I loved it. Slowly, but surely, Adelaide was coming back to me - spitfire attitude and all. I couldn't wait to have every bit of her fiery personality as mine.

Joey and Tristan may not have ever been ready for the kind of woman she is, but I sure as fuck am.

"She's pregnant. She doesn't need to be working on cars." Tristan grumbled in displeasure.

"Not your woman, not your kid," I told him bluntly. He narrowed his eyes at me. I shrugged. Unlike Adelaide, I had no desire to spare his feelings. He ruined his fucking chance with her. I swept in at the first opportunity I saw, and I gave her a taste of what it was like to truly be loved and cared about – a taste of what it was like to be put above all else. "And this is what I'm talking about," I informed him. "The reins were too tight when you were with her. Adelaide needs freedom and independence, Grim. You wouldn't give her that."

"Why didn't you put a bullet through that fucker's head for what he did to her face?" Tristan demanded as he swiftly changed the topic, obviously not wanting to talk about what he did to her. But yet, every time I turned around since he'd walked into my clubhouse, he'd been making my woman feel like shit for choosing me.

And that shit? It wasn't settling right with me.

"I didn't, but I made sure Val did," I told him. "I don't drop bodies in or around my clubhouse, and certainly not around women with sensitive stomachs," I said, referring to Adelaide. I wouldn't run the chance that watching me put a bullet through someone's skull would make her sick.

Tristan just watched Adelaide for a moment. I ignored the sadness in his eyes, not feeling the least bit sorry for him. He brought this upon himself. If he had treated her like a normal human being, he might have still had her. She had been broken and used. She was desperate for someone to just love her and take care of her.

"She's happy." He finally commented, watching her laugh at something stupid Joseph had probably said to her. Joseph was a jokester, but when it came down to it, I could rely on him. He'd make a damn good, patched member once I finally decided to take him off of prospect status and give him a proper cut.

Done talking to Tristan any further, I strode towards Adelaide, watching as her eyes darkened the tiniest bit as she ran her eyes over me, a slow smile twisting her delicious lips. Fuck, she made me hard so fucking easily. I only hoped that it would be like this between us for the rest of our lives.

Her eyes locked onto a worktable almost exactly like the one the Sons of Death had, and her eyes glazed over a little as she remembered our time together. My cock strained in my jeans, begging to be buried deep inside of her.

I wound my arms around her waist, drawing her into me as I lowered my head until my lips were at her ear. "Say the words, and we'll christen that one, too." I huskily whispered in her ear. Her body shuddered against mine in response.

Her beautiful, brown eyes met mine, mischief shining in their depths. She gripped my cut, pulling me harder against her. I growled softly as I lightly pressed my thigh between her legs. Her breath hitched in her throat for a moment. "Send them out." She whispered. "We're closed for business for the rest of the day."

I sure as fuck didn't have to be told twice.

I turned and looked at my crew. "Out!" I barked. "Shut the gates on your way out. We're closed."

With that, I gently pressed my lips to hers, being extra careful due to the bruises on her face.

But when I got her on that worktable, I fucked her so hard that I had no doubt that my club members could hear her screams all the way inside of the clubhouse.

She was mine, and I planned on making sure everyone knew it.

■ ■ ■

My gaze instantly locked on Adelaide as if drawn to her by an unseeable force. She was stepping out of the back hallway from my room, her hair damp from her shower. She was wearing a pair of my sweatpants and one of my shirts. I swallowed hard.

Fuck me; she looked even sexier in my clothes.

Mel was currently holding Tristan's attention, and I was thankful that Adelaide didn't even give him a second glance as she strode towards me, meaning that I didn't have to feel all of that fucking anger and jealousy. I hated it when she looked at him – and even more, I hated the guilt that flashed in her eyes.

I might have been a bit more understanding about the entire situation if he had at least tried to understand her, but he never tried. Fuck, even Joey eventually got the memo with her, but not Tristan.

Adelaide was fragile. No matter how much of a strong front she put up, Adelaide was just a broken woman begging to be loved properly.

I instantly gripped her hips when she got close enough to me, drawing her between my legs as I settled my hands on her ass, squeezing lightly.

Fuck, I loved this ass of hers, and the more weight she gained, the bigger her perfect ass got.

"How's your face feel?" I softly asked as I reached up to gently run my fingertips over her bruises.

She shrugged. "Kind of used to the pain by now, so I'm fine." She admitted.

I clenched my jaw at the reminder that she was so fucking used to physical pain that it didn't even bother her anymore.

Darlin, you'll never have to worry about pain like that ever again. I silently promised her. I was here to protect her now. I'd never let another son of a bitch touch her again – not if I could help it.

"Mel!" Gregory shouted, making Mel jump in fright, snapping her eyes over to my Sergeant at Arms. I smoothed my hands up Adelaide's back, calming her when she tensed in my arms in response to the sudden, loud noise. "Quit fucking around and serve drinks like you're supposed to." He snarled at her.

"Hey, watch how the fuck you talk to her." Adelaide snapped at him, her eyes sparking fire at him. I gently squeezed her waist, hoping to calm her down some. Adelaide was naturally protective over other women, which was understandable. And I would always back her up. "Do you treat all fucking women like shit?" She demanded to know.

I ran my eyes over her face at her words. What the fuck had Gregory done that she hadn't told me about? "Girly, I get that you're River's woman, but you don't get to pop off at the mouth anytime you feel like it." He snapped back at her.

Actually, she fucking did. And as long as she was being reasonable, I would always back her up in whatever the fuck she did or wanted. Old ladies were meant to support their old men, but good old men supported their old ladies, too.

"I knew there was a fucking reason I haven't liked you since I stepped foot in this fucking clubhouse." She sneered back at him.

I tightened my grip on her ass, drawing those beautiful eyes of hers to me. "What the fuck did he do, Darlin'?" I asked her, drawing her furious eyes to me.

"He's just been warning me about my mouth since I stepped in here, and he seems to have a real fucking shitty view on women." She snarled. I knew she wasn't angry at me, but I squeezed her ass again as a quiet reminder that I wasn't the one she was pissed at. Her eyes softened slightly, but her jaw was still clenched.

"She's going to smart off at the wrong person one day, Prez," Gregory stated, but it sounded more like a threat.

And that shit would get his ass killed.

I bristled and narrowed my eyes at him. "Was that a fucking threat?" I snarled as I stood up from my barstool, keeping Adelaide close to me.

Gregory put his hands up in a surrendering gesture, but I didn't miss the heated glare he sent in Adelaide's direction before he walked away, his steps quick and angry.

Clenching my jaw, I nodded once at Tristan as he turned to look at me. I needed to get Adelaide home. Today had been enough for her, and right then, I didn't fucking trust Gregory. I wanted her far away from him.

"Sam will make sure you and your club get settled in for the night," I informed Tristan. His eyes flickered to Adelaide, but I was sure to keep her attention focused on me. I hated it when she tore herself down, and every time she looked at him, that's exactly what she did. "Enjoy the drinks – have fun with the women. I'm taking Adelaide home, and I probably won't be back here at the clubhouse until in the morning once she wakes up for the day."

Tristan nodded in understanding, for once staying silent. I placed my hand on the small of Adelaide's back, leading her out to my bike, not giving her a chance to look at Tristan. I brushed my lips to her temple as we stepped outside. Her body sagged, the weight of being in Tristan's presence lifting from her shoulders.

"Live for me," I whispered in her ear.

She turned to me and pressed her hand over my chest, looking up at me with those beautiful, brown eyes. "Stay with me." She said in return.

I leaned down and brushed my lips with hers. "For as long as you'll have me," I promised.

■ ■ ■

ADELAIDE

My stomach was churning when I woke up the next morning.

Oh, God, it was going to be one of these days. I had thought that these damn days were behind me.

With a gag, I threw myself out of bed, rushing over to the bathroom. I barely managed to kneel in front of the toilet before I emptied my stomach.

River – who I hadn't even noticed got out of bed with me – held my hair out of the way and comfortingly rubbed my back as I dry heaved a couple more times before I got sick again. Tears spilled down my cheeks. Fuck, throwing up hurt *so much*. And my face was fucking *throbbing*.

"You alright, Darlin'?" He asked me once I was done emptying my stomach.

"It's going to be one of those days," I grumbled, my stomach still churning. I gagged again, but nothing came up that time. "I was hoping I'd left them behind in my first trimester, but I guess not."

"Morning sickness?" He asked me with a slight frown on his face as he tried to understand what I was going through. Despite how shitty I felt, it warmed my heart.

I nodded in answer. He leaned down and lifted me against his chest, cradling me in his arms as he carried me to my living room. He gently set me onto the couch and grabbed my throw blanket from the back, draping it over me.

"I'm going to make you some soup. Do you have any saltine crackers?" He asked me. "I heard crackers are supposed to help the nausea."

I shook my head at him. "I ate them all the last time I was sick," I told him, closing my eyes as vomit rose in my throat. I really didn't want to get sick again.

I slowly opened my eyes to see him pull his phone out of his pocket and type out a quick text to someone. After he was finished, he placed his phone back in his pocket and placed a kiss on my forehead before he walked off to my kitchen to make me some soup.

■ ■ ■

RIVER

A soft smile crossed my lips as I walked back into the living room when I found Adelaide asleep again, her hands folded under her head, her lips parted the tiniest bit. At that moment, she looked like an angel – a broken one – but an angel, nonetheless.

Fuck, she took my breath away every time I looked at her, and she didn't even realize it. She was so blind to the effect that she had on me.

I unbuttoned my flannel and slid it off, tossing it onto her coffee table as I walked over to the couch, gently lifting her and setting her onto my lap so I could watch TV while she slept since she didn't have a television in her bedroom.

I would have placed her in her bed, but I wanted to be near her if something happened or if she needed me. And shockingly, despite the location her apartment was in, she had good walls that hid sound pretty well.

I was dozing off myself when Sam entered the apartment with the key that I had given him to her place in the rare case that he may need to get to her when I couldn't. He arched an eyebrow at me in question as he set the crackers on the counter. "Tristan and Jesup have been waiting for you to come back to the clubhouse to finalize shit." He reminded me quietly, seeing as Adelaide was still passed out.

I sighed, leaning my head back against the couch. "She's not feeling good," I told him. "The baby is kicking her ass this morning."

"Baby?" Sam asked incredulously.

Fuck. I had forgotten he didn't know.

I lifted my head to look at him. "She's pregnant," I told him quietly. "And yes, it's mine," I informed him before he could ask.

"Holy fuck, Prez," Sam muttered. He shook his head, laughing softly. "You almost made it to thirty without a kid, huh?"

I chuckled, shrugging lightly. I'd never wanted kids, but when I saw those ultrasound pictures, put the dates together, I'd never wanted anything more.

But it was because it was with Adelaide. I wanted everything with this woman.

Adelaide suddenly gagged, jerking awake from her deep slumber. I quickly released her and followed after her as she rushed to the bathroom, throwing up again.

"You sure that this is just morning sickness?" I asked her as she flushed the toilet.

She nodded. "This is mild." She told me. "It used to be a lot worse. The doctor informed me it may come back sometimes."

I brushed the back of my fingers over her cheek, watching as she slightly tilted her head into my touch, making a small smile touch my lips. Knowing that I was the one that could make her feel comfortable and safe gave me a strange feeling inside of my chest – one I was loving.

"I need to go deal with some shit at the clubhouse. You can stay here if you want, and I can have Sam stay with you, or you can come with me. If you come, you can rest in my room at the clubhouse."

"I'll just come with you." She informed me. "Let me get a shower and brush my teeth. I reek."

I nodded, helping her up from the floor. Leaving her to get a shower, I walked back into the living room, grabbing my flannel off of the coffee table to shrug it on. "She alright?" Sam asked me.

I nodded at him as I buttoned the buttons on my shirt. "She's getting a shower right now, but she's going to come to the clubhouse with us."

"Anyone in the club know that she's pregnant?" Sam asked me.

I shook my head. "The only people that know besides you are Tristan and probably Jesup, and for right now, that's how I need it to stay. I think Gregory is going to pose a problem and a threat to Adelaide, and I don't want him thinking he can use my kid against me or her. I just need him to slip up so that I can boot his ass out of the club. I would do it now, but he's got family with the original members. Shit's a bit more complicated than it looks."

"Got it," Sam stated. He inclined his head to me. "You know I'll protect her and that baby with my life." He told me.

I nodded once, knowing and trusting that he would. It was why he was my VP.

My phone went off in my back pocket, and I quickly snatched it out, seeing Val's name on the screen. "Yeah?" I asked when I answered.

"Red is in town," Val informed me, cutting straight to the chase, knowing how much I hated beating around the bush.

"Fuck." I snarled. This was the last fucking thing I needed right now. "Put up proper safety measures on the clubhouse. I'll be back soon." I told him.

I hung up, reaching up to pinch the bridge of my nose. I fucking hated my brother. Nothing good ever came out of him coming around. I never figured out what he wanted when he held the gun to Adelaide's head – hell, maybe his only plan had been to sabotage what I had going on with the Sons of Death. But the fact that he was now snooping around again was bad news, and it meant my woman was in danger. Red knew she meant something to me.

Sam sighed. "What's going on?"

"Red is in town," I informed him. He scowled. "You're trailing me back to the clubhouse, and Adelaide isn't to be left alone until he's fucking gone and taken care of," I told him.

I wished I could just put a bullet through his skull, but as long as my dad was still alive, that shit wasn't happening. My old man and I may but heads a lot, but the man didn't have many more years left to live. I wouldn't make him miserable in his last years by killing his son.

"He got something for your woman?" Sam asked me.

I shrugged. "Possibly." And that possibility left a sour, bitter taste in my mouth. "He's the reason Grim found out I fucked Adelaide. He watched me fuck her, apparently." Sam's face twisted in disgust. "And he knows I care about her. I don't know what the fuck he wants right now, but I won't take a chance that he'll use her to get what he wants."

Sam nodded in understanding, and I knew he also agreed.

Adelaide was our number one priority.

A few minutes later, Adelaide stepped out of the back hallway with a pair of shorts on with a t-shirt that was a couple of sizes too big for her and almost completely covered the shorts. A pair of plain black sneakers were on her feet. She was carrying a small duffel, and she gave me a sheepish smile.

"I figured I could stay with you for a couple of nights instead of you constantly having to stay over here." She explained.

I grinned as I reached up to cup her cheek. Fuck, she was so perfect, and she had no idea.

I hadn't wanted to ask her to come to stay with me, knowing that she needed to make that kind of move on her own, so I was beyond ecstatic that she had decided to come to stay with me of her own choice.

She felt the freedom that I was giving her. I didn't have to fight to keep her with me.

I took the duffel bag from her and handed it off to Sam. "Darlin', I'm about to be extremely protective and possessive of you," I warned her. "I'm just warning you so that I don't alarm you and you end up trying to pull back from me." She eyed me warily, her guards going up against me. I stayed calm. I knew they would come back down in a heartbeat once I explained what was going on. "Red is in town," I informed her.

As predicted, they came crashing back down. "Your brother – the same Red that held a gun to the back of my head?" She asked quietly.

I nodded as I reached forward and drew her into my arms. I smoothed my hands down her back, holding her with me. "I hope you've got a few outfits in that duffel because I'm not letting you leave the protection of my clubhouse until he's gone," I informed her. "Not without numerous members of my club with you."

She nodded. "Yeah, what I have should be enough." She told me.

I gently pressed my lips to hers, being extra careful of the bruising on her face. "Good; let's roll, then," I said, drawing her tight against my side as I snatched her apartment keys off of the counter.

She drew me to a stop before we could leave. I turned to look down at her. "Thank you." She whispered.

My eyebrows pulled together in honest confusion. "For what?" I asked her.

"For giving me the freedom that I need. No one has ever understood me before." She told me, her voice sounding strangely choked up, her emotions almost overwhelming her.

My woman was finally coming out of her shell and opening up to me. I would cherish every bit of her openness for the rest of our lives.

I cupped the side of her neck, letting my blue eyes meet her beautiful, brown ones. "I stayed back in the shadows, learning all of your quirks, what you needed, and what made you tick," I told her. "I was willing to listen to your unspoken needs, and I will always continue to do that." I brushed my thumb over her jawline. "I never want to smother you, Adelaide. I just want to watch you grow into the woman you've always been meant to be."

EIGHTEEN

ADELAIDE

My eyes instantly landed on Tristan as I stepped into the clubhouse, River close on my heels. Ignoring Tristan's eyes boring into me, I turned away from him and strode behind the bar, heading into the kitchen to grab some cereal as my stomach began to rumble, the morning sickness finally beginning to pass for the day.

"We need to talk," Tristan spoke up quietly from near the doorway to the kitchen.

I stiffened instantly, my guard going up hard against him. I slowly sat down the box of cereal I'd been holding onto the counter, suddenly losing my appetite.

I didn't want to have this talk with him. I wasn't ready. Even if he deserved this talk, it was too hard for me to rip him apart once again, and I knew I would have to. Shit between Tristan and I could never be simple and easy.

Because I wouldn't be able to give him what he wanted. I never could – not after I got with Joey. And now that I was with River? It would *never* happen. River was it for me. I knew it – could feel it deep in my bones.

River was the one Joey had told me about.

"There's nothing to talk about, Tristan," I told him coldly, keeping my gaze fixed on the countertop. I needed to be cold – void of emotion – or I would walk out of here, ripped apart just like he would be.

He gripped my shoulder and spun me around to face him, steadying me as I stumbled at the force he'd used. His dark eyes bore into mine with an intensity only he had ever been capable of having, and I swallowed hard, my heart racing with nervousness at his proximity.

But those feelings that had once been there? They weren't strong anymore – not like they used to be.

I was no longer in love with him. I wasn't sure if that knowledge gave me relief or fucking hurt me. This man used to be the center of my entire universe and now . . . there was nothing.

"Like hell we don't have something to talk about." He softly snarled down at me. "You left me, Adelaide. Not only that, but you fucked one of the men I trusted the most." I flinched, knowing I deserved the cutting of his words. "Why the fuck did you do that? None of this shit has made sense to me."

I ripped myself from his grip, my walls going back up hard against him as I let that familiar surge of rage rush through my veins.

I had to be angry.

If I wanted to get through this conversation with him, I needed to be furious – cold.

I had to break his heart for the final time – get him to finally turn away from me – from what *used* to be between us.

"I left because you're a fucking asshole, Tristan." I snarled at him. He closed his eyes, drawing in a deep breath. "You ruined me four years ago when you dumped me on the night of my fucking birthday. I was still stupid enough to let you back into my heart a year ago, Tristan, but it only bit me in the ass because you refused to understand me. You were trapping me, tearing me down with every passing second. I couldn't - fucking *can't* - do this with you anymore. It's only going to kill both of us in the end."

"I fucking love you, Adelaide." He snapped, his voice rising only slightly before he controlled it again.

I sucked in a sharp breath at his admission. That part of my heart that would always belong to him sliced open, bleeding inside of me. "You love the old me, Tristan," I told him - pleading with him. "You're in love with the eighteen-year-old girl who blushed at the slightest compliment, who needed your constant reassurance and comfort, who needed a hero from the life I was living in." I swallowed thickly. "You're in love with the stupid girl that clung to your every word." I shook my head, letting out a humorless laugh. "Newsflash, Tristan, I'm not that fucking girl anymore. I'm never going to be her again, and it's time that you realized that. I don't need a hero anymore. I'm saving myself."

"I just want *you*, Adelaide. I don't care who you are today. I just fucking want *you*." He breathed.

God, he was killing me.

Tears filled my eyes as my composure slipped. He frowned, stepping closer to me. "Tristan, it can't happen." I choked out, stepping out of his reach as he moved to pull me into his arms. "I'm not in love with you anymore, Tristan." His expression fell as pain filled his gorgeous features - pain that I put there because I was ripping his heart out of his chest. "I fell out of love with you when I realized that you were too controlling for me. I could never just be *myself*, Tristan. We clash way too much."

"Addy baby, please." He pleaded, his expression completely broken.

I sobbed, my heart breaking right along with his.

I shook my head at him, a couple of tears trickling down my cheeks. He shakily reached up to wipe them away, and I let him, letting us have that one last, beautiful moment together before I destroyed both of us completely.

"I will always love you, Tristan, but I don't love you enough to be with you anymore. I'm having a kid with River. Tristan, he makes me *happy*." I choked out, a small, broken smile touching my lips as I thought about how alive River made me feel, how different River was from the other men I'd had in my life.

I looked up at Tristan, reaching up to take his handsome face between my hands as I let my eyes meet his shattered ones. "You have to let me go, Tristan." I softly begged him. "If you love me as much as you say you do, you'll let me go, and you'll let me be truly happy for once in my life."

He squeezed his eyes shut, swallowing hard as he nodded. I reached up on my tiptoes and gently pressed my lips to his cheek. "I will *always* love you, Tristan, but I can't do this with you anymore," I whispered before I stepped around him and moved out of the kitchen, silent tears sliding down my cheeks as I left that piece of my heart that would always belong to Tristan in that kitchen at his feet.

■ ■ ■

I wanted to drink.

Fucking hell, I wanted to do nothing more than get absolutely shit-faced and trash some shit – something – *anything* to get this pain out of my chest.

I wanted to fucking fight.

My hands were itching to destroy something – somebody.

Joseph arched an eyebrow at me as I stepped into the garage. "Something got you worked up, girly?" He asked me, sounding concerned, but I didn't want his concern.

I wanted him to hate me as much as I hated myself because I was a fucked-up bitch with an ugly, dark soul.

I scowled at him. "Fucking call me 'girly' one more fucking time, and I'll shove that wrench so far up your ass that you'll be tasting steel for the rest of your life." I snarled at him.

He held his hands up in a defensive gesture, stepping back from me instantly. "Woah, chill. I was just joking, Adelaide. I'm sorry." He apologized.

I barked out a laugh, slowly feeling my composure slipping. I was hanging on by a thread today, and it was about to snap. And it was going to be ugly as fuck when it did.

"I'm so fucking sick of everyone." I seethed. He eyed me warily. "I can't get one goddamn moment of happiness before someone is trying to fucking slaughter it."

I had been set on what I wanted. I had been secure in what I was doing with my life. I had been completely secure in my relationship with River.

And then, Tristan had to corner me in the fucking kitchen.

I'd been slowly losing my grip on my sanity since then.

I hated it, but it was the kind of effect that Tristan had on me.

"Want to talk about it?" Joseph asked me a bit cautiously.

I snorted. "Do I want to fucking talk about it?" I snapped, another humorless laugh escaping my lips. Tears burned at my eyes, but I forced them to stay back. I didn't want to cry. Did I even have the right to cry? I'd gone behind Tristan's back and slept with one of his own club members, and now, I had just ripped his heart out of his chest a second time.

Should I just have been selfless and stayed with him?

"The one man that I've loved just about my entire fucking life just made me not only rip out his heart but my own with it, and you want to ask me if I want to *talk* about it?!" I finally yelled, completely losing it. "I don't even fucking know why he's *here*! I don't fucking know why the fuck he had to show up!" I screamed, grabbing one of the toolboxes and shoving it to the ground, tears streaming down my face.

There was so much pain in my chest. I wanted it to go away. I didn't want to feel like this over Tristan. I didn't want to hurt anymore.

I was so, so tired of hurting.

Fuck, I just wanted to be happy and secure in what I was doing with River. Joey understood it and what he and I had together ran even deeper than the shit with me and Tristan had. Why couldn't Tristan just accept it and let me move on?

"I want to hate him." I sobbed, tears running down my face. God, I was so fucking weak, and I hated it. "Why can't I just fucking hate him?!" I screeched.

I threw another toolbox to the ground, a scream of rage slipping past my lips as I did so. Suddenly, I felt strong, muscular arms wrap around me, locking my arms against my side. River's cologne surrounded me as he lifted me so my feet were no longer touching the ground.

"Fucking let me go!" I screamed at him, thrashing in his grip, but I knew it was useless. He would never let me do this to myself.

He stayed silent as I continued yelling and kicking, just wanting to destroy something. I needed to alleviate this ache in my chest.

River just effortlessly carried me out of the garage and into the middle of the parking lot, where he finally set me on my feet, gently turning me to face him with a firm grip on my upper arms.

I glared up at him, my chest heaving up and down with anger and sadness. "Who the fuck do you think you are – man-handling me like that?!" I shouted up at him.

He only shrugged at me as he slipped his hands into his pockets, keeping his cool, blue gaze focused on me. I stomped my foot, an enraged scream slipping past my lips as I thrust my hands through my long, dark hair, pulling on the strands.

"Want to tell me what that was all about?" River calmly asked me.

"You can go fuck yourself right along with Tristan and Joseph and the rest of you asshole, biker mother fuckers." I snarled at him, turning on my heel to storm away from him.

I was done talking about it. I didn't want to make the pain worse. I just wanted to do my damnest to ignore it and pray that it would go away on its own with some time.

River growled softly and gently gripped my arm, spinning me back around to face him. I glared up at him. "You're not walking away from me in this state, Darlin', so until you tell me what's going on, we're going to be standing here." He shrugged, stuffing his hands into the pockets of his dark jeans. "I can stand here all day." He reminded me.

I defiantly crossed my arms over my chest, watching as his eyes flickered to my chest where my breasts had been pushed up. I deepened my glare. His heated gaze focused back on mine, and he only shrugged again. But those eyes, they were soft and tender – just like they always were for me. I swallowed hard, the fight leaving me just that quickly. I sighed softly, my shoulders sagging in defeat.

"Tristan talked to me in the kitchen a little while ago." I quietly informed River, my voice breaking.

River stepped up to me, placing his hands on my hips to draw me against him. I leaned into him, needing him to keep me grounded. The ache in my chest eased a little once I was surrounded by him. "Guessing by the mood you were just in, it wasn't that great of a conversation."

I shrugged. "It just forced me to relive some shit that I sure as fuck wasn't trying to," I informed him. "I wanted to leave my memories with Tristan buried deep down." I sniffled, more tears falling from my eyes. "I'm so tired of hurting, River," I told him, my voice cracking. "I just want to be happy. Why is that so hard?"

River gently cupped my face in his hands, turning my head up to look up at him. He gently brushed some of my tears off of my cheeks. "Got to face the rough shit before you can obtain the happiness you want so much." He told me gently.

I sighed, my bottom lip trembling. "River, will it ever stop hurting so much every time that I look at him, knowing the pain I've caused him?" I asked him. "I feel so selfish for wanting to stop hurting, but he just – I just –."

"Easy." River soothed. He leaned down and lightly brushed his lips with mine. I sighed softly, that ache easing even more. "It hurts, but it means you're alive, Darlin'. It means you're doing the one thing I always want you to do."

"Live for you," I whispered, my eyes running over his face.

He nodded, those beautiful, mesmerizing blue eyes locking with mine. "I will be here to soothe all of those heartaches. I know you love him, just as I know you love Joey. And they hold pieces of you that I'll never be able to claim. I'm okay with that just as long as you continue to live for me, Darlin'."

I nodded. "Just stay with me," I begged him, my bottom lip trembling as more tears slid down my cheeks. I don't know if I would ever survive losing him.

"For as long as you'll have me." He promised, just as he always did.

Then, he drew me into his arms, holding me as I finally allowed myself to fall apart.

■ ■ ■

RIVER

I couldn't fucking stand seeing her like this. I hated that even though they weren't together, he was still hurting her.

She felt so fucking guilty, but honestly, in my opinion, she did what any woman who felt trapped and needed an escape did - she did what every woman who just wanted to be properly loved did.

She sought out someone who would take care of her, even if it was only for a brief moment.

I leaned down and lifted her into my arms. She curled her arms around my shoulders, burying her teary face in the curve of my neck. Silently, Sam held the clubhouse doors open for me so I could walk inside.

Tristan's eyes landed on me, his eyes sad as he looked at Adelaide crying in my arms. I clenched my jaw, resisting the urge to knock his teeth down his fucking throat.

I needed to be with her - to take care of her.

Something that he had failed to do when she was his.

Once I stepped into my room at the end of the hall, I kicked the door closed behind us, locking it before I carried her to the bed. She looked up at me through her beautiful, tear-filled eyes as I laid her down on the soft mattress.

I shrugged my cut off, tossing it across the room to the chair in the corner. Kicking my boots off, I also reached down to slide her sneakers off of her feet. She watched me all while those sad tears slid down her cheeks, those perfect lips trembling as she resisted giving into her pain completely.

She was so fucking strong, and she didn't even know it.

I slid over her on the bed, molding my lips to hers. She moaned softly, her hands sliding into my dark hair. "I'm going to take away all of this pain for a little while," I promised as I ran my lips over her jaw. I nipped at her earlobe, drawing a breathless whisper of my name from her lips. "I promise that the only thing that will exist right now will be me and what I make you feel," I swore.

She pressed her palm to my cheek, turning my face to look at her expression. "Just stay with me." She whispered.

I leaned forward and slid my lips over hers, breathing her in, giving her a part of myself to replace that part of her she'd lost to Tristan.

And then, I proceeded to make slow, passionate love to the beautiful woman who was mine - all broken, torn parts of her.

■ ■ ■

I leaned over the bed and brushed my lips lightly with Adelaide's before I walked out of my room, quietly shutting my door behind me. She'd fallen asleep a couple of hours ago, and I had stayed with her, holding her as she slept before I finally decided to have a shower so I could go remind Tristan of his place.

I stepped into the bar room, my eyes instantly landing on Tristan and Jesup who were seated at the bar with Sam. I stalked over, my jaw clenched, that familiar rage I'd felt earlier sliding through me like lava. I stood on the other side of the bar, my deadly, blue eyes locking with Tristan's.

"Let me make something fucking clear." I snarled quietly as I shoved my hands in my pockets. Tristan glowered at me. "If you *ever* make my woman that upset again to the point that she feels the need to destroy my fucking garage to alleviate some of that pain she's feeling, I'll put a bullet in you myself, do I make myself clear?"

Tristan clenched his jaw, his eyes flaring in anger. "What happened between me and Addy was none of your fucking business, River." He snapped at me.

My vision tinted red for a moment before I forced myself to bring my temper back under control. Addy would hate me if I fucked him up for hurting her.

I narrowed my eyes at him, my hands itching to beat the fuck out of him. Adelaide's beautiful face flashed in my mind, calming me enough to restrain myself, but Tristan was treading on *extremely* thin ice. "It becomes my business when my woman is so fucking upset and tormented by whatever you two talked about that she went on a fucking rampage," I told him. "*Everything* surrounding her fucking concerns me. She's been calm and collected since I came back around, Grim, and I promise you, if I think you being here is going to cause too many fucking problems for her, I will send you right back to where the fuck you came from before you can even say goodbye to her."

With that, I turned to Sam, arching an eyebrow at him. I was done with that conversation. If he wanted to continue having anything to do with Adelaide, he had better heed my fucking warning.

"Any news on Red?" I asked him. I'd been patiently waiting for Red to pop up. Normally, he would have by now.

It was slightly worrying that he hadn't yet. Dad hadn't even called me to warn me that Red was in town. Red always stopped in to see Dad. No matter the bad blood between me and Red, we set it aside for our father.

Sam shook his head. "Nothing yet. He's laying low – wherever the fuck he's at."

I pulled my phone out of my pocket, pulling up my dad's number to shoot him a text. I knew he would make sure the message got relayed to Red.

Tell Red I said to get the fuck out of my town before I come to hunt him down. This is his only warning, Dad. He fucked with my woman once, and I won't put it past him to do it again. -River

With that, I slid my phone back into my pocket. Adelaide stepping into the bar room caught my attention. A pair of black slip-on shoes were on her feet with a pair of short, blue shorts and a plain, black t-shirt, her hair swept up into a ponytail. She walked around the bar to me, and as soon as she was within my reach, I drew her against me, pressing a kiss to her temple. She sighed softly, drawing in the comfort that I was offering her before she looked up at me. "I've got a shift at the bar." She informed me.

I blew out a breath, thinking of Red. I didn't like her working while I didn't know what the fuck was going on with Red, but I knew she would fight me and do what she wanted if I tried holding her here at the clubhouse where I knew she was safe. That independent streak of hers might eventually give me gray hairs, but I *never* wanted her to lose it.

I reached up and rubbed her bottom lip with the pad of my thumb, my other arm locked around her waist, holding her against me. "If I let you work tonight, you have to understand that Sam and I will be there with a few other club members to keep you protected," I told her, making her a deal.

She nodded. "Understood." She told me, not putting up a fight.

All it took was a compromise. Adelaide wasn't a hard person to please. You just had to understand her.

I leaned down and gently pressed my lips to hers before I pulled my bike keys out of my pocket. With her hand in mine, I led her outside to my bike, knowing Sam was following close on my heels with Val and Joseph.

I would let her work, let her have whatever freedom I could while still being able to protect her.

I sent Tristan a dark look over my shoulder as we walked out of the clubhouse, a silent warning for him to stay the fuck away from my woman for the remainder of his stay here.

He may be an ally for my club, but if he kept fucking up with her, I would destroy our alliance and fucking kill him with my bare hands.

NINETEEN

ADELAIDE

I glared at the greasy-haired scumbag that tossed his empty beer bottle at me, making it shatter on the floor at my feet. "Watch yourself." I snarled at him. "Throwing your fucking beer bottle at me isn't going to make me get you a fresh one. It's only going to make me bust the fresh bottle over your fucking head." I warned him.

Men like him walked into these bars, acting as if they were a fucking God. They saw a woman like me and instantly thought that I was some nervous little bitch who would trip over her feet to please him.

He had the wrong bitch tonight.

He narrowed his eyes at me in a threatening manner. I wanted to laugh because not only was I dangerous by myself, but I knew River would fucking slaughter someone over me. Pretty sure he had already, but that wasn't a conversation we were willing to talk about.

Rodney was done and over with.

"You better watch yourself, girly, before I make you lose this job, and I ruin your fucking life." He threatened.

I leaned forward on the bar, a humorless smirk twisting my lips as I got in his personal space. Joke was on him. I was the old lady of the bar owner. As long as I wanted this job, I had it.

"Try it, mother fucker." I nodded my head towards River who was watching our exchange with unreadable eyes. I knew he would step in if it escalated, but right now he knew I was handling it. I didn't need a hero, and River knew that. "I'm sure River wouldn't mind hearing what you have to say about my position at this bar."

At my words, the man's face visibly paled, and he swallowed hard before he looked down at the bar, not saying another word. I snorted. "Fucking pussy." I muttered before I stood back up to my full height, snatching a beer out of the fridge and slamming it down in front of him. "Figure out how to get the top off yourself." I snapped at him.

My eyes slid over to someone sitting on a stool a couple of feet down from where the asshole was currently sitting. I clenched my jaw, swallowing hard as my eyes met Red's. The last time I'd run into him, he had cornered me outside, telling me to get him inside that warehouse or he would blow my brains all over the gravel lot.

Red just looked back at me with sad, tired eyes. "I'm not here to cause problems, sweetheart. I just want a beer." He told me, sounding completely nonthreatening, and that just made every alarm in my head go off.

My eyes flickered to River's table, but I did a double-take when I realized that he was no longer sitting there. In fact, Sam, Joseph, and Val were gone from the table, too.

Then, I felt River's hand on my lower back, his dominating aura wrapping around me, protecting me from the sleazebag in front of me. Sam flanked my right, and I knew Joseph was behind me without even having to turn around. Val was leaning beside Red, looking highly amused by the situation.

Glad someone found humor in this shit because I certainly didn't.

"You've got to have a fucking death wish to come in here, Red." River spoke quietly, but he may as well have fucking shouted it in Red's face. I felt that the rage in River's voice when he spoke had the same effect.

Red shrugged. "I knew she was working tonight," he stated, nodding his head towards me, "and I knew that with me being in town, you wouldn't let her come to work by herself. I need to talk to you, River."

River shrugged. "I don't really give a fuck what you want, Red. I'm a hairsbreadth away from bashing your head on this fucking bar top. The only reason I haven't is because this bar is separate from club shit."

"I was given guardianship of my son, River. I need family." Red rushed out, knowing his time was limited. I straightened up as River stiffened beside me. "I can't do this shit by myself, man. He's a newborn, and I'm fucking lost. And I don't want a kid, River."

"What the fuck do you want me to do, Red?" River impatiently demanded. "Fucking spit it out already."

"I want to give you the kid, River," Red stated bluntly. I could practically feel River about to tell his brother no, but I couldn't let that happen. The baby was innocent; it had done nothing wrong. "I can't take care of this baby. He's still in the hospital. His mother died giving birth to him. I can't even fucking name him, River. I don't want any part of him."

Before River could answer, I jumped in. "I'll take him," I told Red. His eyes widened as his eyes locked on mine. "Even if your brother doesn't want him, Red, I'll take him. I promise that I'll take care of him." I told him.

River turned me to face him. "You sure this is what you want, Darlin'?" He asked me, his voice gruff.

I nodded at him. I couldn't let that little boy suffer. I knew if River and I took care of him, he would have a chance at a healthy, prosperous life. If the state got their hands on him, there was no telling what would happen to that boy. "River, you and Red may have your differences, but that little boy hasn't asked to be brought into this world, and he deserves to have someone that will love him and take care of him."

River blew out a harsh breath but nodded his head at me. He looked at Red. "We'll follow you to the hospital." He told his brother. "Make sure you thank my old lady that your son has a home. She's not heartless like I am, and she's the only reason I'm allowing this shit." I warned him. "Once custody is turned over to Adelaide, you get your fucking ass out of this town."

He nodded once as he slid off of his bar stool.

■ ■ ■

RIVER

I stood outside of the nursery at the hospital, my arms crossed over my chest as I stood beside my brother, watching Adelaide talk to the nurse on duty about the baby. I think this was the longest that my brother and I had been civil with each other since we were teens.

Red went off the deep end, and he brought shit on this club all for power and money, almost got our father locked up. He even had a hand in killing our mother. Only for my dad, I hadn't killed him, no matter how badly I wanted to.

Even though he was in the car with the drunk driver that hit our mom as she was crossing the street to the supermarket, dad found it in him to forgive Red.

But I couldn't. I was a bit less bitter about it as time went on, but I could never forgive him for that shit.

After a moment, Adelaide was led over to a clear bassinet that literally looked like a fucking clear tote where a baby in a blue hat was swaddled in a hospital blanket. The nurse said something, and Adelaide nodded. She reached in and grabbed the little boy, cradling him against her chest, a small smile tilting her lips as she looked down at him.

A small smile twitched at my own lips.

Fuck, I couldn't wait to see her holding our own kid.

Adelaide made a fucking stunning mother. It was a sight that would warm any cold man's heart.

She stepped out of the nursery and walked over to us, the baby still cradled in her arms. His lips were slightly parted, his eyes closed as he slept peacefully in her arms. "Guys, meet Axel King Boris," Adelaide announced, smiling down at the baby as she adjusted him to one arm, reaching up to rub her finger over his soft, chubby cheek.

Red shoved his hands in his pockets. "I've signed the necessary documents for you all to be given temporary custody of him. I'll have a lawyer draw up the necessary documentation so you two can adopt him."

I nodded at him, watching as he sauntered off back down the hallway, his back stiff. Adelaide watched him for a moment before she turned those beautiful, brown eyes to me, stepping closer to me as she did so. "Do you want to hold him?" She asked me softly.

I slowly reached out and took Axel from her, surprised at how light he was. I'd honestly never held a baby before, and I was almost thirty.

"The nurse said that he's a little underweight, but otherwise he's perfectly healthy, and we can take him home whenever we're ready." She informed me as she reached out to run her fingertips over his chubby cheeks.

He was perfect. I never thought that I would say that about anything that was a part of Red, but this little boy, with all of his little innocence – he was absolutely perfect.

Red had done the best thing for him by walking away. He would be raised in a loving family with a gentle, soothing mother.

I looked back down at Axel, blowing out a soft breath. Looks like I had a lot of shopping ahead of me – starting with a car seat – and a car for Adelaide.

■ ■ ■

Tristan and Jesup were gone when we got back to the clubhouse, and Sam informed me that they would be in touch to set up our first exchange. Good thing they were gone, too, because I didn't want Adelaide having the added stress of them being here while she was trying to handle taking care of a newborn while still preparing for our own kid.

Tristan was toxic for her. But forcing her to never speak to him again – yeah, that was a fight that would not only cause her to walk away from me, but it would be a pointless one.

When she had gotten settled in with Axel, I had left Adelaide in the clubhouse with him with strict instructions to come get me out of the garage if she needed me, and now, four hours later, I was fucking tired, and I just wanted a hot shower and to crawl in bed with my woman.

As soon as I stepped into my room, I smiled at the sight in front of me. Adelaide was asleep on the bed, propped up the slightest bit on the pillows with Axel resting on his stomach on her chest, her arms protectively wrapped around him as they both peacefully slept.

That was an image I could definitely get used to seeing. Seeing Adelaide being a mom – fuck, it was a sexy as hell sight. I could watch her take care of Axel all day. She was a natural at it. Anyone looking at them would never even think Adelaide wasn't his biological mother.

Turning on the lamp on my dresser, I cast the room in a soft orange glow, breathing a slight sigh of relief as Adelaide and Axel continued to sleep – not stirring the slightest bit.

Someone knocked softly on the door, and I yanked it open to find Reina on the other side, a baby bottle in her hand. Reina was a new girl to the club. She'd come to me, begging for sanctuary, saying someone from the bar had sent her here. So, I'd welcomed her in, though I knew that I made her nervous.

"Adelaide asked me to bring a bottle when it got to nine." She explained, swallowing hard as she cast her eyes from me in submission.

Reina was new to the club still, and I knew that I intimidated her. In fact, I was pretty sure that this was the first time she had ever actually spoken to me outside of me laying down the ground rules for her when she first came to me for help, and I welcomed her into the club.

Something had happened to the woman, but I didn't pry in people's personal shit. All I did was offer protection and make sure no one harmed her again.

I took the bottle from her with a gruff thanks, remembering that Axel needed to eat every couple of hours since he was a newborn. I softly shut the door behind me, setting Axel's bottle on the dresser, deciding to feed him after I got a quick shower so that Adelaide could continue to sleep.

Taking the quickest shower that I had in history, I quickly yanked on a pair of sweat pants before I quickly strode over to the bed. I grabbed the bottle off of the dresser on my way to the bed, preparing myself to wake Adelaide up. I gently shook her awake, not wanting to alarm her by trying to slide Axel out of her arms.

It hadn't even been a full twelve hours since we'd brought him home, and she was already extremely protective of him.

She was a perfect mother, even if she didn't realize it or believe it herself. Axel and our little one would be extremely lucky to have her to call Mom.

I just couldn't wait to see what kind of mom she would be to her own flesh and blood if she was like this with Axel. But something told me that she would always treat Axel with the same love and attention that she would give our own baby.

She blinked up at me tiredly. "What's wrong?" She asked softly.

"Give me Axel so that I can feed him," I told her gently, reaching out to tuck some of her soft hair behind her ear.

She slowly released him, allowing me to grab him off of her chest. He whimpered in protest but quieted as soon as I brought him close to my chest, placing the bottle at his lips. He instantly latched on, his eyes never opening.

"Don't forget to burp him." Adelaide softly spoke up as she slid down the pillows so she was laying down flat on the bed, curling into a ball on her side as she quickly passed back out.

I gently sat on the bed, being careful not to jostle her. I then looked down at Axel, finding him already looking up at me as he drank from his bottle, his blue eyes – that strangely looked a hell of a lot like mine – locking on my face.

"That woman loves you like her own, kid," I told him quietly. He ran his eyes over my face. "Even if your father didn't want you,

233

you're always going to have a family," I swore. "We will love you and take care of you just like the baby she's currently pregnant with - the little one that will be your little sibling," I whispered.

And he would always have a family with us. No matter what happened, Axel would always have a home - would always have people that he could rely on, no matter how old he got.

And knowing Adelaide, she would never turn her back on him, no matter what he may do when he got older. Her love was unconditional.

TWENTY

I pulled my phone out of my pocket as it began vibrating with a call, raising an eyebrow at the screen when I saw who was calling me.

Joey. I knew it was only a matter of time before he got word that Adelaide was with me. I'd just been waiting.

"Been a minute," I said when I answered his call.

"How is she?" He asked, skipping the pleasantries. I knew right away that he was talking about Adelaide. It didn't take a rocket scientist. She was the only woman besides his sister that Joey cared about.

Adelaide was currently holding Axel as he drank the milk out of the bottle she was holding. Reina was sitting next to her, and both women were talking quietly amongst themselves. I smiled. It was nice to see Adelaide finally making a friend here, and it would honestly be good for Reina, too.

My lips tilted up a little more at the corners as her beautiful, dark eyes raised from Axel's face and met mine. "She's doing okay," I told him. She arched an eyebrow at me in question before she turned her head back to Reina. "You're more than welcome to come to see her if you want, but I've got some conditions."

I trusted Joey around her. He'd changed – saw it when he saw her again a few months ago.

He was trying to be better – better for her.

"Name them." He ordered.

This was what I liked and appreciated about Joey. He never beat around the bush. He didn't play fucking games. If he wanted something, he normally got it. And I knew that where Adelaide was concerned, he would do whatever it took to make her happy.

And he knew the meaning of boundaries with her, something that Grim had never grasped when it came to her – never tried to, either.

"Hold on," I told him as I moved outside where my conversation wouldn't be overheard. I needed to inform him of her pregnancy before he got here, but I didn't want anyone overhearing. Adelaide and I had both agreed that her pregnancy needed to be kept under wraps for as long as possible, at least until everyone here got used to her being around.

Once the clubhouse doors were shut behind me, and I was secluded, I began talking again. "She's pregnant, and no one in my club knows except for Sam," I informed him. "I want it to stay that way for right now because I'm pretty sure that I've got an inside problem."

"Understood," Joey stated, the only shock being revealed at the news of Adelaide's pregnancy being his sharp intake of breath when I had first announced it.

"Tristan was just here yesterday, and he fucked her up pretty good when he tried to get her to take him back." Joey softly growled. "If I hadn't stopped her, she would have destroyed my fucking garage. I don't want her that fucking worked up again. The second that I feel that you being here is fucking with her, I'll boot you off of my grounds and out of my town." I warned him. "She comes above all else."

"Got it." He told me. "You can trust me with her, River. I won't do anything to hurt her – not anymore. Anything else?"

"Nope," I told him. "You know how to handle her, so I'm pretty sure your visit will go well."

"Ink and I will be there in a few hours." He informed me before he cut the call.

I walked back into the clubhouse, finding Gregory and Adelaide in a heated argument as Axel cried against her chest. She was trying to get him to quiet down as Gregory got in her face.

My blood ran hot. "Shut that fucking baby up." He snarled at her. "Some of us need fucking sleep, and your fucking brat is disturbing us."

Adelaide tightened her hold on our little boy, her features twisting into a scowl as she lightly bounced Axel, quieting him almost instantly.

"He's a baby, not a fucking brat." Adelaide sneered at him. "Babies fucking cry, Gregory."

"And he's my fucking son, so if you've got a mother fucking problem, you take it up with me, not my fucking woman." I barked, making my presence known. I walked up to them and wrapped an arm around Adelaide's waist, protectively tugging her against my side, my eyes narrowed on Gregory.

He knew that he had fucked up. He'd let me catch him popping off at her after I had already warned him about his mouth around her.

Gregory clenched his jaw. "My bad, Prez." He grumbled.

I gripped his shoulder before he could walk away and swung him back around to face me. I stepped around Adelaide and swung my other fist, clocking him across the face. He crashed against a couple of tables, sending them crashing down to the floor with him. A couple of the girls screamed in fear. Val quickly moved over towards us, ready to back me up if Gregory tried some stupid shit. It was why he was my Sergeant at Arms; he was always ready to protect his president.

I knelt over Gregory, gripping his cut in my fists as I hauled him up off of the floor, bringing his face close to my own. "This is your last warning, Gregory." I quietly snarled. He nodded. "If I catch you disrespecting my woman again when you think I'm not around, I'll cover these walls with your blood. You got me?" I threatened.

He nodded jerkily, knowing from experience not to take my threats lightly. I shoved him away from me, sending him crashing back against the floor. Drawing in a deep, calming breath, I turned to face Adelaide, finding Sam standing beside her, his hand on her shoulder, ready to move her out of the way had that situation escalated.

I ran my hand down my face tiredly, wiping away the anger that I felt as I did so. I wasn't Tristan nor Joey; Adelaide would never be faced with my rage when my anger was for someone else. Even if I was furious with her, I wouldn't raise my voice at her. I would always do my damnest to be reasonable with her.

"I'm going out to the garage for a little while," I informed Adelaide. There was no fear in her eyes, just concern for me. And I loved that about her. She was perfect for me - able to stand by my side as I wreaked destruction. "Remember, if you need me, come get me. And if Gregory or anyone else starts any shit with you, let me know." I ordered.

She reached up with her free hand, rubbing the slight stubble along my jawline. "Grab a beer out of the fridge while you're on your way out." She instructed quietly. "You look like you need it."

I leaned down and pressed my lips to hers, not missing the way she softly sighed against my lips. I moved my head so my lips were at her ear, my stubble rubbing against her cheek. "A beer for now, but later tonight, I want you bent over my bed with those thick thighs spread as I fuck you hard from behind," I whispered huskily, nipping her ear lobe as she moaned softly at my words.

I stood back up to my full height, smirking at her flushed face. I reached up and rubbed her bottom lip gently, watching as she slightly parted her lips on a soft sigh, those pretty brown eyes practically begging me to fuck her.

Dammit, my cock was hard as fuck for her.

Shaking my head with a smirk, I stepped back from her and strode to the kitchen to grab a few beers because after that little moment with her, I was going to need a hell of a lot more than just one.

■ ■ ■

I stepped out of my room in a fresh pair of jeans and a blue and black flannel shirt rolled up to my elbows, my cut on over it. I found Adelaide making drinks with Reina, teaching the newer girl the ropes of mixing drinks. Adelaide laughed when Reina muttered something, her brown eyes lighting up with amusement.

Fucking perfect.

I stepped up to the bar, drawing Adelaide's eyes to me. I reached over to wrap my hand around the back of her neck, drawing her lips to mine for a hot, slow kiss.

I was so fucking addicted to her. It was hard as fuck to keep my hands off of her.

When I pulled back, her eyes were slightly glazed over. She blew out a shaky breath as she locked her eyes on mine. "You have *got* to stop doing that to me, especially when I'm trying to help someone." She said, but there was a smile on her lips.

I smirked at her. "What's the fun in that?" I teased her.

She rolled her eyes, but there was a beautiful smile on her face. Her eyes flickered over my shoulder as the clubhouse doors opened. I turned around and saw Sam letting in Joey and Ink.

Adelaide squealed and ran around the bar. I grinned, loving how happy she looked at that moment. I knew she would always love Joey, but as I told her, as long as she continued to live for me, I didn't care how much she loved him.

She launched herself at Joey, and he caught her, his back slamming against the wall as she locked her arms and legs around him, her shoulders shaking as she began to cry. He released a soft laugh as he locked his arms around her, burying his face in her neck. I smiled, loving how beautiful she looked when she was properly being loved.

How she should have been loved all along.

Surprisingly, there wasn't any jealousy in my veins as I watched Joey settle in a chair in a dark corner. He nodded once at me before he focused his attention on the beautiful, crying woman in his arms.

He'd take care of her, and I was secure enough in my relationship with her to know that she wouldn't be leaving me nor cheating on me.

Those two just had something together that would rip them both apart if they were separated.

She may live for me, but he taught her how to breathe when she felt like her only option was dying.

■ ■ ■

ADELAIDE

Joey ran his eyes over my face, a smile on his lips. I sobbed as I reached up to trace his jawline with my fingers. He grabbed my wrist and pressed a tender kiss to my palm.

"I held you with me." I choked out.

"I told you I'd find you again." He soothed. "I've never broken a promise to you, pretty girl."

A sob ripped from my throat. "It was so hard not to come crawling back to you," I admitted. "But I wanted to show you that I was strong enough to let him take care of me."

Joey kissed a tear off of my cheek as it rolled down. "I'm proud of you, pretty girl. You're glowing, and it's all because of him. He sees you, Adelaide – he sees every part of you, even the parts of you that you've given to me and Tristan. He sees them all, and he loves every single piece."

"It doesn't hurt so much to let you go anymore," I whispered, my voice breaking.

He brushed his nose with mine. "Just hold me with you. It'll make the pain a bit more bearable. We were toxic as fuck together, pretty girl, and I had my own hand in breaking you down, but I'm trying to be better for you, even if you're not mine anymore."

I gave him a broken smile. "I don't care if you move on, Joey; a piece of you will always be mine."

He brushed his thumb over my cheek. "Where did it all go wrong, pretty girl?" He quietly asked.

I shrugged. "From the very beginning," I admitted on a weak laugh. "We fought from day one, but you made me come alive. Some days, it was all I could do to just breathe. But you saw a broken, eighteen-year-old girl who just needed a purpose, and you gave me a purpose. So, no matter how much we destroyed each other, I'll always love you."

"God, he's so fucking good for you, Adelaide." Joey breathed. "Before him, you did your damnest to ignore every emotion you could."

"He's showing me it's okay," I told him. My bottom lip trembled. "He told me that it was okay to still love you both just as long as I lived for him."

Joey smiled, and there was no pain in his eyes as he looked at me – just happiness. "Then live for him, pretty girl."

I swiped at my cheeks with a half-hearted laugh. "I don't know when I got so fucking emotional." I choked out.

Joey hugged me to him, brushing his cheek with mine. I sighed in contentment. "You're living, Adelaide. This – this is what it feels like to live."

■ ■ ■

RIVER

Adelaide walked over to me, Joey following behind her. She looked up at me, a wide smile on her face. I could tell she had been crying, but the fact that she came back to me with a beautiful smile on her lips meant that she was okay.

And as long as she continued to keep him with her, she would be. "Thank you." She breathed.

I reached out and ran my thumb over her cheek. "Anything for you, Darlin'," I told her honestly.

She wrapped her arms around me. I didn't waste a second and securely wound my arms around her smaller frame, burying my face in her hair, breathing her in. We stayed like that for a good minute as Joey spoke to Sam.

Axel began crying, and Adelaide quickly moved away from me and went around the bar, lifting Axel from the pack 'n play, cradling him against her chest.

"Fuck." Joey said, his voice sounding strangled as he stared at her, pain flashing in his eyes for a moment before he smothered it. I remembered she had been pregnant with his baby before she had left that day that caused her to disappear for an entire year. "That's a sight that will warm any man's cold heart," Joey commented, his eyes locked on Adelaide as she cooed to Axel.

Oh, he had no fucking idea.

"Being a mother is an easy feat for her," I informed him. "She does it so effortlessly."

"Always knew she would." He said. "She's got a love that's fucking unconditional." He nodded in Axel's direction. "Your kid?" He asked me.

I shook my head, and he nodded in understanding. He knew that I wouldn't talk about it in here, not with so many ears listening. That was another thing I liked about Joey. One, he respected privacy, and two, he actually fucking listened. He was remembering me telling him about my inside problem.

"Hey, my fucking beer is empty." One of my men snarled as he stepped up to the bar.

Reina paled at his aggressiveness. "I'm sorry, I -"

"Don't apologize to cock suckers like him," Adelaide told her as she reached over and grabbed a beer out of the fridge, still holding Axel in her arms. She slammed it down in front of Holden, her eyes flashing at him dangerously. My dick twitched in my jeans. Christ, she was a sexy as sin spitfire. "Talk to her like that again, and I'll let her bust the next bottle over your fucking head." She snarled at him.

He held his hands up in a defensive gesture, muttering a sorry under his breath as he quickly walked away from the bar. I smirked at Adelaide as she scowled at Holden's back.

"You're turning my men into pussies, Darlin'," I told her, only teasing, though. My men were already beginning to worship the ground she walked on, and I knew it wouldn't be long before they respected her more than they respected me.

She snorted. "Treating women like shit makes them pussies, River." Joey barked out a laugh. "Fucking pisses me off when I see them treating women like dirt."

"Going to straighten 'em out like you did my men, pretty girl?" Joey asked her with a grin.

She smirked at him. Her eyes hadn't lost their shine yet, and I longed to see it stay there. She shined with me, but when she had Joey with her, too, she shined even brighter. "Trying my damnest." She told him. He snorted.

She walked around the bar and handed me Axel. "I need to make his bottle." She informed me. "It's almost time for him to eat. After he eats, I'll take him to our room and change him."

I stood up and leaned down to softly kiss her. "I'll go ahead and change him," I assured her. "Go make his bottle, and I'll feed him."

She chewed on her bottom lip, instantly making me hard. "You sure?" She asked me.

I tugged her bottom lip from between her teeth. "He's mine, too, Darlin'." I gently reminded her. "And grab me a beer while you're at it. I'm going to need it if you keep biting your lip like that." I told her.

She laughed, her eyes beaming beautifully at me. Letting Joey come here had been a damn good decision on my part. Tristan had ripped her apart. She needed Tristan, but he just couldn't get his shit together with her.

But Joey? He could, and he had.

She walked behind the bar and into the kitchen, leaving me to stare after her curvaceous figure with longing in my eyes.

Fuck, tonight couldn't come soon enough.

I was ready to have her beneath me, crying out my name as I made her come over and over again.

TWENTY-ONE

ADELAIDE

I released a tired yawn as I gently set a sleeping Axel in his crib, being extra careful not to wake him up. River was currently working to shut down the party so that people around here could actually catch some sleep – people like me. I was sleeping more and more lately, the pregnancy slowly but surely draining me as the baby grew.

I pressed two of my fingers to my lips before I pressed them to Axel's forehead. His little nose scrunched up, and at that moment, he looked exactly like River. I smiled to myself at the thought of my man.

He was an incredibly good man.

He had allowed Joey to come to visit me all while knowing my history with him, and instead of being all territorial and possessive like Tristan had always been, River invited him here to see me, and he just trusted solely in the fact that I wouldn't fuck around on him.

He'd let Joey and I have our moment together, and there had been nothing but understanding in his eyes when I'd finally come back to him. He really did understand that I would never be able to let Joey go, and he was okay with that.

And Joey – fuck. He had changed so much – changed for *me*. He wanted to be better for me, and I loved him so much for that. We may not be together, but he was trying his damnest to prove to me that he was worthy of remaining a part of my life.

It was why he always reminded me to keep him with me.

"What's got you smiling like that?" River quietly asked as he stepped into our room, softly shutting the door behind him.

I turned to look at him. "You." I honestly answered as he strode towards me.

He quirked an eyebrow at me. God, he was so perfect. How was it possible that a man so rugged could still be so fucking gorgeous? "Me?" He asked as he drew me into his muscular arms.

I wrapped my arms around his neck. "You," I repeated, nodding my head as I smiled up at him. The corners of his lips twitched with a smile. "You're incredibly good to me, River," I told him honestly. "I don't deserve you – not after all of the shit that I've done in my life." I brushed my fingers over the stubble on his jaw, letting it tickle my fingertips. "Thank you for staying with me."

He reached up and gently cupped my jaw. "Always had a soft spot for you, Darlin'." He huskily admitted. "You stole the breath from my lungs the moment you aimed those beautiful, brown eyes at me. I had a soft spot for you even when Tristan dragged you to the clubhouse from Joey's. You were so fucking angry at the world, and yet, I thought you were the most breathtaking fighter I'd ever laid my eyes on. You didn't give up – didn't give in to him."

"How come you never made a move before?" I asked him, honestly curious. If he had, it might have saved me so much heartache. I might have been able to save Tristan from hurting so much, too.

"I had to wait for the right time, Darlin'. I needed you to come to me first." I frowned. He leaned down and lightly brushed his lips over mine. "I knew the moment you came to me first, Tristan would be the least of your concerns. Because I knew when I got a taste of you, it wasn't going to be enough. I was going to want you a hell of a lot more afterward. I was going to want you to be mine in every way possible."

My heart warmed in my chest at his words. "I wish I had made the decision a hell of a lot sooner," I told him honestly.

River's lips tipped up at the corners the slightest bit. I bit my lip at the sight of his beautiful smile lighting up his features. "Everything happens on its own time, and I knew that as long as I stayed patient and waited for you, I would have you here with me where you've always belonged."

Then, River's lips met mine, and I moaned softly as I pressed myself harder against him, allowing him to drag me over to the bed. He quickly yanked my shirt over my head, and he placed hot, open-mouthed kisses all over my skin until he reached the edge of my black bra. With skillful fingers, he undid the clasp and tossed it somewhere across the room.

I moaned softly, digging my fingers into his hair as he let his lips meet mine again as he eased me backward on the bed, his strong, muscular body coming down with me.

■ ■ ■

I groaned in protest when I heard Axel crying, dragging me from my peaceful sleep. I blinked at the alarm clock beside me, only to see that it was just 3:02 in the morning. "I've got him." River whispered before he leaned over to press a kiss to my forehead. He slid out of bed and yanked on a pair of sweats.

I watched him through sleepy eyes as he strode over to the crib and picked Axel up, cradling him in his arms as he strode out of our room.

If he was like this with his nephew, my heart was going to melt at my feet to see him with his very own kid. I knew River was going to shoot Red down that day, but I'm so glad that I stepped in. I knew River would never deny me something that big.

Turns out, it was one of the best decisions I made. Not only was Axel now going to have a warm and loving family, but River had a piece of his brother that would never be tainted by the shit that occurred in their past. And I think he needed that more than he realized.

Our baby suddenly made its appearance by creating a small flutter in my belly. My eyes widened in shock as I stared down at my stomach, unable to believe that had happened. I was barely fifteen weeks now. This wasn't possible.

But then again, the doctor had told me that it may very well be possible that I feel the baby move earlier than usual since I was so small to begin with when I got pregnant.

Then, I felt another flutter. It was unmistakable. Before long, I would actually be able to feel the baby kicking and hitting my belly.

Tears of joy trickled down my cheeks as I quickly flicked on the lamp on my side of the bed and placed my hands on my very slightly rounded belly, laughing softly. I sniffled as River stepped back into the room carrying Axel who was greedily drinking from his bottle.

"Woah, Darlin', what's wrong?" River demanded to know as he quickly strode over to me.

"The baby moved," I told him with a smile. "It was like a flutter – kind of like when I was a little girl, and I would get butterflies in my belly, but the baby is definitely active," I told him. "I'll be feeling the baby kick in no time."

River grinned – an actual full-on smile that melted my heart and soul – and he sat beside me on the bed as he transferred Axel to one arm, adjusting the bottle so it rested against his chest. With his free hand, he rested his hand between mine where I was still cradling my small belly.

"Fuck, I can't wait until I can feel our baby move." He admitted. "I never imagined myself as a dad before you, Darlin'." He admitted, letting those blue eyes that I loved so much meet mine.

"You do incredibly well with Axel," I noted.

"Not even going to lie, Darlin', I probably never would have taken care of him had you not been here to give me the push that I needed." I knew that whether he realized it, though. "I never wanted kids until I found your ultrasound pictures. That day, I suddenly realized that with you, I wanted it all."

I leaned my head on his shoulder tiredly. "I still don't understand how you didn't lose your shit when you found out," I told him. Any normal man would have flipped the fuck out.

River lightly shrugged since my head was on his shoulder. "I told you, Adelaide; I'm not Tristan nor Joey. I could never be angry with you like that, and if I ever got that angry, I would walk away and calm down before I ever exploded at you like that. I made a promise to myself that I would be better than them for you. I'll never raise my voice at you, and I'll do my damnest to always be reasonable with you."

"Guess that explains why you didn't lose your shit about the garage either," I commented.

He released a quiet laugh. "Honestly, Darlin', I was more worried about you and what was going on in that pretty little head of yours than I was about some money I may have had to spend to fix some damages you may have caused." He told me. "For you to lose your shit like that, I knew something had happened – knew you were hurting. I just wanted to help you."

Oh, my heart. "I'm surprised Tristan didn't at least leave here sporting a black eye," I said quietly.

River snorted as he shook his head, clenching his jaw before he forced it to relax. "Trust me, Darlin', I wanted to do more than black his eye, but I restrained myself from hitting him at all. You were hurting enough, and I knew hitting him would only hurt you more." *Why in the hell was River so fucking perfect?* "Instead, I threatened to put a bullet through his skull if he ever made you that upset again." River told me honestly.

I tensed up, hating that I still felt protective over Tristan after everything that had happened between us. But it was my fault that he was hurting this much, why he felt the need to come to me in the kitchen in the first place. River sighed softly as he looked down at me, understanding in his gaze.

"I know that you don't ever want anything to happen to him, Darlin'. I hate it, but I understand it." He admitted. I swallowed thickly. "Tristan has never *tried* with you, so it bugs the fuck out of me that you're so protective of him." I frowned. "However, if someone ever does something to hurt you again – emotionally or physically – I won't be held back, no matter how much they mean to you. And if Tristan ever makes you that upset again, he may not live to see the light of another day." He warned me, his blue eyes flashing dangerously. "You've been hurt enough."

"River, you know that I've got history with him -" I started, but he cut me off.

River shook his head, clenching his jaw. "Adelaide, I wouldn't give a shit if he was currently the father of the kid that you're carrying inside of you. He's known you almost his entire life, and he knows how to get under your skin. What he did the other day – he fucking did that shit on purpose whether you want to admit it to yourself or not. He knew he could get to you. He knows you still feel something for him, and he's going to keep bringing it up to the surface as much as he can. I promise you, he doesn't give the slightest shit how much he hurts you while he does it. Tristan is a selfish son of a bitch, and he will go to whatever means is necessary to take you back home with him."

I instantly went defensive. Tristan and I had our differences, but I knew he still cared about me in his own sick, twisted way, just as Joey did.

"Tristan fucking cares about me, River -"

"Not in the way he fucking should, Adelaide." River cut me off, his voice remaining calm, though I knew if had he been arguing with anyone else, he would have lost his shit already. "You're a woman that deserves to be treasured." I swallowed hard at his words. "I know you're not the easiest woman to please and that sometimes being with you can be like handling the most fragile piece of glass – one wrong move, and it could all go to shit. I know that you've got a temper, and ninety-nine percent of the time, you speak without thinking first." My breath hitched in my throat. He knew me so fucking well. My heart swelled in my chest as tears burned at the backs of my eyes.

He looked at me, letting his blue eyes meet mine. "You're an independent woman, Adelaide, and you don't like feeling like someone is controlling you. You require a certain kind of care and love, and Tristan doesn't give a shit enough to understand that. He never will. As long as he's happy, not a fucking thing else matters to him."

I opened my mouth to speak, but he cut me off before I could. "Adelaide, I love you." He admitted, making my breath hitch in my throat again as those tears I'd been holding back spilled over onto my cheeks. "I love that you're not easy to please. I love that I have to handle you with extra care. I love that you've got a fiery ass temper and that you're not afraid to speak what you feel. I don't mind that you're an independent kind of woman, Adelaide. I don't want a woman I have to control all of the time. I want and need a woman who is capable of making her own decisions and capable of taking care of her family if the time ever comes for it."

He gently set down a sleeping Axel on the bed and reached over and cradled my face in his hands as my tears streamed down my cheeks. "Tristan and Joey never understood you, Adelaide – they never tried to. I think Joey understood to an extent, but both of those men just wanted to keep you on a tight leash, and it made them lose you multiple times." My bottom lip trembled as a quiet sob fell from my lips. "Darlin', you require a special kind of love and care, and I'm prepared to give that to you. You don't need to be controlled; you just need some freedom, Adelaide, and I know that as long as I give you everything you need, you'll be here right beside me where you belong – where I need you to be. And that's something no other man will never understand about you."

"Fuck, River." I choked out as I threw my arms around his neck and pressed my lips to his. He instantly kissed me back as I straddled his lap, wrapping my legs around his hips. "I love you, too."

He peppered gentle kisses all over my face. "Promise me you'll never try to make excuses for Tristan or Joey ever again." He begged me. "Because if I can figure you out, then they could have, too. Joey is trying now; I know that. But when you were his, he still didn't get it."

I nodded, realizing he was right. I had never once felt trapped with River as I had with Tristan and Joey. With River, I felt independent. I could be myself without having to worry about any backlash. I could snap at him without fear of him getting angry at me and trying to dominate me, trying to pull that leash tight around my neck.

I reached over and picked Axel up, holding him in my arms as River leaned back against the headboard, his arms wrapped around me as I leaned my head on his chest, Axel cradled against my belly.

I was home.

■ ■ ■

RIVER

I woke up to someone lightly knocking on my room door. It was times like these that I hated being the president. All I wanted to do was cuddle with my woman and our son.

Was that too much to fucking ask for?

With a soft sigh, I gently moved Adelaide off of my lap and laid her on the bed, placing Axel next to her as they both continued to sleep peacefully, neither of them making a single sound.

Must be nice. But I knew Adelaide needed the rest. Between nurturing a baby inside of her and taking care of Axel, as well as being my old lady and the queen of the club, I knew it was exhausting for her.

I slowly slid off of the bed and walked to the door, opening it just enough for me to slip through before I closed it back, looking at Sam.

"What's up?" I asked him as I stretched out my muscles, wincing when my back popped.

Fuck, I was already getting old.

"Come on." He grumbled, his shoulders tense, his fists clenching and unclenching at his sides.

This wasn't good. Sam didn't get on the edge of losing his shit for anything. He was cool and collected. It was why he was my VP. He was my voice of reasoning.

I followed him to the room that I had given Reina. He pushed open the door, and my eyes instantly fell on Joey who was holding Reina on his lap, whispering soft words to her as she sobbed. She was wrapped in a sheet, her face beaten and discolored, dried blood all over her exposed skin. Hand-shaped bruises were wrapped around her neck and upper arms.

I barely resisted the urge to put my fucking fist through a wall.

"What the fuck happened?" I snarled, looking to Joey, knowing he would know the most.

"She won't talk," Joey told me. I growled. "I went outside this morning to smoke and check up on my club, and she was sprawled out on the back porch – unconscious." He clenched his jaw. "I know you don't want to wake Adelaide up, but she may be able to help with this."

I narrowed my eyes at him. Adelaide was dealing with enough shit as it was. I didn't want to burden her with this shit, too. "How is my woman supposed to help this situation?" I demanded to know.

Joey clenched his jaw, working it around before he forced himself to relax. "She's a rape victim, River." Joey spit, the word rape coming off of his tongue like acid. "Vin got his hands on her a few years ago, and she managed to escape him." He drew in a deep, calming breath as guilt flashed in his eyes. "I didn't protect her enough. She may be able to coax the truth out of Reina."

"Please, no." Reina whimpered as she squeezed her eyes shut, her body beginning to tremble.

"Easy, sweetheart." Joey soothed as he looked down at her. "We'll take care of this; I promise. This won't happen to you again."

I looked over at Sam. His expression was murderous, but his eyes wouldn't leave Reina. There was something there between them, but obviously, Sam hadn't acted on it yet. Probably never would, to be honest. He wasn't an open kind of man.

"Not a single other fucking person comes in here, you got me?" I snarled.

He looked at me and nodded. I stormed off towards my room and slid inside, changing into a pair of jeans and one of my red flannel shirts, throwing my cut on over it before I tugged on my steel-toed boots. I was fucking furious, and as soon as I found out who did this to Reina, I would fucking shove their dick down their goddamn throat.

I gently shook Adelaide awake. She blinked up at me tiredly. Fuck, I hated having to wake her up for this shit, but I needed her help. I only hoped that it didn't fuck with her, too. I knew she'd been raped before Joey had even told me, but I didn't want her having to deal with this.

But I didn't know what other option I had to get Reina to talk.

"Hey." She said quietly, her voice still husky from sleep.

"I need your help," I told her softly. "Get dressed."

Questions sparked in her gaze, but instead of voicing them, she nodded and got out of bed, slipping on a pair of leggings with a tank top, shrugging on a hoodie over it against the slight chill in the air. "I've got Axel," I told her, scooping up the sleeping baby. "Follow me."

When we got to Reina's room, Adelaide gasped. I didn't even have to tell her what happened, and it broke my goddamn heart that this shit had happened to my woman so many times that she picked up the signs in someone else so quickly.

"Oh, not you. This didn't happen to you." Adelaide whispered in horror as she instantly rushed forward, taking Joey's place as he quickly vacated it.

Joey pressed his lips to the top of Adelaide's head. "Help her, pretty girl." He begged her.

She looked up at him – at the guilt in his eyes. She reached up and trailed her fingers down his cheek. "I'll help her." She promised.

Adelaide looked up at me, and I nodded at her, understanding what she needed without her having to voice it.

"Let's give them some privacy," I ordered as I strode out of the room, knowing Sam and Joey were following me.

"Sam, stand guard outside of this door," I commanded, knowing he wasn't going far from this room for a while anyway. He may try to hide it, but I'd known Sam for years – grew up with him. I knew him better than he thought I did. "I'm going to change Axel and get him a bottle. If they finish talking before I finish taking care of him, come find me. Until then, do not move from this door." I commanded.

"Got it, Prez." He told me.

Please, Darlin', find out what happened to that poor girl.

Because I was ready to spill fucking blood.

This shit didn't happen in my club, and I was about to make that message very fucking clear.

TWENTY-TWO

ADELAIDE

I was seeing fucking red, and I was ready to slit someone's fucking throat.

That someone being River's Sergeant at Arms – Gregory.

After finally getting Reina calm enough to talk to me, she spilled everything as she cried while I hugged her, not letting her go. She told me about how Gregory had caught her as she was taking the trash out for the night and that he hadn't taken no for an answer when he had come on to her.

He'd violently beat her and raped her behind the dumpster, using her shirt as a gag to keep her quiet as she screamed for help.

After leaving Reina in her room to try to catch some sleep, I stormed down the hall to mine and River's room, grabbing one of his guns and slipping it into my leggings. I stormed out into the bar room, finding Gregory sitting at the bar, sipping a cup of coffee as if he hadn't just violently taken an innocent woman against her will last night.

I walked calmly around the bar and when I was finally standing in front of him, I grabbed his steaming hot cup of coffee and threw it in his face.

"Fuck!" He roared as he quickly jumped off of his bar stool, making it clatter to the floor as he wiped at his face, hissing out a breath of pain. "What the absolute *fuck*, Adelaide?!" He shouted at me, his eyes murderous as he glared at me.

I pulled my gun out, pointing it at him. Absolute hatred and disgust ran through my veins. I was on a fucking murder spree. He eyed the gun in my hand warily. "You better choose your last words fucking carefully." I snarled at him.

"What the fuck is wrong with you?!" He shouted at me, but he didn't rip his gaze from the gun in my hands, which gave away his true fear.

He knew that I knew what he did to Reina last night.

River rushed towards the bar, coming to stop me, but when I opened my mouth again, he stayed where he was, a murderous, deadly expression crossing his features as he took in my words.

"You fucking raped Reina!" I shouted at Gregory. He opened his mouth, but I spoke first. "Don't you dare fucking deny it!" I barked at him. "It took me almost two fucking hours, but I finally got it out of her." I snarled. "Want to tell everyone what you fucking did? How you wanted a piece of her, but she told you no, so you took it anyway – beating the fuck out of her before you raped her over and over?" I quietly seethed, lowering my voice so everyone else wouldn't hear what had happened to her – no one but me, Gregory, and Reina.

Before I could pull the trigger on Gregory like I so badly wanted to, River slammed his fist against Gregory's face, sending Gregory sprawling across one of the tables next to him, dragging it to the ground with him. River looked at Sam. "Take him out back. No women outside." He ordered.

"He deserves a bullet through his skull." I snarled at River, angry that he was stopping me from delivering justice to the sick son of a bitch. If he did it to one woman, he would do it again, and I would *not* allow another one to fall victim to his shit.

River shook his head at me. "A bullet is a fucking blessing for him." River informed me. "What I'm about to do to him will be ten times worse, and it sends a message to the other men in my club that this shit will *not* be tolerated." He told me.

I narrowed my eyes at him, still seething. "And what are you planning to do?" I demanded to know.

River's eyes met mine, fury making his eyes darken, but I knew that anger wasn't directed at me. He had even said so himself that he would never make me face his anger, especially when that anger was meant for someone else.

"I'm cutting his dick off, and I'm shoving it down his fucking throat." River snapped. He pointed his finger at me. "Stay in this fucking clubhouse, Darlin'." He ordered. This isn't something you need to be watching."

I nodded once, knowing River would do exactly as he said. I watched as he stormed outside where Sam had just dragged Gregory. I heard Axel cry from his pack 'n' play, and I rushed over instantly, lifting him into my arms. Blowing out a soft breath, I walked to mine and River's room and set Axel on his changing table so that I could change him. I was still so angry, but I knew River would take care of this shit.

I heard Gregory scream in pain as I was putting a clean diaper on Axel, and I felt like throwing up at the scream that ripped from the man's throat.

River was a deadly man when he needed to be.

After changing Axel and trying my damnest to ignore Gregory's blood-curdling screams of pain, I walked back out of our room to go check on Reina. She was passed out on her bed, thankfully not having any nightmares. I only hoped that this shit didn't fuck her up inside as it had done me. I didn't wish my shit on anyone.

I quietly stepped back out of her room, jumping a bit in shock when I felt the fluttering in my belly again. I smiled softly to myself and looked down at Axel. His bright blue eyes were open wide, taking in everything around him.

I looked up as the clubhouse doors open, revealing River and Sam. River strode over to me instantly, his expression softening the slightest as he did so. "Has he been giving you any problems?"

I shook my head. "He's just being curious." I shifted Axel to one arm and reached up to rub his stubble-covered jaw. "Everything was taken care of?" I asked him, feeling calmer now that he was standing here in front of me, soothing me.

He nodded. "Kale is taking care of the clean-up." He informed me quietly. "How's Reina holding up?" He asked, his eyes flickering to her room door behind me.

I shrugged. "She's sleeping right now, so it's hard to tell," I admitted. I yawned softly, shocking myself at how tired I felt. I had been up way earlier than I usually was, which probably explained it. It also probably didn't help that I had spent part of the night awake with River.

"I think it's time for you to get a nap, don't you think?" River softly asked me as he reached up to cup the side of my neck, brushing his thumb over my jawline.

Without another word, he placed his hand on the small of my back and led me down the hall towards our room. He took Axel from me, and I crawled onto the bed, snuggling into the pillows, almost immediately falling asleep.

■ ■ ■

RIVER

I released a tired groan as I looked at the screen of my phone, swiping across the screen to answer the call. "Yeah?" I asked gruffly when I answered.

"River, I know you probably don't give two shits," Jesup started, "but Tristan was just shot, and he's in a fucking coma." He told me. He sounded on the verge of fucking losing his mind. "I thought you might want the chance to break the news to Adelaide before she gets wind of it."

"Fuck." I grumbled, looking over at Adelaide who was still sleeping peacefully on the bed. "What's the doctor saying?" I quietly asked him.

Jesup drew in a shaky breath, and I instantly knew he was beginning to lose his composure. "I may be burying my best friend, River. It's fucking bad."

Fuck, this was about to hit Adelaide hard.

"We'll be there within a day," I informed him. I knew that Adelaide would want to go see him, and I wouldn't keep her from doing that. I knew Adelaide well enough to know that she would pack a bag for her and Axel and hit the road to go see him herself if I even tried denying her.

I hung up the phone, and set it on the nightstand, pushing my hands through my hair. I didn't want to tell her this - I really fucking didn't. I knew that even though she was here with me, she still harbored some feelings for Tristan, and I couldn't fault her for that. They had a history that happened long before I ever came into the picture.

But this shit was about to rip her the fuck apart, and I was so goddamn tired of her hurting all of the time. I just wanted her to finally be happy for once.

I stood up and quietly slipped out of the room, going down the hall to knock on the door of the room that Joey was occupying. I hated to cut his time with her short, but I needed to take her to see Tristan. But first, I needed Joey's help breaking this news to her. She would need both of us when she found out. This shit was about to break her.

"What?" Joey grunted as he opened the door, pulling a shirt over his head. He scrubbed his hands down his face, rubbing the sleep out of his eyes.

"Tristan's been shot," I told him. Joey dropped his hands from his face, looking much more awake now. "Jesup just called me – told me he may be burying Tristan. Doctor says it isn't looking good for him."

"Fuck – Adelaide," Joey whispered, his mind instantly going in the same direction mine had gone.

I clenched my jaw, nodding. "This shit's going to hurt her, Joey, but she's going to hate me if I don't tell her. I thought you could help me keep her calm as I break the news to her."

He nodded. "Let me get my boots on and grab my cut." He told me as he opened the door wider, moving towards the bed in the center of the room. He shoved his feet into his boots and snatched up his cut, shrugging it onto his shoulders. He sighed, looking up at the ceiling for a moment. "Not going to be sad to see Tristan go, if I'm honest," Joey told me bluntly. I grunted in agreement, but I knew losing Tristan would make Adelaide lose a piece of herself. Neither of us wanted that for her.

"He keeps hurting her, River. Every time I fucking see him, I want to break his neck. He refuses to change for her." He rolled his shoulders, almost as if he were trying to roll his feelings about Tristan off of him. "Let's go." He told me.

Time to go rip my woman the fuck apart.

■ ■ ■

Joey eased onto the bed beside Adelaide, pain flashing through his eyes for a moment before he smothered it, only showing her the love and happiness that he held for her.

I gently shook Adelaide awake as I sat on the other side of her, and she blinked up at me slowly, a slow smile curving her luscious lips. "Hi." She breathed.

I gently ran my fingertips over her cheek, and her expression instantly fell as she sat up, immediately picking up on my mood. She looked at Joey who was sitting on her other side, and her breathing slightly picked up speed. Joey cupped the side of her neck, locking her eyes on his. "Easy, pretty girl." He soothed. "Breathe."

She looked over at me, swallowing thickly. "River, what's going on?" She asked me, her voice trembling.

Fuck, I didn't want to do this to her; I really fucking didn't. "Darlin', Jesup just called me – Tristan has been shot, and his odds of surviving aren't looking that great." I gently spoke.

Her expression was blank for a moment as she processed what I had just told her. Then, her expression quickly fell, tears filling her eyes as her bottom lip trembled. I instantly pulled her onto my lap and cradled her to me as she burst into tears, her pain-filled wail filling my room.

And my beautiful Adelaide fell apart in my arms.

Joey grabbed her hands in his, bringing her tear-filled eyes to his. "Tristan is not leaving you, pretty girl." He soothed. She sobbed. "He's strong as fuck, and he's stubborn as hell. This isn't going to take him out. Breathe." He coaxed.

"Darlin'," I soothed as I gripped her chin, drawing her broken expression up to mine, "live for me," I begged her. My heart squeezed in my chest as her face scrunched up in pain. "Just live. It's going to be okay."

She whimpered as she squeezed her eyes shut, fucking tearing my heart apart. "Sorry, bro. Kick my ass later." Joey whispered.

Before I could question what the fuck he was about to do, he gripped her face in his hands and soothed his lips over hers. She sobbed. "Keep me with you." He soothed. Her hands fisted in my cut, but she didn't tear her lips from his. I clenched my jaw but managed to keep my temper in check. She needed him; I hated it, but she needed him. "Just keep me with you, pretty girl. You've survived so much shit by holding me with you, so do that. Live for your man and keep me with you."

I gritted my teeth as the urge to break his fucking jaw and his fingers so he'd never be able to touch her again pulsed through my veins like hot, scorching lava. But when her whimpers quieted, her eyes falling shut, some of that anger evaporated. I glared at him over her head, though, but he only shrugged at me. "All for her." He said quietly. I sighed. He pressed his lips to her temple as her cries became a little quieter as well all while she drew herself closer to my body, seeking my comfort. I tightened my arms around her. She only silently cried in my arms as she continued clutching my cut in her fists.

Joey brushed his hand over her dark hair. "Live for him, pretty girl. Let us handle everything else."

■ ■ ■

After I had managed to get Adelaide somewhat calm, Joey had left, promising her that he would come back the moment she needed him to. She'd cried as he walked to his bike. It tore me apart to see her want him with her so badly, but I pushed it down. She needed him. He could help her in ways that I couldn't.

Because he taught her how to breathe.

If it hadn't been for Joey, I wouldn't have Adelaide now.

I slowly eased Adelaide's Nissan Rogue onto the familiar gravel lot of the Sons of Death. I brought the SUV to a stop, looking over at Adelaide who was passed out in the passenger seat of the car as I turned the key in the ignition. Blowing out a soft breath, I looked forward when I noticed someone step out of the clubhouse, my eyes meeting Jesup's.

He looked like shit, to put it lightly. He had a lot sitting on his shoulders now that he had to cover for Tristan. On top of that, he was living with the fear that he may be burying the man he'd known his entire life.

I knew that shit wasn't easy.

I slid out of the SUV, quietly shutting the driver's side door behind me. Jesup walked over to me, his hands stuffed deep in the pockets of his jeans. "The doctor said that I can choose to keep him on life support, or I can just go ahead and pull the plug." He blew out a harsh breath. "I can't make that kind of decision for a guy I've known for my entire life, River." He nodded his head towards the SUV. "I figured I would let Adelaide make that decision."

I nodded in understanding even though I didn't like the idea at all. He was putting more pressure on her shoulders. She was dealing with enough shit as it was.

I walked around to her side and gently opened her door, catching her before she fell out. She snapped her eyes open, locking them on my face. She then looked around her surroundings, her expression falling again, but this time, no tears escaped.

She was living for me and holding Joey with her. I knew she would show no weakness here, and she was clinging onto everything she could to keep up a brave, strong front.

It was one of the things that I loved about her. When the world was an absolute shit place for her, she remained strong.

"Let me out." She whispered.

Nodding, I stepped back, moving around to the back seat to grab Axel. As soon as I lifted his car seat out, Adelaide was next to me. "Give him to me." She quietly ordered.

I took one look at her face and nodded, realizing that she was going to use Axel to try to keep herself held together. I handed her the car seat and watched her as she walked off into the clubhouse, striding past Tank and Dirk with just a nod of her head.

She was on the very edge of that cliff, looking down into the dark abyss. I just hoped that I would be enough to keep her from tipping completely over the edge.

My heart squeezed in my chest for her.

I pulled out my phone, shooting a text to Joey, ignoring Jesup who was watching me. I didn't answer to him anymore, and he knew better than to overstep the boundaries that I had set.

Made it. -River

"A kid?" Jesup asked me as I locked my phone, giving him my attention again.

I shrugged. "Red didn't want his kid, and the mom passed away in childbirth. Adelaide agreed to take care of him and adopt him before I could even form a proper response in my head, so here we are." I informed him as I turned and reached into the backseat to grab our duffel bag and the diaper bag.

"You know, I never imagined you as a domestic kind of man," Jesup admitted as he walked towards the clubhouse, Sam and Val following closely behind us. "Never would have pictured you doing half the shit you've done, actually."

I snorted. *Yeah, me neither, Jesup.*

But I wouldn't change my decisions.

I stepped into the clubhouse, my eyes instantly landing on Adelaide. She was sitting on the couch against the wall, Zyla sitting beside her as they talked quietly while Axel sucked on his bottle, his blue eyes running over his mother's face.

"You two can have Adelaide's old room in the back. Tristan wouldn't ever let anyone else move into it." Jesup informed me.

I nodded without bothering to verbally respond, striding off down the hall to drop our bags. I pulled my phone out to read Joey's message. When it concerned Adelaide, he was quick as fuck to respond.

Tell her to hold me with her and to live for you. -Joey

I sighed, not bothering to respond. I was still pissed about the shit he had pulled with her, but I was forcing myself to shove it aside. It had calmed her – pretty much breathed life back into her because emotionally, she'd been dying in my arms.

I quickly walked back out into the main area. I walked directly over to Adelaide, and Zyla got up, letting me have her spot. As soon as I sat down, Adelaide leaned against my side for support, and I wrapped an arm around her, pressing my lips to her forehead. I unlocked my phone, showing her Joey's message. She sighed softly.

"I'm sorry about what he did." She said quietly. She cast her eyes down to her lap. "And I'm sorry for allowing him."

I tucked my index finger under her chin and tilted her beautiful face up to mine. Leaning down, I softly slid my lips along hers. She released a quiet moan, her body leaning further into mine.

"He helps you breathe, baby. I might be pissed about what he did, but I can't hate either of you." I assured her. "Sometimes, you just need both of us to remind you of who you are."

She frowned up at me. "I just need you." She whispered.

I shook my head at her. "You need him, too, Darlin', and that's okay. He saved your life in numerous ways. I'll never take that from you, and I'll always fight to keep him with you."

She sniffled, her eyes welling up with tears before she blinked them back. "I love you." She choked out.

I smoothed my lips over hers again. "And I love you," I told her. "With every fucking beat of my heart," I promised.

Jesup pulled his phone down from his ear. "That was Joey," Jesup informed us. "He's on his way over here."

I rolled my eyes as my phone vibrated in my lap.

I'm coming to help solve this shit. I may not like Tristan, but she deserves justice for this shit happening to him. I need to know that you'll back me up. -Joey

As long as it's for her, I'll back you up in basically anything. -River

Adelaide's phone went off in her lap. I watched as she adjusted her legs so that they were bent, her feet on the couch. She adjusted Axel was he was settled against her thighs. Then, she grabbed her phone, unlocking the screen. I glanced over to see Joey's name at the top of her message screen.

Brushing my lips to Adelaide's temple, I looked up at Zyla. "How have you been?" I asked her.

She shrugged. "Fine, though it's been a hell of a lot more boring around here without Adelaide to spice things up." She teased. A small smile tilted my woman's lips, but I knew it wasn't because of Zyla.

She was smiling because Joey was reminding her in his own way to keep him with her while she lived for me.

Jesup snorted. "Woman, you're enough for me to handle, and then some." He informed her, drawing her against his side.

"Who shot him?" Adelaide asked out of the blue as she stared down at Axel who was laying across her lap, his blue eyes locking on her dark ones.

"We have an inside problem," Jesup admitted. I glared at him. Jesus Christ, that would have been nice to know before I brought my woman and my child all the fucking way down here.

"Fredrick – you should remember him Adelaide – was doing some shit on the side, and he was telling a rival crew what moves Tristan was making. Tristan confronted him about it, and Fredrick shot him, and then he took off. I found Tristan behind the clubhouse – almost found him too late."

I tightened my arm around Adelaide's shoulders as she stiffened, her hands tightening around her phone. I leaned over and brushed my lips with hers. "Live for me," I whispered. She swallowed past the lump in her throat. "Hold him with you." I coaxed.

"The hospital was able to bring him back," Jesup told us, "but he's on life support, and they don't think he's ever going to come back from it. According to the doctor's, he's completely unresponsive, Adelaide."

Axel reached up and touched Adelaide's face, and she burst into tears. I pulled her and Axel onto my lap, holding them both to me as she cried. She wound her arms around my neck, her tears wetting my shirt. Everyone was silent as they watched the once angry – almost emotionless – woman sob in my arms.

A couple of moments later, she looked up at me through red, puffy, tear-filled eyes, making my heart twist at the sight of her looking so shattered.

"I want him found, and I want him dead." She snapped at me.

"We're doing what we can, Adelaide -" Jesup started.

"No." She cut off Jesup. She looked back up at me, and I knew what she was going to say before she said it.

"You want me to do it," I stated, more than asked, but she nodded her head in response anyway.

I pressed my lips to her forehead. "Anything for you, Darlin'," I told her softly.

And I meant it.

If she wanted me to kill the son of a bitch who almost took Tristan out of her life, then I would.

She leaned her head back in the crook of my neck as she lifted Axel from her legs. My eyes met Jesup's over his head.

"You realize this is our club's problem, right? Not yours." He reminded me, but he wasn't rude about it. Merely stating a fact.

I shrugged. "What Adelaide wants, she gets." I shrugged. "And be prepared, because Joey will be looking for him, too," I warned him.

He nodded once in understanding.

TWENTY-THREE

ADELAIDE

I held Axel tight to my chest as I walked into Tristan's hospital room, swallowing hard at the sight of his pale features. He was connected to an oxygen machine, heart monitors, and an IV machine.

I strode over to his bed, running my eyes over his features. He looked weak – not at all like the strong, dominating man I had known all of my life.

"Darlin' . . ." River drawled softly as he stepped into the room. I slowly ripped my eyes from the pale, weak man lying in the hospital bed to look over at River. "The doctor asked me to come to tell you that he needs to run some more brain scans on Tristan."

My bottom lip trembled as I fought hard to keep myself composed as I stared back down at Tristan's still form. "Adelaide?" River asked softly. He stepped closer to me, shadowing me. My fingers shook as I adjusted Axel to one arm and reached out to run my fingers down Tristan's face. His skin was warm, but with how dead he looked, he might as well had been cold and lifeless.

"Why him?" I asked, my voice breaking as I spoke.

River gently grabbed my arm and pulled me around to face him, pulling me into his arms as I clutched Axel tighter against my chest. Tears streamed down my face as River held me in his arms, giving me as much of his strength as he could.

"I don't know why it had to be him, Darlin'." River said quietly, pressing a kiss to the top of my head. "Tristan is strong. I think you should give him a chance of surviving before you make any kind of decision on pulling the plug on him." He told me softly.

Jesup had informed me of the decision the doctor had put into his hands. I hated that Jesup was now putting it into mine. I would never be able to pull the plug on Tristan. I was selfish enough that I would keep him in that hospital bed – unresponsive – for the rest of my life if it's what kept him here on Earth with me.

I looked up at River through my tears to already find him looking down at me with his understanding, blue eyes, but they were also clouded with the pain of seeing me falling apart. "You really think he'll pull through?" I asked him, my voice breaking.

River nodded as he reached up and gently wiped my tears off of my cheeks. "Tristan is still madly in love with you, Adelaide." River quietly reminded me. "He'll pull through this no matter how long it takes him. He hasn't given up on the idea of you and him yet, and that may be what saves his life this time. Even if it takes him a long time, I have a pretty damn good feeling that he'll make it through this."

I rested my forehead against his chest. "Why are you such a good man?" I asked him quietly. He put up with so much with me. I knew he wanted me all to himself, though he would never admit it. What man didn't? No man wanted to be with a woman knowing she could never let go of the other men in her life.

"I'm not a good man, Darlin'." River told me bluntly as he ran his calloused hands up and down my arm. "I just want to be decent enough for you because I love you, and I hate seeing you like this. I want you to have everything you need – that's all." He said softly as he leaned down and brushed his lips to my forehead.

A knock sounded on the door, and River and I both looked up to see Tristan's doctor stepping into the room. "I'm sorry to interrupt, but it's time for Tristan's MRI." He told us, a silent cue for us to leave the room.

I nodded in understanding and turned around to face Tristan. I grabbed his hand in mine, squeezing gently. "Please pull through," I whispered. "I need you here with me, no matter how much you hurt me," I said so quietly that I wasn't even sure if River could hear me.

Giving Tristan's hand one last, gentle squeeze, I walked out of the hospital room.

■ ■ ■

RIVER

I leaned against the doorjamb of Adelaide's old room, my eyes on her sleeping figure. Axel was passed out in the pack 'n' play next to the bed, and Adelaide was sprawled out under the blankets, her lips slightly parted as she softly snored, the exhaustion of the past forty-eight hours easily knocking her out into a deep sleep.

"How is she holding up?" Sam asked as he came to a stop next to me, peering into the room.

I shrugged. "By a thread, I imagine," I answered gruffly, not drawing my eyes away from her.

"Seeing her this torn up over another man doesn't bother you, River?" Sam bluntly asked me.

I clenched my jaw. "Of course, it fucking bothers me, Sam," I growled. "But at the end of the day, I know who Adelaide will choose. She's known Tristan most of her life, so even if she had never been romantically involved with him, this shit would still tear her up inside." I shrugged, my eyes never leaving her. "Besides, she knows the pain of losing someone. She lost her best friend – Tristan's twin – to cancer, and about a year and a half ago, she thought that she had lost Joey, too – not to mention the fact that she found out she was pregnant with his kid right after that, too."

"Holy fuck." Sam breathed, staring at Adelaide in an entirely different light. "Where's that kid now?"

I shrugged. "She miscarried it," I said quietly. That night flashed to my mind. There had been so much blood – both from her stomach and from between her legs. A chill raced down my spine. Adelaide would never know it, but that night, I had been absolutely terrified that she wasn't going to make it.

Adelaide whimpered in her sleep, her eyebrows pulling together. I instantly walked towards the bed as she whimpered out a 'no', her hands closing into fists on the bed beside her head. I pulled her into my arms, gently coaxing her awake from her nightmare.

When she finally did, tears slowly trickled down her cheeks as she buried her face against my chest. I cradled the back of her head, my other arm wrapping tightly around her body.

I fucking hated that she was going through this shit.

"River, the hospital just called. Tristan is fucking awake." Jesup rushed out from his position at the doorway, making both Adelaide and I jerk our heads up to look at him. "No one knows how, but he's fucking awake, and he's asking for Adelaide."

Adelaide slid off of my lap, and she closed the room door, shrugging out of her plaid pajama pants and into a pair of her stretchy jeans and a tank top. I picked Axel up out of his pack 'n' play. "Tell

Sam I said to head to the hospital with you," I instructed her. "I'll get Axel's shit together and meet you guys there."

Her wide, dark eyes met mine. "Are you sure?" She asked me, her eyes showing how nervous and unsure she was about going to see Tristan without me.

I nodded, leaning down to press a hard kiss to her lips. "Go," I ordered.

She needed to be with him. I may not like how much she seemed to lean on him, but I understood it.

■ ■ ■

ADELAIDE

I stepped into Tristan's hospital room, my heart beating rapidly in my chest, so fucking happy that he was awake, yet, at the same time, I was a little bit nervous to face him without River by my side.

Tristan was sitting up, texting on his phone. He looked up as I entered. "That was pretty fucking fast." He noted, breaking the silence as I let the door fall shut behind me.

I shrugged at him. "River brought me to town as soon as Jesup called him and told him you had been shot."

Tristan shook his head, a scowl on his features. I bristled. "I'll never understand River." He quietly admitted.

I stuffed my hands into the pockets of my leather jacket. "River is secure in the knowledge that I'll never leave him or cheat on him with another man," I informed him. Tristan scoffed. That familiar guilt surged within me. "And he knows that despite mine and your past, I do still care a lot about you, and I worry about you."

Tristan leaned his head back against the bed, seeming to drop that specific topic of conversation. "Dumb of him to let you come here by yourself considering the mother fucker that shot me is still running around," Tristan grumbled.

I scowled, defensively crossing my arms over my chest. "For your information, River had Sam bring me up here since he had to get Axel's shit together." I snapped.

"Who the fuck is Axel?" Tristan demanded, his eyes flickering to my stomach only to see that I was still very much pregnant.

"My nephew." River spoke up as he strode into the room, holding Axel's car seat in one hand with the small diaper bag in his other hand. He set Axel and the diaper bag down and pressed a light kiss to the top of my head, relaxing me.

I knelt and unhooked Axel from his car seat, lifting him and cradling him in my arms as he opened his beautiful, blue eyes and looked up at me. I smiled down at him as I rubbed my fingers over his chubby cheek. He gurgled as he reached up to put his hands on my face.

"Kid looks a hell of a lot like you, River," Tristan admitted as he looked at Axel.

River shrugged. "Red didn't want him, so Adelaide told him she would take him. We're parents a bit earlier than expected." But River smiled at me – that smile that told me everything was okay – that everything would continue to be okay.

I looked at Tristan. "So, Jesup said that Frederick was doing some shit on the side, and when you confronted him, he shot you," I said, spiking up that conversation. I wanted to know what the fuck was going on.

Tristan shrugged. "Something like that." He said gruffly – evasively.

Fuck, I hated it when he did this shit. He didn't like anyone outside of the members that sat at his table knowing anything, and he liked even less when women tried getting in the middle of things.

"Spill." I snapped at him.

Tristan scowled at me. "You're in no fucking position to be making fucking demands, Addy." He snarled. "You're a club woman. Remember your fucking place."

I glared at him, opening my mouth to snap back at him, but River beat me to it. "Watch your fucking tone with her." River warned coolly. "What exactly happened, Grim?" River demanded to know. "And don't you dare fucking hold back information just because she's in the fucking room. She's my old lady. I determine what she knows and doesn't know. She deserves to know this."

Tristan glared at him for a moment. River's expression didn't change. He just looked at Tristan with cool eyes, waiting on Tristan to begin explaining what the fuck had happened.

Finally, Tristan grunted in displeasure. "Some fucking how, he got wind of Adelaide's pregnancy, and he was under the pretense that it was my kid." I tensed, and I felt River step closer to me on instinct, his hands settling over my hips. "I confronted him to tell him to keep his mouth shut about it – that no one else was supposed to know. Frederick is being paid by someone to get his hands on Adelaide because they know I would go to extreme lengths to make sure that she's safe and protected." Tristan clenched his jaw. "I don't know what they want from me, but Adelaide isn't safe – especially not here."

River stepped around me, his glare fixed on Tristan. The door opened behind me, and Joey stepped in. He flashed me a warm smile that made my heart flutter in my chest before he focused his attention on the scene in front of him. "You should have fucking called me the second someone got wind of her being pregnant!" River barked at Tristan.

"Woah; what the fuck is going on?" Joey demanded as he stepped to my other side, his muscular arms crossing over his chest.

River released a humorless laugh. I swallowed thickly. River angry and pissed at Tristan? I could handle it. I knew he wouldn't hurt Tristan because River loved me too much.

Joey, though? He may love me, may have changed for me, but putting my life in danger drew the line for Joey. He would drop bodies regardless of the pain it caused me.

"Fucking dimwit here decided that instead of informing me that someone is after Adelaide to get to him, he would take care of shit himself. Now, the mother fucker – the only person we know that holds the answers we need – is fucking MIA, and Tristan got himself shot trying to *talk* to the fucker instead of getting the answers he needed and putting a goddamn bullet through the traitor's skull."

Joey moved to lurch forward, but River intercepted him despite the pure rage simmering in his gaze. "You hurt him, you're fucking hurting her." River growled at Joey.

Joey's eyes flashed dangerously. I shifted Axel to one arm and settled my hand over Joey's bicep. His jaw flexed as he turned to look down at me.

"I'm holding you with me," I whispered, willing him to stay with me and to not hurt Tristan, silently *begging* him not to.

He leaned down and brushed his lips to my forehead. My heart squeezed in my chest. "I'm stepping out. River, I'll catch up with you in a bit. I need to cool the fuck off, or I'll be eliminating one dumb fuck from your woman's life." He growled.

I frowned after Joey as he stormed out of the room.

"I was trying to do fucking damage control without worrying Adelaide." Tristan snapped at River, drawing River's attention back to him. "I knew the second I told you, you would tell Adelaide because you just can't keep your fucking woman out of club shit. Adelaide is too unpredictable – can't fucking trust her to not take shit into her own hands. This is club shit."

"This *club shit* involves her!" River roared at him, stepping back from me as he started losing his cool.

I reached out to River, gripping his cut. He swung his burning, blue eyes to me. "Stay with me," I whispered.

He drew in a deep breath, nodding once at me before he turned his attention back to Tristan.

"Fucking hell, Tristan, I tell Adelaide shit because if she knows, then she can take necessary measures on her part to keep herself safe, and she won't feel fucking trapped when I do what I have to do so that she's protected." River growled, but he wasn't shouting anymore. "You still haven't grasped that fucking concept when it comes to her. Keeping her in the dark about shit will only get her stuck in the same fucking position she got herself into a year ago, or it'll send her back into that same fucking hole she got into with Joey."

"River," I called softly, knowing his words were cutting me, no matter how true they were. I was doing my damnest to not be that woman anymore, and he knew that.

River shook his head at me, his blue eyes blazing with rage. I swallowed thickly. "Nah, Darlin', he needs to hear this shit. You and everyone else has sugar-coated this shit way too much. Yes, you made some dumb ass decisions on your part, but Tristan played a fucking hand, too. I don't give a fucking shit how close you two are. I will *never* trust him to keep you safe because he just can't seem to fucking understand how to do it."

Axel began crying in my arms, and I bounced him gently, quieting his cries. "Watch yourself, River," I warned him softly, my guard going up hard against him to protect myself.

River stepped up close to me, his hands clamping down on my hips as I moved to take a step back from him. His grip held me in place. "Remember what I told you?" He asked me gently. "I will *never* lash out at you, Adelaide. But you and Tristan are extremely toxic for each other. I promised you that I would never make you choose between me and someone else, and I'm not going to, but I will step in when it's necessary to make sure that you, Axel, and our unborn baby are safe, and right now, Tristan needs to understand that this was a dumb ass fucking decision on his part. He put you in grave danger. It's not just you that all of us have to worry about anymore. You're pregnant, and you're Axel's mom. He should have been thinking clearer instead of being prideful and deciding to not reach out for help."

He pressed his lips to my forehead for a moment, and he didn't move back until he felt me relax some. "There you go." He whispered. He gently pressed his lips to mine before he turned to face Tristan again. "I want to know how anyone found out about Adelaide being pregnant in the first place." River ordered. "She fucking lives with me, Grim, and not a fucking person besides Sam knows she's pregnant, so how the fuck did the news get out in your fucking club and Adelaide isn't even fucking here with you?"

Tristan fisted his hands on his lap, and I knew he was restraining himself from destroying something. He wasn't used to people talking to him like this, but he knew River was a force to be reckoned with. It was one of the reasons he had always trusted River with me over anyone else, even his own VP.

His only mistake was that River had betrayed him by sleeping with me because River's loyalty to me ran a hell of a lot deeper than it did to his president.

"Frederick has to have people in his pocket." Tristan finally told him. "I don't know how the fuck he found out, but he knows,

River, and Adelaide is in danger. He had no idea she was with you, so that may work in your favor."

A smirk twisted River's lips as he looked over at me. I already knew what he was thinking before he even spoke.

"You want to finally let people know that I'm with you and that the baby is yours," I stated more than asked.

River nodded in agreement. "It's time to let everyone know that you're mine, Darlin', and any mother fucker that tries to fuck with you has another thing coming for them because everyone knows that I'm *not* the one to be fucked with."

Joey stepped back into the room, looking a lot calmer this time. I honestly hadn't expected him to come back to the hospital at all. He said he wouldn't get back with River until later.

"Include me in that," Joey said, looking to River. River nodded once. "Someone wants to be stupid enough to fuck with her, they fuck with my entire club." He growled.

Joey looked at me, his dark eyes clashing with mine.

He was letting me keep him with me.

I let a small smile touch my lips. He nodded once at me, his lips twitching, but he didn't smile. "Always, pretty girl." He promised.

My heart swelled in my chest.

Tristan looked between the three of us with confusion in his eyes, but River only slid his hand along the back of my neck, drawing my lips up to his for a soft, slow kiss.

"Hold him with you." He whispered against my lips.

TWENTY-FOUR

RIVER

Three weeks.

It had been three weeks since Tristan had gotten shot and since I had made it known that Adelaide was *my* woman – not Tristan's.

Someone could try to fuck with her if they wanted, but she would be the last person they would go after. Either Joey or I would make sure of it. It all depended on who got to the dumb son of a bitch first.

After what I had learned in the hospital room, I had taken Adelaide home the very next day, not wanting to risk something happening to her or Axel because of the shit Tristan had going on with Frederick. His dumb ass hadn't even told his own VP what was going on with Frederick – not the full extent.

Secrets in a brotherhood led to deaths, and I didn't want my woman around that kind of shit.

I held Axel on my hip as I shook his bottle. Sam was leaning against the kitchen counter in front of me while Reina made breakfast for all of us. She seemed to be dealing with what happened to her okay, though I knew she still went to Adelaide a lot when she felt bothered by it.

"Is Adelaide up yet?" Sam asked me as I shifted Axel in my arm so I could feed him since he was still too young to hold his bottle.

I shook my head at him. "Jaxon kept her up a lot last night," I informed him. "So, she didn't get much sleep."

About a week ago, Adelaide went in for her monthly check-up, and we were able to find out that she's going to be having a boy. Without hesitation, she named him Jaxon Tyler Boris. It felt nice to finally call our kid by a name instead of always calling him 'the baby'.

"I'm awake," Adelaide grumbled as she stepped into the kitchen.

I let my eyes run over her. She hadn't bothered to brush her hair yet and had instead just thrown it up into a messy bun on her head with a few strands falling out around her face. She had a red line on her cheek from where she had obviously slept in one position for too long. Her belly was rounded out now, and she couldn't hide it anymore, so she was just wearing a plain black tank top and a pair of stretchy shorts since it was pretty warm outside.

Fuck, even though she had just rolled out of bed, she was still the most beautiful woman I had ever laid my eyes on. Without any effort on her part, she always made the blood in my veins head straight to my cock.

She placed her hand on her belly at the same time that I saw Jaxon swipe either his hand or his foot against her belly. "He's awake." She mumbled, making me laugh softly as I leaned down to press a kiss to her sweet lips – always so sweet.

"I swear, you get bigger by the day," Sam commented, watching her belly with fascination as you could clearly see Jaxon move one of his extremities again.

Adelaide scowled at him, making me bark out a laugh. She had a low tolerance for little comments like that, even if they were harmless. "Thank you for stating the obvious." She snapped. Sam laughed. He got a kick out of getting on her nerves. "There *is* a growing human being inside of me." She reminded him.

He rolled his eyes at her, already used to her smart-ass mouth by now. One of the men stepped into the kitchen and put an arm around Adelaide's shoulders, giving it a gentle squeeze. "Ma, River," Henry started, speaking to both of us, "Olive mentioned to me that there's a small fair happening in town today, and they still have a spot open. I think it would do us all some good to raise some money for the kids in town here."

I looked at Adelaide only to find her already looking at me. She shrugged at me. "I think it's a good idea." She told me. "It's a nice day out, and I could use some sunshine." I pursed my lips, not sure about having her out in that heat or Axel. It was already hot outside, and it was only going to get hotter as the day wore on – somewhere close to a hundred degrees.

She pouted at me. I sighed. She knew that look would work ninety-nine percent of the time. "They'll have plugs out there, so we can have a fan blowing on Axel while he's in his pack 'n' play to keep him cool, and we can just drape a sheet over the pack 'n' play to keep the sun off of his skin." She reasoned with me.

I looked back at Henry. "If she's in, I'm in." I finally told him. He grinned, knowing I only agreed because Adelaide wanted to go and help the community. "Tell your wife to secure us that spot."

He nodded, and with another gentle squeeze to Adelaide's shoulders, he released her and pulled out his phone, walking back out of the kitchen. Adelaide shook her head slightly. "It's going to take me a minute to get used to all of the men calling me Ma." She admitted.

I smiled down at her. "You're my woman now, Darlin'." She smiled at me, making my heart swell in my chest. "The men will look to you as a mom - a guider of sorts." I reminded her.

Since I had made it known that Adelaide was carrying my son and that she was definitely around to stay, the men had taken to her a lot better. I get why they were a bit hostile towards her - besides Val and Joseph, of course. She was an outsider, and not to mention they all knew she was the reason I got kicked out of the Sons of Death, though it had all been worth it to have a taste of her.

Because now, Adelaide was by my side where she had belonged all along.

I caught her laughing at her phone a moment later. She flashed me a grin. "Joey said to make sure I don't get sunburnt and that I better get sprayed with sunscreen every hour." She told me, a teasing smile playing on her lips.

I rolled my eyes. "Tell him to mind his own fucking business." I retorted.

She only giggled before she leaned down to press a kiss to Axel's forehead since he was still drinking his milk. She blew me a kiss before she sauntered out of the kitchen, gently pulling Reina away from the stove and ordering another club woman to finish breakfast as she did so.

God, she was perfect.

■ ■ ■

I stood to the side of the section we were assigned on the fairgrounds. It'd taken a little less than thirty minutes to unload all the tables and grills and get them set up. The club had jumped in to help, and some of the men even scolded Adelaide and Reina when they tried to help. Some had gotten their heads bit off by my woman, but when one of them ran and grabbed her a corndog, she settled down.

Women were a different level of crazy when they were hungry – and pregnant.

I watched as Adelaide and Reina talked to the people in our town that came up to the table to buy burgers and hot dogs. Sam and I were manning the grill, leaving the two women to deal with everyone else.

Adelaide was a natural at this shit. You wouldn't think so when you first met her, but she had a way with people that had them wanting to talk to her despite how blunt she was.

The people in this town looked up to the Fathers of Mayhem. We didn't bring trouble here, and we helped out when we could by doing things like this for the community. Though my club dealt with illegal shit, never – not in the thirty-something years this club has been established – has shit ever come home.

And it was going to stay that way because I wanted this community to continue to be able to rely on us and trust us.

I looked over at Sam to find his eyes locked on Reina, his eyes unreadable as he watched her. "You would be good for her," I commented, making him drag his eyes off of her to look at me.

He arched an eyebrow at me. "What the fuck are you talking about now, River?" He demanded.

I shrugged, gesturing towards Reina with the hand holding my water bottle. "Her." He grunted. "I caught you staring at her, Sam. You know shit doesn't slide past me."

He stuffed his hands into the pockets of his jeans. "That woman is going through too much shit right now to want anything to do with a man," Sam informed me. "Gregory made sure he fucked her up good."

I walked over to the grill to flip the burgers and turn the hot dogs. Sam followed me. "You won't know unless you try," I told him. "Adelaide went through her own shit, and she still let me close." I reminded him.

"Adelaide is different from Reina, River." He reminded me.

I looked over to where the two women were laughing at something together. Adelaide placed her hand on her belly right as I saw Jaxon move, and I felt a smile twitch at my lips. She had a second sense for when he was about to kick or hit her belly.

"Just give it a try, Sam." I told him as I closed the lid back on the grill and moved over to check on Axel who was sleeping peacefully in his pack 'n' play.

"River!" A woman exclaimed loudly, making me jerk my head up. A blonde woman was making her way over to our table. She launched herself at me and wrapped her arms around my neck. I narrowly missed her trying to kiss me.

With a growl, I pried her off of me, scowling down at her. "What the fuck do you think you're doing?" I demanded of my ex-wife as I crossed my arms over my chest, glaring down at her.

"I told you that I was coming back to town to make things right between us, River." She told me, making me only arch an eyebrow at her considering I had never gotten a text or a phone call. "You told me okay, so here I am."

I shook my head at her. "You had the wrong number, Lindsey," I informed her. I jerked my head in the direction of Adelaide who was helping a customer, but I could tell her body was tensed. She was aware of what was happening behind her, and I hated that my fucking crazy ex-wife was the reason why my woman's mood soured. "Because even if you'd had the right number, I would have told you to keep your ass right wherever the hell you ran away to when you signed your name on those divorce papers."

Hurt flickered across her face at my words. Adelaide stepped up beside me, looking Lindsey up and down, taking in her dyed, blonde hair and make-up-caked face. Lindsey was slim, and she had obviously toned up over the years. She looked a hell of a lot different from the young, eighteen-year-old girl that I had married all those years ago.

But she didn't compare to the woman at my side – never would be able to. Adelaide was it for me.

"Who the fuck are you?" Adelaide demanded, her beautiful, brown eyes flashing dangerously.

"River's wife," Lindsey spoke smugly.

I opened my mouth to correct her, but Adelaide beat me to it. "Lie one more time, and I'll knock your teeth down your fucking throat." Adelaide snapped at her. Lindsey's eyes widened at her words, fear flashing in them as her face paled. I smirked. "Now, who the fuck are you?" Adelaide repeated.

"River's ex-wife." Lindsey corrected herself. I wrapped my arm around Adelaide's waist, leaning down to press my lips to her temple. She relaxed a little.

"River doesn't want you here, and I sure as hell don't, so turn the fuck around and go back to wherever the fuck you came from," Adelaide told her.

"And who the fuck are you?" Lindsey demanded, surprising me with the curse word that came out of her mouth.

The old Lindsey would have never even dreamed of speaking like that, and she had always hated that I did. It was one of the biggest causes of our fights. She wanted me to change, to be a gentler kind of man, and I refused to.

The woman you fall in love with isn't supposed to make you change your entire personality. She might change you just enough to make you a better man, but not an entirely different person. Lindsey wanted me to be someone new – someone that wasn't me.

"Adelaide is my woman," I informed Lindsey. "And she's the mother of both of my kids," I told her, thinking of how much of a mother she was to Axel even though she wasn't even blood related to him.

Lindsey looked down at Adelaide's belly, and I saw her face pale again. Me never wanting kids had been one of the reasons she and I had divorced. We both had so many conflicting views after we signed our marriage certificate that our marriage hadn't lasted very long at all. She wanted kids, a happy marriage with a house surrounded by a white picket fence, and nine to five jobs.

I was never that kind of man, and I never would be, though Adelaide had changed my mind about never wanting kids. I wanted a house full of kids, and I was already on the hunt for a house big enough for the number of kids that I wanted with her.

Another thing Lindsey could never wrap her head around was that I lived and breathed this club. Adelaide understood that, and she took to her role well as my old lady. She was a fucking natural at it all, and my club loved her – fucking worshipped the ground that she walked on.

"River." Lindsey spoke up, her voice trembling, and I saw her blink back tears. "I - I thought -"

"People change, Lindsey," I informed her. "And you and I would never work out, even if I gave you everything you wanted because then that would mean I would have been miserable. You could never embrace this life. You hated it way too much. You were demanding too much from me, and I couldn't give you everything that you wanted."

"I just wanted some of your time, River." Lindsey choked out.

I shook my head at her. "I couldn't give you as much as you wanted." I reminded her. "You wanted all of it, and my life revolved around the club – it still does."

Adelaide reached down and gently squeezed my hand before she went back to the table where a small line was forming for food. I watched her as she smiled and laughed with the customers, her pretty face lighting up. "Her, River?" Lindsey asked, drawing my eyes back to her bitter face. "She's nothing like the kind of women you normally settle for."

I looked back over at Adelaide for a moment before I looked back down at Lindsey. "She's everything I want in a woman and more, Lindsey. She's fucking remarkable. She knows the club life, and she embraces it. The club loves her, and they worship the ground that she walks on. She understands the role I play as the president. She's strong, and she doesn't crumble under the pressure that's put on her as my old lady." I shook my head. "You could never be even half of the woman that Adelaide is in my eyes."

Because Adelaide was my entire fucking world.

Lindsey shook her head and swiped at her cheeks as tears fell down her face. I just watched her, not feeling anything at how upset she was. "I had so much hope, River." She said, her voice breaking.

I stuffed my hands in my pockets. "I don't know why you did, Lindsey, because even if I wasn't with Adelaide, I still wouldn't take you back." I bluntly told her.

"I can handle it this time, River." She pleaded with me.

Nothing was going to change my mind. Even if Adelaide and I weren't together, I still wouldn't take Lindsey back. We were oil and water – toxic – never mixing.

"Really?" I demanded, not believing her for a second. "You would crumble at the slightest bit of fucking pressure." I reminded her. "You always have."

She shook her head and turned on her heel, walking off. Blowing out a harsh breath, I turned towards the grill where Sam was taking the burgers and hot dogs off. "Well, that was definitely unexpected," Sam commented.

I grunted. "I don't know why the fuck she thought I would have wanted to work shit out with her," I told him. "When we signed those divorce papers, we fucking hated each other."

Sam snorted. "Hate is a nice way to put it." He stated, obviously remembering the shouting and the destruction that happened almost daily between me and Lindsey. I broke so much shit when she and I argued that it was a miracle I ever had furniture in our damn room at the clubhouse - another place she fucking hated living in.

There were so many damn times that Sam had to get me out of the clubhouse and away from her before I did something I would have regretted.

Granted, I was a lot calmer now than I was back then, but I knew that Lindsey had a way of pushing all of my buttons.

"So, your ex seems . . ." Adelaide trailed as she stood next to me, trying to find the right word to use.

"A stuck-up bitch?" I asked as I wrapped an arm around her waist, turning to face her as I wrapped my other arm around her so her belly was pressed against my abs. Jaxon kicked her belly, and I smiled. I loved that feeling.

Adelaide shook her head. "More like a fucking cry baby." She corrected me. I barked out a laugh. She arched an eyebrow at me. "You actually went for women like that?"

I snorted. "Both of us didn't start showing who we really were until we were married," I told her. "Shit was too quick between us. But we were both young and stupid."

"Yeah, those two were toxic as fuck." Sam commented as he walked past us, going to take the hot dogs and hamburgers up to the table where Reina was at.

I leaned down and kissed Adelaide, groaning softly as she opened her lips beneath mine, allowing me to slide my tongue with hers. She moaned quietly, her hands sliding under my shirt and running up my muscular back, making my muscles quiver beneath her touch.

I slowly pulled back from her, not wanting to end the kiss. But we were in public, and we also had people to feed. I pressed a kiss right beneath her ear, causing her to release a breathless moan. My cock twitched in my jeans. "I'll finish this tonight," I whispered into her ear before I pulled back from her, watching as her eyes slightly glazed over. She aimed a slow, sexy smile in my direction that made my blood pound for her.

Fuck. When would this damn event be over?

■ ■ ■

I stepped into the bathroom after laying Axel down in his crib, letting my eyes run over Adelaide's naked figure under the water in the shower. Her breasts had gotten bigger, and they seemed to increase in size the bigger her belly got. Her hips were also widening slowly, growing in size to accommodate Jaxon.

She continued to look even more beautiful every single day. I loved watching her body grow and change to accommodate our baby.

I pulled my clothes off and stepped into the shower with her, watching as she slowly opened her eyes and looked up at me, her beautiful, dark eyes locking on mine. She ran her eyes over my body, and she slowly licked her lips, making me groan slightly.

This woman was fucking insatiable, but I didn't mind. I enjoyed every moment of pleasing her perfect body.

I reached out and drew her against me, leaning down to press my lips to hers. She stopped kissing me all too soon, but she began trailing kisses all over my chest, making me close my eyes as I relished in the feeling of her lips moving over my body.

I released a low growl and closed my eyes as I felt her palm my cock, her lips following soon after. "Fuck!" I moaned, throwing my head back against the wall of the shower as she began giving me the best fucking head of my entire life. Her tongue slid along the underside of my cock before she drew me as deep as she could, my cock hitting her tonsils. She didn't even gag. She fisted the part of my dick that she couldn't fit into her mouth, working it in tempo with her mouth.

When I felt myself getting close to coming, I pulled back from her and reached down to pull her up from her kneeling position, roughly slanting my lips over hers, yanking her hard up against me. I quickly slipped my hand between her legs and slid a finger between her wet folds. She gasped, moaning loudly. I tightened my arm around her as I watched her face contort with pure bliss as her lips slowly parted as I slid a finger in her slick heat.

Fuck, she was so wet for me.

"Fuck this shower right now," I grumbled, reaching forward to shut the water off.

I quickly swept her up into my arms and aggressively kissed her as I carried her into the bedroom. I laid her down on the bed and came over her, using my arms to keep my body weight off of her as I placed my lips on hers again.

"River, please." She begged me, her hands running over my body almost frantically.

I lifted one of her legs so it hooked around my hips, and I swiftly entered her. She dug her nails into my back as I pushed in and out of her, being careful not to hurt her, but still managing to fuck her the way she loved to be fucked.

She wanted to feel like I was claiming her as mine all over again.

When we finally came, we came together, and it was a goddamn explosion when we did.

■ ■ ■

Adelaide was passed out next to me despite the sheets and blankets being wet from us having sex without drying off from the shower. Me? I couldn't sleep on this fucking cold, wet bed. I didn't know how the fuck Adelaide was managing to.

I shot a text to Sam asking him to have Reina bring some fresh sheets and blankets. I got out of the bed and slid on a pair of sweats and covered Adelaide up with a small throw blanket before I lifted her out of the bed right as Reina lightly knocked on the door.

"Come in." I gruffly called back.

She stepped into the room, her cheeks flushing red as she quickly figured out the reason the sheets and blankets had to be changed. Sam leaned against the door frame, a smirk tilting his lips.

I just rolled my eyes at my VP. He released a quiet laugh as he shook his head.

Axel began whimpering, and without having to be asked, Sam walked over to him and lifted him from the crib, instantly quieting him since my hands were full with Adelaide. Reina made the bed in record time, and I gently laid Adelaide back down, covering her up with the blanket. Brushing my lips over her forehead, I softly whispered that I loved her before I walked over to Sam. He handed me Axel. "I'll go make him a bottle," Reina told me.

"Thanks." I gruffly told her.

She left the room, and Sam watched her until she disappeared from sight. I just shook my head, hoping he would stop being stupid soon and make his move before one of my other men did.

"Been meaning to ask you a question, Prez," Sam said quietly as he looked down at Axel. Axel stared back up at him in open curiosity.

"What's that?" I asked him, grabbing the spit-up cloth from Axel's changing table to clean his mouth where he had drooled a little.

"When you step down, is Axel or Jaxon getting the president position?" Sam asked me.

"Axel," I told him. There was no question about it. He may not biologically be my son, but he was the first born of my children, nonetheless. When he was old enough, he'd have an option – leave when he was eighteen to lead a clean, legal life, or stay here and learn how to be a better president than I was.

Sam nodded. "If you raise him to be anything like you and Adelaide, River, he'll make a fucking damn good president."

I grunted in agreement. If I had anything to do with it, he would be one of the best damn presidents this club had ever seen.

TWENTY-FIVE

I crossed my arms over my chest as I stood outside of my clubhouse doors, watching Tristan and Jesup ride onto my lot unannounced. To say that I was pissed that they hadn't told me they were coming was an understatement.

Anyone could have followed them up here. At least if they had informed me, I could have put up proper safety measures around town and my clubhouse to make sure that they weren't tailed by anyone.

But no, just as it was always Tristan's style, he did whatever the fuck he wanted to do without regard to the woman he was supposedly in love with. I was at my goddamn wits end with him.

"What the fuck are they doing here, River?" Sam asked as he stepped up beside me, his eyes narrowed on the two idiots riding onto my lot.

"Fuck if I know," I answered gruffly. "I had no fucking idea they were riding in," I informed my VP. I clenched my jaw.

Reina poked her head outside, and I met her eyes coolly, arching a single eyebrow at her in question. She swallowed nervously but kept her gaze on mine. I felt proud of her. She was slowly coming out of her shell, being braver, and I had my woman to thank for Reina finally becoming stronger.

"River, Adelaide just got sick all over the kitchen floor." She informed me.

"Fuck." I cursed. I looked at Sam. "Don't let them into this clubhouse until I come back out to find out what the fuck they're here for," I ordered before I turned around and strode into the clubhouse, heading for the kitchen to go take care of my woman.

Adelaide was bent over, dry heaving into the trash can that Reina had probably put in front of her. "Reina, get one of the women to clean this kitchen up, and then make Axel a bottle. It should be almost time for him to eat." I knelt so that I was at eye level with Adelaide. She looked up at me through teary eyes, breaking my heart. Her face was pale, and she gagged again, squeezing her eyes shut as she did so. "Can you make it to our room if I carry you, Darlin'?" I asked her gently, reaching out to push some of her dark hair behind her ear.

She nodded, slowly standing back up to her full height. She was pale and swaying slightly on her feet, her hand reaching out for me to hold herself upright. I quickly slid my arms under her back and her knees to lift her against my chest, striding out of the kitchen to take her to our bathroom. Her skin was practically on fire, and I knew if I couldn't get this fever to break soon, I would need to take her to the doctor.

Adelaide *hated* doctors. Hell, she barely tolerated her OB.

I pressed my lips to her forehead before I sat her down on the closed toilet seat. "Sit right there for a minute," I told her before I strode back into the bedroom and grabbed some Tylenol for her to take to see if I could get the fever to break. Tylenol was safe for her to take during her pregnancy, and I knew if I had to take her to a doctor, this is what they would prescribe her for her fever anyway.

When I strode back into the bathroom, she was leaning her head back against the towel rack behind the toilet, her eyes closed.

Sweat trickled down the side of her face. I frowned. Fuck, I hated that she felt like shit. "Adelaide, Darlin', I need you to take this." I coaxed as I knelt in front of her.

She slowly opened her eyes, taking the bottle of water I had grabbed and the Tylenol from me. "Do you want to lay in here, or do you want me to put you in bed with a trash can?" I asked her as I soothingly rubbed her belly, feeling Jaxon kick beneath my hand. Adelaide moaned in discomfort, her hand weakly reaching up to wipe the sweat from her face.

Jaxon moved under my hand again, already seeming to know my touch. "Bed." She grumbled. "Is Axel going to be alright?" She asked.

I lifted her easily, loving that she was such a good mom that she was still worried about him despite how ill she was. "Yes, Darlin'. Reina has him, and I'll take over from her when I find out why Tristan and Jesup are here."

She looked up at me tiredly. "They're here?" She asked, a frown marring her forehead. She didn't look happy that they were here, and that surprised me. Normally, she would be ecstatic.

Guess after what Tristan did to try to 'protect' her, she wasn't too happy with him.

I nodded, clenching my jaw. This was the last damn thing she needed on top of her being sick. "I'll come in to check on you in a little while, Darlin'," I told her as I laid her on the bed. "Try to get some rest," I instructed as I grabbed the little trash can and set it beside the bed.

"I love you, River." She mumbled, her words almost incoherent as she snuggled into my pillow, passing out almost immediately.

A small smile touched my lips. "I love you, too, Darlin'." I softly told her, though I knew she wouldn't hear me. She was already lightly snoring, her illness making her extremely tired.

When I stepped outside, Tristan and Jesup were standing beside their bikes talking to Sam. "What the fuck are you doing here?" I demanded as I strode up.

All three men turned their eyes to me as I strode across the gravel lot towards them. "We need help," Tristan told me. "This conversation can't happen over a phone, and I couldn't warn you in advance that I was coming. My club is fucking falling apart. I've got a rat, and I don't know who the fuck it is. We were fucking ambushed yesterday on a run - lost three fucking guys. Three days ago, my fucking clubhouse got shot up."

"They took Zyla." Jesup interrupted him as he shoved his hands through his hair. He was stressed and tired. Dark circles were imprinted under his eyes, and he looked like he hadn't slept in days. "Goddammit, River, even if you don't decide to help the club, just help me get Zyla back." He begged me.

I'd always liked Jesup more than Tristan, and if you asked me, I always thought Jesup would have made a better president than Tristan. He was calmer and more collected than Tristan - better at making decisions - and he was damn good at reading people. I also had mad respect for him for keeping his mouth shut even though he figured out with only one look that I had feelings for Adelaide.

"How long has she been missing?" I asked, giving Jesup my undivided attention. I frankly didn't give a fuck about what Tristan had to say. I would help Jesup because no woman deserved to go through the hell that Zyla was probably going through at that moment.

"She was taken yesterday when we got ambushed. I can't track her cell phone. Whoever took her left it lying in the club parking lot.

Everyone is claiming they didn't see her get taken. I'm at my wits fucking end, River." Jesup told me, sounding panicked.

"First, calm the fuck down," I told Jesup. "Panicking and losing your head isn't going to get her back home to you." I reminded him. He drew in a deep breath, nodding his head.

I looked at Sam, and he met my eyes, inclining his head to me, already knowing what I was thinking. I looked at Jesup. "I'm going to make some phone calls – see what I can find out. Give me three hours, and then we'll ride out of here back to your territory. I'll see what I can find out there." I told him.

"And do what with Adelaide?" Tristan demanded, finally speaking up, though I was enjoying his silence.

My eyes flashed with anger that he had the fucking audacity to question me about my woman – overstepping my boundaries about her. Only Joey had that privilege, but that was because he really did put her first, and he held her together – breathed life into her so she could live for me.

"Don't worry about what I do with my woman, Grim." I snapped. His eyes flashed dangerously at me, but I didn't give a fuck. "She's not your fucking concern anymore."

I turned on my heel and strode into the clubhouse. Reina was holding Axel in her arms as he played with a lock of her hair. "You," I told her as I walked up. She snapped her eyes up to me. "I need you to take care of Axel until Adelaide gets better. I've got to ride out in a few hours – don't know when I'll be back." I warned her. "Adelaide is sick as fuck. She's not capable of taking care of him right now."

She nodded in understanding. "I'll take care of him, River." She promised.

I nodded at her before I strode down the hall to my room, quietly opening the door so I wouldn't wake Adelaide up. I quickly packed a small duffel, and once I was done, I strode over to the bed, gently shaking her awake. I didn't want to disturb her, but I wouldn't leave without first letting her know where I was going and what was happening. She was my old lady – she needed to know – deserved to know.

She blinked up at me slowly, her tired eyes meeting mine. I ran my fingertips over her cheek, noting that her skin was still hot and clammy, but it wasn't as bad as before. The medicine was beginning to take effect. "I've got to ride out, Darlin'," I told her quietly.

"Why?" She asked, moving so she was closer to me. I slid my hand over her body, soothing her, wishing I could take her illness away and make it my own.

I ran my hand over her hair. "Zyla is missing," I informed her. She sucked in a sharp breath of air at the sound of her friend being missing. "Jesup needs my help."

"Find her, River." She begged me, those beautiful, exhausted brown eyes locking on my face.

"I will; I promise," I assured her as I ran my fingertips down her back. "I'm going to call Joey – have him ride in to keep an eye on things around here – keep you and Axel protected while I'm gone."

She nodded. I leaned forward and pressed my lips to her forehead, thankful that her fever seemed to be breaking. "Get some rest, Darlin'. I love you. Call me if you need me." I reminded her.

She nodded. "Be careful, River."

I smiled softly. "Always, Darlin'," I promised her.

I grabbed my duffel bag off of the floor and strode out of my room, quietly shutting the door behind me. I dropped my duffel at my feet so I could call Joey.

He answered on the first ring, just as I knew he would if I called him. "What's up?" He asked.

"I need you to ride up here," I told him. "I have to help Tristan and Jesup. They have someone on the inside ratting to outsiders. They've lost three members so far, and now Zyla is missing – been missing since yesterday."

"Can't believe you're helping that fucking asshole," Joey growled. I released a long sigh. This was why Adelaide was still my woman despite Joey changing. He would have put a bullet in Tristan's skull a long time ago for the shit he's done to her. "He does nothing but tear her down, River."

"She loves him." I reminded him. Because she loved him, I wouldn't let myself nor Joey harm Tristan. Even if she gave us the order to, I wouldn't let us. Because after he's lying cold and dead in front of her, she would lose a part of herself – the part of herself that had and would always belong to Tristan.

Joey sighed. "I know, and that fucker has no idea how precious that fucking love is." That, Joey had right. He didn't, and he never would. Adelaide didn't give her love freely, but when she did give it, she loved deep and hard. "Fuck. Yeah, I'll head up with Ink and a couple more of my men within the next fifteen minutes."

"Adelaide is sick," I informed him. Joey muttered a 'shit' under his breath. "High fever – throwing up. Reina is taking care of Axel until she's better. Just keep an eye on her – try to keep her fever broken so I don't have to haul her in to see a doctor."

"That woman hates doctors," Joey grunted. I laughed quietly. At least he knew that as well. "I'll take care of her, River. You can trust me." He reminded me.

"I know. That's why you're getting this phone call." I told him. "Shoot me a text when you've got your eyes on my woman," I ordered.

"Understood," Joey said.

I hung up and began making more phone calls, trying to get as much intel as I could before I rode out to the Sons of Death's territory – rode into a fucking war zone.

I knew Tristan's club wouldn't survive this. If it did, it would be a miracle, and there would only be a small ass club left behind – not the one he's built up over the years.

The Sons of Death's days were limited.

■ ■ ■

ADELAIDE

I groaned when I felt someone gently shake me awake. Blinking slowly, I looked up to see Joey knelt beside the bed. "Joey." I breathed, my voice sounding hoarse.

He gave me a small smile. "Hey, pretty girl." He greeted me as he reached out and tucked my hair behind my ear. "River told me you were sick. You feeling okay?"

I shrugged. "Could be better, but not as bad as earlier," I told him. "River gone?" I asked him.

He nodded. "He told me to tell you he would call as soon as he got to the Sons of Death's clubhouse."

I sleepily rubbed my eyes as I sat up, my belly prominent with the t-shirt I was wearing. I moved to slide out of bed, and Joey gripped my hands, helping me up. I smiled up at him as he chuckled. "You get bigger and bigger every time I see you." He told me. "You look beautiful, pretty girl. Got a pretty ass glow about you."

I ran my hand over my belly, feeling Jaxon move under my hand. "He's strong," I told Joey. He caressed my belly for a moment, that small smile for me never leaving his face. "I'm measuring pretty big – he's going to be as big as his damn dad when he gets older."

Joey chuckled as he laced his fingers through mine to lead me out of the room. "You need to eat so you can take some more medicine, pretty girl." He told me. I groaned. I hoped I held it down this time.

When I walked into the bar room with Joey, my eyes instantly landed on Reina. She was holding Axel on her hip as she shook a bottle. I walked to her and gently took Axel from her, smiling down at him. "Hey, little man." I cooed, taking the bottle from Reina as she handed it out to me. He instantly latched on when I put it to his lips, his beautiful, blue eyes – strangely so much like River's – staring back up at me.

Joey grabbed his little fist, smiling down at him. "Hey, kiddo." Joey greeted. He looked over at me. "Don't overdo yourself." He warned me.

I rolled my eyes at him. He only grinned before he leaned over and pressed his lips to my forehead. "I'm going to find you some soup. Sit your pretty little ass down somewhere." He ordered.

My phone went off as I was taking a seat on the couch, and Reina grabbed it out of my pocket for me and answered it, placing it on speaker for me. "Hello?" I asked as I finally sat down, adjusting Axel into a more comfortable position.

"Hey, Darlin'." River responded, making me smile.

"Hey." I breathed. "Everything good?" I asked him, so happy to hear his voice. He'd made it safely.

"Clubhouse is fucking trashed." I frowned. "Zyla's room has blood on the carpet – sign of a struggle. She didn't go calmly."

Fear for her settled in my gut. Zyla had already gone through so much hell. I only prayed that she didn't go through it again. "River, you have to find her," I begged him.

"Trying my best, Darlin'." He reminded me. I sighed. "Everyone is silent – won't even meet my fucking eyes. Someone here knows what happened." He told me. "No one was expecting Tristan to bring me in. They remember what I was like when I was here – how much I noticed. I'll find out who did this, Darlin', I promise."

I racked my brain trying to think of something – anything that could help him find her. "Fuck." I muttered. "It's got to be someone from Vin's circle," I told him. "It's the only thing that makes sense to me. They had to get power situated within their circle again, which is why it's taken them this long to do anything, but it makes sense why they were trying to come after me to get to Tristan. Tristan pulled that trigger."

"But Jesup was with him." River finished. "So, they went after the next best option to get their hands on Tristan and Jesup. Fuck." He muttered. "Not even going to lie, Darlin', I'd forgotten about him – been so fucking long since anyone heard from them, but I don't have a doubt in my mind that they haven't forgotten about what happened to Vin."

"Fredrick wouldn't go to these lengths to draw me out," I told River. "Something in my gut tells me that whoever is in power now is behind this, and if Zyla isn't found soon enough, she's never going to be coming back home," I warned him, fear settling in my gut.

A chill went down my spine as I remembered what Vin's men had been capable of doing to me when Vin had allowed them their turns with me.

It made me sick just to think about it.

"I'll find her, Darlin'. You've got my word. And when I find her, she'll be alive." He promised.

He hung up a moment later. Joey strolled over to me, his eyes narrowed down at me. I closed my eyes and drew in a deep, shaky breath. Joey knelt in front of me, his hands lightly gripping my thighs. "Talk to me, pretty girl."

I opened my eyes to look into his warm, dark eyes, holding him with me. "I think Vin's men may have Zyla." I swallowed thickly, tears filling my eyes. "She might die all because Tristan was so desperate to save me." I sobbed.

Joey sat on the couch next to me and lifted me onto his lap, wrapping his arms tight around me. Reina quickly lifted Axel from my arms, allowing me to tightly wrap my arms around Joey, sobbing into his shoulder.

Zyla, I'm so sorry. This is all my fault.

■ ■ ■

RIVER

I shoved my phone back into my pocket, hating that I wasn't there with Adelaide right now, but I knew Joey would take care of her. I knew this shit was going to hit her hard – after all, the only reason Vin's men wanted retaliation was because Tristan was an idiot and allowed himself to be seen when he sent a bullet through Vin's skull.

Which put him and all members of his club on their radar – not to mention anyone that might be attached to them.

I strode into the clubhouse. "Call church," I ordered Tristan, not giving a fuck about the boundaries that I was overstepping. They wanted my help? They were getting it – my way.

I strode into his chapel without waiting for another word. Jesup was sitting at the table with a glass of whiskey in front of him, but he hadn't touched it. "I think I've got something," I told him. "Adelaide thought of it." He looked up at me with hope in his eyes. I only hoped that my woman was right and that I wasn't giving the broken man in front of me false hope.

Men began to file into the room under Tristan's command. Tristan took his seat at the head of the table, but I remained standing. Sam stood at the door with Henry and Val. "Let's cut to the chase." I started. "All of you sitting here know I'm not fucking stupid. Somebody better speak up about their ties to Vin's men and you better tell me who the fuck is behind this shit."

Sam coughed slightly, and I looked over at him. He inclined his head to Dirk. I arched an eyebrow at Dirk. Sad to see him as a traitor, but every man had a price. My men kept their loyalty to me because I kept my payment high. Tristan had never learned that. "Something you want to share with me?" I asked him.

He clenched his jaw and shook his head. "I'm not a fucking traitor - unlike you." He snapped at me. I snorted. "Don't come making commands when you fucking betrayed the goddamn president himself."

Anger roared through my veins. Dirk had once been a pretty damn good friend of mine, but obviously, that had changed. And Tristan betrayed himself before I ever betrayed him. He betrayed himself by not loving a good woman correctly.

"At least I owned up to my shit, Dirk." I retorted. He clenched his jaw. "I was prepared to take the bullet in my skull for sleeping with her." I reminded him. "So, what the fuck do you know?" I asked him again.

He stayed silent. I looked up at the ceiling, slowly losing my fucking patience. The only person I had patience for was the woman currently waiting at home for me to come back to her.

"Aright, then." I snapped, pulling out my gun. Everyone squirmed uncomfortably, even Tristan. "I'm about to just start dropping fucking bodies." I snarled. "So, if someone values their fucking life, they better speak the fuck up *right now*," I ordered.

"I saw Dirk and Winston meeting up with a man named Calhoun a few nights ago – the night the clubhouse got shot up." Tank spoke up. Dirk's and Winston's eyes flashed with rage before they smothered it, but it was there long enough for me to catch it. "They caught me eavesdropping. I was going to call you with all of the information so you could protect Adelaide, but they saw me, and Calhoun threatened Adelaide if I opened my mouth, so I kept it shut."

Jesup got up and sent a right hook against Dirk's face. I heard a bone crunch in Dirk's face – most likely his nose – as he flew out of his seat to the floor. Winston got up, but Sam sent a solid punch against his temple, sending him crashing to the floor knocked out cold. "Get Tank out of the room," I ordered Henry. "Keep him isolated from the rest of the club because if there's more than one traitor, someone is going to shut him up," I told him.

Henry nodded, motioning for Tank to follow him. I clapped a hand on Tank's shoulder, bringing him to a stop for a moment. Like me, his loyalty had always resided with Adelaide. Fuck the President. Protect the woman. I had always had respect for him for that.

I nodded once at him in thanks. He clapped my back on his way past me as he continued following Henry out of the room.

"There are two of your traitors," I told Tristan. "Find out where Zyla is and find the rest of your traitors. Guarantee by the time you find all of them, you'll barely have a club left."

I strode out of the room, pulling my phone to my ear. Joey answered on the second ring. "Yeah?" He answered, his voice hushed. Knowing Adelaide, she had probably cried herself to sleep.

My heart squeezed painfully in my chest for her.

"You got your eye on Adelaide?" I asked him.

"Always." He responded. "She's passed out on the bed with Axel on her chest. I'm sitting in the rocker. What's up?" He asked.

"Tank caught Dirk and Winston talking to a man named Calhoun – said Calhoun threatened Adelaide if Tank opened his mouth. Don't take your eyes off of her and get one of your men on Reina." I told him, thinking of Sam and the attachment he seemed to be forming with her. "I want tight fucking security on my goddamn clubhouse," I ordered.

"You got it," Joey told me. "What are you going to do about Tank?" He asked.

"See if he wants to switch clubs," I told him honestly as I moved through the clubhouse, wanting some fucking fresh air. This clubhouse was fucking trashed and so were its members.

"What about Tristan?" Joey asked me. I grunted, frankly not giving a fuck about Tristan and his thoughts on it. "It's his choice in the end if he wants to let go of one of his members." Joey reminded me.

"Fuck Tristan." I snapped. Joey laughed. "Tank has always done a good job of protecting Adelaide, and Tristan doesn't treat his fucking men like he should. Besides, once this shit is taken care of, I doubt Grim will have much of a club left." I told him.

Gun shots rang out on the other end of the phone. I stopped in my tracks, my hand tightening around my phone. Joey shouted 'fuck' at the top of his lungs. "Adelaide, get the fuck up!" He roared.

My blood ran cold in my veins. This shit didn't happen on my territory. Someone had notified either Fredrick or Calhoun that I wasn't at the clubhouse anymore – that I was down here – a few hundred miles away from Adelaide.

"They'll be safe, River," Joey informed me before he hung up.

"Fuck it all to hell!" I roared, storming back into the chapel, fear and anger rushing through my veins. If something happened to my woman or my kids, I would tear this goddamn world apart. I slammed open the doors. "Put your fucking hands on the table!" I roared.

I pointed my weapon at Tristan when he didn't move with everyone else. "That includes you, Grim." I snarled. "Hands on the mother fucking table."

He warily eyed the gun in my hand as he did as I instructed. I was pissed. I didn't give a fuck anymore how Adelaide felt about him. Joey and I could bring her back to us, but Tristan was a hairsbreadth away from getting a fucking bullet put through his skull.

Tristan could tell I was at my fucking wits end. "Who the fuck snitched that I wasn't at home?" I demanded. No one spoke. "Fucking speak!" I roared.

"Fucking shoot." Jesup spoke up. "Zyla is at your clubhouse with Calhoun. I got it out of Dirk right as you burst through the doors."

I put a bullet through Dirk's head and one through Winston's, cleaning up the trash for Tristan. "I'm taking Tank with me." I snapped as I strode out of the room. "Jesup, if you want your woman, let's go. My clubhouse just got fucking ambushed." I turned my angry gaze to Tristan, letting my eyes meet his. "If Adelaide or Axel is hurt, or if she loses our baby, Tristan, I'll fucking kill you, do you understand me? I don't give a fuck *what* you mean to her right now. So, you better hope and pray that Joey fucking protected them." I snarled.

■ ■ ■

ADELAIDE

I held Axel tight to my chest as I paced the floor of the waiting room of the hospital, barely holding myself together. I was worried sick. Ink hadn't gotten to Reina in time, and she had taken a bullet to the shoulder and one to the thigh.

And she was in surgery for it.

"Pretty girl, you need to sit down before you walk yourself into an early labor," Joey commanded as he stood up and gently gripped my hips, stopping my pacing. "River isn't far out." He assured me.

"I'm scared for her, Joey," I told him, my bottom lip trembling. "She's already been through so much."

The doctor said she lost a lot of fucking blood – almost didn't make it to the hospital alive.

God, and then there was Zyla. She was bloody and unconscious when two of the club men found her behind the clubhouse.

Ink strode over to us. "The doctor just informed me that Zyla is going to be alright, and she'll be waking up in the next few hours."

I nodded at him. "Any word on Reina?"

He shook his head at me. "Afraid not." He said quietly. Guilt flashed in his eyes. "I'm sorry I didn't protect her, Adelaide."

I shook my head at him, blinking back the tears in my eyes. "It's not your fault." I hoarsely whispered. "She was showering. No one could expect you to be in the bathroom with her."

Axel began crying, and I bounced him up and down, wishing I could calm down so he wouldn't feel my stress. Joey drew me to him, holding me with my back to his front, his strength wrapping around me, holding me together as I tried my damnest to calm Axel. But his wailing only intensified, making a tear run down my cheek.

River strode through the waiting room doors at that moment with Sam, Jesup, and Tank behind him. A sob ripped from my throat as soon as I saw him. Joey quickly pressed a kiss to the top of my head before he let me go. I rushed towards River, and he met me halfway across the room, wrapping his arms around me tightly, sandwiching Axel between us as he pressed his lips to the top of my head.

"Still no news on Reina," Joey informed them. "Zyla will be awake in a few hours according to her doctor."

Jesup took off for the nurse's station. "What do we know about Reina so far?" Sam demanded to know as River led me over to a chair and forced me to sit down, taking a now whimpering Axel from my arms, instantly calming him down.

"She took a shot to the shoulder and to the thigh," Joey informed him. "She's in surgery, and she's lost a lot of blood. The doctor told us she barely made it here alive."

Sam swung his angry eyes to Ink who was meant to be protecting her. Ink swallowed thickly. "Why the *fuck* weren't you with her?" Sam snarled at Ink.

"She was coming out of the bathroom from a shower, Sam." Ink informed him. "I swear to God, I tried to get to her in time, but I'm not as fast as bullets." He told him.

Sam clenched his fists at his sides, his eyes flashing dangerously. "Sam." River snapped, drawing his VP's eyes to him. "Cool it down. I know you want to bash his face in, but this isn't the time nor the place."

Sam stepped back from Ink and stormed over to one of the windows to look out at the darkening sky, his back rigid with tension.

I rubbed my hand over my belly and winced in pain as I got a cramp. River's eyes instantly locked on mine, nothing getting past him. I shifted uncomfortably as the pain worsened. "Adelaide?" He asked as he moved closer to me, kneeling in front of me, his worried eyes running over my face.

"I think I need a doctor," I whispered, knowing this cramp all too well.

I only prayed that it wasn't what I thought it was – that I wasn't miscarrying. Not this late in my pregnancy.

I whimpered, tears filling my eyes. I couldn't lose Jaxon. I wouldn't survive the heartache.

Sam instantly took Axel from River. River lifted me into his arms, striding to the nurse's station. My eyes met Joey's. He watched helplessly, pain for me shining in his dark eyes.

Hold me with you, he mouthed.

I sobbed. River clutched my body tighter to his chest. "I need a doctor." River snapped at the nurse working the desk.

"I'm having contractions," I informed her when she opened her mouth to inform him that he would have to wait, as was normal protocol.

Her eyes widened, and she instantly paged for someone from labor and delivery. I whimpered as I got another strong contraction. River's jaw clenched as he pressed his lips to my forehead, trying to console me as much as console himself.

We were both terrified that I was losing our baby.

"They'll pay for all of this hell, Adelaide." River promised me as he laid me on the stretcher that a nurse brought over to us. "They'll pay." He swore.

I resisted the urge to wail as another contraction tightened my belly. The pain in my stomach was nothing compared to the pain in my heart. I was terrified.

"River," I cried, "stay with me," I begged him. "Fuck, please stay with me."

He brought my hand up to his lips as he hurriedly walked with the nurses beside the stretcher. "Always, Darlin'." He promised. "For as long as you'll have me."

TWENTY-SIX

RIVER

I closed my eyes, leaning my head back against the back of the chair that I was sitting in as I held Axel's sleeping form in my arms. Adelaide was passed out on the hospital bed. She had gone into labor, and the doctor had to give her a shot to stop her contractions.

I wanted to fucking drop bodies for the hell that she was going through right now – for making us almost lose our son.

Axel yawned as he came awake, his blue eyes locking onto my own instantly. "Hey, kid," I murmured.

He smiled his adorable, toothless smile at me in response. Adelaide whimpered, her features twisting with pain. I instantly got up from the chair and strode over to her. She whimpered out a 'no' before I gently shook her awake. Her beautiful, dark eyes snapped open, locking on my own. "You're okay." She breathed, her eyes welling up with tears.

I reached out and gently ran my thumb over her cheek. "I'm alright, Darlin'." I gently assured her. "You okay?" I asked.

She nodded. "I just had a nightmare." She said quietly. She held her arms out for Axel, and I handed him over, watching with soft eyes as she lifted Axel and blew on his belly, making him giggle.

She was a fucking incredible mom.

"How's Zyla and Reina?" Adelaide asked me, not taking her eyes off of Axel as he smiled up at her, his hands reaching for her hair.

"Zyla woke up for a little while," I told her. A tiny bit of tension left her shoulders. "She took a damn good beating, but she'll be alright. Her doctor is keeping her overnight for observation, but she'll be released sometime tomorrow morning most likely. Reina is awake, and she did fine in surgery. Sam is with her."

Adelaide's lips twitched with a smile as all of the tension finally left her shoulders, making her look so much more relaxed. "Think Sam will come around finally?" She asked me, not having missed the way my VP was with her friend.

I snorted. "The way he's ready to fucking bury Ink in a shallow grave for Reina being hurt? Pretty sure he's already come around, Darlin'."

"Tell me what happened at Tristan's." She ordered as she finally drew those beautiful, brown eyes over to me.

"Tank saw everything go down – Dirk and Winston met up with a man named Calhoun a couple of nights ago. Tank caught them. They threatened you if Tank told anyone, so Tank kept his mouth shut – wanting to protect you the best that he could."

"He always had a soft spot for me." She noted.

"I know, Darlin'," I told her. "Tank is back at the clubhouse doing some clean up with some of my other men. I'm patching him over." She smiled up at me for a moment before she suddenly frowned.

"What's going to happen to Tristan's club?" She asked me.

"Not much of a club anymore," I admitted to her. Her frown deepened. "So, we'll see what happens."

Someone knocked on the door, and I walked over to open it, a scowl settling on my features as my eyes met Tristan's.

Hadn't he done enough shit to her as it was? Couldn't my woman have one goddamn moment of peace before he came and destroyed it all?

"If I let you in this room, you need to watch what the fuck comes out of your mouth." I snapped at him. "She's going through enough shit without you adding onto it."

I wanted to send him away. Fuck, I didn't want him anywhere around her, but Adelaide would want to talk to him, especially after he'd just had his entire world flipped upside down.

She would want to comfort him.

I hated that she wanted to when she was the least of his concerns anymore.

Tristan nodded in understanding, but I knew him well enough to know that he was going to do something fucking stupid – just like he always seemed to do around her.

Nonetheless, I allowed him into the room, shutting the door behind him. Adelaide watched him with guarded eyes as she held Axel against her chest a little tighter. I stepped next to her bed on instinct. She was uneasy around him, and that had bells ringing in my head – bells of alarm. She knew something was wrong.

It was both an advantage and a disadvantage of her knowing him so well.

"What do you want, Tristan?" Adelaide asked him.

"I've fucking lost everything," Tristan told her. I growled softly. I knew he wouldn't keep his fucking word. "I've lost you, the club – every fucking thing. I don't even have my fucking sister anymore."

Adelaide swallowed hard, flinching at the mention of his sister – her best friend. Axel whimpered, picking up on her stress

317

instantly. She bounced him gently in her arms, quieting him almost immediately. "Tristan . . ." She trailed off, her tone giving off how nervous she was.

"I've got nothing to live for, Adelaide."

She snapped her eyes up to his, fear shining in their depths – fear that she was going to lose him, too. "Tristan, don't do anything stupid." She snapped as she clutched Axel to her, her breathing picking up speed as she began to panic. "River, don't let him do anything stupid." She desperately choked out, her eyes never leaving Tristan.

I ran my eyes over Tristan, watching as his fingers twitched. "Tristan, if you touch that fucking gun in your cut, I'll beat your fucking ass." I snarled at him as I stepped towards him, watching his hands for more movement.

"You've got her, River. What fucking more do you want from me?!" Tristan roared at me, completely losing his composure.

If Joey and I had our way, he'd no longer be a part of her life. But goddammit, she wanted him here with her, so he had to stay alive.

"I want you alive because you fucking mean something to her, dammit!" I snapped at him. "If you fucking kill yourself, Tristan, it'll fucking destroy her. She lost your sister; don't make her fucking lose you, too."

He barked out a humorless laugh as he threw his hands up in the air before letting them drop back to his sides. "Doesn't matter how I go out." Tristan snapped at me. "I've got the same fucking cancer my sister had." Adelaide sobbed. My heart broke for her. She was going to lose him, no matter how hard she tried to keep him alive. "I've got fucking cross hairs on my back. I'm going out soon no matter what."

"I can give you fucking protection in my club, Tristan," I told him, no matter how much I didn't fucking like it. "I can pay for your treatments. Shit doesn't have to end like this." I tried reasoning with him.

Tristan shook his head at me. "I wish it were that easy. I caught it too late. I'm on borrowed time. The cancer wasn't detected until I got shot. With something that sensitive and since the chances of me surviving were already slim to none, the doctor didn't inform anyone, though he did make note of what he found. I'm in stage five. It won't be long before my lungs collapse."

"No." Adelaide choked out.

We both turned to look at her. My heart shattered. Her expression was completely broken, tears pouring down her beautiful face. "I'm sorry, Addy baby," Tristan whispered. "I'm so fucking sorry. I fucked up everything between us. You've been trying to hold me with you, and I've destroyed all of that. I'm so fucking sorry."

A sob ripped from her lips. The machine that was monitoring her baby and her belly began to print out lines indicating a contraction, and the baby's heart rate spiked up – dangerously high. Adelaide cried out in pain, and I instantly rushed forward and took Axel from her. "River -" She gasped, fear filling her eyes.

I was lost. I didn't know what to do.

I didn't know how the fuck to help her.

"We need you gentleman to leave the room." The doctor stated as he rushed into the room to help her.

Adelaide cried out in pain again. Axel wailed, and I quickly bounced him. I pressed a kiss to Adelaide's forehead. "Live for me, Darlin'," I whispered. "Hold Joey with you."

She only screamed as I was shoved out of the room.

■ ■ ■

I held Axel to my chest as I paced the floor out in front of Adelaide's room. I'd never been a religious man, but at that moment, with her wails sounding out of the room through the closed door, I found myself praying for a fucking miracle.

God, please, don't take her from me.

Tristan was sitting on the floor, his head back against the wall. Joey was standing against the wall, his arms crossed over his chest. His jaw was clenched as he stared at the door, almost as if he were trying to will her pain away.

I only wished it were that fucking easy.

After what felt like an eternity, the door opened, and the doctor stepped out. "Mr. Boris?" He asked.

"Is she okay?" I asked him, so fucking nervous that I was actually sweating. I needed to know that she and Jaxon were both alive. If she lost him but survived, I would lose her. Joey wouldn't be able to breathe life back into her. She would be lost to both of us.

He smiled at me and nodded. "She's going to be just fine, Mr. Boris." I breathed a sigh of relief. Joey stood up from his leaning position and scrubbed his hands down his face, his shoulders deflating. "She's asleep right now, but she should be waking up in a little while. She went into premature labor, and I'm assuming she had an anxiety attack because she was saying that her chest was hurting – that she couldn't breathe, but we were able to stop her contractions and place an oxygen mask over her face. She's fine now." He assured me when I gave him a worried look. "I just ask that you keep visitors out of her room until we feel that her blood pressure won't spike again, which I'm inclined to think are causing the contractions."

I pointed to Joey. "Can he see her for a few minutes?" I asked the doctor. "You don't have to worry about him; I promise," I assured the doctor.

"Only for a few minutes." The doctor ordered. "If she wakes up while he's in there, try to keep it light-hearted. She's been under way too much stress."

Joey nodded his head at the doctor before he quicky slipped into the room. I stepped into Adelaide's hospital room with him, leaving Tristan on the floor in the hallway. If he had just fucking listened to me, this shit wouldn't have happened to her again.

My eyes instantly landed on Adelaide's pale form. I could tell that she had been crying before she passed out, and her hair was an absolute mess.

"Mommy's okay," I whispered to Axel. "Fucking hell, she's okay."

Joey's hands shook as he reached down to grab her face in his hands. I knew he was going to kiss her. I only gritted my teeth. Adelaide needed this.

"Breathe," Joey whispered. He soothed his lips over hers, barely letting them touch.

She slowly woke up, her eyes locking on his. He cupped her cheek, letting his other hand drop. "I need you to breathe, pretty girl, so you can live for River." He softly spoke. "Can you do that, pretty girl?"

She nodded, her bottom lip trembling. "He's leaving me." She choked out, referring to Tristan.

"Easy." Joey coaxed. "I know it's hard, but try not to think about it. Just focus on staying healthy for your family. River and I will do whatever we can to try to keep him here with you. We can't make promises, but we will try." He promised her. "Just hold me with you."

She nodded. He pressed his lips to her forehead. "The doc doesn't want you to have any visitors except for River, so I have to go, but I'll come to see you soon – I promise."

She nodded at him again. He pressed his lips to her temple. "Live for him." He whispered.

I dragged a chair over to her bed as Joey quietly slipped out of the room. Holding Axel in one arm, I held Adelaide's hand in the other, pressing my lips to the back of her hand. "Hold him with you," I whispered to her.

"I'm sorry he kissed me again."

I shrugged. "He does it to remind you that you can live," I told her. "When shit gets this bad for you, Darlin', you start dying inside. We both just want you to live."

"I'll always live for you." She told me.

I pressed my lips to the back of her hand again as I slouched down in my chair, getting comfortable. "That's all I ever ask, Darlin'."

I finally allowed my eyes to shut for a little while.

Thank you, God.

■ ■ ■

REINA

I groaned in pain as I slowly ripped my eyes open, wincing at the bright light in the room. My shoulder and my thigh were burning in excruciating pain. Was this what hell felt like? I was pretty sure it was.

"Fuck, you're awake," Sam grumbled from across the room.

I slowly turned my head to look at him, wincing when the movement only made pain flare up all over my body. I was both shocked and excited to see him here. I'd wanted Sam from the moment I laid my eyes on him, but he tended to avoid me like the plague.

He was coming out of the bathroom. He didn't have his cut on, and his hair was a mess, like he'd been running his fingers through it for the past few hours. "How are you feeling?" He gently asked as he came closer to me, running his dark eyes over me.

"Like hell," I muttered, a thrill running through me that he seemed to at least care about how I was feeling. "I'm in a tremendous amount of pain."

He brushed some of my hair out of my face in a tender gesture that had my heart rate spiking on the heart monitor. My lips softly parted. He glanced at the heart monitor for a moment before he looked back down at me. There was no amusement in his eyes to my reaction to his touch – ever the serious one.

It was one of the things that drew me to him. He seemed strong – capable of protecting me from the demons that haunted my soul. The real ones were dead, but the ones inside of me? They would never go away.

"To be expected." He said quietly. "You had to go through surgery for both of your gunshot wounds." He informed me.

I winced. That explained the burning, excruciating pain that I was feeling.

"Is everyone okay?" I asked him.

He shrugged. "Adelaide is facing some trouble." I frowned. Sam brushed his thumb over my cheek. "Too much stress. River is with her. Tristan has tipped over the fucking edge." I shrugged one shoulder at that, making him laugh huskily. I had never really liked Tristan. He was a complete dick, and he treated Adelaide like shit. "Jesup is with Zyla. She'll be released later on today."

"Why are you here with me?" I asked him quietly, asking the question that I was dying to know the answer to. Sam normally only interacted with me if he absolutely had to. I was ecstatic that he was here, finally showing me some attention, but I was curious, too, about why he suddenly decided to be around me.

Unless he was only following River's orders. That made me frown, dampening my mood.

He sighed. "When I got here and found out that you'd been shot – that you were in fucking surgery and no one had heard anything about you yet," he shook his head as he grabbed my hand in his, playing with my fingers, "I fucking saw red. I wanted blood for what had happened to you, and had I not been held back, Ink would be in a room here instead of walking around."

My breath hitched in my throat at his fierce words. He cared; he really fucking gave a damn. "He tried to protect me, Sam," I told him. "I promise that he did." I didn't want Ink getting in trouble for the shit that happened to me.

Sam shook his head, his jaw clenched. "He didn't fucking try hard enough, Reina. Almost losing you made me realize a fucking lot. I don't ever want to lose you, and I'm fucking done playing games – beating around the bush with this shit – trying to ignore it. I hope you're ready to stick around because I want you. I'm claiming you as mine."

My heart rate picked up speed again, doing double time in my chest. Sam gently gripped my chin between his thumb and index and slanted his lips across mine, kissing me like I'd wanted him to do from the very moment I laid my eyes on him.

I was lost in him – a complete fucking goner.

TWENTY-SEVEN

ADELAIDE

I held Axel on my hip as I walked into Tristan's room near the back of the clubhouse. He was having another one of those days I remembered his sister having all too well.

The days where he could barely find the energy to get out of bed.

It had been almost four months since Tristan had informed River and I of his condition. I was getting hopeful. He didn't seem that sick even though he was in stage five of his cancer. River had him religiously going to cancer treatments. Hell, even River and Joey had managed to talk Tristan into handing over his cut and giving Jesup the reins on what was left of the Sons of Death.

But I was hoping with every fiber of my being that he could beat this.

Tristan slowly opened his eyes as I opened the door to his room. He gave me a small smile, holding his hand out to me. I quickly moved towards him, placing my hand in his. My belly was swollen. I was honestly due any day now. My due date was only a couple of days away, but my doctor had a feeling that I was going to go past it. Jaxon wasn't settled correctly yet.

Being stubborn just like his damn father.

"You should eat something," I told him, watching as he only shut his eyes again.

"I'm not hungry, Addy." He told me gruffly. "I just want to sleep."

I sighed, taking a seat on the bed beside him as I held Axel on my knee. Without opening his eyes, Tristan settled his hand on my belly. Jaxon nudged his hand. "Tristan, not eating isn't going to help you keep any energy." I reminded him. The cancer treatments really fucking drained him.

He groaned. "It's only feeding the fucking cancer, Addy." He told me, his tone harsh. I sighed, staying silent. "It's killing me anyway." He grumbled after a moment.

I frowned. "Don't talk like that." I scolded him. He slowly opened his eyes. "You can't leave me, Tristan," I told him, my voice breaking.

"I'm sorry, Addy baby." He whispered.

A tear slid down my cheek. He reached up and brushed it away. "I wish I had done shit differently, even if you still ended up with River. Joey got it, but I never did – never wanted to. Now, your memory of me will always be tainted with the pain that I caused you."

"No." I choked out. "You got me out of that trap house when we were teenagers, Tristan." I reminded him, more tears sliding down my cheeks. "There were plenty of happy moments between us. This shit between us, it'll never taint those memories."

The door opened again, and River's large frame filled the doorway. He shook his head at me and stepped into the room. Leaning down, he brushed my tears off of my cheeks. "Don't cry, Darlin'." He soothed.

I sniffled. He leaned down and lightly brushed his lips with mine. "Easy." He crooned. I nodded my head at him. He stood up and looked at Tristan. "Come on, Grim. Up off the bed. Reina hasn't been barking orders at the women about breakfast for half the morning for no damn reason." River told him as I stood up from the bed.

River pressed a kiss to my temple. "Go eat." He told me before he looked down at Tristan. "Come on, Tristan. Get the hell up." River ordered.

Tristan huffed and sat up, coughing as he did so. It was a bad cough, too. His whole body shook with it, his face screwed up in pain. I stopped on my way to the door, worry clenching my chest.

River nodded his head towards the door. "Darlin', go." He coaxed. "I've got him."

With a sigh and a clenched jaw, I left the room, worry settled deep in my bones for Tristan.

I hadn't heard him cough like that before, and now I was worried that he had been leading me to believe he was still mostly okay.

Because a cough that bad? That meant the cancer was worsening.

All of my hope rushed down the drain.

■ ■ ■

RIVER

I watched as Tristan snatched the trash can from beside his bed, spitting out blood into it as soon as Adelaide stepped out of the room, shutting the door behind her. "How much longer do you have?" I asked him as he set the trash can back down and ran his hands down his face.

Tristan shrugged. "Doctor is giving me a month, two if I'm really lucky," Tristan informed me. "Lung cancer of all fucking things. I don't even fucking smoke." He released a bitter laugh. "What a fucking way to go out," Tristan grumbled as he shook his head.

"How do you plan on telling her?" I asked him, referring to Adelaide.

Tristan sighed. "I don't fucking want to, River. She doesn't need to worry about how much longer she has with me while she's pregnant and trying to take care of Axel. Fuck, man, she can have Jaxon any damn day now." Tristan looked over at me with tired eyes, and I realized right then how much he had been hiding from all of us. He looked fucking exhausted – like living right now was just too much for him to do anymore. "I know you tell her just about everything, River, but I don't want her to know this. Don't breathe a fucking word in her direction."

I blew out a harsh breath, knowing that what he was requesting was going against everything I believed in. I never kept shit from Adelaide. I told her everything. She and I had one hundred percent honesty with each other.

"River, I mean it. It's my one fucking death wish." Tristan told me. "I just want her to relax as much as she can. Can I please just let her have that after all of the shit that I've done to her?" He asked me.

Since Tristan finally saw what the fuck his selfishness did to her, he'd been different – gentler with her. He was careful about trying his best to stay calm, though they both always had a way of pressing the other's buttons.

Honestly, Joey punched Tristan in the face one day when Tristan and Adelaide were arguing about her needing to eat. When Tristan had angrily told her that she was a selfish mother, Joey had snapped and knocked Tristan unconscious. I hadn't been close enough to do it myself. But I did get my ass over there to hold her as she cried.

Adelaide ate when she was hungry, and Joey and I both knew that.

Tristan was just being a normal, overbearing asshole.

But despite him being an asshole, I would give him his one, dying wish.

I ran my hands down my face and nodded. "Alright, Grim," I grumbled. "I won't tell her."

He nodded in thanks and pushed himself up off of the bed with a groan, his arms shaking. He was getting weaker with each day that passed. It wouldn't be long before Joey and I stood next to Adelaide as she set up funeral arrangements for him.

"Let's go before she gets suspicious," Tristan grumbled as he walked towards the door, forcing his body to stand like he always had, no sign of how sick he actually was showing through his mask. And when he turned to look at me, his eyes gave nothing away except the confidence and dominating attitude he'd always had.

Finally, he was doing something for her.

I stood up from the bed and followed him out into the bar room.

■ ■ ■

ADELAIDE

River wrapped an arm around my waist as soon as he stepped up behind the bar and pulled me into him, pressing his lips to mine. I gripped his cut in my fists, tugging him up harder against me – well, as far as I could with my large belly between us. He pulled back gently and pressed a kiss to the tip of my nose, a smirk on his lips.

"Always so fucking needy." He whispered, his eyes gleaming with mischief.

I heard a bang from the kitchen, and something fall to the floor. "Fuck! River!" Reina screamed from inside of the kitchen.

We both rushed in, and my heart stopped at the sight of Tristan passed out on the floor. "Tristan!" I screamed, rushing forward. I fell to my knees beside him, shaking his shoulders. Panic clawed at my throat, fear filling my veins. "Fucking wake up, Tristan!" I screamed.

This couldn't be happening. I couldn't lose him. God, no, not today. Please let him live long enough to meet Jaxon. Please.

"Tristan, don't leave me!" I screamed, tears pouring down my cheeks.

I heard Sam talking to a 9-1-1 operator. River pressed his fingers to Tristan's pulse, nodding something to Sam. I gripped Tristan's pale face in my hands, tears blurring my vision, making it so hard to see him. I sobbed. "Tristan, please." I wailed, something in my gut telling me that this was bad. Really fucking bad.

My gut was telling me what my heart wanted to deny.

I was losing him. This was it.

Since we weren't that far from the hospital, paramedics were already rushing into the kitchen. River tried pulling me back from Tristan, but I screamed at him to let me go, to put me the fuck down.

"Darlin', come on. Let them get to him. They have to help him, Adelaide." River told me soothingly.

"River, let me go!" I screeched. "Tristan!" I yelled, sobs wracking my chest. "*Tristan!*"

"Patient is breathing. Pulse strong. Get me a stretcher." One of the paramedics commanded.

"Darlin', come on. Stay with me." River begged me, but I was losing it.

"No!" I wailed when they lifted him onto a stretcher. I tried getting up, but River held me with him on the floor. "Tristan, please, God, no!" I screamed.

River lifted me into his arms and carried me out of the kitchen as the paramedics began to wheel Tristan out of the clubhouse. Reina was holding Axel, trying to quieten his cries. "I've got him," Reina told River over the sound of me crying. "Go on to the hospital."

River nodded in thanks, but I continued sobbing, begging for Tristan to come back to me.

■ ■ ■

RIVER

Adelaide was a zombie.

I leaned against the wall outside of Tristan's hospital room, listening to the steady beat of his heart monitor as I watched Adelaide through the glass window. She was holding his hand, staring at his face as silent tears streamed down her cheeks.

She had lost all color to her skin. All she could do was stare at him, and occasionally, she would beg him in a whisper to come back to her.

But she'd lost him. I did my best to save him, but all I could do was extend her time with him.

She'd been like this since the doctor had told her that they would put Tristan on life support, but there was no chance that he would wake up again. The cancer had eaten away at him. There was no way to save him. If they cut the machines off, that was it.

He was dead.

"How is she?" Sam asked as he strode up beside me, holding a cup of coffee.

I shrugged. "She's fucking shattered," I grumbled, clenching my jaw. "I don't know how to help her. She's lost to me, Sam. She's dying inside. I knew this would happen, but fuck, nothing could have prepared me for it."

Sam sighed. "I called Joey for her." He told me. I looked over at him, nodding once in thanks. I hadn't even thought to call Joey with everything going on. "He's on his way now. He was on a run, but he's got his Sergeant at Arms and a couple of other patches handling the hand-off for him. He and Ink are high-tailing their asses here."

I nodded once. "Thanks, brother," I grumbled.

We were silent for a moment. "Is she ever going to come back to you, River?" Sam quietly asked me, worry for my woman in his voice.

I drew in a deep breath. That question scared the fuck out of me.

"I don't know," I told him quietly. "I'm praying that Joey can help her. He has a way of breathing life into her that I don't. He's her survival mechanism."

Joey, save her before it's too late. I silently begged him even though he wasn't even here yet.

■ ■ ■

A couple of hours later, Adelaide still wouldn't respond to me. I had tried everything I knew to try, but she only blankly stared back at me.

Joey, how the fuck did you save her last time?

As time dragged on, I got more and more scared that she wasn't going to come back to me. There was a blank - yet haunted - look in her eyes when she looked at me. It was almost like she was there, but all she could do was relive painful memories.

She was breaking, and I was helpless to stop it from happening.

I knelt in front of her. She drew those empty, brown eyes to me. Sadness settled there as her gaze landed on mine. Her bottom lip trembled, but she held herself together. My heart shattered in my chest. "I can't lose him, too, River. I don't think I'll survive it this time." She whispered, her voice cracking. "I feel empty - hollow."

I pressed my lips to hers tenderly. "You will, Adelaide, because I won't let you spiral down again," I swore. "You have to live for me, Darlin'. You've lived before, remember?"

She sniffled. "I don't think I can." She croaked.

Joey walked down the hallway, Ink right behind him. He didn't even say anything to me. He just strode into the room that Adelaide and Tristan were in, leaving Ink outside of it with me and Sam.

I stood up from the chair I had commandeered, watching as Joey gently lifted Adelaide into his arms. I didn't give a fuck what he did with her right now as long as he brought her back to us.

Honest to God, he could make love to her right there in that room, but as long as he got her to breathe for us again, to live for me, then I could be okay with it.

Joey, I don't care what the fuck you have to do. Save her.

■ ■ ■

ADELAIDE

I whimpered as Joey settled down in the chair that I'd been occupying, his arms cradling me on his lap. "Pretty girl, you're stronger than this." He soothed.

"It's over for him, isn't it?" I asked him, my heart breaking more. "This is it?"

Joey nodded. "Yeah, pretty girl, this is it for him. He fought hard for you for as long as he could, but he got tired of fighting to survive."

I sobbed. "I don't want to lose him, Joey."

He held me tighter. "Pretty girl, I'm sorry to say it, but you already have. He's gone. There's no saving him, and you're just holding his soul here on Earth - torturing him. Let him go, pretty girl. Let him be with his sister. It's time for them to be reunited again."

I looked up at Joey, my eyes awash with tears, making his face blurry. Joey slid his arms from beneath me and cradled my face in his hands, leaning down to kiss me. I sobbed against his lips as I kissed him back. My tears mixed with our lips.

"Let him go, pretty girl. It's okay." Joey whispered, his lips rubbing against mine.

"I'm not ready." I whimpered.

He brushed his nose with mine before he stole another kiss. "We never are. No one is ever ready to lose someone they love. But Tristan wouldn't want you to be like this." He reminded me. "Let him go, pretty girl. It's time."

"No." I cried.

Joey kissed me again, forcing my lips apart so he could kiss me deeply, his tongue sliding with mine. My chest felt like it was going to cave in, but I clung to him, breathing him in, holding him with me.

"Let him go, pretty girl."

■ ■ ■

I sat wedged between River and Joey as the doctor handed me the clipboard to take Tristan off of life support. My tears dripped onto the papers.

"Let him go, pretty girl," Joey whispered as he brushed his lips to my temple. "He's always with you, but he's going to be happy with his sister." He assured me. "It's okay to let him go."

I nodded my head, a sob falling from my lips. My hand shook, keeping me from signing the paperwork. River gripped my face in his hands, turning my head to face him. He took my lips in a soft, slow kiss, his tongue tangling with mine, forcing my heart to beat a little faster. "We're still here with you, Darlin'." He reminded me. "Hold on to Joey." He reminded me.

"I'm trying," I whispered.

"Then I'll force you to keep me with you," Joey told me. I looked over at him. "You're not losing me, pretty girl. I won't let you. And River will force you to keep me as well, just as I'll always force you to live for him, no matter how many times I have to remind you how to do that."

"Don't make him suffer any longer, Darlin'." River coaxed. "Sign the papers."

Tears slid down my cheeks, but I signed my name at the bottom of the papers, ripping that part of my heart that would always belong to Tristan out of my chest.

Then, as I was watching the nurse pull all support from Tristan, both Joey and River held me, sandwiching me between them as I cried, wails and sobs ripping from my lips.

EPILOGUE

I held River's hand in mine as we walked down the winding path in the graveyard that led to the Groves's plot where Tristan and Helene were buried next to each other. Axel ran along ahead of us, his childish laughter filling the air as he chased after a butterfly. I smiled as I watched him. He was such a happy child, and according to River, he was outgoing just as Red had been as a child.

Jaxon walked along much slower, still trying to become familiar with walking on uneven terrain. He had been walking for a couple of months now, but ground like this was still hard for him to walk over.

"Axel, don't go over there." River commanded, his voice stern but gentle as he spoke to our oldest son.

With a pout, Axel walked back over to us and away from the tree line that he was headed towards. Axel was the adventurous child – he didn't ever really fear anything.

Jaxon was our quiet, calm child for the most part – much like his dad. Even as an infant, he had never really been a crier.

Both of the boys were daddy's boys for sure, though.

"I can't believe it's been a year," I whispered as we stepped up to the plot where Tristan was buried next to his twin sister – my best friend.

A year ago, I had signed papers that took Tristan off of life support.

Three days after that, I had watched him get lowered into the ground and his casket covered with dirt. Every man in the Sons of Hell and the Fathers of Mayhem grabbed a shovel and covered his casket while I stood on the sidelines with silent tears running down my face.

That night, I couldn't sleep. I just cried. Joey and River laid beside me with me sandwiched between them, both of them holding me together the best that they could while every part of me tried to fall apart.

I swallowed the lump in my throat as River pressed his lips to the top of my head, my eyes not leaving the plot in front of me. "I've got the boys." He quietly spoke up. "Take all of the time that you need, Darlin'."

I nodded in thanks, not able to form words yet since there was a huge lump in my throat. River lifted Jaxon onto his hip and took off at a slow jog, making Axel laugh as he ran after them, somehow managing to keep his balance on the uneven path.

Joey had offered to come with me today, to be my support, but I'd told him no.

This was something that I had to do by myself.

And it was going to hurt like hell, but I was hoping it would give me some closure.

I looked back down at the headstones in front of me and sat down on top of their graves, knowing neither one of the twins would have expected anything less from me. In fact, I could picture Tristan reprimanding me right now, but Helene would only laugh and tell him to leave me alone.

"I never thought I would lose either one of you," I admitted in a whisper. "God, Helene, we were supposed to be best friends forever. We even had plans of being in the same nursing home when we got old, causing ruckus together." I admitted with a soft laugh. A tear trickled down my cheek. "But you got taken away from me before you could ever really live."

Another tear slid down my cheek, my heart squeezing painfully in my chest. "I'm so sorry that I never came to visit you after you were buried." I apologized, more tears raining down my cheeks. "I couldn't bring myself to. I was so damn *angry*." I choked out. "You promised me that you were getting better, and then you left me - you *lied* to me." I shook my head. "I wish you had told me how bad it was - maybe I could have prepared myself for your death. Losing you was one of the hardest things that I've ever faced." I admitted. "And because I was so angry, I let myself self-destruct."

I sniffled. "And when you finally stepped back into my life, Tristan," I said, beginning to speak to him, "it was already too late. I had ruined myself. You never destroyed me, Tristan. I destroyed myself - destroyed every part of me that made me a decent human being. I was so caught up in my own misery that I never realized that I was the main cause for all of the pain and suffering I had gone through. I was so focused on being miserable that I wouldn't allow myself to heal - to live."

I looked up at the sky that was shining blue, the sun warm on my face. "I wish I'd had more time with both of you," I whispered. "But now, I know you're both happy, wherever you are now, and I hope that you're finally together again." I laughed. "You two really were always inseparable." I swallowed thickly. "And I hope neither of you are in pain anymore."

I looked down the graveyard and saw River rolling around in the grass with Jaxon and Axel crawling over him, their laughter ringing out over the otherwise silent area. "He convinced me to come here today, you know?" I informed them. "I didn't want to come here

- I really didn't. I wasn't sure I could handle it, honestly, especially after I pulled the plug on you because you were only getting worse, Tristan." I shook my head with a small smile. "But somehow, he knew what was best for me - what would really help. And if you two can see me, I hope you know that I'm okay. River has taught me to live, and Joey continues to make sure that I breathe. I'm in good hands with them."

I swiped at my cheeks. "I know that's what both of you had always wanted for me - to be happy, to be safe and well. I am. For once in so many years, I'm finally okay." I admitted. "Some days are still extremely hard, not going to lie, but every day gets easier to get through."

I pressed my fingers to my lips and pressed them to each of their headstones. "I'm just happy that you two are finally together again, and I'm hoping that you both smile when you look down at me," I whispered. I swallowed past the lump in my throat so that I could speak again. "I love you both. I'll never stop." I promised.

I stood to my feet, and as I did so, my eyes met River's as he stood up from the ground as well. He knelt and whispered something to Axel, and Axel squealed loudly right before he took off running up the path to me. With a laugh, I knelt and swept him up into my arms, pressing a big kiss to his cheek.

"Momma!" He squealed, his smile as wide as the Grand Canyon. God, I loved how happy of a child he was. I prayed life never dimmed the spark in his eyes.

I met River halfway down the path. As soon as he reached me, he reached out and tucked some of my hair behind my ear. "You cried." He murmured as he brushed his fingertips over my cheek.

I reached up with my free hand and covered his larger hand with my smaller one, squeezing gently. "I'm okay," I assured him.

He gently tipped my chin up and pressed his lips to mine right before our two little boys shoved our faces apart. River grinned and shook his head, his eyes shining with love as he looked between the two of them.

"Let me love your Momma." River playfully growled.

Axel hugged me tightly, glaring at his dad. "No. Momma is mine." He said, sticking his tongue out at River.

He laughed softly as he reached up to ruffle Axel's dark hair. "She's ours." River corrected. "Which means you have to *help* me love Momma."

Axel nodded his head. "I can do that."

I reached out and linked my fingers with River's, and together, we walked back up the path to the SUV.

And somehow, I knew Tristan and Helene were smiling down at me from wherever they were.

SNEAK PEEK
SAVED: BOOK TWO

Link to Pre-Order: https//mybook.to/savedtosmith

A loud knock sounded on the chapel doors, dragging me from the books that I was working on. Yeah, I had a secretary and a treasurer, and yeah, I trusted them, but I always did a check over the books after they did their work.

I was thorough kind of man – sue me. I didn't become one of the most feared leaders of organized crime in this country by not being careful about shit.

"Ink, what the fuck is the matter now?" I snarled as I looked up from the paperwork scattered in front of me to where someone was pushing open the meeting room doors. I knew it would be Ink. He was the only fucker in my club brave enough to face me when I was in the middle of doing something important.

I had a rule. If someone wasn't dying, don't fucking bother me.

Kyle and Roger held both doors open as Ink strode into the room with a woman hanging limp in his arms. She had blonde hair that was tangled with leaves and sticks, some of it streaked with blood from her face. She was small – tiny really – and young, probably not much older than nineteen or twenty if I had to guess.

I abruptly stood up from my chair, my eyes trained on Ink, waiting for an explanation. "Found her outside behind the clubhouse." Ink gruffly informed me as he gently set the young woman on the table. "She's unconscious. Somebody beat her half to death." He told me, though I could clearly see that for myself. The woman was in horrible condition.

I strode around the table so I was standing beside the unconscious blonde. "Kyle, get me a bucket of warm water and a washcloth. Roger, get me the fucking first aid kit." I barked as I gently pushed the woman's hair away from her face.

She was actually beautiful beneath all of the blood, bruising, and swelling – made me wonder who the fuck hated her enough to want to do this to her. You didn't see women like this getting the fuck beat out of them very often.

She groaned softly, her face scrunching up with pain as my fingers skimmed lightly over a bruised part of her forehead. "It's alright, sweet girl." I crooned as Kyle rushed back into the room with a plastic bowl of warm water and a washcloth. "I'm going to take care of you," I assured her.

Goddamn, what was it with me and the fucking damsels in distress?

Adelaide, my ex, had been the first woman I had taken in – taken under my wing. She'd been so broken. Tristan – her ex – had fucking destroyed the life inside of her. And I couldn't turn my back on her; I couldn't let her go.

A pang sliced through my chest at the thought of the woman that would always hold a piece of my heart. I'd go to the ends of the fucking world for her even though she was no longer mine.

And here I was, yet again about to fall into the same fucking trap.

But I couldn't fucking help myself.

The blonde's eyes slowly fluttered open, revealing the most beautiful, blue eyes I'd ever seen in my life. They were a startling shade of blue – as blue as the ocean on a bright, sunny, Summer day.

They stole the damn breath from my lungs.

She jerked back from me in alarm, her chest rapidly rising and falling as panic set in. Those blue eyes darkened the slightest bit, terror flashing in her eyes. She quickly scrambled into a sitting position, and I could see her heart thumping wildly against her breastbone.

I quickly reached out and gently grabbed her shoulders, halting her movements before she toppled onto the floor on the other side of the table. "Hey, hey," I soothed as I gently ran my hands down her bruised arms. "Easy now. I'm not going to hurt you, sweetheart. I just want to help you."

She swallowed hard as her eyes ran over my face. After a moment, she silently nodded. I looked at the men behind me. "Leave us," I commanded.

Ink's eyes met mine with a questioning gaze before he left the room with the other two men, knowing better than to question me. If it was something extremely serious, he would go against me. Something like this, though? He trusted my judgement.

"Can you walk?" I asked her once the chapel doors shut behind Roger, and we were alone in the chapel.

Instead of answering, she slowly slid to the edge of the table, and I stepped back, allowing her to stand. As soon as her feet touched the floor, she cried out in pain, her legs crumpling beneath her. I quickly caught her in my arms, desperately trying to ignore the soft curves pressed against me. Despite her being so small, she had little dips and swells to her body that were already driving me wild.

Fuck, I needed to get laid. I couldn't remember the last time I had gone balls deep in pussy. It was beginning to fuck with me.

I quickly set her in one of the more comfortable chairs. "I'm going to clean your face up, okay?" I told her. "Just relax." I coaxed. "Do you know who hurt you?" I asked her as I dipped the cloth into the warm water and rung it out, gently wiping the dirt and blood from her face.

"I was kidnapped." She told me quietly. I let my dark eyes meet her blue ones, rage pulsing through my veins on her behalf. "My dad – he's the president of The Outlaws MC." I barely resisted the urge to scowl, instead keeping my face impassive. The Outlaws MC was nothing but fucking trouble. "I left a few months ago – trying to escape him and his bullshit – but he tracked me down."

I'd never dealt with The Outlaws, and I made sure none of my men or women got tangled up with them either. But I had always kept my eyes and ears open for them, making sure to keep them as far away as I could. But I knew I couldn't send this girl away.

Now, it looked like I was going to bring them right to my front door.

"I managed to escape, and I just kind of ran through the woods until I passed out here before I could knock on your door." She finished.

That explained why she was found behind the clubhouse, and it explained why she knew she could run here for protection. Being as she was the daughter of The Outlaws MC President, she would know who her father had alliances with and who he didn't.

And we certainly were not on speaking terms with Yeller Giddons.

"My VP found you," I informed her. "His name is Ink."

"And yours?" She asked me as I gently began cleaning her cuts with alcohol wipes, making her wince slightly.

I shot her an apologetic smile for hurting her, surprising myself with how gentle I was being with her. The only woman who I'd ever truly been able to be gentle with was Adelaide.

I ignored the pain in my chest at the thought of that beautiful woman.

"Joey," I informed her. "I'm the President."

"Joey Dirks?" She asked me as she swallowed hard, nervousness flashing in that pretty, blue-eyed gaze.

I nodded, watching as fear momentarily slid through her gaze. I frowned, wondering what had her afraid of me. Sure, I had a shitty reputation – was known for being cold-blooded and ruthless, but I would never hurt a woman.

"Something on your mind, sweetheart?" I asked.

She swallowed hard. "I met your woman Adelaide a few years ago."

I snorted, my heart twisting in pain at her words. Adelaide was far from my woman since she was now married to River and carrying their second child together. I held in a fuck ton of feelings around her when I went to visit her and when she came here with River. But she was happy. She was taken care of. That was all that fucking mattered to me.

I had promised Adelaide that I would always force her to keep me with her. I was her reason for still breathing. And I wouldn't ever break that promise to her, no matter how much it killed me inside.

After everything that I had put her through, she deserved for me to give her the best parts of myself.

"Adelaide hasn't been my woman for a few years now," I informed her. "She's married to another man with two kids and one on the way." I let my eyes meet hers again. "What's got you so afraid of her?"

When Adelaide had been here, she'd been a monster – a monster I created. When I took Adelaide in, she had lost all of her fight – all of her purpose.

So, I gave her a purpose. I taught her how to breathe again.

"When I turned sixteen, I was going to see if I could come here for protection, but Adelaide turned me away at your gate – told me that if I knew what was good for me, I'd go back home." She swallowed thickly. "She's certainly a force to be reckoned with."

I released a soft laugh at that. That, Adelaide was – even now. She loved hard, and she loved deeply. And she would destroy the fucking world for those she loved. Now, though, River just did it for her.

"I can assure you that Adelaide doesn't live here anymore," I informed her. "So, what's your name, sweetheart, and how did you escape?" I asked her, wanting to steer the conversation away from the one woman who would always be my first love – the woman who would always be a piece of me. Nothing and no one would ever change that.

She looked down at her hands. "Elaina." She murmured. Fuck – a pretty name for a beautiful woman. It suited her. "And it sounds stupid, but I managed to kick him in the head when he had me down on the floor. I took off for the woods, knowing he wouldn't think to look there for me."

I gently hooked my index finger under her chin and raised her face to meet my eyes. Those blue eyes sucked the air from my lungs again. I barely resisted the urge to rub my chest. I knew this girl was trouble, but I couldn't fucking help myself.

I don't know how I always found myself in these damn predicaments, but I was already falling in deep with this woman.

It was dangerous, but if there was one thing about me, I fucking had a thing for danger.

"Sweetheart, nothing about that sounds stupid," I assured her, my tone gentle. "That was incredibly brave, and as long as you'll stay here, you'll have protection within my club."

"Thank you." She whispered, so much relief flooding her stunning features at my words that it tugged at my soul.

I could see it clear as day on her face. She had been through too much shit for such a young age, but I knew better than most people what the fuck could happen in such a little amount of time. I mean, fuck, look at the shit that my sister and Adelaide had both gone through.

Adelaide had been kidnapped, beaten, stabbed, raped, and miscarried a baby all before she hit twenty-five.

My sister – Jessie? She had been kidnapped, sold to numerous men, raped and beaten. She still wasn't the same; I wasn't sure if she ever would be again.

The chapel door opened, and Ink strode in. I ripped my eyes from the pretty blonde in front of me and glowered at him. "One of these days, you mother fuckers are going to make me install a fucking lock on that door." I snapped at him as I stood up to my full height to face him.

I crossed my arms over my chest, waiting on him to tell me why the fuck he'd interrupted my discussion with Elaina. "River is riding in with Sam and Adelaide in a few hours." That familiar ache settled in my chest. His eyes were understanding as he met my gaze. He knew how much it hurt me to have her around, but I would never walk away from her; he knew that – understood it, even. Which was another reason he was a damn good VP. "They've got a shipment coming in close to here, and they need a place to crash for the night. I told River it was fine." Ink informed me.

I felt the tension radiating from Elaina's form, and I gently placed a hand on her shoulder. "Make sure the spare rooms are prepared," I told Ink. "And inform Jessie to cook extra."

Ink nodded and strode from the room. "I thought you said -" Elaina choked out as soon as the door was closed back behind him.

"I said she doesn't live here anymore." I reminded her. "Not that she doesn't visit." I shrugged. "Besides, you'll find that she's mellowed out a hell of a lot," I informed her. "Now come on. You need a shower. I should have some clothes you can fit into. If I don't, I can ask Jessie - my sister. You two are probably about the same size."

Elaina slowly stood up from the chair, her legs holding her up this time. With my hand on her lower back, I led her from the chapel and down the hall to the very end where my room was located across from my sister's. I pushed open the door and allowed her to go in first before I stepped in behind her and shut the door behind me. "The bathroom is through there," I told her, pointing towards the slightly open door. "Towels are in the cabinet above the toilet. Feel free to use whatever is in the bathroom. I'll have the clothes on the bed by the time you get out." I informed her.

I turned away from her, striding towards my dresser. I had her alone in my room, and temptation was fucking knocking, begging me to make a move. But she was hurt - injured - and had just gone through something traumatic. The last thing she needed was an asshole, territorial president like me making bold ass moves on her - wasn't even sure if she was the kind of woman to move so fast with a man.

"Joey?" She softly called as I turned my back to her.

I looked over my shoulder at her, silently arching an eyebrow at her, waiting on her to continue. "Thank you." She murmured before she strode into the bathroom, shutting the door behind her.

Fuck me; I really did have a thing for the damsels in distress.

I stared up at the ceiling for a moment, drawing in a deep breath as I reached up and rubbed my chest, that familiar pang slicing through my heart. *Adelaide, pretty girl, I'm going to need your help. I fucked up with you, but goddammit, I don't want to fuck up with her.*

I drew in a deep breath, closing my eyes as I gripped the top of my dresser, seeing the pain in Adelaide's beautiful eyes as I closed my own. "Pretty girl, please don't let me fuck this up with her, too," I whispered. "Only a few minutes with her, and I can already feel that I'm in deep."

■ ■ ■

I watched as Ink let River, Adelaide, Sam, and the kids into the clubhouse. Axel instantly ran over to me, squealing with happiness. I couldn't help the grin that stretched over my face at the sight of the little boy. I had a special place in my heart for Adelaide's kids. And seeing her as a mom? It did some shit to my cold heart.

"Uncle Joey!" Axel screamed as he catapulted himself into my arms.

"Hey, kid." I laughed as I settled him onto my lap. "Have you been good?" I asked him.

He enthusiastically nodded his head, but I knew that was a lie. Every time I was around, he was giving *everyone* a run for their money. The kid was trouble, and he was always doing some shit he shouldn't be.

River snorted. "He got into the cookies in Adelaide's nightstand drawer, and he's been a nightmare ever since." He informed me as he strode over to the bar, going straight for a beer that my sister slid to him without him even having to ask.

I smiled at Adelaide, ignoring the pang of hurt in my chest as she settled herself in between River's legs. He placed his hand over her small baby bump. "Life treating you good?" I asked her as I watched Sam scoop Jaxon up into his arms out of the corner of my eye.

She shrugged. "Morning sickness is kicking my ass, but I'm doing good otherwise." I frowned slightly. I hated it when she went through anything that made her the slightest bit uncomfortable.

I opened my mouth to respond before I saw a blonde-haired, blue-eyed woman step out of the back hallway wearing my clothes. My mouth ran dry as all of my blood rushed straight south to my dick.

Holy fuck, she was beautiful – and sexy as fuck wearing my clothes.

I gently set Axel on the floor as I stood up and strode over to where she was standing. She was nervously scanning the room. I could feel Adelaide's eyes on my back, but for the first time in history, I didn't feel like shit for having eyes for another woman.

Elaina was something else entirely for me.

A small smile tilted Elaina's lips as her eyes landed on me, and my heart raced double time in my chest. Fuck. I was in deep – real fucking deep with her. How did this shit happen to me so fast?

"You good?" I asked her, cursing myself when my voice came out gruff. But this woman in front of me was so damn clueless, she still hadn't picked up on how much and how easily she affected me.

"The shower was great." She informed me, a little more comfortable now that I was there with her. My heart swelled a tiny bit at the fact that I was the one able to bring her comfort – to make her feel safe. "I wasn't sure what to do with my clothes, so I left them in your hamper."

"All good, sweet girl," I told her. Without thinking about it, I grabbed her hand in mine and led her back over to Adelaide and River. Adelaide was watching me curiously, and River had a knowing smirk on his face. I rolled my eyes at River, and his smirk widened.

He knew I was in deep without me even saying a word. It was the first time I'd willingly walked away from Adelaide to go be with another woman.

I felt Elaina stiffen next to me as soon as Adelaide turned her brown eyes to her. I clenched my jaw, protectiveness swelling inside of me for the blonde at my side. I gently squeezed her hand – a silent reminder that I was still right there with her.

"I remember you." Adelaide abruptly spoke up, as was her true style. She didn't beat around the bush for shit. Elaina squared her shoulders and tilted her chin up at Adelaide, and pride swelled in my chest. Not many people had the balls to stand against Adelaide. She was a dangerous woman by herself. With River and his club backing her up as well? She was practically untouchable. "Somebody fucked you up pretty damn good, huh? Tried poaching on another woman's territory again?" Adelaide asked her, a careless, humorless smirk twisting her lips, that monster I had created flashing through for a moment.

"Calm yourself." River sternly ordered, his hands squeezing her hips. "Elaina, been a minute." River greeted. "Last I heard, you had run off from your old man."

"You know her?" Adelaide demanded as she turned to face her husband, her eyes narrowed at him. I clenched my jaw. I may love Adelaide to fucking death, would go to the ends of the fucking world for her, but she was treading on thin ice right now.

River nodded at her. "Elaina Giddons. Her old man is a nasty fucker. I deal with him because his territory is so close to mine, but he's mostly a problem that I'd like to eliminate."

"How'd you end up back here?" Adelaide asked as she swung her angry, brown eyes to Elaina. Elaina flinched at my side, stepping closer to me on instinct. I tightened my hand around hers, narrowing my eyes at Adelaide.

"Adelaide." I snapped at her, slightly pushing Elaina behind my body as I narrowed my eyes at the beautiful woman in front of me. "That's enough," I growled.

"You suddenly protective over a bitch that's going to ruin you soon?" Adelaide snapped at me. I growled – a soft warning for her to shut her fucking mouth while she was ahead. "I know all about Yeller Giddons and his fucking MC. I can fucking guarantee you that she's making you play right into her hands." She snapped at me, her eyes burning with fire.

"You don't know a damn thing about me, Adelaide." Elaina snapped as she came out from behind me. Her face was pale, but despite her fear of the woman in front of me, she was standing strong. I squeezed her hand again, pride swirling in my chest for this little spitfire beside me. "And you don't know the first thing about Yeller nor what he's capable of."

Adelaide stepped up closer to us, and River quickly yanked her back to him, his hands tightening on her hips. "Oh, I know plenty of what he's capable of, sweetheart, and I saw you in that same room with him, watching as he beat the fuck out of me." Adelaide snarled at her. I bristled, a thousand conflicting emotions swirling inside of me. "Watch yourself, bitch."

Elaina snatched her hand away from me and stormed out of the clubhouse. I didn't know who the fuck to be angry with. But I had promised Elaina protection within these walls, and unfortunately, that also meant that I had to protect her from the woman in front of me.

I pointed my finger at Adelaide, my hand shaking with my rage. "You need to learn to keep your fucking mouth shut." I snarled at her. She glared up at me, hurt flashing in her eyes, but I tamped down my need to comfort her. "River, get your fucking woman in check." I barked at her husband.

352

With that, I stormed out of the clubhouse, running to catch up to Elaina. She was power walking through the gravel lot, heading straight for the gate.

Fuck, she couldn't leave here. She'd have no fucking protection out there. Her old man would fucking kill her.

I caught her around the waist and pulled her around to face me. "Hey, hey, don't go anywhere," I begged her. "Adelaide doesn't know a fucking thing about you." I reminded her, trying to calm her down.

"She was right." Elaina snapped up at me. My blood ran cold at her words. That's the exact opposite of what I was hoping to hear. "I did stand there and watch as he beat the fuck out of her," Elaina informed me. I clenched my jaw, momentarily tightening my hands on her waist before I forced myself to relax. "But I had no damn choice, Joey. And that's something she'll never listen to."

"Why didn't you tell me that?" I asked her, tightening my hands on her waist again when she tried to move away from me.

"You're still in love with her, Joey." I closed my eyes, drawing in a deep breath. Fuck, I was hoping she wouldn't catch onto that. "I knew it the moment I brought her up in your chapel. I need protection, and I wasn't going to jeopardize that by telling you."

Adelaide could frankly kiss my ass at this moment because there was a beautiful, blonde-haired woman standing in front of me who was making me feel more than Adelaide had ever done the entire time we had been together.

How this shit was possible this fucking fast – I didn't know. But I wouldn't question it.

I gently drew Elaina against me. "And if I told you next to nothing would stop me from protecting you, Elaina?" I softly asked her. I ran my eyes over her bruised face, looking for something – anything – that I could use to make her want to stay.

She swallowed hard, tears burning at her beautiful, blue eyes as she swallowed thickly at my words. "Joey . . ." she whispered, her sweet voice breaking on my name.

Our tender moment was interrupted by the sound of motorcycles tearing onto my lot, and I threw us both to the ground right as gunshots rang out around us. Elaina's loud, terrified scream ripped through the sound of the gunshots, almost bursting my eardrum. My blood pounded in my veins as rage – fucking white-hot rage – pulsed through my body.

Someone was looking to fucking die today.

OTHER MC ROMANCE NOVELS BY T.O. SMITH

Protecting Natalie

https://mybook.to/protectingnatalie

Kaden Brookes never bothered with any female outside of the club women.

Until he crashed into Natalie - quite literally.

Her fiery attitude amuses him, and he wants more. But he quickly realizes there is a lot more to Natalie Farmer than quick wit and a temper that rivaled even his.

He wants Natalie as his woman, and he will make her his.

But Kaden has his work cut out for him because Natalie isn't as easy to claim as he thought she was.

Because when her life is on the line, she will do whatever is necessary to protect herself.

That includes leaving those she loves behind.

Little Reaper

https://mybook.to/littlereapertosmith

Amberosa Calloway betrayed the Reapers to protect them, but now her betrayal has caught up to her.

Now wanted dead by one of the most dangerous gang leaders in America, Amberosa needs protection.

And who better to be protected by than Jayden King - her brother's Vice President?

Ink: Savage Crows MC Book I

https://mybook.to/inktosmith

"Me nor this MC is turning their backs on you, Reina. I'm claiming you as my old lady, and the MC has to respect that whether they like it or not." - Ink (Ink ; Savage Crows MC Book 1)

INK

She ripped my heart out five years ago when she left to be with my brother.

Now she's back, and she's asking me for protection.

~ * ~ * ~

REINA

Five years ago, I left to chase a life with a man that I thought loved me.

I was a fool.

Now I'm on the run, and Ink is my only chance of survival.

PLEASE LEAVE A REVIEW!

I would love to hear your thoughts on the book!

Please leave a review. I would love to see your thoughts, whether you liked it or disliked it.

https://mybook.to/ruinedtosmith

FOLLOW T.O. SMITH

Facebook page: https://www.facebook.com/tosmithauthor

Facebook group: https://www.facebook.com/groups/TOSmith

Instagram: https://www.instagram.com/authortosmith/

Twitter: https://twitter.com/TOSmithauthor

TikTok: https://www.tiktok.com/@authortosmith

https://www.patreon.com/authortosmith

ABOUT THE AUTHOR

She resides in Georgia with her fiancé, four cats – Tyson, Nightmare, Midnight, and Kream, and her dogs – Bailey and Mocha. She can normally be found in her office on her big, comfy chair with her laptop on her lap as she dives into her next creative world.

She writes a variety of books, and most readers are bound to find their favorite kind of romance novels on her website.

https://www.tosmithbooks.com

Made in the USA
Middletown, DE
05 January 2025

68895653R00215